JOHN STONE AND THE CHOCTAW KID

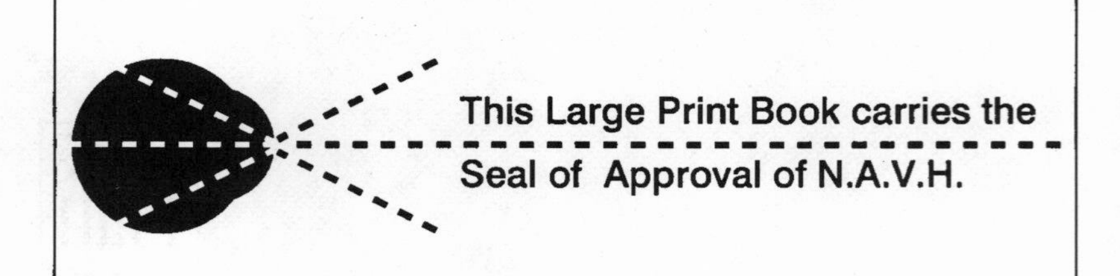
This Large Print Book carries the
Seal of Approval of N.A.V.H.

JOHN STONE AND THE CHOCTAW KID

Wayne Davis

G.K. Hall & Co. • Thorndike, Maine

Published in 1999 by arrangement with M. Evans & Co., Inc.

G.K. Hall Large Print Western Series.

The text of this Large Print edition is unabridged.
Other aspects of the book may vary from the original edition.

Set in 16 pt. Plantin by Rick Gundberg.

Printed in the United States on permanent paper.

Library of Congress Cataloging-in-Publication Data

Davis, Wayne.
John Stone and the Choctaw Kid / Wayne Davis.
p. cm.
ISBN 0-7838-8728-0 (lg. print : hc : alk. paper)
1. Frontier and pioneer life — New Mexico — Eddy County Fiction. 2. Eddy County (N.M.) — History Fiction. 3. Large type books. I. Title.
[PS3554.A93786J64 1999]
813′.54—dc21 99-38420

Dedicated to the memory of Arthur J. Mayes
(born September 28, 1882;
died September 18, 1962)
*He shared his memories with the big-eared kid
who rode the LA Bar bay.*

Author's Note

This story and the main characters herein are products of the author's imagination. Wherever actual residents of early Eddy County, New Mexico, come into the story I have endeavored to depict them as accurately as possible based on what I have read about them as written by themselves and/or others or what I have been told about them by those who knew them. However, I make no claim to biographical accuracy for *any* of the real-life characters depicted in this work of fiction.

The author wishes to express his gratitude to a number of people who were involved in the gathering of information and inspiration for this novel: to Tom Cotton and the other members of the Southeastern New Mexico Historical Society, as well as the gracious staff of the Carlsbad Municipal Library and Museum; to Virginia Ballard for providing a base of operations (C. B. Eddy's original stone ranch house still stands in a pasture back of her home despite the ravages of time and the elements); to Jim Ballard for the provision of horses and equipment, and guidance on various expeditions into the Guadalupe Mountains; to Stacy Bieble for entrusting me with the family's only copy of the story of her great-grandmother, Barbara Jones; and to all the "old-timers" of Eddy County who took the time to share their recollections.

A special thanks is due a number of persons who've provided encouragement and admonition over the years, especially Joe Lansdale, Ardath Mayhar, Barbara Puechner, and finally and most profoundly, my wife, Joan.

Chapter One

John Stonecipher knew he was dying. It was about time, he reckoned. Not that he wouldn't like to live on and on, if he could be young again. Or even as an old man, if a reasonably healthy old man. The eight decades of his recollection were not very much time when you looked back on it. And when he looked back, he remembered that it came very near to ending on a number of occasions. At least on those occasions it would have been swift, with a last breath of fresh desert or mountain air intermingled with gunsmoke. Not like this! He would have breathed his last with his back against a boulder instead of a sickbed, or with the feel of a strong, young horse between his knees. Or better yet, lying in the tall grama grass away upon the mountain. Even face down with caliche dust in his nostrils would be better than this. Oh, he appreciated the extra years, but . . .

If only he could rise and somehow make it to the little place he still owned on the edge of town. He'd continued to keep a few head of horses around, even after the sawbones forbade him to do any more riding. If he could only make it that far, and manage to get a saddle on one of them. At least he could ride out and find a place somewhere in the sand hills east of Carlsbad. Then his final breath would be carried away on the wind instead of being lost in the stagnant atmosphere of the sickroom. But where he really wanted to be was high up on that mountain amidst the smell of pinyon, juniper, pine, and cedar.

For awhile his mind lingered on the high-country hideout that figured so prominently in eighty-some years of memories; then he contrasted that scene with the plot Grace had reserved for them in the Salt Flat cemetery, among the sandspurs and goatheads that prevailed in spite of the efforts to establish Bermuda grass.

The sky pilot who came around every week had assured him that it really didn't matter where the body was laid to rest. That may be, but he wanted to experience the mountain one more time. It had been so long. Just once more, and he could leave it all behind with peace in his heart and a smile upon his weathered face.

His large nose crinkled as he squinted his faded blue eyes in search of the writing materials among the various articles on the bedside table. There might be a way. If he could hold on long enough. There was someone who would see to it, if he possibly could. Someone who owed him, owed him a lot. Even if it wasn't for that, he'd still do it.

It had been a long time, but John knew where he was. Nobody else did. No one else knew he was still alive. Almost everyone thought he'd plunged to his death from Lonesome Ridge. But John knew. And he would come, too. He was almost as old as John, but he would come. If there was any way at all, he would come. Of that there was no doubt.

Fingers that had once been strong and nimble fumbled to get paper and pen into position. The nurse would mail the letter for him. Now he was glad they had made him learn to read and write, made him attend that one-room school at Salt Flat.

Salt Flat would seem an unlikely spot for a school, or anything else for that matter. Four or five acres of light-colored gyppy soil that was reminiscent of the real salt flats on the other side of the mountains, beyond the ridges of the Guadalupes and the chasm of Dog Canyon, clear on the other side of the Brokeoffs, in Texas. That was genuine salt for which men had fought and died. But no one would fight over the so-called salt flat of the solitary school house, with its absence of graze and surface water. It was an ideal choice for the ranchers of the area, what with their recurrent disputes over range and water rights. And it was the most centrally located site for the majority of the participants.

Several of the ranchers' wives alternated days teaching classes, and the ranchers decided among themselves which months or weeks of the year the wives and children could be spared from the business of running a ranch. The fact that they organized the school shows they were concerned about the education of their children. But the success of the family cattle operation was the main concern, and this priority coupled with the occasional interference of extremely bad weather limited the school terms to a total of five or six months out of the year.

As Johnny Stonecipher nudged his father's mule up the rocky slope east of the family homestead on the Black River, he periodically glanced over his shoulder toward the Guadalupes, which cast an eerie blue silhouette upon the western horizon in the early morning haze of late summer. He'd much rather be headed in that direction. And before long he would be, for school would be interrupted by the annual fall roundup. All the ranching families of the upper river would be busy gathering their market stock from the vast open range. Everyone's cattle would be thrown together and herded to a holding pasture near the newly incorporated town of Eddy, New Mexico territory. From there they'd be consigned to a larger herd for the three-hundred-mile drive to market at Amarillo, Texas. For the roundup and the drive to Eddy, John would be a-horseback instead of on a silly mule.

He was too big to go to school, anyway. If they'd gotten it organized sooner he'd already be finished. If pa was going to make him go, the least he could do was let him ride one of the cow ponies. Pa said a mule was more surefooted and not nearly as excitable. They were always so worried about him. Just because they'd lost the other son, his brother. It was a wonder they let him ride a horse when they gathered cattle. He felt like a sodbust farmer, riding to school on a plow mule.

Wally Bledsoe had his own horse to ride to school, and he was slightly younger than John's eighteen years. Gracie sure perked up and took notice whenever Wally came sashaying in on that blaze-faced black. He always arrived at the last minute, so everybody would be there watching. He'd spur the black headlong across the flat and pull to a tail-dragging skid in the schoolyard with all eyes upon him, making a flamboyant dismount before the horse was even stopped. Then he'd pay out his stake rope, pull the saddle and bridle and swagger away without even cooling his mount. Maybe the black didn't get all that hot galloping across the flat, but darned if John would treat his horse like that, if he had one.

Johnny pulled out for school even earlier than usual on that late-summer day in 1893, for it was his turn to clean the cistern. It had to be checked every day school was in session, for somehow small creatures from the desert seemed to find their way into the cistern to die. The precious rainwater was funneled into the reservoir from the roof of the schoolhouse by means of a crude gutter. Rains were infrequent, so now and then it was necessary to haul a barrel of drinking water to the school. The summer of 1893 was an exception, for the rains had come in torrents. The irrigation dams on the Pecos washed out, Eddy was flooded, and many a disillusioned farmer was ruined. The abundant downpours were welcomed by the Black River ranchers, many of whom recalled "The Big Die" of '86, when many of the cattle herds of the Pecos Valley perished from drought and overgrazing. The September grass of '93 was the best in ten years.

There was nothing to do to the cistern except to skim off a slight scattering of debris from the surface of the water. No matter how tightly a structure was built in this country, the wind always managed to penetrate. Johnny replaced the lid and sat down upon it to await the arrival of the teacher and the rest of the students.

His mind returned to Gracie and Wally. Mostly Gracie. Seemed that she was always on his mind, even when he was asleep. Seeing her was the one thing to which he looked forward on every school day. And during the times that school was out, he constantly wondered about her. Where was she? What was she doing? Did she ever think about him? No matter how busy he was, there was always that gnawing loneliness in his breast. At least he got to see her once or twice a month even when school was out, when a circuit-riding preacher held services at the school house. She was his only incentive for attending those affairs, also. And occasionally there would be an all-night dance and social at one of the larger ranch headquarters, usually around Christmas and on the Fourth of July.

Always there was Wally. Dark hair so perfect, black eyes flashing, acting so grown-up. Flirting with her and yet somehow remaining aloof, which seemed to tantalize her all the more. There was no mistaking the uplift in her spirit and the direction of her sidelong glances whenever he was around.

John had long since admitted to himself that he held a grudging admiration for Wally. After all, if Wally represented the qualities Gracie admired, then he wanted to be more like him. When he lay awake at night with visions of himself and Gracie in his mind, did he not picture himself as having the same dashing bravado? Yes, he liked Wally, and the surest way to be noticed by Gracie and to be able to enjoy her company was to stay close to Wally. This he had done, and he and Wally had become "pardners."

If Wally sensed John's feelings for Gracie, he regarded it as no cause for concern. No moreso than John's obvious envy of the magnificent black gelding.

Wally made his usual showy arrival just as John was about to strike up a conversation with Gracie, who'd arrived earlier on her little palomino mare. She turned her back on John as a piercing rebel yell attracted all eyes to the far side of the flat to watch the shiny black horse race its own dust cloud to the schoolyard.

Gracie's eyes continued to stray to Wally all day long. She didn't even try to hide it. At least John tried not to be obvious when he sneaked his looks in her direction as he constantly adjusted his lanky frame to the schoolroom furniture. It had not been designed for youngsters of his size and no position was comfortable for very long. He felt like a bumpkin.

Finally the school day ended. John and Wally charged out the door and into the schoolyard ahead of the younger students. Gracie was the last one out. She headed straight for Wally. John could sooner make himself jump off Signal Peak than take his leave as long as she tarried to talk with them, notwithstanding the fact that her attention was mostly for Wally.

Wally always seemed to have the option of doing whatever he pleased when class was finished. He suggested they ride over to the distant grove of cottonwoods on Black River, where the horses could graze along the banks while they enjoyed the shade and the water. It was in the opposite direction from the Circle S, and John's conscience burned with the thought of expectant family and undone chores awaiting at home. But the picture of Wally and Gracie alone together in the cool grassy shade of the river bank sucked his gut dry and made his heart tremble with apprehension. He caught the disappointment in Wally's expression when he agreed to go along for awhile and he knew he was bound to stay at the grove as long as they did.

Chapter Two

The brush-scarred green pickup with welded side racks was similar to others that could be seen on the streets of Carlsbad on any given day, except for the Arizona plates. Texas plates were not uncommon in the southeastern New Mexico town, for it was the nearest town of any size to many of the ranchers just acrosss the Texas line. Some of them even owned homes in town in which their families lived most of the school year. Arizona plates were not often seen, especially on a vehicle so obviously accustomed to the rocky, brush-choked trails of back-country ranchlands. But a fellow rancher would only wonder casually at a work truck so far from the home range, and the average citizen wouldn't even notice. So it was of no concern to Wallace Bledsoe as he steered his vehicle through the gathering twilight in search of the Riverside Nursing Home.

The town had been named Eddy at first, back when Wally had known it, a cowtown that was making a tortured attempt at also becoming a farming community. Now it was known as the potash mining capitol of the world and the old "bat cave" had become a major tourist attraction. But he wasn't entirely unfamiliar with the modern town, because he'd returned several times over the years. Just to see the country again, to reminisce, and to see old friends. He'd seen them, but he never let them see him. He'd let John know how he could be reached, just in case.

Grace saw him this time, in the lobby of the nursing home. But he turned away before she recognized him, if indeed she could after all these years. After she passed through and on out the door, he hurried down the hallway to John's room.

John was awake, Gracie having just left, and the faded blue eyes brightened with the recognition of the jaunty form that silently slipped in the door. His weathered face conveyed a gratified welcome as he extended a trembling hand.

Wally's grip was swift and firm, and John silently marveled at the difference in degree of preservation between two men of the same generation. He would have recognized Wally anywhere, even if he wasn't expecting him. His hair was silvery, but when he eased his black Stetson back and leaned upon the siderails of the bed, John could see that it still had the fullness of youth. The black eyes, still efficient without glasses, flashed the old mischievous fire as they laid their plans.

Wally hid in the closet when the nurse came for the evening bed check and dispensation of medication. Then he helped John into the striped shirt, Levi's, and boots that had been stored in the closet for many months. He placed the sweat-stained, silverbelly Resistol on John's shiny crown, eased him to a seated position on the edge of the bed, and assumed his vigil against the wall by the slightly opened door, watching patiently for an opportune time to slip past the office and out the main door.

By the time their chance finally came, John was slumped over on his side, snoring blissfully. Wally gently shook him to semiconsciousness and helped him into the flannel-lined denim jumper he'd found in the closet. He was groggy and weak as a fresh-dropped calf, and Wally had to half-carry him outside. He shook his head at John's lightness as he lifted him onto the sun-faded vinyl of the truck seat. He banged the door shut, hurried around to the driver's side, and slid under the wheel. It took several grinding cranks to start the cold engine. They exited the parking lot with John mumbling directions.

Wally cut the lights and killed the engine and coasted the truck to a stop on the side of the road a hundred yards short of the corral, for although the house was yet another hundred yards or so up the road, John divulged that Grace had become a light sleeper in her old age. The pounding of hooves on a truck bed or the squeak of a tailgate would carry in the still night air.

John described the two mounts he judged the best trail horses, and remained in the truck as Wally made his way through the darkness to the barn. He lured the horses into the trap with the sound of feed being scattered along the trough, then eased around behind them and pulled the gate. The line-back dun and the blue roan were not difficult to catch and he soon had them bridled and saddled. He quietly led them out to the truck and loaded them with as little commotion as possible. It was a tight squeeze and a heavy load, even for a long-wheelbase wide-bed with overload springs, but Wally managed it. Then the overloaded pickup with two old men and two young horses eased through the blinking traffic lights of the sleeping town and headed south as a rosy fringe of dawn seeped into the blackness on the eastern horizon.

Johnny had left for school as the sun rose beyond the Pecos and it was setting behind the rugged silhouette of the Guadalupes as the mule picked its way through the mesquite, greasewood, and prickly pear on the slope above the Circle S headquarters. Occasionally old Cletus broke stride to rip off a mouthful of tobosa grass or some other succulent morsel still green from the unusually abundant rainfall, each time flopping a long ear in the direction of his rider. But the anticipated tug on the reins and kick in the flanks were not forthcoming, for Johnny's mind was not set upon the task of getting home in time to accomplish his chores before nightfall. He'd already dallied so long there was no way to justify his tardiness and he wasn't good at making up excuses.

An icy fist wrenched at his insides each time he contemplated how Gracie had leaned against Wally as he helped her down from the sidesaddle of her little palomino mare. And how, in spite of his presence, Wally had dared to lift her golden curls and kiss her neck as they finally said their farewells. And her smile of obvious pleasure at the gesture. Perhaps at the same time she was laughing at him as he turned with burning cheeks toward his shameful mule. He felt the bile rise in his throat at that revolting thought and, fighting down the nausea, he yanked Cletus's teeth just short of the next morsel and gigged him into a rough trot toward the corrals.

Many times John had fantasized that Gracie would come upon the scene when he was working cattle a-horseback near one of the wagon roads just as he became involved in some dangerous situation, usually something which threatened her safety. With courage and expertise he would quickly neutralize the threat and she would be filled with new-found admiration and affection for him.

In reality she'd never even seen him on horseback. Just on that broken-down mule. And in the wagon with the rest of the family when they all went to a preaching or a social. Always with the family, like he was nothing but a big ol' kid!

John's brow was furrowed by such disconcerting thoughts as he unsaddled Cletus and turned him into the corral. He fetched a bucket of barley from the barn and poured it in the trough as the old mule rolled in the dust; then he pitched several forkfuls of hay. At the same time he glanced toward the house, his scowl deepening at the silhouette of his father leaning against the jamb of the kitchen door with the lamplight behind him. He knew he'd have to make confession before he got his supper. All during the meal there would be reminders of how worried they were, and how unthoughtful and uncaring he was to go off gallivanting around the country with that undisciplined Wallace Bledsoe, and neglect his responsibilities.

Well, he'd take care of the chores after supper. There was enough of a moon that it wouldn't be too difficult. Just take a little longer. He'd be relieved to be out of the house and away from all the talk. He'd do his homework, too, by lantern light after they'd gone to bed. That is, if he could keep his mind off Gracie and the events of the day. He wasn't worried about sleep; it was doubtful he'd do much sleeping on this night anyway.

Chapter Three

Wally glanced over at the shell of the man that had been his friend when it mattered the most, pale and drawn as he sat hunched over, chin on chest, sleeping away the slowly passing miles. His black eyes became shiny with moisture as he thought of the tall, rawboned youth he'd known, and the quiet courage and unbending loyalty he'd treated with such flippancy. He never realized the value of true friendship until it was too late for requital. The enormity of his indifference had haunted him during all the years since. They'd been lonely years, years of obscure ranch jobs in isolated areas where he wouldn't have to establish background or identity, jobs that asked few questions and required little contact with others.

It was the loneliness that had driven him back here from time to time, just to see how fared the only ones to whom he'd ever accounted for anything. He wasn't so presumptuous as to complicate their lives by making known his presence. Not anymore.

When John's message arrived he'd trembled at the opportunity to do something to compensate for having been remiss. He did not think to balance the debt; he never considered it possible to do so. Just, at long last, the opportunity to do *something,* a thing that would really mean something to John. His white-knuckled grip on the wheel and the beads of sweat on his forehead were owing as much to his determination to see this last request fulfilled as to the unsteadiness of his load.

Nervously he watched the asphalt ribbon of the El Paso highway fall away behind him in the rearview mirrors on the doors of the battered Dodge pickup. The reflection of the mirror in the cab was blocked by the two saddle horses that were neck-roped to the siderails. Ahead and off to the southwest the distant ridges of the Guadalupes rose up on the horizon. He'd ridden this country with an eye on his back-trail before, when there was no pavement, and the quickest method of escape was on the back of a fresh young mustang.

The autumn sun shed its splendor on the scrubby terrain by the time the overloaded pickup rolled across the dry wash where the Black River flowed underground beneath the highway bridge. One of the horses shifted its weight and the truck lurched toward the shoulder. Wally straightened it with an iron hand on the wheel and glanced at John, who was shaken from his sleep by the sudden swaying of the vehicle.

"Them ol' ponies's gettin' restless, I reckon," Wally said, breaking the thirty-mile silence that had ensued since John had fallen asleep. "Can't drive more'n thirty, or they're liable to turn us over."

John grunted a response as he began to shake off the effects of the previous evening's sleeping pill. He'd tried not to swallow it, but the nurse had made sure. He pawed at his eyes with fingers that somehow seemed steadier, then focused upon the rugged silhouette to the southwest. Blue and inviting in the distance, he knew the appearance of the escarpment would change to a forbidding drab as they drew nearer. But for one who dared to enter its deep canyons and scale its dizzying heights, there awaited many an exhilarating surprise.

Anticipation stirred his vitals. He straightened up against the back of the seat, rolled the window down a bit, and lifted his head to fill his lungs. It felt as if the crisp desert air inflated his heart as well; the oxygen seemed to pervade his disease-ravaged body and a feeling of revitalization gradually spread to his extremities. Laughter swelled his chest and he couldn't suppress a spontaneous chuckle. He'd felt the same way seventy-some years ago when they'd escaped to the mountains for the first time.

The fall gather was underway. Pa always tried to stay close enough to keep an eye on Johnny, but that was hard to do when you were working cattle, and John was always on the lookout for an excuse to edge farther and farther away. He completed his escape when Pa was obliged to return to the holding pasture with a bunch of cattle just at the time Johnny managed to busy himself helping the Bledsoe hands head up some contrary animals that had broken away from the herd. When the bunch-quitters were finally turned he and Wally held back, reasoning they were not needed to trail the strays back to the herd, and assigned themselves the chore of scouting a canyon that sliced back into the towering escarpment of the mountain.

There were no cow paths or cow piles, not even any tracks except for a few of the mule deer. Soon the terrain became so steep and rocky that it would be foolish to expect to find a stray longhorn. Still they explored on, dismounting to lead their horses across areas of slick or loose rock, angling back and forth on the steep slopes of the canyon wall, totally mesmerized by the thrill of discovery as they climbed ever higher.

It wasn't until they rimmed out and gazed back down upon the lower elevations where they'd worked earlier in the day, nearly two thousand feet below, that the gravity of their situation permeated their awestruck minds.

The enormity of the expanse that at this late hour separated them from any of the wagons was self-evident, yet they could but stand and stare, silently marveling at the vast panorama of rugged hills, canyons, draws, and flats that spread out below them into the infinite distances until lost in the blue haze of the far horizons.

"We come a ways," Wally finally broke the

silence with an understatement.

"We'll play hell gettin' back down before dark," John responded, squinting at the sun.

"Best get started," agreed Wally with a disappointed sigh. "I'd purely hate to have to cross them slickrock places in the dark. A feller could lose a horse off the sides of them ridges even in daylight if he wasn't extry careful." Wally, always the leader, reined his horse around and headed back down.

John lifted his hat, rubbed a sleeve across his sweaty forehead, pulled the hat snug again and after a final look, turned his mount to follow.

The short days of late October have a way of ending rather abruptly, and by the time the pair wended their way back to the mouth of the canyon, darkness was fast overtaking them. Before the inky blackness of night completely obliterated their vision they selected a protective bend in the canyon's dry wash, gathered a pile of sotol stalks for campfire fuel and settled down to await the dawn.

"That ol' soto' makes a good fire, but it's sure 'nuff got a odor," commented Wally.

"Wish we had somethin' to cook," Johnny replied. "Sure am hungry."

"Got a six-shooter in my saddle pocket," Wally divulged, "if we'd seen anything to shoot."

"Oh, well, it's worth goin' hungry to see what we seen!"

"I'll allow that," agreed Wally, "but is it worth what you're facing when we get back?"

"What about you?" countered John.

"I finally come to realize that I'm gonna get treated about the same no matter what I do, so I mostly do what I please," said Wally with a scowl. "But you're really gonna catch hell!"

The fire in John's eyes was not entirely a reflection of the firelight. In his mind Wally and Gracie and just about everyone looked upon him as a wet-eared kid tied to the family. His face burned with anger and disgust as the image whirled around and around in his mind and a tide of rebellion swelled in his chest.

"Ain't gonna be hobbled no more, Wally!" His voice was choked with anger and desperation and Wally raised an eyebrow and cut his eyes at John in a look of surprise. He'd not expected his offhand comment to arouse such ire in his usually mild-tempered friend.

"Durn!" John blurted, "I'm man-growed! I swear, I'll leave if I have to! I'll hire on somewhere else!"

"Ain't much future in workin' for wages," Wally stated flatly, as if such a factual statement would ease the timbre of emotion.

"Well, what choice is there?" responded John in a more subdued but still desperate tone. "Way things are I can't see myself workin' with my paw 'til he gets so old I can take over!"

"They's other ways," Wally gravely replied, "to get your own outfit. . . ."

Wally hesitated and studied John for a few seconds as if considering whether he should go on.

"You see, in a way I'm in the same predicament," he confessed.

"What do you mean?"

"Well, my big buds'll see to it I never own no part of the Bar BX."

John accepted the revelation in silence, returning Wally's somber look and waiting patiently for him to get to the point.

Wally picked up another sotol stalk, broke it and studied the splintered ends for a moment before adding it to the flames. He threw an impatient glance at John, then ducked his head as he blurted out what was on his mind.

"Well, how did half the outfits in this country get started? You know as well as I do!"

John still didn't respond for a minute or so. He looked at the ground between his legs, picked up a twig and began to doodle in the sand as he gathered his thoughts. His voice was calm and deliberate when he responded.

"Times are changin', Wally. Folks don't take kindly to branding mavericks these days."

"And them *same* folks is the ones got their own start doin' just that!" Wally countered hotly. "*Now* they don't want to give another feller a chance!"

"Well, that's the way it is, and you know it. Can't be changed."

"Shoot, we wouldn't vent no brands, John. Just claim unbranded stock that nobody knows who it belongs to anyhow. We got as much right to claim them as anybody. I tell you, John, it's the only way! We won't brand anything that's follerin' a mammy cow, just weaned stuff that's been overlooked."

"Now that's an almighty scarce critter in these parts!"

"They'll not be easy to find, I'll allow that. But they're out there. In out of the way places. Like where we been today. It would be a start and a feller's got to start somewhere!"

"We'd have to have a brand. How would we go about registering a brand?" Suddenly John seemed to be going along with the idea. Wally's enthusiasm was contagious and his argument convincing. And the idea of further ventures into heretofore little-explored territories was virtually irresistible.

"I talked my paw into registering my own brand for me," Wally hastened to reveal, "like he did for my brothers. He's been letting them put their own brand on a few head and see 'em through to market. Teaches responsibility, so he says. But my brand'll never singe a hair on one of his steers. . . . You and me can use it together to get started if you're willing."

"I'd say you been studyin' on this for a spell," pronounced John with a knowing look.

"A man's gotta plan ahead," Wally admitted matter-of-factly.

Chapter Four

Wally momentarily relinquished his scrutiny of the highway to raise a hoary eyebrow at John. "Well, ain't nothin' wrong with your giggle box, ol' son. That's a good sign! You hangin' on all right?"

"Feelin' right pert at the moment, Wallace," John responded, a distinct cheerfulness in his raspy voice. "By damn, we've done it!" he exclaimed with a slap to his knee.

"Ain't there yet, compadre."

"We'll make it," John said evenly.

"We could've taken the road through Queen and driven all the way to the top."

"More chance of bein' spotted," said John with a negative shake of his head. "Besides, the country this side of the mountain was our home range and I'll be obliged for one last scout."

"You got it, amigo. . . . You hungry? They's vy-eena sausage and sody crackers in that there greasy-sack." Wally gestured his chin toward a canvas drawstring bag lying on the floorboard between them.

"Where'd all this come from?" asked John as he fumbled among the canned goods in the mouth of the sack.

"Stopped at White's City and stocked up. Reckon you never missed a snore."

"Them sleepin' pills *do* pack a wallop. Not to mention the pain pills," said John with a grunt as he fished his pocket knife out of his Levi's.

"By the way, you got any of them pain pills *with* you, pardner?" queried Wally with a concerned voice.

"Nope . . . only thing hurtin' right now's my hungry," John proclaimed as he undertook to open a can of sausages. He managed the task without spilling too much of the juice on his jeans, lifted the first link to his mouth with the pocket knife and settled back to gaze at the western horizon as he consumed the pappy meat. His thoughts returned to another hungry morning years ago.

Jerked beef and hard bread eaten in the saddle was the only noon meal possible on "the works," as the ranchers called the semiannual roundups, and most days there wasn't time for that. The young men hadn't eaten since breakfast. Gnawing hunger made sleep difficult and their bedrolls were at the wagons. They spent most of the night scouting the perimeters of the firelight for more sotol stalks and other dry brush to fuel the campfire against the autumn night's chill, and talking. At first light they drank the last of their water and headed out with full intentions of making as short a trip as possible to the Bar BX wagon to rustle some grub.

They approached a *rincón* which resembled a hill that had had about a third of its structure removed, leaving a perpendicular bluff plummeting into a brushy thicket which filled the flat bottom of the chasm. They skirted the edge of the thicket and began to climb a rocky slope to the rim. Suddenly there was the sound of popping brush. They drew rein simultaneously with questioning looks at each other.

"Mule deer?" suggested Wally.

"Maybeso . . . or could be a ol' mossy horn got wind of us and hid out. We spooked *somethin'*, that's for sure."

"Might as well punch 'im outa there and have us a look-see!"

They pulled their hats down tight and crashed their broncs into the mass of thorny vegetation, ducking as they fended branches from their faces and peered from beneath extended arms for a glimpse of the quarry. From the fusillade of popping brush they knew they'd jumped a sizeable group of animals.

The cattle broke from the thicket with Wally and John charging after them, whooping their delight and working their mounts to a lather by the time they managed to keep the wild longhorns from scattering. When the cattle were finally bunched and pointed toward the holding pasture they reined their ponies toward each other behind the herd.

"Wha'd I tell you?" Wally beamed. "I count six head of mother cows, two calves that's less than yearlin', three twos and a three. All the younger stuff is slick eared and unbranded! And most of 'em's heifers! How'd that be for starters?"

"Almighty temptin'," John admitted. "Should be more calves," he added in a concerned tone, "with that many cows. Hope we didn't lose 'em in the brush."

"Naw, we'd still be havin' a time keepin' them cows from turnin'. . . ." He took a long look at the *rincón,* barely visible on the horizon, and added: "And we could hear them calves a-bawlin' for their mammies, the way sound carries on these flats. . . . Naw, they prob'ly lost 'em to the panthers this close to the mountain."

Most likely screwworms, thought John. They were more of a problem than usual in wet years, and the blow flies were prone to lay their eggs in the bloody navels of newborn calves. Sadly, the little fellows didn't stand much of a chance with the onslaught of the flesh-eating larva. Even mature animals were in danger when the flies attacked an open wound or a sore. *Them bothersome flies could be another explanation why they was shaded up this early in the day.* But John didn't challenge Wally's adventurous explanation for the absence of calves.

"Well, now we got a good excuse for bein' out of camp last night," he said.

Wally had been toying with the idea of "sleepering" the bunch, driving them back into the brush and leaving them until they could get back and put his brand on the weaned stock that had not been claimed.

"First we gotta get 'em to the hold-up," he acquiesced, turning the black after the dispersing herd. "Next time we make a welty over this way we'll bring a extra cinch ring!"

"And find out where the critters have been going to water!" John shouted after him. He touched the spurs to his own mount and they continued their wild and desperate riding to keep the herd bunched and pointed.

When they were finally in the brush-fence wings of the trap leading to the holding pens, a couple of riders eased out to circle around and assist in driving them into the primary enclosure.

As soon as the gate was pulled behind the reluctant longhorns John and Wally dismounted, loosened their girths and led their mounts toward the Black River, which skirted the eastern boundary of the holding pasture. The horses were breathing normally by the time they walked to the water, so they allowed them to drink and knelt alongside them to slake their own thirst.

Wally dipped his bandana in the river and used it to wipe the dust from his face and neck. "Seen the XT wagon over yonder a ways," he said, glancing over his shoulder. "Ol' Jake Holderman sent a few hands over in case we happened to scare up some of his hosses on this cow hunt. His cookie always rustles more grub than them boys can eat."

John cleared the grit from the corners of his eyes with a fingertip, pausing after each swipe to examine the finger as if to ascertain just what it was that had obscured his vision. "Now, that's the kind of outfit I'd *really* like to have. Nothin' but hosses."

"Ain't no maverick hosses in these parts that I know of," replied Wally sardonically. "Our prospects are limited to cow-brutes."

"I reckon," John replied with a sigh. "Well, let's go see if that ol' belly cheater's got any leftovers."

The XT cook supplied cold biscuits and bacon wrapped in a kerchief. The boys carried it back to a small campfire near the cow pens where the hands kept a huge pot of coffee warming. They squatted on their spurs to wolf down the overdue vittles, then selected from the tin cups perched on the rocks surrounding the fire. They lingered with the strong brew, hoping to revitalize their weary minds and muscles.

One of the hands who had ridden out to help pen the cattle sauntered up and hunkered down to pour himself a cup of the steamy black liquid. He was of medium height and build, like Wally, also with dark hair and eyes, but several years older, a stranger to the boys.

"Much obliged for the hand with the critters, mister," said Johnny.

"McDaniel," the newcomer replied with a curt nod of his hatbrim, "Rafer McDaniel, reppin' fer the MDX."

"I'm John Stonecipher from the Circle S and he's . . ."

"I know," interrupted McDaniel. "Stonecipher's been askin' after you boys."

"Well," Wally interjected, taking up the conversation before John could reply, "we cut the sign of that bunch a-ways out, headin' west, and by the time we caught up to 'em we knowed it was too late to get 'em headed up before nightfall, so we just staked out and commenced the job at first light."

John knew that Wally felt safer relating the subterfuge himself. He was glad Wally took the initiative, for he'd never been any good at lying.

"Wasn't no trouble mothering up them sucklin's," said McDaniel, "but there's no way of knowing who those four big calves belong to."

Wally glanced at John with a smug I-told-you-so grin.

"The *patrones* will have to figure it out," continued McDaniel. "Meanwhile, we'll just put the Bledsoe road brand on 'em."

"*Holding* brand," corrected Wally. "In New Mexico we call it a holdin' brand. I can see you come over from Texas for the roundup."

John's heart quickened when he saw the color rise in McDaniel's face and realized he'd taken immediate offense at being so tersely corrected by the younger man.

"What's it to you, kid?"

Sparks flashed in Wally's black eyes as they followed the deliberate motion of McDaniel's right hand returning his cup to a stone, missing the simultaneous easing of the thong from his pistol with the left.

John, gaping wide-eyed at the sudden turn of events, missed nothing, and sprang to his feet as the two dark-featured cowhands rose to face each other. He knew of men who'd killed and those who'd been killed over some imagined insult.

"Now y'all just rein in there a minute," he said, holding up a palm toward McDaniel. "Wally didn't mean nothin' — shoot, most of the folks in these parts are most recent from Texas, leavin' out them farmers and promoters over on the Pecos. . . ."

"I can handle it, John," Wally pronounced evenly.

"*He's not carrying,* McDaniel!" Johnny persisted.

"So I see," sneered McDaniel. "Too damn wet-eared to tote a gun, I reckon."

"Got one on my saddle," said Wally. "I'll go . . ."

"McDaniel, I know you've seen his brothers around here," John interrupted. "I'd caution against gettin' them riled."

"The Bledsoe boys wouldn't even miss the half-breed whelp, way I hear it," quipped McDaniel with a smirk.

John shot a surprised glance at Wally. He saw the truth of the statement reflected in the hurt and shame that washed over Wally's face. His shoulders slumped as he unlocked his eyes from McDaniel's accusing glare. He stood with hands on hips, staring at the ground as McDaniel slowly relaxed and turned toward the cowpens with a snicker. Wally watched him go from beneath a downcast brow, then turned and strode quickly to his horse. John scrambled after him.

"It makes no *difference!*" gasped Johnny, catching up.

Wally flung the stirrup leather over the seat. "*You* don't have to *live* with it!" he snapped.

"Wally, I didn't even . . . *know.* Sure, I know your ma's kinda dark, but I — Wally, *it just don't make no difference!*"

"Ma's the half-breed," Wally replied bitterly as he tightened the girth with a jerk. He pulled the stirrup back, gripped the horn, and leaned against his mount with a sigh. "Half Choctaw. Paw married 'er up in the Nations after Ben and Charlie's maw died. That's why they hate me — her too. Part Injun. Shame to the family. That's the main reason I'll never get my part of the ranch," he concluded with a slap of the right palm to the leather. He wearily mounted and turned the tired black in the direction of the Bar BX wagon.

John scrambled to pull the slack from his own latigo, mounted, and trotted to catch up. He came abreast, but the morose figure slumped dejectedly in the saddle next to him didn't encourage conversation. Suddenly it occurred to

John that Wally's usual air of self-assurance and swagger was likely a cover-up for an underlying feeling of inferiority. They rode on in silence.

John kept mulling over the incident in his mind. "No call for him gettin' proddy over a little thing like that," he mumbled to himself.

"Trying to pick a fight," quipped Wally, overhearing.

"Now why would he want to do a thing like that?"

"He just as well's admitted he and my half brothers done had 'em a little palaver about me."

"You think they put him up to it?"

"Maybe . . . more likely just made it plain they wouldn't count it no skin off their backsides, if you know what I mean."

"Why did they tell 'im about your Injun blood? Seems like they'd want to keep it quiet, feelin' the way they do about it."

"They used to . . . and Paw kept them in line. But I've seen it comin'. Ever since this ol' black cayuse . . ." Wally's voice trailed off with a tremor. He patted the gelding on the neck and John sensed that the gesture was more for his own solace than the black's.

"What's Ebony got to do with it?"

"He came in with bunch of green broncs Paw bought from the XT," Wally explained, releasing pent-up breath. "Ben and Charlie both wanted him. Paw said whichever could top 'im off would get 'im. Ben got the first chance, 'cause he's oldest. The ol' horsecolt could *some* pitch," he exclaimed, a tinge of pride intermingling the bitterness in his voice.

"Ol' Ben couldn't stay with him, and Charlie neither," guessed John.

"Nope."

"And you did!"

"Well, it wasn't all that simple," replied Wally. "You see, I wasn't a part of that deal at the start," he explained, warming to the story. "But Ma was out there at the corrals takin' it all in and I reckon she seen the look in my eye and knowed I wanted this here ol' bronc as bad as anybody. So she up and says to Paw in that quiet way of hers that he ought to give his youngest a chance at the jackpot."

"Reckon Ben and Charlie took to the notion about like the cat does to a rainstorm."

"They wasn't about to set still for it. Wanted to keep on takin' turns between the two of them till he got tired enough for one of 'em to stick. But Ma shamed them into it, accused them of bein' scared I could ride him when they'd already been bucked off. Wasn't no way they could get out of it — Paw neither — and you could tell them boys hated her even more because of it."

"And you rode him!" John repeated.

"Wasn't easy, but I done it. They let 'im rest up a spell before I got my turn, but *I done it,*" Wally asserted with an iron voice.

"I reckon they've been after you like a bunch

of heel flies ever since," said John, bringing the conversation back to the point.

"After that's when they commenced talking like I'm not a real Bledsoe," Wally bitterly affirmed. "Commenced just callin' me 'the Choctaw's kid,' like I'm somethin' one of their cows dropped and who knows what bull it's out of."

"*You* know who you are, Wally. That's all that matters," said John consolingly.

"Yeah, I reckon," said Wally with a sigh, "and *I'll* not have to put up with it much longer. But Ma, she's got no place to go, and it's gettin' so they treat her like a damn housenigger!"

"But your Paw . . ."

"Gettin' too damn old, John. He's lots older'n Ma. Them boys're man-growed bigger'n he is. Used to, he could make 'em show a little respect, but he's losin' control. Plus, he don't have much reason to, now that the lust's all gone."

John felt his cheeks redden at Wally's unabashed revelation about his parents' sexual relationship and fell silent as they rode on to the wagon.

It seemed Wally sat his saddle a bit straighter now that he'd gotten a few things off his chest.

Chapter Five

Wally slowed the pickup almost to a stop as they approached the turnoff. The "rip . . . rip" of the tires crossing the pipes of the cattle guard marked the transition from paved highway to the gravelly surface of the Bureau of Land Management road that zigzagged a southwesterly course toward the distant peaks.

John retrieved his bifocals from their case. Wally had had the presence of mind to stuff them in the chest pocket of his jacket before they'd sneaked out of his room. He hung them on ears and nose and peered southwest to the eerie blue outline of the most distant and tallest peaks, just the other side of the state line.

"Still there, just like always," commented Wally. "Never change."

"From here they don't," agreed John. "Yet at the same time, they're constantly changing. Rocks move, caves get uncovered, others get stopped up; trees die, new ones grow, springs go dry . . ."

"Yeah, downright mysterious sometimes."

"Still, like you said, they're always the same. Sorta . . . eternal-like, I guess you could say. Anyhow, that's where *I* want to face eternity,"

John chuckled. "The sky pilot told me it was time I's thinkin' seriously about makin' peace with my Maker. I told him I'd never had any trouble with Him that I know of. Fact is, *somebody's* helped me outa lotsa jackpots over the years, and I always gave Him the credit."

The intervening years seemed to melt away as the two old men shared their laughter in the same way they'd mixed humor with crisis in times long past.

John gazed intently through the top part of his lenses at the sprawl of country sloping off toward the Black River bottoms. In his mind he could picture the vast herds of bygone years strung out across land unfettered by tumbleweed-choked fences as the drovers pushed them toward Eddy, where they would be consigned to a larger herd for the three-hundred mile drive to the market at Amarillo, Texas.

The herd that trailed to the holding pasture north of Eddy in the autumn of 1893 was much smaller than most. The financial panic that gripped the nation that year left the ranchers with meager expectations for the price of beef. Most were consigning only as many as necessary in order to get by until the next year.

The ranchers looked forward to shipping their stock on the Pecos Valley Railway, which was called the "PV" or the "Pea Vine." It had reached Eddy from Pecos City, Texas, nearly three years previously, but would not connect with the rails from Amarillo until 1899. The floods of '93 even interrupted the rail service for several weeks. Mining impressario J. J. Hagerman, who had joined forces with C. B. Eddy of the sprawling Eddy-Bissel Livestock Company for the irrigation, promotion, and development of the Pecos River Valley, financed repairs to the railroad and the irrigation dams. He did so despite the devastation of his New Mexico land investment, the flooding of his famous Mollie Gibson silver mine in Colorado, and the depreciation of silver all in the same year! Even his power plant, which was already providing limited electrical service to the fledgling town of Eddy, was washed away.

The problems of Mr. Hagerman and associates were of no concern to young Johnny Stonecipher and Wallace Bledsoe. Their thoughts were centered on the town two miles south of Eddy, east of the tracks, and on the opposite side of the dry arroyo of Dark Canyon.

Phenix had sprung up during the past year for the specific purpose of providing the very things that the founding fathers of Eddy forbade in their town — saloons, gambling, wheeliego girls, excitement!

The short stroll up the boardwalk from where the horses were tied could not account for the quickness of John's breath. Nor could the fact that he knew he wasn't supposed to be here. He'd opted to remain at Owen's wagonyard with the rest of the cowboys when his father and some of the other ranchers had gone to the Hotel Hagerman for the night. Under cover of darkness he and Wally slipped away and followed others of the trail crew to Phenix. John was about to see the inside of a saloon for the first time and, he hoped, more female flesh than arms and face and the occasional "well-turned ankle."

Wally pushed through the batwings of Barfield and Rhodes' Saloon like it was something he did everyday, but John knew he was feeling the same nervous anticipation. The smoky room was buzzing like a swarm of bees. Liquor, gambling, dancing, and more were available for the asking. And, of course, the paying. Wally swaggered toward the bar. John tried to keep up with him and at the same time peer about from beneath his hatbrim at the women.

"Well, I'll swun, if it ain't young Johnny Stone!" John abruptly turned around to face the sluggish voice, eyes wide at being so quickly recognized. "Stone*cipher,*" he corrected automatically.

"Whatever," sneered Rafer McDaniel, hanging a bootheel on the rail as he leaned against the bar and folded his arms across his chest.

Suddenly Wally sensed that John was no longer with him and turned to go back for him.

"Well, well. If it ain't the Choctaw," chided McDaniel. "Don't you know they don't allow 'breeds no firewater, kid?"

Wally was not to be nonplussed by the accusation again. No sooner had McDaniel's whiskey-slurred words escaped his lips than Wally's right fist exploded into his midsection just beneath his folded arms, doubling him over like a jackknife springing shut and knocking every bit of the air from his lungs. The smelly contents of his stomach immediately followed, spilling over his grounded hat. The putrid whiskey streamed from his mouth and nose, and his black eyes held a glassy stare as he cocked his head at Wally and made a tentative effort to stand and defend himself. Wally's whole body spun with the punch he aimed at the pallid face and McDaniel was sent sprawling belly down in his own vomit.

One of the house gamblers burst through the gathering onlookers and pinned Wally's arms in a bear hug.

"That's enough!" he shouted in Wally's ear. "He'll die if you don't let him get his breath. You don't want a murder on your hands, now do you?"

"Aw, let the kid go, Eli," yelled a savage voice from the bloodthirsty crowd.

"*Do* you?" the gambler repeated.

Finally the fire in Wally's eyes cooled and he quit struggling. Eli relaxed his grip, but kept a hand on Wally's arm.

"Someone help that fellow get his wind or he's gonna strangle!" he said with a nod in McDaniel's direction. Then he turned Wally so he could look him in the face. "I'd advise you to ease on out of here before you attract the attention of Sheriff Kemp."

Wally nodded, shrugged free of his grasp and sauntered out the door.

"Thanks, Mister," said John, stepping past the gambler to follow.

"Eli Shavalda," the gambler said, laying his hand on John's shoulder as he passed. "Best get your friend out of Phenix before this fellow gets his noggin' cleared and comes hunting him with a shootin' iron."

"Yessir . . . thanks. . . ."

Wally was leaning against the adobe wall of the saloon at the corner nearest their horses, alternately shaking and flexing his right hand when John caught up to him.

"Sum-bitch got a hard head, I'll allow 'im that," he said, blowing on his knuckles. "Well, I reckon we'll just have to try our luck over at Lyle and Kemp's Saloon."

"Bad idea, Wally. That Kemp is one and the same as that sheriff Mr. Shavalda said to steer clear of."

"To hell with Shal . . . whatever the hell his name is. A little light work like that in there makes me thirsty sometimes."

"Y'all could ride to the Lone Wolf." The high-pitched voice from the darkness at the corner of the building gave the boys a start. "They got the same things up yonder as they got in Phenix. Gals ain't as purty, but —"

"What the hell are you *doin'* out here a-settin' in the dark? Waiting to scare folks or what?" responded Wally as the short, bandy-legged old man arose from where he was seated around the corner of the wall in the shadows.

"Nope. Just doing what you saddlebums is merely talkin' about," he said, displaying a long dark bottle.

"Scenery's a lot better inside," stated John.

"I swanny, do believe 'tis," agreed the old man, "but some of them cowprods don't cotton to the smell of goat. Don't see how they make it out amongst their own stink, but that's their excuse, anyhow. So, it sounds like you *muchachos* are in the same fix. That is, unless you've a mind to ride all the way to the other side of Eddy and up to the town of Lone Wolf."

" 'Tain't *that* far," Wally replied.

"No, it ain't really, but it's a dry ride for a thirsty feller like you."

"Sooner we start, sooner we get there," said John, turning to the horses. "C'mon, Wally."

"Now, now, don't go taking the bit in yer teeth," said the old man. "You could start the party before you leave and make it a warmer ride."

"Oh yeah? You gonna share your bottle?" asked Wally sarcastically.

"Uh-uh!" answered the old man, clutching the bottle against his round belly. "But they like my *dinero* in there almost as much as they *dis*like my company. I'll fetch y'all your own bottle for a little extra."

"Well, *that's* a new way of bummin' the price of a drink," said John disgustedly. "Come *on*, Wally."

"Just a minute, John. How *much* extra?"

"How much you fellers got? You trailbums even got enough for a bottle?"

"How much you got on you John, lemme see," said Wally, holding his palm out and digging in his own pocket with the other hand.

"I swanny, just like I figgered!" exclaimed the disappointed old man when they'd finished pooling their resources. "Just barely enough to buy a bottle."

"Well, will you get us one?" asked Wally impatiently.

"Not for nothin', I won't," was the quick response. "What else you got to trade?"

John and Wally looked at each other and slowly shook their heads. Neither one could think of anything else with which he was willing to part in return for the service.

"Ain't gonna do it for nothin'," the old man repeated. "Every time I go in there I take a chance on one of them scoundrels a-boppin' me on the noggin or somethin'. Ain't gonna do it for nothin. . . . Onliest way I'll do it is if y'all will share it with me."

"Alright, okay!" Wally agreed impatiently. When the old man reached and took the money Wally snatched his bottle from the other hand. "Just to make sure we get *something* for our money," he said.

"Why, I wouldn't cheat you boys!" said the old goatherd indignantly. "Just go ahead and start enjoyin' yourselves and I'll be right back.

If'n I don't get bopped on the noggin or somethin'," he mumbled as he waddled toward the entrance.

Wally wiped the mouth of the bottle on his cuff, took a swig and muffled a cough with his shirtsleeve as he passed it to John, who lifted it for a tentative taste. The contents sloshed loudly when he lowered it.

"Not a lot left, Wally," he said, holding the bottle up as if he could determine the amount in the meager light. "It's a wonder that old coot's got enough sense to haggle like that." He took another sip and passed it back to Wally.

"So much rotgut's prob'ly passed through 'im that his gut's seared over," speculated Wally before taking another long pull.

By the time the old man returned, his bottle was empty and John had had enough. He paced the alleyway between the saloon and the building next door while the old man and Wally slowly consumed the fresh bottle and carried on a desultory conversation about the pros and cons of cattle versus goats.

"Come on, Wally!" he said after awhile. "That sheriff might come by any minute and wonder what we're doin' back here."

"Kemp?" said the old man. "Don't worry about him. Way things are a-bustlin' in ol' Phenix tonight, he'll stick to his own place like a old settin' hen on the nest."

"You talk like you know a lot about him," said John dubiously.

"Enough," replied the old man. "Me and his chief deputy's got a little deal a-hatchin'," he added smugly.

John ignored the comment. "Wally, the worst enemy you've got on this earth is just the other side of that wall you're leanin' on and pretty soon he's gonna come outa there with blood in his eye and a pistol in his fist. Let's *go!*"

Wally hove up and staggered to his mounts. John followed, breathing a sigh of relief. When he saw Wally fumbling with his saddle he rolled his eyes and stepped over to help him mount up. But Wally whirled around to face him, brandishing the pistol he carried in his saddlebag.

"Well, let 'im come," Wally countered, "he ain't the only one's got a gun!" He poked at his midsection with the barrel, vainly attempting to place the pistol in the waistband of his trousers. Finally he grabbed his belt with his left hand and pulled it out far enough to jam the barrel behind it.

"You call that ol' relic a *gun?*" asked the old man incredulously. He'd followed them to the horses and was squinting pointblank at Wally's belly while leaning forward with the bottle clutched in his fist behind his back. "I swanny, what *is* that ol' thing, anyway? A old Patterson cap and ball? You'll be lucky if that old thing even fires!"

John marveled anew at the old man's ability to hold his whiskey with so little effect on his perceptive powers.

"It shoots," Wally firmly retorted.

"*Most* of the time it does. But mark my words, she'll let you down just when you need 'er the most. Now if you wanna see a *real* pistol, you come on out to the river with me and I'll show you a real pistol."

"You got a camp over there?" asked John.

"Yep. Got me a throw line staked out. A feller needs somethin' besides red meat every once in awhile."

"And you left the pistol out there," John stated in a dubious tone.

"Shore! I go struttin' around Phenix with it and somebody'll hop me on the noggin to get it away from me."

"That special, eh?" John was still doubtful. "So what makes you think we won't go out there with you and do the same thing?"

"I swanny! You just might at that! Reckon I done got so drunk I ain't thinking straight. . . . But if you's a mind to do it, you wouldn't of told me about it, now would you?"

Drunk like a fox, thought John. But it was a way to get Wally out of Phenix, so he went along with the idea.

The old goatherd extracted his reluctant little mule from among the horses lined up at the hitchrack and slowly led the way with a constant prodding of his heels and tapping of a stick he'd pulled from where it was wedged on his saddle. The mule stopped when they reached the old man's "camp," although there was no indication of a campsite on the clean, rocky banks of the Pecos. John and Wally followed his lead and dismounted.

By the light of the brilliant stars and a fingernail moon, the old man went straight to his fishing line. "Well I swanny," he said with disappointment as he pulled up the empty line. "Wrong phase of the moon for fishin' I reckon. . . . Naw, them damned ol' turtles done stolt my bait again."

"Where's the gun?" asked Wally, making an unsteady dismount.

"Now just hold yer hosses and let me bait up again right quick." The old man fumbled among the rocks at the edge of the water, came up with a rusty tin can and proceeded to impale chunks of a smelly concoction on the naked hooks as he continued talking. "This here's my own secret recipe. The catfish can't resist it."

"Turtles neither," commented John dourly, with no effect upon the old man's enthusiasm.

"This here ol' Pecos River's plumb chock full of fish," he went on. "Biggest catfish I ever seen! Folks hereabouts can live on fish if the price of beef gets too high!"

"Right now beef's cheap enough to use for bait," said John with an impatient sigh. "Let's have a look at that pistol and we're gone."

"Just a secont." The old man flung his line out with a plop, rinsed his hands in the river and briskly rubbed them together to dry as he clambered up the rocky slope. He went to a certain pile of rocks, did a little rearranging and withdrew a rolled-up buffalo hide that contained all his "possibles."

"You fellers he'p me rustle up some brush," he said. "Y'all need more'n starlight to fully 'preciate what y'all are about to *be*hold."

When he considered the campfire sufficient he motioned them to kneel before his roll as he spread it out part way and extracted a black, silver-studded gunbelt. From the scabbard he carefully withdrew a long-barreled Colt's Peacemaker, engraved and silver plated, replete with carved mother-of-pearl grips.

Drunk as he was, Wally whistled through his teeth at the sight. "Ain't that a dandy piece!" he exclaimed.

"I do believe somebody just might lay a gun barrel across your conk for that, after all," admitted John. "Unless you've got a reputation for bein' handy with it."

"Can't hit the side of a barn with a pistol," the old man said disgustedly. "I can shoot my old carbine, but a durn pistol just squiggles around on me."

"Why you hauling it around, then?" Wally wanted to know as he held out his hand.

"Can't leave it up there in the *choza,*" he said passing the flashy firearm to Wally. "Melda just runs and hides in the brush if a stranger comes by. She couldn't do nothing about it anyway if somebody came messin' around. Get herself raped, maybe. She'd probly *like* that."

John shook his head. A man shouldn't talk about his woman like that. By the name he assumed she was Mexican, but that was no excuse. He took the gun from Wally's extended hand.

"Well, if you're not a *pistolero,* what are you doing with a piece like this?" he wondered as he ran his fingers over the eagles that were carved into the grips.

"Found it on a dead man up to the Cappy-tans during the Lincoln War."

"Why you old bone picker . . ."

"Well, I swanny! Wasn't no use burying it with him! He owed me *somethin'* for puttin' him in the ground! Didn't have no money on him to speak of."

"Well, you *are* a old bone picker! It's a wonder the feller that shot him didn't take the pistol." He started to hand it back to the old man, but Wally reached for it again.

"If he was still standin' hisself," he commented, turning the pistol this way and that to catch the reflection of the flames upon the bright finish.

"It looked to me like he'd traveled awhile since he'd been shot," explained the old man.

"Why haven't you sold the durn thing?" John wondered. "Must be worth a pretty penny, a gun like that."

"I was afraid somebody'd think I had something to do with the killin'. Folks notice a flashy pistol and remember who it was totin' it. If I wasn't so drunk I wouldn't of showed it to y'all."

"Got to have this six-gun, John." Wally's inebriated voice was nonetheless determined.

"We barely had enough between us to buy a bottle. How you gonna talk Mister — whatever his name is — out of that pistol?"

"Got to have a dependable sidearm," persisted Wally undaunted. "McDaniel will come after me with a gun next time. He knows now he can't best me with his fists."

Hell, the man was drunk as a polecat, Wally! John thought to himself. *He didn't have a chance!* Yet John knew Wally was right about the likelihood of gunplay the next time they met.

"Well, what're you gonna do, Wally? Shoot the old feller with his own gun so's you can have it?" asked John sarcastically.

"Ain't loaded," the old man rejoined. "Got a-plenty of them forty-five central fire cartridges for it, but I ain't drunk enough to hand it over with ammo in it."

John looked at the old man and his eyes narrowed as the thought struck him: *Drunk like a fox! You're already working up to a deal! You see the chance to unload that pistol on someone who's too young to have any recollection about who that dead gunman might have been.*

"Mister, what *is* your name, anyway?" was what John actually said to him.

"Abels!" was the enthusiastic reply. "Augustus Alonzo Abels. Triple A, that's me! You can call me 'Gus,' or you can call me 'Lon,' or you can call me anything you's a mind to, as long as you calls me fer chuck!" he concluded with a high-pitched laugh.

"Well, Mr. Abels," said John, "I'll allow you this, if I'd drunk as much as you have I'd still be back in that alley in Phenix. But I don't think you're any drunker than I am and I'm not drunk a-tall. I think you slickered us out here on purpose just to sell that fancy shootin' iron to someone too young to know enough to ask very many questions."

"Well ain't you the owl-head!" admitted Abels. "Nothing wrong in it. Anybody can see ol' Wally's too young to've had anything to do with a killing way back in '80."

"What if we told where he got it?"

"My word against yours. Nothing to prove I ever had the durn thing. Anyway, by then y'all won't have no idea where I'm at. Me and them goats changes ranges from time to time."

"We don't know where you're at *now.*"

"No, but you will. See, I knowed you fellers didn't have no dinero. Hell, what cow-prod does? But me and ol' Walker Bush has us a little deal a hatchin'. . . ."

"You mean Kemp's chief deputy you's talking about before?"

"Was I? Yep, that's him."

John doubted he'd forgotten a single word of what he'd said earlier.

"Anyhow, ol' Bush, he's a-fixin' to start up a butcher shop in Phenix, maybe even in Eddy. Cowden and Green's is the onliest shop now and it's run by that sawed-off little runt of a Dee Harkey that the Eddy bunch put up for deputy U.S. marshall."

"What's all this got to do with the price of pistols?" interrupted John impatiently.

"I'm getting to that. See, Harkey knows his business. He's already run two other shops off. So Bush is calculating to get the advantage on him by slaughtering nothing but young stock; yearlin's and such."

"Sounds like a good way to go broke to me," John commented.

"Depends on how you come by the calves," said Abels with a wink. "That's where I come in. He wants me to be on the lookout for unbranded calves to sell him."

"We've had some experience at finding them," Wally interjected.

"I figured you had," said Abels with another wink. "That's where you fellers come in. I can sell them calves cheap to ol' Bush 'cause I ain't got nothing in them except the catchin'. But I ain't no cowboy and besides, I've got my goats to see to."

"You want us to maverick some calves for you for the six-gun," stated John flatly.

"Zackly! Fair and square business deal!"

"No deal!" said John emphatically.

"I'll do it!" Wally proclaimed just as positively. "Got to have that pistol," he told John again before he could object. "You tell my paw I got a little cow huntin' job on the side. Be on home in a week or two. I should be able to find enough mavericks to satisfy Mr. Abels' attachment to the pistol in a coupla weeks."

John was doubtful of that. He expected the old goatherd would exact as much tribute as possible before he said "enough." But he was also aware that McDaniel would probably be at the wagon yard in the morning if he recovered from his drunk early enough. It would be a good idea for Wally to be out of the way for awhile to allow some time for McDaniel to cool off. Maybe he'd drift on out of the country now that roundup was over. John raised no objections to Wally's plan.

Wally's choking gasp interrupted John's musing. His face turned pale and he grabbed his mouth, jumped up and stumbled down the bank to the water. John went with him and held him from falling in the river while he puked his guts out.

Abel's shrill laughter pealed forth into the night air. "Alls we'll have to do now is scoop them fish offa the surface," he whooped, and continued to cackle and slap his thigh while Wally alternately retched and gasped for air.

Chapter Six

Wally eased the top-heavy pickup over the low-water crossing of the Black River. Then he reached under the seat, pulled out a dark flat bottle and offered it to John.

"Chaser, pard?"

"Naw, the doc said — aw, to hell with the doc; won't be seein' him no more." He took the bottle and uncapped it and sampled the fiery liquid before handing it back.

"It's the only painkiller we got from here on out," Wally reminded him after he'd had his turn.

"It'll do," John assured him, smacking his lips over his second taste.

Wally reclaimed the bottle and took an exceptionally long pull. He caught the concern in John's watchful eye.

"Don't worry ol' pard. You held my head while I puked up my toenails for the last time a long, long time ago." He capped the bottle and crammed it back under the seat. "I decided way back then that I don't *ever* want to wake up again feelin' like I did that morning in that 'ol goatherder's camp by the Pecos!"

The new day revealed that the camp of Augustus Alonzo Abels was by no means the only one with a view of the Pecos.

Among the cargo and passengers that the PV regularly deposited and loaded at the Eddy terminus was a constant flow of people who had contracted the dreaded "lung fever." They came to pitch their tents around the fringes of the town, hoping that living outside in the dry semidesert air would bring relief. Some were restored to good health. Many came too late, and their bodies were shipped home for burial among family and friends.

The tents that were perched upon the high elevations adjacent to the Pecos south of Eddy caught more than the early morning breeze. The horizontal rays of the rising sun reflected from the white tent cloths with a glare that stopped young Wallace Bledsoe in his tracks. He put a hand to his forehead to shield his bloodshot eyes and to massage his throbbing skull. He fought down a wave of nausea, then continued his drag-foot stagger toward his partner.

John jerked his girth tight, tied off the latigo, and was pulling the stirrup back when he heard Wally's boots on the rocks. He turned and chuckled at the comically painful progress of the approaching figure.

"Need some help?"

"No. . . . Well, prob'ly. But I got to learn to walk again *some*day. Might as well be today."

"I can throw you a rope!" said John, laughing aloud.

"Naw," Wally grinned sheepishly, "I'll just want to be right sure we got everything straight before you ride outa here. I don't recollect last night none too clear."

"Purty simple. I'm 'sposed to tell your paw you got a little job on the side for a couple of weeks or so, and you'll be on home afterwards. Do you remember what you're fixin' to do and why you're doing it?"

"Oh yeah, sure," said Wally, stopping before John and putting his hands to his temples. "Ain't that pistol just about the dandiest thing you ever saw?" Even a pulsating headache and a sick stomach couldn't dampen his enthusiasm for the fancy Peacemaker. "I'll bring it over and let you shoot whenever I get back."

John turned and swung astride the Circle S sorrel. "You keep a owl neck when you're around that old man," he warned solemnly with a farewell nod of his hatbrim.

When John rode up to the southeast corner of Mermod and Main he was delighted to find the *patrones* had not yet returned to the wagonyard from the hotel. He surmised they'd lingered in order to treat themselves to a leisurely breakfast at the Hagerman Hotel. John gave the sorrel some special attention with brush and curry-comb to insure that his father would never suspect it had been anywhere but right there in Jake Owen's wagonyard where it was supposed to have been last night.

John looked forward to a few days in Eddy. His mother and sister would be arriving in the wagon soon. Driven by Lalo, the wizened little Mexican national who always showed up every fall to help his father with the chores that the cowboys disdained, they would follow the herd in, leaving a day or so later in order to be sure the dust had settled ahead of them. The family would enjoy the town for a day or two and stock the wagon with enough supplies to last until spring before returning to the ranch.

The twice-yearly visits to town were a pleasant change of pace. The little town was growing rapidly and it was interesting to note the new homes and businesses that had been added during each six-month absence. They always looked to see how much the young cottonwoods that lined the downtown streets had grown. The town planners had laid out a network of aceequias to irrigate the young saplings they planted and tied stalks of ocotillo cactus around them to protect the tender posts from rabbits and foraging livestock. They would grow into mighty trees that would form a canopy over city streets.

The Eddy trip of the autumn of '93 would not be a pleasant one for John. For although McDaniel did not come back through Eddy when he left Phenix, the story of what the Choctaw kid had done to him was discussed among the cowhands and others. When rancher Stonecipher overheard it, he also caught the mention of his son's name. The confrontation that followed spoiled the return trip for the whole family.

John rode along in sullen silence until they stopped to camp overnight at the Blue Springs, about half the distance back to the Circle S. The one good thing he'd learned from his father's telling and retelling of the story he'd heard about their Phenix adventure was that McDaniel had been so drunk he remembered little of what had happened. He had the physical marks to prove what had happened, but he was used to waking up after a night on the town with cuts and bruises and no recollection of how he'd gotten them. It seemed his animosity for Wally was no more or less than before the incident.

John felt that Wally needed to know about McDaniel's present disposition. He was afraid their trails would cross after Wally had heeled himself with the Peacemaker and he would assume it was a shoot-on-sight situation when it really wasn't. The result might be that Wally would be guilty of murder or be killed himself.

The old goatherd had been persuaded to reveal the location of his goat camp. John insisted on knowing where his friend would be. Blue Springs was due east of the canyon Abels had described.

John slipped out of camp and rode by the light of the waxing moon as far as the mouth of the canyon. There he waited for daybreak to illuminate the search for the abandoned *choza* the old man claimed to have found for his camp.

The *choza* was simply a dugout with a small,

sod-roofed picket cabin built onto the opening. It was situated on the side of a little hill in the mouth of a header canyon which branched off of the main gorge. When it suddenly came into view from behind a prominent slope of the canyon wall, John noticed that Wally and Abels were already standing before it with hands on hips gazing in his direction. He didn't think the clink of horsehoes on rock should have carried so far ahead of him, but sound sometimes travels in odd ways in the canyons.

A scattering of Angora goats grazed across a grassy bench that extended from the hill, and the old man had fashioned a brush corral a little further up the header.

As he rode up to the men John could hear the calves bawling in the corral and he knew why they were so watchful. "Wally, them calves ain't weaned yet!" he accused without even a howdy-do.

"They are now!" was the firm reply.

"But Wally, you promised —"

"This's got nothin' to do with *our* deal. . . . John, if I don't get a good pistol *pronto*, I'm dead. I got no choice. It's just this once, I swear!"

"That's what I come out here to tell you, Wally. McDaniel don't remember a thing. He's no more proddy then he was before."

"Well, *that* was proddy enough. Besides, he might be foolin'. Anyway, it's done!"

"Wally . . ."

"I'm gonna *have* me that pistol, John!" The

fire in Wally's eyes and the set of his jaw reflected his fierce determination. John could see there was no sense in further argument.

With the conversation ended they could hear the distant clink of scattering stones on the canyon wall. All three turned to watch a willowy Mexican girl as she scurried down the slope and ran toward them. A medium-size black and white dog bounded ahead of her. When she drew nearer John noted the spyglass clutched in her hand and understood how they'd known he was coming. They weren't taking any chances.

The girl's face was flushed with excitement as well as exertion and her firm bosom heaved beneath the flimsy cotton dress. *"Viene jinette . . . trae la estrella metálica en el pecho!"* she gasped.

"Damnation Melda!" said Abels with exasperation. "I swanny, when she gets excited she cain't talk nothin' but Mes-kin," he complained to Wally and John.

"She said a rider's coming," offered John.

"I figgered that much. What else she say?"

"He's packin' a badge," said John with a smug look and a hint of satisfaction in his voice.

"I wouldn't be a-braggin' about it if I's you," retorted Abels. "You're standing right here with the rest of us."

John realized he was right. He'd have the devil of a time convincing the lawman he'd just ridden up.

"Prob'ly Walker Bush," said Abels confidently. "So what's she so excited about. She knows Bush. He's been here before."

"No es Boosh!" exclaimed Emelda, clasping the spyglass with both hands and jumping up and down. *"Es un chaparrito! Muy flaco!"*

"Ain't Bush!" Abels interpreted correctly, and cut his eyes at John.

"Short feller, skinny."

"Hot damn, it's Harkey!" said Abels with alarm.

"He have a cow!" Emelda volunteered, beginning to catch her breath and calm down.

"Why that owl-head!" exclaimed Abels. "He happened on that cow and knowed from the way she was a-lowin' that she's missin' her youngun. He's pushin' her up here to see if he can pair her up with somethin'!"

"If he's close enough for Melda to make out that tin star, I'd say you fellers better rattle your hocks," John opined.

"*Us* fellers," corrected Abels. "Melda! Take that hound and round up fifteen or twenty head of them goats! You waddies rope them dogies and drag 'em down here and help me stuff 'em in the *choza.* A calf don't beller when he's shut up in the dark."

Wally fetched his horse and they unlimbered their ropes as they rode toward the corral.

Like hell they're dogies! John thought. "What am I *doin'?*" he said aloud. "Hiding stolt cattle from a deputy U.S. marshall? Durn!"

"It's my *neck,* John," Wally soberly reminded him.

The calves were barricaded in the *choza* and the goats were run into the corral, milled around a bit, and rescattered on the bench before Harkey and the cow hove into view. No calves. No tracks. They even made sure the droppings were obliterated.

Emelda and the dog disappeared into the brush, Abels sat in front of the *choza* pretending to clean his carbine, and Wally and John leaned upon the corral as if in conversation with their backs to the approaching lawman.

"I didn't know you spoke that much Mex'can," said Wally.

"I have to work with Lalo a lot. You either learn it from him or you don't have anyone to talk to. He sure as hell ain't gonna learn English." John noticed that Wally had the old Patterson stuck in his belt. "What're you gonna do with *that?*"

"Abels said to show it."

"You always do what Abels says?"

" 'Til I get what I come for, I do."

"Durn!"

Out of the tails of their eyes they could see Abels arise to greet the deputy marshall with mock surprise, then follow along within earshot with the carbine held loosely in the crook of his arm when Harkey nudged his horse in their direction. They turned and said their howdys as he rode up to inspect the corral. When he asked what brought them to the goat camp they explained that Abels had befriended them in

Phenix and bought them a bottle when they were thrown out of a saloon, so they'd decided to drop in on their way home.

Harkey's steely blue eyes focused on Wally, taking note of his dark features. "You must be the one nearly killed that McDaniel fellow. The Choctaw Kid, I believe you call yourself."

Wally's mouth fell open.

"That's the *last* thing he'd ever call hisself," John exclaimed.

The probing blue eyes shifted to John, causing him to think of a passage he'd heard at some of the preachings: *Thou art weighed in the balances and art found wanting.*

"John Stone?"

"Stone*cipher*."

Harkey backed his pony a few steps and shifted in the saddle to study the *choza* for a minute. At the same time he kept the three men on the ground within the scope of his vision. When he moved out he managed to hold his mount in a sideways prance that permitted him to keep them in view until he'd withdrawn to a point downhill beyond the cow, whereupon he turned and rode away without another word.

As he faded out of sight John suddenly felt a presence at his elbow. He realized Emelda was standing there and his heart quickened. *How come a young woman like her up here with a old man like Abels?*

Wally interrupted the thought with his own question. "How'd he know about the fight?

They's lots of fights in them saloons."

"But you two were with the trail crew and it seems McDaniel had made out like he was a *mal hombre* amongst the hands," John explained. "So natur'ly they talked it up. Harkey musta heard the tale."

"Well we sure nuff slickered the ol' lawdog this time!" said Wally with a guffaw.

Abels maintained a serious expression. "Didn't fool nobody! You seen 'im eye-ballin' that there *choza*. He *knowed* they's in there. But he didn't figger on nobody but me when he come up here. He ain't fool enough to take on the three of us."

"Two," John corrected. "I've got no gun."

"Far's he could see," said Abels. "He didn't know for sure. You coulda had a hideout."

"*Durn!* I'm gettin' out a here before I get im . . . they've got a word for it I heard down at the new courthouse. . . ."

"Implicated?" suggested Abels with a wicked laugh.

"Yeah. Before I get *implicated* any more than I already am."

He mounted the sorrel, but before he turned it down the canyon he ventured an appraisal of Emelda's curvaceous backsides as she walked away. She glanced over her shoulder as if she felt his eyes upon her. It was nothing more than a flash of eyes in an oval face framed by dark hair, but the look said enough to keep his imagination active all the way home.

Chapter Seven

When the overloaded pickup topped out of the river bottom John peered across the oncoming flats to the grove of trees surrounding the cool waters of Rattlesnake Spring. Nothing short of death itself could ever erase the painful memory of Christmas, 1893, at the old Harrision place.

The Harrison place wasn't really old, but it was the oldest among the ranches of the upper Black River. Hank Harrison was the second person to file a claim in extreme southeastern New Mexico. That was in 1880, when all of southeastern New Mexico was still a part of Lincoln County, Eddy County being formed in 1889. The first claim was taken out at Blue Spring in 1873 by William Brady, who abandoned his claim and went to Lincoln town to become county sheriff, a career abruptly ended by the bullets of Billy the Kid.

The Lincoln War was a dozen years past when John Stonecipher rode to the Christmas party on the flaxen-maned sorrel that was his favorite of the Circle S remuda. The rest of the Stonecipher had gone ahead of him in the buckboard. He was taking a lesson from Wally, choosing to arrive late when all would be there to see him ride up. It was a typically crisp but bright December day, and he expected the majority of the partygoers would be on the leeside of the house, out of the wind and in the sunshine. One, in particular, he hoped would see him.

She did. Just a glance and her gaze was refocused upon Wally, who stood by where she sat on a low wooden bench with her legs crossed beneath her skirt and her hands clasped about her knee.

John staked the sorrel on the long, dry grass beneath the elm trees and sauntered over to them. She greeted him with a brief smile and again lifted her eyes to Wally.

"Last I seen of you, you was riding off on the same horse with your tail between your legs," he said, effectively destroying the moment for John. His heart seemed to deflate within his chest and his stomach turned sour. He suddenly felt just the same as when he was obliged to ride in the wagon like a kid.

"Didn't want no part of that kind of trouble," he mumbled.

John detected a glimmer of alarm in Wally's eye. He certainly didn't want his affair with the stolen calves made known. Yet he'd unwittingly broached the subject himself.

Gracie's mother appeared in the doorway and summoned her to help with the fixings. Both young men considered the intervention a timely happenstance.

"Well, did you get the gun?" John asked flatly as soon as Gracie was out of earshot.

"The gun? Oh, yeah," Wally replied uncertainly, as if surprised by the question.

"I'm surprised you're not wearin' it around to show it off."

Wally ignored his peevish tone. "Got nothin' to put it in," he admitted. "I got the gun, all right, but not the rest of the outfit. Abels said I didn't hardly do enough for the pistol, even. Ol' Harkey a-comin' up there that day made him *some* nervous. He was so afraid he'd sneak around and catch us pullin' a calf off the tit or somethin' that he just up and canceled the whole deal."

"The U.S. marshal's office don't usually concern itself with rustlers, Wally. Stolt cows are the sheriff's lookout and Abels said Bush is in on the deal, and that likely includes Kemp. Harkey just happened on the cow and got curious."

"That's about the way I had it figgered. But Abels said they'd been some talk about making Harkey inspector for the Cattle Raiser's Association. Maybe he's already been appointed or maybe he's just practicing up. Anyhow, him knowing about the goat camp sure did spook ol' Abels."

"Well, I reckon you'll have a gun for both saddlebags," John chided.

Wally ignored the jibe. "He said he'll keep the gunbelt til I get some money or he'll think of something else I can do."

"I like the first idea best. No telling what ol'

Triple-A's got up his shirtsleeve. Bound to be a skunk in the brush *somewhere,* when it comes to any of his deals."

Wally looked over at the grazing sorrel. "I see they've cut a little slack in the apron strings." He continued to act as though his first statement had been nothing more than a casual remark.

"Well, it's not exactly like that." John had been waiting a long time to tell Wally about what had happened. Miffed as he was at Wally for throwing cold water on his "grand entry," he was his only confidant.

"My paw was trying to track me up the canyon when Harkey came out. That durn marshal told him what he thought we were up to and told him not to go up there or he'd likely get hisself shot before we saw who he was."

Wally muttered a string of expletives under his breath. "I reckon every goose in the county knows what I done by now!"

"No, no. Pa's not one to go a-scatterin' everything he hears tell of. He wouldn't be a echo to anything like that without a heap more to go on than what Harkey told him."

"I'm obliged to 'im fer that!"

" 'Course, that don't mean he don't believe it hisself."

"I reckon your paw never did put a gold star by my name, but it's a marvel he'll let you in hollerin' distance of me now."

"Well, if he had his druthers . . . but, things've changed."

"How's that? What happened?"

"Well you see, I came outa that canyon right soon after Harkey. Pa was on his way to Abel's camp in spite of the warnin', I'll give him that. But I got to him before he got there. Course, he lit into me right away. I think I convinced him I only went up there to tell you McDaniel wasn't huntin' you, but he badgered me all the way back to the wagon just the same."

"So how come you're ridin' the sorrel?"

"It's no less than he'd allow another hired hand," said John dolefully.

"*Hired* hand?"

"Yep. He gave up trailing me a long time ago, but after we got to the house he just kept on ranting and raving about my shenanigans in Phenix and how I insist on running with owl-hoots and rustlers and how I'm a shame to the family and the Stonecipher name. I finally got a crawful and told him he wouldn't have to worry about that any more because they've been calling me John Stone anyhow, so from now on I'm John Stone and if he'd be right neighborly and loan me a horse, or even the mule, I'd be obliged and I'd return the critter soon as I found me a job."

"I'll swun, I don't believe it!" There was both surprise and a grudging admiration in Wally's tone. "I thought I'd be the one gettin' pecked out of the nest. But you ain't completely flew the coop, have you? What's this hired hand business?"

"Well, Pa commenced to backwater just a little when he saw I was serious about leaving. And yet he wasn't about to let on like he was giving in. So he says fine, he needs somebody to help Lalo build ditches this winter and he'd just as soon hire me as another Mexican, so if a job's what I really wanted, then I had me one. Chances of gettin' a riding job this time of year's about as slim as a cottontail's in a coyote den, so I took him up on the deal."

"Seems to me you're doing the same as always and gettin' paid for it."

"Well, living in the bunkhouse with Lalo ain't exactly like living in the house."

"He put you out?"

John answered with a slow nod to the affirmative. "I'm almighty tired of Lalo's frijoles, tortillas, and chili peppers; and the bunkhouse ain't what you'd call warm and comfortable, but I'll not give in."

"Leastways you'll have money to buy you a six-shooter," asserted Wally enthusiastically.

"What I need is a horse. I can't go just anywhere I want to on his. At least my saddle don't belong to the Circle S. It was given to me for my birthday four years ago. But I've got to get my own bronc."

"Maybe he'd let you work it out for that streak-face sorrel you're so partial to, sorta like the deal I made with Abels."

"I already mentioned it." John revealed with a negative wag of his head. "Says he can't spare any of his cowponies."

"But you'd still be using it on the ranch."

"And for other things. That's why he says he can't spare one. And he says he'd just be making it easier for me to get into more trouble. That's the real reason. He wants to keep my wings clipped as short as he can." John spoke hastily, for the women were calling for everyone to line up for the big feed. "Wally, you keep a eye peeled for a good pony for me, will you?"

The partygoers filled their plates with barbequed beef and sweet potatoes that were roasted in the ashes. There was a big kettle of frijoles with garlic and chilies, and a tubful of stew that had been made by finely chopping heads of cabbage in a barrel with a spade and mixing it with sour cream dressing. For dessert there was gingerbread topped with cream.

After everyone had eaten their fill the dancing began. Parties were few and far between and just about everyone wanted to participate while there was the opportunity, but the men far outnumbered the women. So they worked out a system whereby each man took a number and awaited his turn during the waltzes. A man could dance with a lady until his number was called out, then he had to relinquish his spot on the dance floor to the one with the number next in order. Of course, some would try to trade numbers in order to dance with the lady they preferred.

Wally constantly tried to juggle his position so he could be next in line after whomever happened to be dancing with Gracie, but he was not very often successful. Gracie, in addition to her sweet smile, green eyes, and golden curls, had a way of maneuvering her lithe and lively body so that even the most stumble-footed cowboy in the room felt like a prince when he danced with her. Very few were willing to forego their turn.

Wally was every bit as agile as Gracie on the dance floor. They were a graceful pair and sometimes others would stop waltzing just to watch them. You could see with one eye that she enjoyed dancing with him more than anyone. Wally mentioned the fact when he tried to talk John out of his turn with her.

To John it was an opportunity to be close enough to Gracie to smell the fragrance of her hair, to actually touch her and look directly into those limpid green eyes without feeling sneaky about it or fearing to offend her.

"Well, maybe I don't cut a rug like you, but I can durn sure hold on to 'er whilst *she* dances, and tromp her toe now and again to let her know I'm still with her," he said, trying to make light of Wally's request.

"She'd be as obliged to you as me," Wally persisted. "She figgered out of all these waddies you'd be the most likely to give us a extra turn, you and me being pardners and all."

"You saying it's her idea, too?" John already knew if it wasn't her idea it would no doubt be her preference.

"Now it ain't like she don't want to dance with

you or nothing like that, John. You'd most prob'ly be her first pick, next to me. It's just that the chance of the draw don't get around to us enough, and you know how 'tis with me and her."

Yeah, I know how it is, thought John. *And I'd not give in except she might think less of me if I don't.* "Aw, all right," he said irritably, "what's your number?" At least he'd get to touch her occasionally during the square dances.

More than half of the dances were square dances or "b flats," as they were called. One reason they were so popular was because everyone could participate at the same time. Some of the men tied bandanas on their arms to signify that they were taking the part of women and everyone had a stomping good time as those who could play fiddle, guitar, bass, or accordion provided the rhythm.

When the stomping and do-si-doing began to raise the dust on the hardpan floor of the ranch house, they paused long enough to sprinkle it with water and smooth it with a big heated shovel. They stopped to eat again at midnight and then went right back to dancing. Not until the new day dawned would the party break up and the buckboards, buggies, and saddle horses drift away toward their home ranches.

John lingered with the vittles as the little band started with a few waltzes to get folks warmed up again. All this prancing around to music made him hungrier than digging out Lalo's aceequias.

He planned to get back in the swing when they got to the schottishes and b flats again. Even if he should get a waltz with Gracie, Wally would just hound him out of it. This way at least he wouldn't be helping him get close to her. And he'd have more time to watch her swinging hips and exquisite moves as she danced with the others. His eyes searched for her among the swaying figures. She wasn't there. Nor anywhere in the room. Well, maybe she'd stepped out to the privy. There must be a waiting line out there by now. He went on with his feasting, unconcerned.

By the time he'd satisfied his appetite the music was changing rhythm. There was still no sign of Gracie. *And no Wally.* He glanced about the room, double checking. Suddenly he realized he hadn't seen Wally for some time. The men were not obliged to wait their turn at the privy. A clump of turpentine bush served the purpose just as well, and this time of year you didn't even have to worry about snakes and scorpions. *What could they be doing out there?*

He headed for the door, his blood racing in his brain and blurring his vision. It was none of his business, he knew that, and yet a team of wild horses couldn't have held him back. *He had to know.* When he was outside he paused in the shadow of the ramada and filled his lungs with the cold December air. He expelled the breath in a cloud of vapor and told himself to settle down. You couldn't just go out blundering around the place, making it obvious. He stayed in the shadows, moving cautiously among the trees and outbuildings and corrals, pausing frequently to stand and listen.

He was easing quietly from the shadow of the harness shed along a picket corral when he heard them — Wally's heavy breathing intermixed with small ecstatic female sounds. He froze and fought down the impulse to clamp his hands over his ears and flee, forcing himself to peer between the slats. A half-dozen two-year-old heifers stood at the far end of the enclosure, rolling their eyes at the two humans writhing in the spilled hay, barely visible in the shadow of the hayrack.

A brief look was all John needed to confirm what his ears had heard. In spite of the trembling in his knees he managed to backtrack quietly to the shadow of the harness shed and slip silently out of earshot before he let go of the excruciating sob that was jammed in his throat.

"*Puta!* Whore!" He spat the words, and doubled over with hand on knees, jamming his eyes shut against the scalding tears and shaking his head as if to rid his mind of the terrible vision. When he straightened up he threw his head back, willing himself to turn the tide of the angry tears as he stood with hands on hips, staring at the stars and breathing fast and hard. *You just wish it was you rolling in the hay with her instead. You've dreamed about it more 'n once,* a voice at the back of his consciousness accused. It was true and he knew it, but it didn't make it any easier to accept what he had seen. *It would be different with me. It would mean something to me. Wally won't never do right by that girl. I'd do anything for her. . . .*

Impulsively he jerked himself from his trance and plodded toward the elm trees where the sorrel stood hipshot and lazy beneath the naked limbs.

Chapter Eight

The restless blue roan shifted his weight and the unsteady pickup swerved to the left on the washboard surface of the unpaved road. Wally wrestled the steering wheel to realign the swaying vehicle between the rocky shoulders. He allowed it to coast to a slower speed before reapplying his foot to the gas pedal.

"Reckon I better ease off the foot-feed a little more."

"These ol' BLM roads just get worse the closer you get to the mountains," John agreed. The lurching of the truck had caused his bifocals to slip to the end of his nose and he pushed them back with a stab of his forefinger. Through the windshield he could perceive a light haze of dust rising above a group of cattle pens that had been set up just off the road. He squinted at the late-model pickup and homemade stock trailer parked near the pens to see if he could recognize them.

"How'd you know I's still alive?" asked Wally abruptly.

John gave him a dumbfounded look. "Well you wrote me you'd let me know if anything special happened . . . you know, like an emergency or something."

"I reckon cashing in the chips is one emergency I'd have a little difficulty letting you in on," said Wally with a tremble of mirth in his voice. "I don't know that a feller can send a message from the happy huntin' ground!"

John started to giggle. "Hadn't thought about that," he said sheepishly, and they both burst out laughing.

John finally stopped laughing enough to explain. "Bad a shape as I've been in, I just never thought about the possibility of you going first."

Wally placed a hand on John's knee. "Facts of the b'iness, you'd of knowed, ol' pard. Every place I worked at over the years I told 'em who to get in touch with, just in case the ol' pony stepped in a hole or something. Far's I'm concerned, y'all are the only family I've got."

"I'm proud to know you feel that way, Wallace."

John focused teary eyes on the pickup and trailer which were now much closer. "Wallace, if you'll take a gander over yonder at the squeeze chute, you'll see a feller who's got some of the same blood as you in his veins."

Wally almost lost control of the steering wheel again for gawking at the man as they rumbled past the corrals.

"That's your brother Ben's grandson, his daughter's boy, Winston Brittain," explained John.

Wally drove on in silence, lost in the thoughts conjured up by the sight of a blood relative after all the years.

John felt the air turn cooler as they passed by a hayfield on the right and he rested his eyes upon the green terraces of irrigated alfalfa. He recalled the irrigation ditches he'd help to build on the Circle S, and how the pain of the blisters where pick, shovel, and crowbar wore holes in his gloves had been nothing compared to the pain in his heart.

Mounted on the black, Wally appeared atop a knoll overlooking the flat where John and Lalo were building the ditches and check-borders that would direct and control the irrigation water for the Stonecipher's new hayfields. With pinky and forefinger stuck in mouth, he issued a shrill whistle that caused Lalo such a start that he lost his footing and fell into the newly excavated aceequia. John recognized the call immediately. It was amazing how Wally could make such a loud, disconcerting noise with fingers, teeth, tongue, and breath. He climbed the knoll, his somber expression contrasting Wally's mirth over Lalo's reaction to his arresting signal. Even with two months to think things over, John still didn't have a very charitable feeling toward Wally. He steeled himself to control his agitation lest Wally should suspect his eavesdropping, only to be at once confronted with the question which challenged that very subject.

"How come you left the party so all-of-a-sudden?" Wally asked the question as if the party had been just yesterday. It was the first time they'd seen each other since, for neither had returned to class when it was reconvened after the roundup.

"Belly commenced to griping me. Must've ate too much," John explained. "Decided I'd best get on to the house before I took the green apple trots." It wasn't far from the truth, although his nervous stomach had been brought on by something more than overeating.

"Found you a pony!" Wally proclaimed.

"That so?" The prospect began to take the edge off John's antagonism.

"Yep! I was over to the XT the other day."

"Holderman don't deal in nothing but prime stock, Wally."

"So? You want a good-un don't you?"

"*Es cierto,* but I've not been drawing wages but three months and they've been at *mexicano* ditch-digger scale."

Wally threw his head back and laughed harder than he'd laughed at Lalo. "Well, look at it this way — you could be starting one of them *careers.* Hell, you might even graduate to working for the Pecos Irrigation and Improvement Company!" He cut short his cackle when he noticed John's deepening scowl. "Hey, I's just guyin' with you!"

"Yeah, I know. But the *dinero* is gonna be a *problema.*"

"I think I better get you away from Lalo before you forget how to talk American." Wally used the humor of the statement to finish getting the chuckle out of his system, then turned serious. "You might have enough to pay for a good mare. Mare's ain't worth near as much as hosses. Ol' Jake's got a dandy bay filly he's ridden about a dozen saddles."

"She must be special; he don't generally break his mares to saddle."

"He said when he was working the brood-mares he commenced to notice how cat-footed this filly was and allowed he'd make an exception."

"Reckon he'd let her go *muy barato?*"

"I don't reckon he'll sell her *real* cheap, but he ain't spent much time on her yet, so that's in our favor. You'd have a lot of work to do, her being just barely green-broke and not knowing anything." He could tell by the look in John's eyes that he keenly anticipated spending his every spare moment working with the animal. "Tell you what, you give me all the money you've got and I'll go make the best deal I can. Me and ol' Jake get on like a couple of pups in a basket; I know I can work something out with him."

"Sure you won't run off up to Abels' and buy that gunbelt?" said John with a mischievous grin. The thought of finally owning a horse, and a promising young mount at that, was a tremendous tonic for his disposition.

Wally laughed, happy that the unexplained tension he'd sensed earlier had dissipated. "Already been back up there," he revealed. "Not a sign of 'em. No goats, no nothing. I thought maybe he'd have a little something I could do for him, enough to earn some more shells, at least. I don't even have enough bullets to do any practicing as it is. I should've knowed he wouldn't hang around after ol' Harkey boogered him. Like he said, they's plenty of good goat country on public land that's too rough to interest the cowmen."

"He's up in the mountains somewhere," agreed John.

"Well, after we get you outa these ditches and proper mounted so's we can sashay over yonderway and start building our herd, maybeso we'll run on to him one day."

John hoped not. Although he wouldn't mind seeing Emelda again. Reflecting on the feelings Emelda aroused in him had made it easier to accept what Gracie had done with Wally. The pure passion he felt for the little *Mexicana* and what he felt for Gracie were altogether different. Oh, he'd had the same fantasies about the both of them, but with Gracie it would mean something; it would be for all time. If he could have her he wouldn't need anyone else. Knowing she felt that same way toward Wally was not a pleasant thought, but it helped him to understand why she did it and to deal with the situation.

Wally whiled away the remainder of the afternoon hovering around John and Lalo as they worked on the ditches, distracting John with his talk of Holderman's horses and some maverick calves he'd seen riding to the XT and back. He spent the night in the Circle S bunkhouse. In the morning John turned all of his hard-earned wages over to him as Lalo looked on with a concerned frown creasing his dark features. John only hoped it would be enough.

It was. "Just barely," said Wally, as John extended his hand to let the mare get acquainted with his scent. Wally had led the prancing bay pony up to the Circle S headquarters just as John and Lalo were pulling in from the day's work on the ditch. John ran a hand across the sleek hide of the mare's neck and shoulder, then stepped back and walked around her, appraising the filly's conformation with a knowing eye.

"Proud as a chaparral bird with a fresh-kilt snake," Wally chuckled to himself. "She's coming three year old this spring," he raised his voice to John, "just right for some good hard riding."

"She'll get it," John assured him enthusiastically. "Just hang on to her til I get old Cletus unhitched and help Lalo with the chores, will you, Wally?" he added with a nervous glance toward the house. Wally followed his look and saw Mr. Stonecipher standing with hands on hips, glaring at the scene from the back porch. "Cert'inly, I'll just take her on around back of the corrals," he said, nudging the black away from the disapproving audience at the house.

Wally stayed for supper and spent the night with John and Lalo in the bunkhouse. They were the only occupants, as the Circle S was a family operation and Mr. Stonecipher rarely hired any cowboys except for the roundups. Occasionally an unemployed cowboy riding the winter grub line would spend a few days. When Wally left after breakfast the next morning Lalo hoped he would not have to cook for him again this winter. This hope was to be sorely disappointed.

Chapter Nine

Winston Brittain slammed the curved pipe down behind the poll of the next Bar BX heifer, secured it with a wire noose, and shouted for O. C. Kirkes to leave off with the hotshot. O.C. was always overenthusiastic with the electric cattle prod; he liked to see 'em pitch and hear 'em beller. O.C. desisted, shoved a slick pole through the rails ahead of the posts that were just behind the cow's rump to keep her from struggling backward against the head gate, and leaned his narrow body against the chute.

"We fixin' to take a coffee break after this-un, ain't we, Win?"

"I reckon," Winston responded, and shook out a disposable rubber glove as he squinted into the distance across the river at the dust cloud approaching on the road from the highway. After he'd stretched the glove to the elbow of his bare left arm and greased it with Vaseline he stepped back to the chute and gently rubbed the heifer on the top of her tailbone with his right. "Atta girl," he cooed, as she hiked her tail and voided her colon. He expertly slid his hand into the opening before she could even detect the one sensation from the other.

"Ol' man Bledsoe always said a *real* cowman can tell whether or not a cow's bred by lookin'," O.C. dryly commented. "He don't have to go a-pokin' around in her guts."

Winston ignored the comment and went on with his probing. The palpability pregnancy test wasn't the only thing he'd learned at the university that Grandpa Bledsoe hadn't agreed with, he reflected. It had been impossible to get close to the quarrelsome old man, and he'd tried very hard because he'd never known his father. Tom Brittain had perished in 1941 on Bataan along with many other soldiers from Eddy County, not even knowing he had a son.

O.C. popped the pearl snap on a shirt pocket and gouged out the makings for a roll-your-own. Ben knew he was anxious to take the break moreso for the smoke than the coffee. If he'd just buy regular cigarettes he'd have time to light up and smoke while he was working. But O.C. wasn't about to change the way he'd done a thing for at least forty of his fifty-some years merely for the sake of convenience, not even his own.

"That's one of the heifers sluffed her calf, ain't it?" he guessed.

"Yeah, but she was too young the first time. She'll do all right this time." Winston wished he felt as confident as he sounded. So many cows had aborted the past year that he'd been afraid he was facing an outbreak of Bang's disease. It was typical of the way things had been going the past few years. He withdrew his arm and checked the progress of the oncoming vehicle as he stripped off the glove. An outsized stainless steel syringe lay on a towsack nearby and he stooped to retrieve it and set the plunger for the correct number of cc's. After he'd administered the serum he released the head clamp and startled the whitefaced cow into backing up in the squeeze chute. O.C. clamped his cigarette between his teeth and continued sucking smoke in his mouth and blowing it out his nose as he pulled the side gate and goosed the grey-eyed critter into the cow lot.

"She's open," Winston yelled to Julio, and motioned to him to haze her into the left-hand holding pen. The heifer balked at being herded into the holding pen with the other unimpregnated cows and Winston was helping Julio turn her when the vehicle lumbered past the corrals.

"You see that?" O.C. screeched, staring after the departing dust cloud.

"No, what about it?"

"That old pickup damn near turned a wheelie. They got two ol' ponies in the bed and they was swerving and a-swaying and churning up the road like a coyote dodging bullets. I thought they was gonna lose 'er for sure. They oughta know better'n to overload a old truck like that."

"Well, maybe they're not hauling them very far," said Winston on his way to his own pickup.

"Prob'ly some city fellers going up to scout some territory for deer season. One of them ponies was a blue horse. You don't see very many of them around."

Winston opened the door and pulled a large thermos and three tin cups from behind the seat. "Yeah, those blue roans are pretty rare. I wouldn't mind having one myself."

Winston filled his own cup last and leaned his flat belly against the hood of the truck as he squinted at the disappearing cloud of dust. He judged they were just about where the road dipped into the dry wash of Slaughter Canyon.

O.C. lounged on the fender of the late-model Chevy stepside, holding his cup in both hands and breathing on the steamy liquid to cool it. "Yep," he said through the vapor, "I reckon old Ben would roll over in his grave if he knowed his grandson was sticking his arm up a cow's ass for any reason but to pull a calf."

Winston sighed and took a sip of the hot brew. Once O.C. got something in his craw he wouldn't let go of it short of getting a response. "Well, O.C., Grandpa Ben *is* in his grave, God rest his soul, and *I'm* ramrod of the outfit now!"

"May God rest his soul," murmured the mourners as the preacher ended his graveside spiel and the pallbearers began to lower the plain wooden coffin into the gyppy soil of the Salt Flat Cemetery. Tally Bledsoe's black eyes were moist, but no tears coursed her prominent tan cheeks and she did not vary her straight-backed posture and stoical silence. Ben and Charlie stood with heads reverently bowed, the April breeze teasing wisps of their yellow hair back and forth across their foreheads. John doubted they were truly any more sorrowful than Wally, who kept turning his hatbrim in his hands and glancing surreptitiously off into the distance.

The pallbearers backed away and Tally dipped her knees to secure a handful of soil, allowed it to trickle through her fingers upon the coffin and turned away from the gravesite with her long black skirts trailing in the dust. The late Anson Bledsoe's three sons followed in his widow's path in the order of their birth until the youngest stepped out of line with a relieved expression on his face and veered off in the direction of his friend.

"Gimme a leg-up." John was just about to turn the blazed-face bay mare onto the road back to the Circle S when Wally called out.

John reined around to face him with a look of questioning surprise. Wally quit trotting when he saw John respond, and approached the fidgety young mare more cautiously. "Gimme a leg-up," he repeated.

"You're not riding home in the buckboard with your family?" John asked incredulously. Wally was grinning as if they'd just bumped into each other at a Fourth of July picnic.

"New, I decided to fade outa that bunch of fakers. Gimme a leg-up?"

John noticed a number of people had turned to watch Wally's not-so-subtle escape and decided that "fade" was not an apt description. Gracie was among them, but of course, she always had her eye on him.

"The ol' mare's never rode double before. She might pitch."

"Well, hold a tight rein and don't let her swaller her head. But if she does, I'll take over when she shucks you and come back for you after I've learned her better," bragged Wally, extending his left hand. John gripped it and gave him an empty stirrup. When Wally's weight slid onto the mare's back behind the cantle she humped up a bit and John thought they were in for it. But after a little spell of nervous prancing, eye rolling and ear flicking she decided to accept the extra burden.

"Cut across the flats to the house and I'll saddle my black and our dust'll be settled before they get in sight of the place in that buckboard."

"But you should be with your family at a time like this, Wallace. Out of respect for your father, if nothing else."

"*Respect?* Then I'd be a-fakin' too. Far as he was concerned, I'm just a aggervatin' leftover from his lust for dark sugar; like a cow pile comes from a craving for grass, you know? Only cause I got for being sorry he's gone is Ben and Charlie's bound to make it even tougher on me now."

Wally settled into the bunkhouse with John, taking to Lalo's spicy cooking with gusto. Nobody turned a grub line rider away and Wally at least made a pretense of helping with the ditch digging. The aceequias were almost completed. The last project was to install the main head gate at the shallow rapids they'd selected on the river, and to dam the spot with rocks. It would only be necessary to impede the flow enough to raise the water level sufficiently so that a portion of it could occasionally be released through the head gate and down the ditch to the hayfields. Alfalfa was one crop that was impervious to the late frosts of southeastern New Mexico.

Wally was a better hand when it came to loading the rocks on the wagon and hauling them to the river bank. He enjoyed testing his strength against the weight of the rocks, but was prone to waste time challenging John and Lalo to see if they could lift some particularly ponderous stone as many times as he could. John kept advising him to save his energy for carrying them out into the stream.

By the time they'd hauled as much material to the river bank as they thought they'd need, one of those April cold snaps blew in. The cold river and the cold air would make a miserable combination, so the dam building was postponed for a few days. As usual, John took advantage of the slack time to further the training of his flashy bay filly.

The bay mare's coat was already summertime slick and shiny, due to the recent warm spell and John's currying and brushing. The nippy spring morning following the passage of the cold front might give her cause to regret the loss of her winter coat, thought Wally, admiring her conformation and travel. The muscles rippled beneath her cherry-red hide and her shiny black mane and tail whipped in the wind as she quick-stepped through the scrubby brush on agile black-stockinged legs. He reined the black in closer when John turned to speak.

"I thought I seen a little smoke a-driftin' outa them trees down yonder on the river by the deep hole. Let's mosey on over there and have us a look-see."

"Whatever suits yer fancy," Wally agreed. "We need to take that ol' mare off yonder where we jumped them mavericks last fall and get her rope wise."

"Yeah. We'll go soon's we get the dam built. She'll do just fine," John said, patting the bay affectionately on the neck. "Yep, she's a reg'lar ol' owlhead."

"Wha'd I tell you? I know how to pick 'em! What're you calling her?"

"Chris. Short for Christmas. On account of she's so red and flashy and also because of when I asked you to start looking for her."

"John, we better ooze into them trees yonder real careful-like. We just might surprise a brand burner." Wally twisted in the saddle and dug the fancy Peacemaker out of his saddlebag and stuck it in his waistband.

"Si, muy despacito," agreed John. "I doubt anybody'd be changing labels this close to head-

quarters, but there's no telling what they're up to." They rode into the edge of the trees and pulled up to listen.

"I can smell the smoke," whispered John, "but if they was working cows you'd hear 'em tromping 'n' bellering. Better let 'em know we're coming in or we might get shot at." He hallooed the camp and they moved on through the trees to the riverbank. All they saw was a campfire with a black coffeepot suspended over the flames from a crude tripod of cottonwood branches.

"That there's fur enough. Y'all just ease yer hands up where I can see 'em, now," commanded a familiar voice.

John and Wally reached for the sky with an exaggerated motion, exchanging knowing glances and laughing out loud as they did so. Abels stepped out from behind a big cottonwood with his carbine to his shoulder and a fierce, no-nonsense look on his face. The expression was immediately transformed into a gap-toothed, eye-crinkling grin. He swept the rifle aside and leaned it against the tree.

"Well I swanny! If it ain't John Stone the Implicated and Ol' Choctaw!"

A distasteful grimace flashed across Wally's face at Abels' last word, but he followed his partner in dismounting to shake hands. He knew John wasn't as happy to see Abels as it appeared, but Wally was real glad to have happened upon him, and his reason was in plain sight in his waistband.

"You better watch out where you pointin' that hawg-laig, Choctaw," said Abels with a cackle. "You liable to git yo'self *de*horned if you ain't real careful!"

Wally gave him a tolerant grin and got right to the point. "You got what I need to remedy the problem. What's it gonna take to get you to hand over that gunbelt?"

"Well, I 'spect we can work something out."

"You still got a deal working with Walker Bush?"

"Naw! Got my goat camp set up near to the state line now. Too far away to deal with the Phenix crowd." Abels moved away to pull his mule out of seclusion and stake it out on the green of the riverbank.

"What, then?" asked Wally when he came back.

"They's always a market," Abels assured him.

"C'mon Wally, let's light a shuck. There's got to be another way."

"Ol' John the Implicated's still kind of squeamish, ain't he?" chided Abels.

"Yeah," Wally sighed, giving John an exasperated look. "He gets about as cheerful as a bloodhound's eye when it comes to branding mavericks."

"Wally, them wasn't mavericks we hid in that *choza,*" he said evenly.

Wally turned to John with a direct and appealing look. "They'll be mavericks from now on, John, I promise."

"Well, now that's settled; let's have us a little breakfast!" said Abels with a satisfied chuckle.

"You just now getting around to breakfast?" Wally inquired with a look of dismay.

"Had to catch it first!" exclaimed Abels, and waddled down to the bank to retrieve a stringer of small-to-middling-size catfish. "They's biting kind of slow this mawnin', too. Change in the weather, I reckon. Ain't caught no real bigguns, yet. Maybeso they all swum down to the Pecos 'fore they got growed."

"Fish for *breakfast?*" John asked disbelievingly.

"Fellers, I can eat catfish three times a day and extra on Sunday," was Abels' enthusiastic reply. He looked down at his protruding belly as if he'd just noticed it for the first time. "Ya'll know what that is?" He gave it a satisfied whack with his free hand. "That there's a catfish graveyard!"

John and Wally joined in heartily as he cackled at his own joke, but tactfully declined his offer to share the fishy breakfast, explaining that they'd already eaten and needed to be getting on about their business.

"I been saving that there fancy gunbelt for you, Choctaw. When you get ready to dicker, come on up to the goat camp."

Wally knew if he let on how much it rankled him to be called Choctaw, Abels would just use the name all the more. Besides, he didn't say it in a demeaning way, as did McDaniel. "Where's the camp at?" he asked.

"It's in the last big canyon this side of the state line. About as far in as you can go a-horseback. Just foller the main arroyo up past the headers and you'll see a pointy knob away up on the south rim. Right down below on a sort of a bench next to the arroyo they's a little seep spring. We got us a lean-to right close by. Can't see it for all the trees and brush, but it's there. Give us a 'halloo the house' when you get close, if we ain't already seen you."

Wally stood knee-deep in the middle of the river holding a rock against his thighs and gazing at the distant blue outline of the tallest peaks of the Guadalupes.

John bent over the last chunk of rough stone Wally had handed him, wedging it into a close-knit position among those they'd already deposited in the streambed.

"All right, hand me another'n," he said. When Wally didn't answer he looked up and, noting his friend's trancelike demeanor, nudged him on the leg with an elbow.

"Huh? Oh! Here you go."

"You ain't dreamin' about that li'l *Mexicana* up to the goat camp, are you?" Many times John had wished someone would attract Wally's attention from Gracie.

"Naw. She's a fetchin' li'l splittail tho', ain't she?"

"You ever find out what-all she's doing up there with that old codger?"

"Oh yeah. Abels said he bought her."

"*Bought* her? You can't buy people no more, Wally!"

"Well, he sorta bought her. You see, he bought that goat-herding dog from her *padre* and the girl and the dog sorta went together. I mean, she was attached to the dog; you know how that is. And the dog worked best for her. Near's I could figure it, the old Mexican had more kids than he could feed and he reckoned she'd stand less chance of starving with Abels, so he snookered him into taking her to get the dog."

"You reckon anything's going on 'twixt her and that old man other'n her taking care of the goats and him feeding and sheltering her?"

"Don't seem to be. Old as he is, he prob'ly ain't capable of much. But you can't never tell about them old he-coons."

Wally saw that John was putting the final touches on the rock and slogged to the bank where Lalo had rolled another stone within reach. John was ready for it by the time he got back. After passing it to him, Wally again turned his attention to the southwestern horizon.

"What say me'n you saddle up and make a little welty up that canyon ol' Triple A was telling us about, soon as we finish this here dam?"

"Don't know, Wally. I thought we'd have some time, but that li'l norther set us back more than I expected. The way Pa talks, they're fixing to start rounding up right away soon."

"You going on the works with your paw this spring?"

"That's when he'll need me the most," John affirmed.

"Reckon he'd hire me on for one of his extra hands this time?"

"I reckon he'd be obliged to, seein's how you've helped out on this here doings for nothing more'n beans and bunk." John wasn't surprised by the request, but he asked the obvious question anyway. "You won't be helping your brothers?"

"Naw, why should I?" Wally splashed over to get another rock and brought it back to John.

"John, are you going on to Eddy after the branding when they all go in for supplies?"

"Always have. But I don't have to. Wha'cha got up yer sleeve?"

"Well, with most all of them off to Eddy, we could scout around for mavericks a little closer without arousing suspicion."

John concentrated on the rock and didn't answer.

"That way," said Wally, "I could get something to trade with Abels for the gunbelt."

John kept on working. Wally fetched him another rock.

"And," he added, "you could talk me out of it if I was to get the temptation to fudge just a little about what is and what ain't a dogie."

"I suspect you talk me *in*to more things than I talk you out of," John replied dryly.

Chapter Ten

Winston helped Julio haze the morning's last cow through the proper gate. "Time for *lonche,*" he said, gesturing toward his mouth.

No one had to tell O.C. when it was "dinner-time." He was already lifting the Styrofoam cooler out of the bed of the pickup and setting it on the ground on the leeside by the rear wheel out of the wind. "What kind of *sand*wich did the li'l woman fix for us today?" he wondered aloud as he pulled the lid and claimed two of the wax paper bundles. He opened a door and slid onto the seat, pulling a wrapper away with his teeth as he clicked the key into the power position and turned on the radio. Within a half a minute he was mumbling angrily to himself.

Winston took a seat on the running board between the door and the fender after digging out a sandwich for himself and one for Julio, who squatted on his heels nearby.

"Something wrong with your sandwich?" he responded to O.C.'s grumbling.

"Naw. It's just this damn radio! All you can get at noon is the news and that damn crazy music. Can't pick up no Western music nowhere. That damned rock 'n' roll stuff has done took over! I'd sooner listen to the news than that stuff," he said resignedly, and left the dial on a local "news at noon" program.

Winston chuckled and shook his head as he consumed one of the sandwiches Barb had prepared for them before she left for her job as a junior high school history teacher in Carlsbad. He hated she had to work outside the home, but her salary was very important to them for the time being. She enjoyed her teaching, but she would rather be home with their three-year-old son. At least the boy had his grandmother to care for him while his mom was at work. Barb would have to take some time off toward the end of the current term for the arrival of their second child.

"One bucking and one in the chute," was O.C.'s way of describing their family situation. He liked to use terminology that alluded to his professional rodeo background. He was one of those old-timers who "almost rode Midnight," the famous black bucking horse of the twenties.

Aside from Midnight, O.C. had indeed been able to ride anything that bucked, and Grandpa Ben had so admired him that he'd offered a job to the aging rodeo performer when his bones and been broken too many times to stand the jolting of the rough string any longer. O.C. had had a lot to learn, for the ability to rake the spurs while staying close to the saddle or surcingle doesn't necessarily qualify a man for ranch work.

"You hear that?" he queried, poking his head out of the cab.

O.C. had the radio turned up loud enough, but the newscaster's humdrum summation of local events had encouraged Winston to become lost in his own thoughts as he munched through his second sandwich. "No, what'd he say?"

"Old John Stonecipher's done disappeared. Just plumb vanished out of that nursin' home where they had 'im. When they went in to check on him this mornin' he wasn't there no more. Neither was his clothes."

"Probably became disoriented from some of the medication and wandered off in the night."

"That's what they figger, but not a soul has seen hide or hair of him. They gave a *de*scription of what he's wearing and asked for anybody who thinks they might've seen him to call the police or the sheriff."

It crossed Winston's mind that if old John was finally dead, maybe Mrs. Stonecipher would sell him some of their deeded property. That is, if he could swing another loan. He already had most of the Circle S range under lease.

"Sheriff might be callin' you in on this'n, Win, seein's how you been knowing old John and leasing from him," O.C. opined.

"Oh, I doubt it," disagreed Winston. He'd been appointed as a special deputy for the isolated southern end of the county. It was a part-time, on-call position that usually required very little of his time. The meager salary for his services was nonetheless a welcome addition to the family budget. He'd taken some law-enforcement courses at the university and this, along with his location and his friendship with several of the department's officers, had influenced his selection for the post. He'd already been a member of the Eddy County Sheriff's Posse, a support organization that promoted gymkhanas; competitive riding games for the youth of the area.

"Yep, the old scudder must of went daffy and wandered off somewhere," O.C. went on, "but seems like somebody would of seen him. . . . Say, wasn't he a friend of your gran'pappy's way back?"

"Well, not exactly. He was friends with Grandpa's half brother."

"I didn't know ol' Ben had a brother."

"Had two, counting the half brother."

"What happened to 'em? They still living?"

"No, both of them died in 1894. The half brother shot the full brother, then was killed himself in . . . an accident, I guess you could say. Grandpa always believed it was actually someone else who was killed in the accident."

Winston would never forget the periodic nighttime disturbances that had awakened the household over the years, and the old man's drunken rantings: "That renegade Choctaw's alive, I tell you! He's still up thar in them mountains jest a-waitin' to pounce! Wasn't him they found, I tell you! That John Stone knows where he's at, but he won't tell nobody! He's still up thar, and he's a-coming for *me,* I tell you!" Winston often wondered if Ben Bledsoe might have managed to hold on to more of the original Bar BX holdings were it not for his obsession that his vengeful "half-breed" brother was still out there somewhere.

The cogs of O.C.'s imagination were set awhirl by Winston's unearthing of the family skeletons. "Well, I'll be switched! Quicktrigger doin's in the good old two-gun times! So what kind of a accident was it, then? And how come him to shoot his own brother? How come old Ben didn't believe it was the half brother got killed in the accident?"

"I'll tell you what I know about it, sometime. Mom can probably tell you more. Right now we've got to get back to work if we're going to finish with this bunch of cows before dark."

The smell of seared flesh and singed hair accompanied the sound of bawling protest as Wally described his WX connected brand on the side of the big calf that was stretched between the two horses. The single-bar iron he used had been fashioned from a handle that had broken off one of the Circle S branding irons. Thereby the WX could be burned with six swift impressions, much easier than using a heated cinch ring or a running iron.

The black maintained the tension on the rope stretching from the horns, but the bay responded to the consequent tug on her saddle-horn and moved forward a step. John waved his arms with a sharp "back-up!" and she immediately took the slack out of the rope that had the calf's rear feet captured.

"She's catchin' on purty quick," said Wally, stepping away from the freshly branded calf.

"I figgered she would," agreed John, and kneeled to quickly transform the young bull into a steer with his razor-sharp pocket knife, eliciting another indignant bellow.

"Dope 'im good," instructed Wally, "we don't want them confounded blowflies gettin' to 'im."

"I reckon this'n'll go up the canyon to pay for that gunbelt, eh?"

"Shouldn't take more'n a couple or three steers," Wally assured him. "It's good we're finding so many heifers," he added.

"We're gonna have to start studyin' on staking a claim to some water around here somewhere if we're gonna make this a legitimate outfit."

"Gonna have to do somethin' purty soon," Wally cheerfully agreed, "at the rate we're accumulatin' a herd."

The number of cattle wearing the new WX connected brand was growing much faster than John would have ever believed possible. He and Wally had packed enough provisions on their saddles to last for several days of scouting the countryside for unbranded cattle and ridden straightaway for the outer fringes of the area that had been canvassed by the spring roundup.

They immediately began to find a few head scattered here and there. At first John was amazed that so many had been carelessly overlooked during the recent cow hunt. Then he began to notice that Wally seemed to have an uncanny knack for directing their search into the areas where they happened to find the strays. It occured to him that Wally had worked by himself a good deal of the time during the roundup, and a dark suspicion had crept into his mind. He decided it was time to air it out.

They mounted their horses, nudged them forward and flicked the slackened lariats off the steer before it could struggle to its feet.

"Wally," said John, nudging the mare closer as he coiled his lariat, "You sleepered most of these cows when you was on the works, didn't you?"

Wally's silent look was answer enough, but John would say no more until he responded. "We got just as much right to claim 'em as anybody, John," he said finally.

"You was drawin' Circle S pay and workin' for yourself!" John accused.

"For *us,*" Wally reminded him. "But it didn't take no time a-tall to turn a head or two back every now and then. And you remember I came in later than anybody else of a evening a bunch of times."

Not much later, thought John. But it was no use to argue with Wally's self-justification. And he had to admit he was pleased with the results.

They stayed out three days and came back to

the Circle S to rest the horses two days and restock their provisions before going out on another foray. The Stoneciphers would be returning before they got back this time, so John left a note saying he'd return in a few days to see if his father had anything for him to do. They rode beyond the area they'd previously scouted and continued to rope and brand everything they could find that was weaned and unbranded. They set up a base camp in the lee of a small *rincón.* It was not nearly as large as the one where they'd found the strays during the fall roundup and had only a scattering of trees and brush.

On the third night out, after staking their horses out to graze and eating the last of their beans and salt pork, they reclined against their saddles and watched the campfire slowly burn down before turning in.

"Gonna have to get us a pack horse so's we don't have to go back for supplies so often," observed John, stifling a yawn.

"If we had a good carbine we could shoot a young mule deer for camp meat now and then."

John lifted his hat and ran his fingers through his sandy hair as if the enormity of what they'd begun was just beginning to sink in. "We'll have to have more cow ponies, too. These'll stay rode down all the time if we don't get some others. Shucks, on the works each man has six or eight or more apiece."

"We'll have to gather a few steers to sell from time to time and gradually accumulate what we need. We can drive 'em south across the line somewhere and sell 'em to keep from showing our hand around here too soon. Pecos City maybe, or Toyah. Or maybe we can work something out with ol' Abels to move them for us. Won't get much for them that way, but we'll just have to do the best we can for starters. Whatever it takes."

The mare whickered softly in the darkness and at the same time they heard the unmistakable sound of metal on rock. Both men sprang to their feet and started to move away from the firelight, but a familiar voice caused them to stop and relax. "It's alright, jest stand easy. I'm coming in." A white horse materialized out of the night.

Wally assumed a hands-on-hips posture with his head slanted in a disgusted attitude. "What the hell you doing out here Charlie? You liable to get yourself shot, riding up on a man's camp in the dark like that without a halloo or a by-your-leave, don't you know that?"

"Don't see no guns," jeered Charlie, "not to mention no men." He swung off his mount and walked into the circle of firelight and leaned forward to spit a stream of tobacco juice into the flames. The fire illuminated a sneering look of contempt upon his face.

"Don't recall inviting you to light and set, Charlie," Wally flatly stated. "What cause you got to be a-slinkin' around out here in the dark like a polecat anyway?"

"Ain't fixin' to set," answered Charlie. "Just been trackin' some Bar BX stock that's been missin' ever since the funeral." He turned and raised an eyebrow in the direction of the grazing horses.

Wally's eyes flared. He dropped his hands from his hips and took a step toward his brother. "What the . . ."

"Both o' them ponies is wearin' the XT brand," interrupted John.

"Stay out of it Stonecipher. The Bar BX is holding a bill of sale describing that black horse and it's signed by Mr. Jake Holderman hisself."

"Now Charlie, you know that horse was give to me a long time ago!" Wally moved a step closer.

"Not by me. Ben didn't give it to you. We're the owners of the Bar BX and I'm taking that black horse back where he belongs!"

"You bastard!" shouted Wally. He took another step and slammed his palms into Charlie's chest, knocking the larger man off balance for an instant.

Charlie's lip curled even higher, exposing tobacco-stained teeth. "Why you little half-breed pissant!" he blurted. A looping backhand shot out and smacked Wally across the mouth, drawing blood and spinning him around. Then Charlie drove the toe of his boot into Wally's crotch, sending him sprawling face down on the rocky ground near his saddle.

John lunged at the big raw-boned man, but

Charlie stepped back and tripped him, at the same time clubbing him on the back of the neck. John hit the ground and rolled over and started to spring to his feet, but Charlie pulled the short-barreled six-shooter he wore waist high and butt forward on the left.

"You best stay where you are, Stonecipher," he warned. "This here's fam'ly b'iness and you just stay out of it if you don't wanna get hurt."

John eased back on his haunches, yet kept his hands on the ground ready to push into action.

Charlie took several steps backward and reached to loosen his horn string and take his lariat from the saddle. He holstered the pistol and shook out a length of rope as he moved toward Wally's prostrate form. "A good horse whippin'll take the rooster outa you," he proclaimed with a sweep of his hand. The knotted end of the rope slashed viciously across Wally's back, tearing his shirt and drawing blood. John lunged at Charlie again, but Charlie anticipated the move and whirled to deliver a brutalizing kick to John's sternum, knocking him down and momentarily taking his breath away. "Try that again and I'll use the pistol." He punctuated the warning with a stream of tobacco juice and turned back to bring the rope slashing across Wally's back a second time.

John gasped for breath and was making ready to try again when he saw that Wally had crawled upon his saddle and was digging in the saddle pouch. "Wally! No!"

Charlie swung the rope for another stroke. Wally rolled over with the shiny Peacemaker held in both hands and thumbed the hammer back. Charlie's mouth dropped open and he let go the rope in midswing, grabbed the holster with his left hand and jerked out the pistol with his right.

"Drop it Char . . ." the blast of the forty-five overrode Wally's warning.

Charlie's face turned gray in the flickering firelight. He stood slack-jawed, staring down at the crimson stain spreading across his shirt just below the left pectoral. Then he looked at his pistol, unfired in his hand, as if he wondered how it got there. He glanced at Wally, who remained with his back against his saddle, still clutching the long-barreled six-gun in both hands between his knees. It was recocked and holding a steady aim on his chest. With another confused look at his own gun, he stabbed it into the holster and turned to his horse, which sidled about nervously but did not spook. Grabbing a handful of reins and saddlehorn, he dragged himself astraddle and took one more disbelieving look at Wally before socking the spurs to the beast and galloping away into the night.

Chapter Eleven

The blue roan stood with head down and sides heaving when Wally reined in for a rest stop and dismounted. He noted the paleness of John's face and moved quickly to assist him as he laboriously hauled his right leg across the cantle to effect a painful dismount. His steadying grip on John's arm was all that prevented him from staggering to a rocky spill on the narrow trail. When John was securely seated on a flat-topped boulder with canteen at hand, Wally turned to loosen the cinches.

"Better give these ol' ponies a chance to blow before we go on up to the ridge. I can tell they've not been rode much of late. They's well-fed but shy on condition."

"Who's to ride 'em, with me shut up in that calaboose of a nursing home? Grace don't ride no more, and I was told not to, even before they locked me up. I just kept 'em around for the company, I reckon."

"You always was one to make pets out of horses," said Wally with a reminiscent smile. He pulled the black Stetson from his silver crown and tilted his head to survey the heights that towered over their position on the side of the mountain. "The last couple of hundred yards was always the worst," he recalled.

"Steep, and lotsa slickrock," John agreed. "We'd best lead the horses the rest of the way."

Wally gave him a suspicious eye. "You up to climbing, pard?"

John scrutinized the steep tangle of rocks and scrubby brush that obscured the dim switchback trail to the rim. "I don't rightly know, Wallace. But I do know if that ol' town horse there was to lose his feet I could let go the reins a lot quicker'n I could shuck the saddle. I come up here to die *on* the mountain, not from falling off of it," he said with a chuckle, and turned his head to squint at the sun. "We got plenty of daylight, so we can just take it a little bit at a time. . . . We'll be campin' on Lonesome Ridge tonight!" he said with a grin.

"I'm gonna see if I can find Abels' camp," said Wally finally, after what seemed to John an eternity of sitting next to his saddle and staring at the pistol in his hand.

John was standing before the campfire, staring into the flames and pondering their situation, not knowing what to say to break the silence that ensued Charlie's departure. A short time earlier they were eagerly planning how they were going to make their dreams come true. A few seconds of sudden violence reduced them to a loss of words as each absorbed the shock of what had happened and contemplated the effects the tragic confrontation might have and what their next move should be.

"If Abels told us straight," John mumbled, "he shouldn't be too hard to locate."

"You going with me?"

John slowly wagged his head to the negative, still staring into the flames. "No, I reckon not. I expect we'd best know how bad Charlie's wounded and what they aim to do about it before we make any more plans."

"He was plugged good enough to make him leave us alone," said Wally with a tremor of satisfaction.

"For the time being." John shifted his gaze to his partner. "But you know them boys won't let it go at that."

Wally raised the pistol in a menacing gesture. "They better learn to leave me alone!" he proclaimed in a voice choked with emotion.

John frowned and looked away. "Come daylight I'll follow Charlie and make sure he got back to the Bar BX. I'd go right now but I'm afraid I'd miss him in the dark if he happened to pass out and fall off his horse somewhere betwixt here and yonder."

"Well, you be careful, John. If he sees you on his trail the only thanks that onery skunk'll give you for your trouble will be a bullet in the gut and spit in yer eye while he watches you die." The Peacemaker gleamed in the firelight as Wally carefully returned it to the saddlebag. Then he untied his soogans and began to spread his bed. "You'll come up to Abels' after you find out about Charlie?"

John got his own bedroll and shook it out. "Soon as I know something worth tellin' I'll be there."

There were no drops of blood to be seen on the rocks and vegetation along Charlie's trail, and John took that to be a good sign. Keeping a wary eye for Bar BX riders, he eased to within sight of the ranch headquarters. If Charlie fell off his mount close to home, the riderless horse surely went on to the corral and alerted the crew. Satisfied that Charlie had indeed reached help and haven, John turned the bay and drifted away toward the Circle S, thinking to use his father's ranch as a base while keeping an ear to the ground for information about Charlie's condition and any plans for retaliation.

He wondered what Charlie's version of the incident would be. And what would John's parents say when they heard the story? It was too much to hope that Charlie wouldn't mention his presence. No doubt he'd exaggerate John's part in the fray in order to save face in coming off the loser. His parents would suspect he was there, anyway. They knew when he wasn't at home he was always with Wally. There would be enough questions even before they heard about the shooting. With that thought he abruptly reined the mare to the opposite direction. It would probably be a few days before any news of how Charlie fared reached the Circle S, so why face the interrogation sooner than necessary?

For awhile John drifted aimlessly to the south, away from the river, lost in thought and not going anywhere in particular. He had some provisions on his saddle, so he figured he'd just wander until he found a likely spot with good grass and camp for a day or two. There was a stock tank in a draw not too far from the Lazy P which usually held some water, so he pointed Chris in that direction. The Lazy P belonged to the Porters, Gracie's family. Thoughts of her were the only ones appealing enough to divert his concentration from the problems evoked by the previous night's episode.

The fact that she was on his mind as he approached the brink of the draw in which a dirt dam had been built to form the tank could not diminish the jolting impact of the scene that greeted his eyes upon his arrival. The mare smelled the water and quickened her pace and he let her lope to it. Flashing suddenly into view was a palomino mare tied to a bush draped with clothing and a horrified Grace Porter standing knee-deep in water, clutching at her own body in a futile attempt to hide her nakedness. John viciously yanked the slack out of the reins and pulled the bay to a tail-dragging slide down the embankment. Grace splashed for deeper water as he spun his mount and hightailed it back toward higher ground as if shots were being fired.

"Johnny! Wait!" Were his ears deceiving him?

He hauled on the reins again, coming to a standstill on the brow of the slope with his back to her. "I mean . . . wait until I get dressed!"

He dismounted and loosened his girth, keeping his eyes averted and listening to the swish of fabric being hastily pulled over wet skin. The palomino mare interrupted with a shrill whinny. "*Now* you sound the alarm," laughed Gracie. "All right, you can come on down." John led the bay to water, still not looking directly at Grace. When Chris had had her fill he pulled the bridle and hung it on the saddle horn and turned her loose to graze.

Grace was seated on the grass Indian fashion, chewing on a stem of grama. "She must not be hard to catch," she commented as he walked toward her.

"Naw, she's tame as a puppy dog." John was glad to have something to talk about besides what had happened. "She won't try to roll while she's totin' that saddle, neither." He stood before her, fidgeting with his empty hands and trying to pretend he didn't notice how her wet skin plastered the blouse to her breasts. She gave him a searching look, his obvious discomfort bringing an amused smile to her lips. "I didn't know you could swim," he said, as if that was all he'd noticed.

Gracie took a deep breath and mercifully turned her scrutiny to the pond. "I love to go swimming. This ol' tank finally caught enough water last summer. But it's starting to dry down again so I ride over here every chance I get."

John took advantage of her diverted gaze to do some scrutinizing of his own. "Why don't you just go to the river?"

"I do when the tank's too low. But there's less chance of privacy at the river." She turned her calculating gaze upon him again. "I like to go naked, too."

John felt the color deepen in his face. "So I noticed," he admitted, raising his eyes to the sky.

Gracie could contain herself no longer and burst forth with a resounding peal of laughter. John joined in heartily and, wagging his head, he took a seat on the grass beside her. "I don't know who was surprised the most," she said between chortles, "me . . . or you . . . or that poor thirsty mare when you practically snatched her head off."

The laughter finally subsided. Wiping the tears from her cheeks, Gracie once again gave him a sober look. "So, what have you and Wally been up to? I haven't seen him since the burying."

Wally! All the mirth suddenly escaped John's heart and the all-too-familiar emptiness seized him like an icy claw. For a few minutes there was a world with just him and Gracie. Now Wally intruded again. Sure, that was the only reason she'd stopped him from riding away. She wanted word of Wally.

"Johnny, what's the matter? Why the somber

face? Has something happened to Wally?"

"Uh . . . no! Wally's all right . . . it's, ah . . . *Charlie.* Something happened to Charlie. He's been shot."

"Killed? Did Wally do it? Oh, no, John!"

"No . . . I mean yeah, Wally did it; but no, Charlie wasn't killed."

Grace breathed a sigh and put a hand to her forehead. "Thank God for that, at least. Is he gonna be all right? How did it happen?"

"I think he'll be all right. He jumped on his horse and rode home . . . and he didn't bleed much. Leastways I didn't see no blood on his trail."

"You followed him? So you were there. Where was it? And *what happened?*"

"If you'll just quit asking questions for a minute, I'll tell you!"

"All right. I'm sorry," said Gracie in a subdued tone.

"Yes, I was there. And I followed Charlie to make sure he made it back to the Bar BX, which he did."

"*When* did it happen?" she persisted. John raised his brows and cut his eyes back at her. "I'll be quiet," she promised, "go ahead."

"I just now come from the Bar BX. It happened last night over west of the Bar BX headquarters, about halfway to the mountain. I didn't trail him until daylight so's I wouldn't miss him if he lost consciousness and fell off his horse in the dark."

"Good thinking. So what . . ."

John raised a palm to cut her off. "So here's how it happened: Charlie come to our camp and tried to take Wally's black horse away from him. Said it belongs to the Bar BX and Wally can't use it no more."

"But Wally broke that horse himself! It's *always* been his mount!"

"I know, but that don't mean anything to Ben and Charlie. They was always jealous of that horse and with the old man gone they figured on taking it. Anyhow, Wally bucked up to Charlie and Charlie pulled a gun on us and commenced to give Wally a lickin' with his rope, so Wally crawled to his saddle pocket and got his own pistol and plugged Charlie in the side and Charlie took off."

They sat staring at the ground in silence for a few moments while Grace digested John's story. John's ironical chuckle broke the spell. "I'll never forget the look on Charlie's face when that flashy hogleg come around. He —"

"Flashy? That old pistol of Wally's? It's a wonder it even fired! What do you mean, *flashy?"*

So John was compelled to tell her about the fancy Peacemaker Wally had acquired from the old goatherd, although he left out the details of just how Wally managed to pay for it. "Wally's gone up the old feller's camp in the big canyon near the Texas line to wait for me to find out how bad off Charlie is. Maybe them boys'll leave him alone now," he said hoping to allay her worry.

"You know better'n that, Johnny."

"Yeah, I reckon," he admitted. "Well, at least maybe I can let him know when they're coming so's he can stay outa their way. Now don't you go and tell nobody where he's at."

An injured expression flashed over Gracie's face. "Aw, I know you got better sense than that; I'm sorry I even said it. *Lo siento mucho.*"

"Well, since you apologized in two lingos, I guess I'll let it pass this time," she said, giving him her amused smile. Then turning serious again, she added, "But, knowing Wally, I don't think he'll go to a lot of trouble to stay out of their way, if you know what I mean."

"I know," said John with a sigh. "I'll stick with 'im and do whatever I can . . ."

"*There's* something else that goes without saying. You're a loyal companion, Johnny Stonecipher, and Wally and I are lucky to have you as our friend."

John knew that statement was supposed to make him feel good, but it didn't, for it paired Wally and Gracie and relegated him to a purely platonic role. He wanted to be more to Gracie than just her friend, *much* more. He followed her as she arose and walked to her mare.

"I suppose you'll be staying at home until you get news of Charlie," she guessed. John mumbled the affirmative and assisted her to horseback. "If I hear anything I think you should know, I'll get word to you somehow," she said as she gathered the slack from the reins. She readied the palomino to leave, paused, and looked somberly into his eyes. "Thanks, John," she said huskily, and kicked the mare up the slope and over the rim. John scrambled to the edge of the draw and watched until she was out of sight.

Chapter Twelve

The Bar BX pickup swept out of the draw in the early morning darkness, the headlights reflecting brightly from the snow-white rumps of a group of surprised antelope as they dashed headlong down the fence row that paralleled the right hand side of the BLM road. Winston slowed the truck and allowed them to cross into the unfenced pasture on the left. "A mule deer would've cleared that fence without even breaking stride," he commented to Barb, "but not an antelope."

"They're so pretty," she responded. "I wish we had more of them in our part of the country."

"What we *don't* need is more nondomestic grass-eaters," disagreed Winston.

"Oh Win, you're so darn . . . *practical,*" she said, nudging him in the ribs with an elbow. She still liked to sit close to him when they traveled without the baby.

"Sorry to get you up so early, hon," Winston apologized for the fourth time, although it had been her idea.

True to O.C.'s prediction, the sheriff called after they'd gotten home from the cattle pens and asked Win to visit Mrs. Stonecipher. The other officers had gotten very little response to their questions. Barb volunteered to go with him, thinking the old lady might open up more readily to another woman, and especially since Barb already had a certain rapport with her.

In order to make the subject of history more meaningful for her students, Barbara developed a class project wherein taped interviews were conducted with old timers in the area. For the most part the questions were about the old folk's rememberances of events of history that were covered in their textbook, with the most elderly encouraged to relate any recollections that would help the youngsters to get a sense of what life was like in bygone eras. The Stoneciphers were not socially inclined, but Grace had reluctantly agreed to some interviews. Because of her extreme age and the delicate situation Barb always accompanied the two students who interviewed her. She actually seemed to enjoy the attention once she got used to the idea.

Winston and Barb had decided to travel together, leaving early enough to see Mrs. Stonecipher before school started. Winston would stay in town until her classes were over in the afternoon.

Barb had readily adjusted to ranch life, although she'd grown up a city girl in Alamogordo, another town founded near the end of the last century by the enterprising Charles B. Eddy. She and Winston met at the University, and in her senior year they decided they couldn't wait any longer and were married on an impulse by a

Justice of the Peace, much to the dismay of her parents. She managed to get her teacher's certificate in spite of her ensuing pregnancy. Winston, studying on a meager Vo-Ag scholarship and a shoestring, and besieged by the problems resulting from O.C.'s inefficient management of the ranch in his absence, was forced to drop out short of his degree.

Barb twisted her body to keep her knees clear while Winston shifted the floorboard gear stick to bring the pickup to road speed on the El Paso highway. "We'll be in Carlsbad by daylight," he estimated.

"Do you think we'll be too early for Mrs. Stonecipher?"

"Naw. These old cow people been up and at 'em ahead of old Sol all their lives. Most of them couldn't lose the habit if they tried, even after they've retired and moved to town."

"It's not just the '*old* cow people' who've acquired the habit, I've noticed," remarked Barb with raised eyebrows.

"I sure hope she'll open up to you."

"Oh, I think she will. She even told me some rather confidential things when we interviewed her for class. Off the record, of course."

"Confidential eh?" It was Winston's turn to raise the eyebrows. "That old couple hasn't said much more than 'howdy' and 'adios' to anybody as long as I can remember. All my dealings with them have been strictly business. She was always cut and dried and tough as bull hide. She must've really took a liking to you."

"It was as if she'd never had anyone she could talk to before. I mean another woman, you know? Like she'd kept all the loneliness bottled up inside for all those years."

"Well, they always seemed to prefer to keep to themselves, sorta like they had some dark secret or something they were afraid somebody'd find out."

"I believe the reason for that goes back a long, long way into the past. . . . Do you know what she told me one day after the kids had left?" asked Barbara indignantly. "People used to call her Racy Gracie."

"I always heard she had a certain reputation," Winston admitted.

"Well, I think that's just awful! She's been faithful to her husband for what . . . close to seventy years? Just because she had an immature fling with some peter-do-well before she got married, she's had to carry the stigma all her life."

"She told you about *that?*" Winston was incredulous. "There's hardly anyone left who knows about it!"

"But everyone of their generation knew about it, all of those who might otherwise have become their friends, anyway. *You* know about it, I gather," she added with an expectant look.

"Guess I never told you that story. Obviously, one thing Mrs. Stonecipher *didn't* tell you is who the desperado was!"

"She mentioned some Indian name he was called. He didn't like it because he was ashamed of his Indian blood. Choctaw, I think it was." Barb looked expectantly at Winston.

Winston cut his eyes at her in order to see her mouth fall open when he said it. "The Choctaw Kid . . . also known as Wallace Bledsoe!"

"*Bledsoe?* You mean . . . ?"

"Yeah. Grandpa's half brother. I reckon that'd make him my great uncle."

"No wonder she didn't tell me who he was!" A silly grin crossed Barb's face as she gazed at Winston. "My husband, the grand nephew of the Choctaw Kid!"

Barb pursed her lips and wagged her head in mock derision. "Bad seed."

Winston feigned an offended expression, "*I'm* no owl-hoot. I've got a badge to prove it!"

When they'd finished laughing Winston's face turned sober. "The memory of Wallace Bledsoe haunted my Grandpa to his dying day and now I'm on my way to track down the one person who could probably tell the truth about the Choctaw Kid."

"You mean . . . ?"

"Yep, the Choctaw Kid's closest friend was *John Stonecipher.*"

John awoke with the break of day, anxious to be moving on. He'd spent most of the night lying awake in his soogans on the bank of the stock tank gazing at the stars and trying to reconstruct the details of his brief visual encounter with Grace Porter in the nude. He regretted that his surprised mind hadn't done a better job of capturing the image. No sense torturing himself by hanging around where the memory of her was so fresh, he decided. Might as well go on home and see if Pa could find something else to occupy his mind while he waited for word about Charlie.

He hadn't long to wait.

The following Sunday after his return to the Circle S a circuit-riding preacher was scheduled to hold a service at the school house. John sat in the early morning sun in front of the tack shed repairing a bridle as the family filed out to mount the wagon for the ride to Salt Flat. He knew from their sidelong glances they were hoping he'd come too, thinking a good preaching might help him mend his ways.

John had considered going, although he didn't feel like he was ready to face Gracie so soon after the incident at the stock tank. Seeing her wouldn't make it any easier on his tortured mind. Also, he'd probably blush every time she happened to look at him. She probably would look at him, too, since Wally wouldn't be there to occupy her interest.

The main reason he'd considered going to the preaching was to see if word had spread about the difficulty between Charlie and Wally, and if so, to learn the news about Charlie's condition. On second thought he realized if his part in the incident was known he might be compelled to answer a bunch of questions. Or, if Charlie had exaggerated John's participation in the fracas, the would-be gossipers might be reluctant to discuss it at all in his presence. He decided it wasn't necessary for him to go, for he could rely on his parents to convey any gossip that involved himself or Wallace Bledsoe.

His faith in that fact of life was not disappointed. He knew they'd heard the news when the sound of the wagon's returning rumble came sooner than was to be expected and he looked up to see that the old mule was being urged on in a way not typical of a Sunday-go-to-meeting drive.

John walked over and held the mule's cheek strap while his mother and sister dismounted, then followed the wagon to the barn and began unhitching Cletus before his father could climb down. Might as well be doing something while he heard him out, he thought. Pa immediately demanded to hear his version of the incident, but John was just as anxious to know what the elder Stonecipher had heard.

That information had John saddled up and heading for the mountains soon after Pa threw his hands up and went to the house to finish venting his exasperation by rehashing the whole affair with the rest of the family. They would expect him to pull out after a row, so he didn't bother with explanations or goodbyes.

The big canyon Abels had described sliced

into the mountains just short of the Texas line. The sun was out of sight behind the ridges by the time John entered the chasm and urged the mare through the brush along the bank of the dry wash that threaded the bottom of the canyon. He hoped he could find the goat camp before the deepening shadows of the narrowing gorge completely obscured his vision. Presently he descended the bank into the wash. The rocks would make for treacherous footing for his mount, but their whiteness would reflect the dim light and help him to hold a course to the main branch of the canyon, in which Abels said the camp was located. John peered up at the dark silhouette of the southern rim as Chris picked her way through the rubble, looking for the outline of the pointed knob Abels had given as a landmark. About the same time he thought he had a fix on it he smelled woodsmoke. When the arroyo had led him to a point below the knob he reined in next to the bank and hallooed the camp.

"It's John!" he heard Wally's voice exclaim from the brush above his head. "We heard you coming, John. Just set tight and I'll come down and show you how to get up here."

Wally shinnied down the embankment and swung up behind John to show him the way to an obscure path up the side of the wash and through the brush and trees to the tiny clearing on the bench next to the canyon wall where Abels' camp was located beside a small seep spring.

“Well, dang my eyes!” exclaimed Abels from behind the campfire. “It *is* ol’ John the Implicated, for shore! Light down and line yer flue, boy; they’s plenty of vittles left.”

“Don’t mind if I do,” John responded as Wally slid off the bay’s rump. Emelda slipped out of the shadows to take charge of the mare as John stepped down. He wasn’t accustomed to having someone else care for his mount, but a timid flash of her dark eyes told him she really wanted to, so he surrendered the reins and went to take the tin plate Abels was offering him.

In his concern about finding the camp before it was too dark to see, John had forgotten about his gnawing belly. The juices boiled up anew as he loaded his plate with beef and beans. He was glad Abels preferred to make commissary from the calves that strayed into the mouth of the canyon instead of eating his own goats. Lalo had told him many times that *cabrito* was the choicest of meats, but John preferred the old standby rations of the cattle-raising fraternity.

Wally squatted next to him and patiently nursed a cup of coffee while John took the edge off his appetite. As soon as John’s wolfing of the food slowed to a steady mastication he inquired about the repercussions of the fight with Charlie.

“Well, I saw to it he made it to the house all right,” replied John between swallows. “Then I went on home to lay low and keep my ear to the ground.” He didn’t mention his detour to the stock tank, for how do you tell your best friend you've seen his sweetheart in the altogether? It had nothing to do with the subject at hand, anyway.

"So what did you find out?" Wally knew he wouldn't be here if he didn't have news.

John hastily chewed another mouthful and swallowed it down. "Charlie's alive and kickin' and bellerin' about how we ganged up on 'im and you pulled a fancy, long-barreled Colt's you had hid out and blasted him whilst he wasn't lookin'."

Wally ducked his head and slammed his coffee cup down, splashing hot liquid on his hand and wrist. He left the cup on the ground and put his hand up to his mouth.

"Well, least he ain't dead, Wally. Ben took him straight away to Eddy and the doc's been taking care of him ever since. Best thing for you to do now is to go on in and tell your side of it. I'll back up your story." Wally immediately began wagging his head to the negative.

"Mebbe you orter listen to him, Chocktaw," said Abels with a studious scowl. "Most times I don't hold with trustin' to the law, but —"

"But what if I give myself up and Charlie dies?" Wally interrupted. "He ain't kickin' too high, if he's so bad off he's gotta stay where the doc can watch over him. He's jest liable to kick the bucket. They'll have me up for murder!"

"Shucks, they's all-time indicting somebody for a shootin', but the jury pract'ly never convicts nobody," Abels proclaimed. "Besides, John is a eyewitness to the fact of self-defense."

"They'd say he's lying, us being pardners and all."

"Not necessarily," John disagreed.

"Oh, Ben'd see to it," Wally insisted. "He'd go to bellerin' an' spoutin' off and have them all thinking you're the shadiest thing since the Santa Fe Ring, next to me myself."

"Aw Wally, Charlie'll pull through it." John didn't see how anybody as mean and tough as Charlie Bledsoe could succumb to a single gunshot wound.

"I dunno, I plugged him purty good." Wally didn't try to hide the satisfaction in his voice.

John glared at Wally's smug expression for a moment. "Well, if Charlie does give up the ghost, it couldn't do nothin' but help your case if you'd already come in to settle the difficulty."

Wally stared into the campfire around which the three of them were huddled and slowly wagged his head. "Nope. Wouldn't help me none when it's all said and done. 'Cause it won't never be settled but one way as long as Ben's alive."

"Now, he's got a point there," Abels sided with Wally.

John rose to his feet with an exasperated sigh and flipped the dregs from his coffee cup into the flames. "Well, at least you'll be in the clear as far as the law's concerned," he persisted.

"Maybe so, maybe no," Wally replied, also rising. "But as long as Ben ain't had his satisfaction, I'm a hunted man anyhow, so it don't make no difference and I don't see no percentage in taking a chance on the law."

"So are you just gonna wait for Kemp and a possee to come after you, or what?"

Wally's hand caressed the pearl grips of the Peacemaker, which he now carried in the holster of the silver-studded black gunbelt around his hips. "Kemp's posse or Ben's posse, they's all the same to me."

It was Abels' turn to stand up. "Now Choctaw, you know I don't want no gaw-durned posse up heah!"

"They don't even know where he's at, Abels," said John disgustedly. "As for Ben, he's got no posse. He don't even have any friends that I know of."

"They'd be bought and paid for — Bar BX hands, maybe — but Ben won't hunt me by hisself," countered Wally. "They'll be a posse, law or no law!"

"Well, let's just hope ol' Charlie don't cash in his chips," said John resignedly.

"If he don't they'll *both* be after me. Only Charlie'll not want any outside help," predicted Wally.

"Still and all, that's the best we can hope for," conceded John.

Abels bobbed his head in agreement. "Won't be no posse thataway, no law dogs."

John heaved another sigh and lifted his eyes to

the glittering stars which appeared to be suspended just out of reach beyond the canyon's rim in the clear mountain sky. "For the time being all we can do is wait and see what happens. I'm the scout, so come daylight I reckon I'll sashay back to the ranch and keep my ear to the ground."

John turned to fetch his bedroll and Abels headed for the lean-to with a yawn and a belch. Wally eased off thru the brush toward the arroyo, to answer a call of nature, John assumed. Out of the tail of his eye he caught a glimpse of a lissome shadow stealing away in the same direction. John grimaced and wagged his head. "*I* wouldn't want anybody else if I had Grace," he muttered to himself.

Chapter Thirteen

Grace Stonecipher sat with her spine as rigid as her old ladder-back chair, her hands folded on top of the cane across her lap, staring out the window at the sun rising above the sand hills that ran east to the Texas line. She didn't get up to open the door — just hollered for them to come on in, it was open. She knew why they'd come.

Winston stopped in the middle of the room, turning his hat in his hands and peering at her from beneath his brows. She was one of the very last of the generation that had seen the country when the grass was hock-high on the flats and the streams and springs were not encumbered by irrigation dams and artesian wells. *Cut and dried and tough as bullhide* was how he'd described her business dealings with him, and the persona by the window fit the description.

Barb caught his eye and nodded toward the door. "Miz Stonecipher —" she stepped around the coffee table and sat down on the end of the divan near Grace and gently clasped a pale, blue-veined hand between her own — "Miz Stonecipher, is there anything that needs doing around the place that Winston can take care of for you?"

Grace started to shake her head no, then stopped. "Come to think of it, I didn't feed Johnny's ponies yesterday. There was such a hubbub around here and all, you know," she explained in a voice made throaty by the years.

Winston bobbed his head and moved toward the door, "I'll see to it ma'am. Anything else?"

"Not as I know of," she replied, finally turning her snow-white head from the window. "There's plenty of alfafa. Just go ahead and fill the hayrack. And scatter about five scoops of Omolene in the trough — one for each head, if you please. Maybe a little extra. The poor things are prob'ly starved by now." Her next comment was directed at Barb. "I don't know why he insists on keeping so many horses. The old scudder can't even ride anymore . . ." Her voice broke and she bowed her head. Winston raised his eyebrows as he slipped on out the door. It was the first slack in her austerity he'd witnessed in all the years he'd known her.

Winston reentered the house sooner than Barb expected and she could tell from his expression that something was amiss. "What's the matter?"

He ducked his head and glanced out the window toward the corrals. "Miz Stonecipher, didn't you say there were *five* horses out there? Five scoops of feed, one for each? Well, there's only three in the corral now. An appaloosa, a bay, and a bald-faced sorrel."

A frown deepened the wrinkles in her forehead

and she withdrew her hand from Barb's to position her cane. "They all came up for feed day before yesterday."

Winston extended a palm. "Now, just stay where you are, ma'am. I'll check it out. If someone took those ponies they must've left tracks. Might be some kids let 'em out. Whatever's happened, we'll find 'em for you."

"Well, I hope you do a better job than they've done for poor old Johnny."

Winston failed to suppress a grin. *That* was the Grace Stonecipher he knew. "Can you describe the two missing horses, ma'am?"

"I described what Johnny was wearing and it hasn't done any good. . . . You'd be looking for a line-back dun and a blue roan."

A blue roan?

The bay mare rested in the Circle S corral and recovered from the hard ride to and from the canyon hideout. John was sure she got an ample daily ration of feed and went about the work his father assigned him, studiously avoiding confrontation. Word of Charlie Bledsoe's condition circulated to the Circle S from time to time with the passing of weeks. The news was always the same. Charlie was recovering, but the doctor was alarmed that his recovery was so slow. Perhaps there was more internal damage than he'd first thought. He insisted on keeping Charlie under observation in Eddy.

To John it seemed like the world was on hold,

waiting for the outcome when Charlie was well enough to return to the Bar BX. In the meantime, Ben Bledsoe kept an impatient rein on his seething anger and divided his time between the ranch and frequent trips to Eddy to check on Charlie. But John knew it was only a matter of time before the inferno of Ben's wrath — and Charlie's too, if he was able — would be unleashed in an all-out manhunt for their despised half brother. He also knew the flames of that explosion were bound to engulf him as well.

When news worth taking to the canyon finally came, it wasn't what John had expected. It most certainly wasn't what he wanted to hear.

When John told his father he had to leave for a few days, the elder Stonecipher didn't even bother to object. He knew John was bound to carry a warning to his friend and he couldn't stop him short of hogtying him. As he watched the lanky youth ride away on his beloved bay mare he admitted he'd have to have a lot of help these days to hogtie a young man such as that. Unexpectedly a feeling of pride welled in his breast. *"Que vaya bien, hijo mio,"* he muttered as he turned toward the house. Maybe if that boy would settle down and quit causing him so much worry he'd start digesting his food a little better, he thought, and put a hand to the burning sensation in his chest.

The mouth of the big canyon was discernable among the many serrated clefts in the drab wall of the escarpment when John noticed the dust of a herd of trailing cattle. The herd was bound in the same direction as himself and he gradually overtook it. The sounds of the bawling cattle and the shouts and whistles of the drovers reached his ears as he edged closer to see if could recognize any of the drovers before being noticed. He was so intent on squinting through the veil of dust that he failed to check the mare in time. She betrayed their presence before he could jerk the reins to stifle her neigh. This could be trouble if they were moving stolen cattle. One of the riders turned out and rode toward him. At first he thought it was Wally, but the man sat his saddle a little differently. John held the bay to a nervous strut as he approached. She could probably outrun the other horse, but a bullet travels a mite faster.

"Well, I'll swun, if it ain't ol' John Stone. Choctaw said you'd be along directly."

John relaxed, but not completely. "McDaniel! Durn! You mean you've seen Wallace and both of you are still able to tell about it?"

"Pshaw, I's just funnin' you boys that day at roundup. No call for him to go and take it so serious. Anyhow, we got us an understanding now. Facts of the bidness, these are his cows we're pushing."

"We ain't got that many cows yet. . . ." John peered into the dust. "Why, they're Bar BX cattle!"

"I do believe the boy can read a brand,"

laughed McDaniel. "It's about time we collected Choc's share of the Bar BX herd, I reckon!"

John decided he'd best save his comments on this development for Wally. "Where is Wally, anyway?"

"He went on ahead to the goat camp to make sure Abels ain't got no undesirable visitors, if you know what I mean. We're gonna hold these beeves in a little grassy cove near the mouth of the canyon and rest 'em up a little before we take 'em to Texas to turn 'em over to some friends of mine. For a price, of course," he added with a wily sneer. "Lend us a hand," he said, turning back to the herd.

Help handle stolen cattle again? At first John thought of making the excuse that he needed to talk to Wally as soon as possible. Then it occurred to him that by rights a fourth of the Bar BX herd really should belong to Wally and there was no other way he would ever get it, especially in light of the news John was bringing. They were almost to the end of the drive, anyway. He fell in and helped them push the cattle on to the holding ground, but left the others to turn the leaders and settle the herd while he rode on to the goat camp in search of Wally.

As the bay breasted her way through the brush obscuring Abels' camp by the spring, John observed Wally coming up from the arroyo, buckling his gunbelt around his hips as he strode toward the lean-to. John suspected he hadn't been alone down on the sandy bank of the gulch.

"Well, John!" Wally was still seeing to his gunbelt. When he looked up and his hatbrim cleared his face, John noticed his recently cultivated mustache.

"Wallace," said John with a nod, and paused as if scrutinizing his face. "I do believe you've done rubbed your upper lip whilst you was blacking your boots." Actually, Wally had attained a splendid growth of black lip hair in John's absence. "No cause to black yer boots up here," he laughed.

"Shoot, a feller could grow hair like a 'Pache waitin' for you to show up." John dismounted and began knocking the dust from his clothes with his hat. "We've got your cows captured," he said matter-of-factly.

Wally waited for him to have his say about the rustling operation, but, much to his surprise, John went on to the reason for his visit. "I'm afraid I've got some bad news, Wallace. Charlie's dead. Got the ague on top of being gunshot, or maybe because of it. Anyhow, betwixt the two ailments he finally passed in his chips."

Wally put his hands on his hips and angled his head to spit on a small stone. "Bad news," he repeated as if giving careful consideration. "Well, I reckon that all depends on how you look at it."

"I suppose to you it means the Bar BX owes you a third of their stock instead of a fourth," John had hoped to parley without the censuring tone, but there it was.

"The Bar BX is a lot more than just livestock,"

Wally reminded him. "But you're right about one thing; that's the only currency they've got that I can get aholt of for my rightful share."

John couldn't argue with that. "Durnit Wally, I just hate to see you slippin' to the darker side of the pale."

"Now that's a mighty hazy line, John. Some folks see it one way, others see it another. They's prob'ly more folks on the river sees it my way than Ben's."

"Maybe. Anyhow, let's us go on in and get this shootin' b'iness straightened out. Then at least you won't have the law doggin' you on that account."

"Now John, you know Sheriff Kemp ain't nobody you can trust. If Ben got to him I wouldn't even get a hearing. They'd shoot me and say I tried to escape or something."

"We'll go to Harkey. Talk is, he's a fair man. *He'll* do you right."

"No, John, I reckon not. The way the Eddy crowd and that Phenix bunch is at one another's throats, there's no telling what's liable to happen. From the way I hear it, Kemp and Harkey's liable to be slinging lead at one another before it's over." Wally cocked his head and grinned. "Now wouldn't that be lovely? A couple of law dogs on the prod for each other." He laughed at the prospect.

"I think you've been sharin' camp with ol' Triple A and that Rafer McDaniel too long." John said it at the risk of sounding reprimanding again, but Wally just kept on grinning. "So are you just gonna wait around up here 'til a posse comes for you, or what?"

"Nobody's posse's gonna surprise us in this canyon." Wally raised his eyes to the precipice overlooking the camp. "Not with Melda up there on the lookout."

John couldn't resist the impulse. "If you let her outa the draw long enough, that is."

Wally's face fell apart, first with dismay, then with mirth. "Why, you eagle-eyed son-of-a-gun! Maybe we ought to put *you* up on the bluff!" He poked a friendly fist at John's shoulder. "By the way, I think she likes you, too, John." John responded with a nervous chuckle and commenced studying the toes of his boots.

Wally moved on toward the lean-to. "I better roust Abels and get him to start some chuck. I reckon the boys're hungry as a pack of gainted wolves in a hard winter."

Abels waddled about the fire, stirring the beans in a cast-iron caldron that hung from the tripod he'd rigged with green manzanita limbs and frying steaks for the hungry rustlers, who stood around with tin plates in their hands and expectant looks on their faces. "Here's one's about half-way cooked if any of you fellers just cain't wait."

"I'll take it," volunteered John.

"I swanny, John, you ain't nothin' but a appetite with a hide stretched around it!"

"Naw," said Wally, "that's just the way he likes 'em. All's you need to do to suit ol' John is drag 'er up and cut 'er throat and let 'er drain a whilst." The aversive looks on the other faces revealed that John was the only one who liked his beef rare.

"Speakin' of slaughtering beef, whose brand was this here calf-awearin', Abels?" The inquirer was a slim, freckle-faced redheaded drover.

"Why, I plumb disremember now that you mention it, Speckles," asserted Abels with an innocent look.

They all laughed in unison. Oates, the pudgy, tow-headed youth McDaniel sometimes called "Grassbelly," spoke up. "Well, I hope it wasn't a Bar BX calf. We wouldn't want ol' Choctaw knowing what his own beef tastes like," he joked, alluding to the cow country adage that a man never slaughtered his own beef for home use. After another round of laughter Abels rejoined the banter. "Oh, I reckon he's ate with his neighbors enough times to figger that one out." More laughter, and Abels added, "These steaks'll be done soon and the rest of you boys can see if you can recognize the brand by the taste. John Stone don't know it, 'cause he don't never eat with his neighbors."

John almost choked on the mouthful he was just swallowing. Then he relaxed. "Whose leg you think you're pullin', Abels? Ain't likely any Circle S beef would stray up to these parts."

"Who said it strayed?" replied Abels with a

complacent smile. John still didn't believe him.

"Beasley," said McDaniel to the sullen-looking puncher who rarely spoke, "you take first nighthawk after we get done eatin'." He was obviously in charge of the three drovers, and John surmised they'd been his gang since before he struck his deal with Wally.

Abels finally pronounced the steaks "cooked enough for normal folks" and the others gathered around for their portions of beef, beans, and hot coffee. Wally squatted on his spurs next to John, and McDaniel took up a position next to him. After the rest of the drovers and Abels had filled their plates and hunkered down to satisfy their hunger, Emelda materialized out of the shadows. She took a plate, quietly helped herself to the victuals and sat down Indian style just outside the circle of men. As she ate, her dark eyes recurrently flashed in John's direction.

"Melda sure is giving you the scout," said the observant Wally. "Told you she likes you."

"Naw, it's you she's eyeballin', Wallace. Anyhow, I'm sure you can take care of her without any help from me."

McDaniel was grinning his wily grin. "Tarnation, boy! The man's willing to share with you. You ain't gonna turn down a offer like that, are you?"

It seemed to John that McDaniel was always smiling. It reminded him of the perpetual close-mouthed smile of a rattlesnake, except McDaniel could vary the intensity of his. And

McDaniel's darting black eyes were like the snake's tongue. "Some things are not for sharing, I reckon," John mumbled.

"Why, I can't believe my ears," McDaniel mocked. "The boy must have that ol' mare stump-broke!"

John slammed down his plate and made a move toward McDaniel. Wally clamped a restraining hand on his shoulder, juggling his plate in the other hand and rocking forward on one knee to get in front of him. "Now John, ol' Rafe's just a-funnin' you, that's all."

John relaxed a bit. "Yeah, Rafer's always on the guy, ain't he?" He and Wally settled back to their former positions. Rafer just kept on eating and smiling as if nothing had happened. Wally decided it was time to change the subject. "Say, you're going with us on the drive *mañana,* ain't you, pard?"

Abels had been listening to the exchange and proceeded to take his jibe at John. "Ain't likely he'll go with you, Choctaw. He's scared he might git hisself *implicated!*"

For once Wally came to John's defense. "Well, why the hell *should* he go, Abels? The cards've already been dealt on this herd and he wasn't here to get any, so they's nothing in it for him this time. I shouldn't of even asked him." Abels looked surprised and suddenly became very interested in his supper.

At Wally's sally a warm feeling of camaraderie stirred in John's breast. "I'll go with you, Wally.

I know you got a natural right to some of the Bar BX stock. Y'all got a sizeable herd and it's gonna raise some dust — just might stir up some curiosity. I'll be your scout, so's nobody can slip up on you unexpected-like."

Abels shot him a surprised look. "Well I swanny!"

Chapter Fourteen

"Durn!"

At John's mild expletive, Wally arose from his seated position on the rim overlooking the precarious trail they'd climbed the previous day and walked back to their makeshift camp among the rocks and thorny brush. They'd planned to go on to a more sheltered campsite, but John was exhausted by the time they rimmed out and they were obliged to spread their bedrolls at once.

"You all right, pard?" inquired Wally as he squatted to pour John a cup of coffee from the pot that was warming over a small campfire. John had tossed the flap of his sleeping bag aside and was propped up on an elbow squinting at the sun.

"Was you gonna let me sleep *all day?*"

Wally handed him the cup. "I aimed to let you get your sleep out," he admitted. "Figured you need it. Are you okay?" he repeated.

John drained the cup, set it aside on a rock, tried to rise, grunted, and sank back to his elbows. "Sore as a boil, durnit." Wally reached a hand and helped him to his feet. He tried a tentative step and staggered. Wally kept a hand under his arm and guided him to a juniper tree he could use for support. "I'll be all right," said John confidently. "My head just wakes up a little faster than the rest of me." He held on to the tree with one hand and massaged his thighs with the other. Then he twisted his torso, stretching the brittle muscles of his back. "Legs're sore from climbing and my back's sore from sleeping on the ground."

Wally retrieved John's cup and refilled it. "Been worse if I hadn't had them sleeping bags stashed in the pickup." He handed John the cup. "You hungry? I'll open a can of something for you. I already ate."

"Whatever you got. Can't be no worse than that nursing-home feed." John let go of the juniper and made it to a rock and sat down without spilling his coffee. "I expect you've been up for a spell, Wallace. Whatcha been doing, just settin' over there on the bluff watching the sparrows and the buzzards?"

Wally laughed. "Mostly. And looking down yonder and thinking that somehow it don't seem so long ago when we was pushin' stolt cows across them flats."

The whistles and shouts of the drovers punctuated the din of lowing cattle and clattering horns as the gang roused the herd and pushed it toward Texas. They pointed the cattle to the southeast, hoping to make a hard, fast drive to the Delaware River, a tributary of the Pecos, by nightfall of the first day or early the next.

John helped them get the herd started, then rode off to the east and climbed a rocky knoll that provided a vantage point for surveillance of the surrounding territory. Any pursuit of the stolen cattle would most likely come from the northeast. Wally had cajoled the reluctant Abels into the loan of his extra spyglass and turned it over to John for his reconnaissance. John removed it from his saddle pocket and commenced a systematic visual patrol of the rugged terrain. The hours dragged by. Besides the ever-present jackrabbits, he saw nothing moving on the land except a chaparral cock, a pair of hunting coyotes, and a rare daylight appearance of a bobcat. When the sun neared its zenith he decided he'd take one more survey, then ride across country on an angle that would bring him closer to the herd and locate another likely watch point. He was about to lower the glass when he glimpsed movement atop a distant rise. At first he thought it was a mule deer. The color was right, but deer seldom travel during the heat of the day unless disturbed. Suddenly there were two more flashes of color — horse colors — brownish, probably a sorrel and a dark bay. The red shirt of a rider was visible. Then he realized the animal out front was also a horse, a mouse-gray horse, the color locally known as a "gruyer." Ben Bledsoe had a gruyer in his string! Well, so did a lot of cowboys. But what if it was Ben? The riders were headed west, therefore they were not closing on the herd's present position. But they might be following yesterday's trail to last night's bed ground. It was imperative that John find out if the riders were from the Bar BX. He nudged the bay mare off the hill and rode north to cut their trail.

When John judged he was close, he left his mount ground-hitched at the base of a slope of rising ground and, taking the spyglass, made his way to the apex on foot in order to reconnoiter from behind the camouflage of rock and brush. He didn't even need the glass to locate the riders coming along the trail of the stolen cattle. And one quick look through it was all that was necessary to confirm what he'd already guessed; it was Ben Bledsoe and two Bar BX hands. He felt his pulse quicken and the burning in the pit of his stomach wasn't entirely because he'd had no noon meal. This was a dangerous turn of events. He'd have to do something about it.

John lowered the telescope and watched their approach with the naked eye. Durn! It didn't take them long to miss those cows. Well, that tallied with the fact that the herd was all Bar BX stock. The gang must have turned them out pretty close to headquarters or they would've been mixed with other brands from the open range. The Bar BX crew would trail the cattle on to last night's bed ground and pick up today's trail to the Delaware. They'd catch up to the rustlers tomorrow for sure, because the boys planned to take it slower the next day, drifting east and slightly north along the river before leaving the water the day after to make a hard drive across country to Pope's Crossing on the Pecos.

John had come a good distance north to identify the riders, but he thought he could catch up to the herd by nightfall or early the next day. At least he'd make it ahead of the trackers. But what then? Forewarned, the gang would surely stage an ambush. Someone he knew would likely be killed. The discomfort in John's stomach intensified like a flickering flame.

The danger existed for either side, for the wary Bar BX men had trailed rustlers before. They were not the sort who'd blunder aimlessly into an ambuscade. It would be better if John could somehow divert the hunters before they closed on their quarry. He retreated to his horse, trying to think of some sort of delaying tactic he could use. He mounted the bay and urged her up the slope, thoughts racing through his mind but forming no feasible plan. Well, he'd just have to see what happened and play it by ear. Showing himself here should at least preclude any suspicion that he had anything to do with the rustling. And if he was unsuccessful at creating a diversion, he could still make a run for the Delaware to sound a warning. The mare crested the knoll and John lifted a hand in greeting as she carefully picked her way down the other side to intersect the approaching riders.

"Stonecipher!" exclaimed Ben as he drew rein. Both his tone and his look emphasized his surprise at being accosted by the young man who'd had a part in the incident which led to his brother's death.

John howdied the other two riders with a nod of his hatbrim. "I reckon ya'll are out looking for Wally," he said as innocently as he could.

"Wal, we ain't just sure; maybe we are and maybe we ain't. I s'pect we are." John feigned a confused look. Ben spat a shot of tobacco juice at the bay's right front hoof and continued. "Anyhow, it ain't none of yore bidness." His pale blue eyes gleamed at John and the color in his ruddy face brightened in sharp contrast to the straw-colored hair of his temples. "Charlie died, you know," he said abruptly in a voice that trembled with bitterness.

John detected more rage than bereavement in Ben's emotional demeanor. For a disconcerting moment he thought Ben might burst into angry tears, and self-consciously shifted his gaze to his horse's ears. "Yeah, I know," he quietly affirmed. "I'm trying to find Wally myself, before you do. Maybe I can get him to go in and give hisself up." Well, it wasn't entirely a lie. Even so, John was glad he wasn't looking at Ben when he said it. He cut his eyes back to Ben. "I was hoping I could talk you into laying off 'til I get a chance to talk to him. How about it?"

Ben nearly swallowed his cud. His eyes glistened hatred and his face turned even redder. He considered John's request too absurd even to be acknowledged. "We should take *you* in, Stonecipher. You was a party to that shootin', in case you've done fergot. I can't *believe* you rode up here bald-faced and purty as you please and commenced to parley like you's just passing the time of day and didn't have nothing to do with it!" He deposited another spurt of tobacco juice on the mare's hoof.

John felt his hackles rise and reminded himself that it was Ben's purpose to provoke him. He must pretend not to notice and keep him talking instead of tracking. "I just happened to be there, is all. A feller can't be arrested just because he saw something."

"Yeah, you jest *happened* to be there, all right, like you jest *happen* to be out here looking for Wallace. Now that tells me you got a purty good idea of where to find him. How 'bout it, Stonecipher? You spit it out now, boy!"

John hesitated, his mind racing. This could be the hook he was hoping for! The honest hesitation made his ploy all the more convincing. "Well, I . . . ah . . . yeah, we got us a couple of places. But I just come from where I thought he'd be and there wasn't a sign of him. I figger he's already heard about Charlie and run off to Arizona or somewhere, like he was talking about doing." John tried to sound like he was anxious for Ben to believe Wally had already gone. He held his breath, hoping he'd take the bait.

The cowhand wearing the red shirt took it instead. "Sure, Stonecipher. You're so convinced he's done took off that you're still out here looking for him," he said with a sneer, "and on your way to check out that *other* hideout you forgot not to mention," he concluded triumphantly. He cut his eyes at the boss to be sure he got credit for his savvy.

"My sentiments exactly," agreed Ben with a condescending glance at the red-shirted puncher. His eyes swung back to John and his hand simultaneously came up with his pistol. "So let's go check it out, Stonecipher. We'll keep you comp'ny."

John tried to appear reluctant. "Aw, I don't think he'd be over there. It's over north of here. If he was still around he'd been back yonder where I came from."

"Well, let's go check it out, *jest on case,*" jeered Ben, motioning with the gun barrel for John to move out. "And just remember what I'm holding, in case you get any wild ideas about leading us on a wild goose chase."

The other Bar BX hand finally spoke up. "But Ben, hadn't we better stay on the trail of them longhorns? One of us, at least?"

"Muncie, you always was a little shy when the guns come out," accused Ben. "Now what would you do if you caught up to 'em all by yerself, huh?"

"I'd come fetch you!"

"Now tell me, Muncie, what advantage would that have over all of us going after them rustlers when this little jag's over, huh?" Muncie slumped his shoulders and gathered his reins to move out. "Besides," Ben continued, "when we find that half-breed I'm thinking we'll of found someone who can tell us right where that bunch of cows is at!"

"Now Ben," said John, sounding anxious, "you gotta promise me you'll take him to Eddy to stand trial!"

"Why shore," promised Ben. "Sheriff Kemp'll take *real* good care of him." A humorous twinkle flashed in his eyes and he licked his lips as he gestured again with his pistol.

John moved out with Ben right behind. Redshirt followed closely and Muncie came along several lengths off the pack.

John led them northward, farther and farther away from the trail of the rustled cattle. Occasionally he glanced back at Ben to see if his gunhand was becoming weary. It was, but he was keeping close attention on John and every time he saw him look he raised the gun in a menacing gesture for him to lead on. John pushed ahead, angling all the while closer and closer to the escarpment. He stopped glancing at the pistol in Ben's hand and began to concentrate on the location of the canyon he and Wally had explored the previous autumn. The afternoon sun beat down upon the riders, drawing perspiration which darkened underarms and dribbled beneath hatbands and other areas not exposed to the dry air. John sensed the anticipation his subterfuge had kindled in Ben for catching up to his younger brother was wearing thin, and therefore his patience also. He was determined to string him along as far as he possibly could. Every minute wasted on the false trail was a minute gained by Wally and the boys.

"Whoa-up there!" Ben finally exclaimed in an irritated tone. John reined the bay to a standstill and twisted in his saddle to flash his best innocently questioning look. The two cowhands seized the opportunity to dismount and ease their bladders. "I'm smellin' a skunk in the brush, Stonecipher," Ben declared. "Just where do you pretend to be taking us, anyhow?"

"Right to the mouth of that canyon over yonder," John confidently replied, gesturing with his chin. "It's a place Wally and I've used for a camp." He could look Ben hard in the eye when he said it, for it was truth. "Mind if I bleed my lizard?" he asked, nodding toward the two cowhands who stood with their backs to them. He stepped down without waiting for permission, and Ben followed suit, dropping one rein on the horse's neck and transferring the other to his gunhand in order to leave a free hand for his personal ministrations.

The beat of John's racing heart thudded in his ears and his breath quickened. He'd planned to wait until they were closer to the canyon, but this was a better chance than he'd ever hoped for. He turned his back, then glanced over his shoulder at Ben. "I can't while you're lookin at me," he said. He really wasn't even trying, and had made no preparations to do so.

"Then you'll jest have to tank it up and hold it," Ben retorted. But he couldn't resist one glance at his own manipulations and at that moment John let out a war whoop and sprang for his saddle.

The whoop and sudden burst of action had two effects — John's mare was already in motion when he grabbed the saddlehorn and Ben's mount was startled into jerking the rein away from his hand, which caused him to drop the pistol. By the time the Bar BX hands got things put back in place and caught Ben's horse, John had a good head start. He was confident the mare was faster than anything the Bar BX crew had, except their bullets. But cowhands don't have much time for target practice or money for bullets, and most of them can't hit the side of a barn with a six-gun. John hoped the Bar BX hands were typical, including Ben. He hoped Ben was a poor shot all the way around, for he carried a Winchester on his saddle.

When John finally ventured a look behind him there was no one in sight. His exit was so abrupt and left enough turmoil in its wake that not a shot was fired. As soon as he reached the mouth of the canyon he rode to a vantage point on a slope and retrieved the spyglass from his saddlebags.

He didn't locate them at first because he expected them to be much closer than they were. When he finally made them out in the distance, his heart swelled with pride over the superiority of his mount. Of course, their horses had been traveling all day, while Chris had rested at the lookout most of the morning. But even so, she'd sure gotten him out of their gunsights in a hurry. He wondered why they were moving so slowly. Then he realized that, having lost sight of his dust, they were compelled to track him across the rocky terrain because they couldn't know for sure where he would go. John lowered the glass and peered up the canyon he and Wally had so eagerly explored several months before. The Bar BX men would find the tracking even slower up there. He was sure he could elude them. But after he rimmed out, where would he go? He assumed he could ride the ridge to the south, but how would he get off the mountain without doubling back to this canyon? They might anticipate that move and post a sentinel to watch the canyon. He'd heard there was an old Indian trail on the side of the escarpment somewhere near the Texas line, but the chances he could find it were slim to none.

John had successfully lured the trackers away from the trail, wearing their horses out in the process and allowing the rustlers to get away with the herd, but Ben would take it up again as soon as they had time to regroup. It was imperative that Wally be apprised of the situation as soon as possible, else the gang might ride into a trap on the way back.

As he glanced about the canyon and considered his alternatives, John recalled that several of the short header canyons which branched off the main gorge were choked with small trees and brush, some of it tall enough to obscure a horse. He decided he would try to use this camouflage to save time and avoid the possibility of getting trapped on top of the mountain. One more look through the glass reaffirmed his lead over the pursuit. He spurred the mare into the canyon, blazing a trail along the southern slope and leaving enough sign of his passage that it would not be missed. When he estimated he'd gone about as far as he could go and still have time to get back near the mouth of the canyon before the others entered, he selected a likely spot and reined Chris to a precipitous sliding descent into the rocky wash at the bottom of the gorge. He followed the wash back toward the entrance until he found a place they could ascend to the other slope. He picked their way along the slope to a brushy header he'd selected, ventured another peek through the spyglass to make sure they were still coming, and dismounted to lead his mount into the tangle of thorny brush.

With the spyglass in one hand and the other on the mare's nose, he watched them approach. Ben was in the lead, spurring and thrashing the weary gruyer and, from the way his jaw was working, cursing as hard as he was chewing. His face was almost as red as the shirt the second rider wore. Muncie plodded along in their wake.

When they'd disappeared around the bend of the canyon, John replaced the glass and led

Chris from the thicket. He mounted and made his way out of the canyon as hastily as he dared, then set the mare into her ground-eating trot toward Texas.

Chapter Fifteen

"Take it easy, cowboy, you'll get me to school on time," cautioned Barbara when Winston sped through an intersection after the traffic light had turned amber.

"I didn't mean to cut the time so close," he apologized. "I just got engrossed in tracing out those tracks."

"So what do you think?"

"Well, it appears that one person took the horses and led them down the road a ways and loaded them onto a truck or a trailer. I studied the tire tracks real careful, but the shoulder's hard and gravelly and several vehicles have strayed off the pavement in the same area. I really couldn't discern anything from the tire tracks."

"She said the missing horses were a dun and a blue roan."

"Yep, and those blue horses are pretty rare. That's my best lead. That and the fact that O.C. saw a pickup pass the corrals yesterday with two horses and he mentioned that one of them was a blue roan. I'm sure anxious to find out what color the other one was. It's probably just a coincidence, but it's worth checking out."

"Is O.C. working close to the house today?"

"Yeah, this morning I've got them replacing the boards on the horse corral where that ol' cribbing sorrel chewed them up last winter. I'll call Mom and get her to fetch him."

"If the other horse O.C. saw was a dun, Sheriff Hawkins may want you to go back out there right away to try to find that truck."

"Most likely." Winston sighed and cut his eyes at Barb. "Barb, I didn't mean for you to have to ride the school bus home, but if I'm not there to pick you up. . . ."

"Oh, that's all right, Win. I can grade papers on the bus just as well as at home. I just hope you can get those horses back for Mrs. Stonecipher. More than anything, I hope they can find Mr. Stonecipher and he's okay."

"You better brief me on what she told you so I can pass it on to Carl. I don't suppose there was really much of anything she could add to what we already know."

"No, not much. She did say he's commented several times lately as to how he'd rather been shot in a gun battle or bucked off on his head than to die in that nursing home. She's not so sure he wandered off in a stupor. He may have done it on purpose."

"That's important, Barb. If he's actually trying to avoid detection it would explain why nobody's seen him. But how could a sick, stove-up old man like that . . . ? Poor old John!"

The breaks of the Pecos were dimly visible on

the far horizon by the time John saw the riders approaching. He pulled out the spyglass long enough to make a positive identification and waited for them to ride up to him. They'd disposed of the rustled cattle somewhere east of the Pecos and were on their way back to New Mexico with money in their pockets and self-satisfied smiles on their faces. Except for Beasley. He had his share of the proceeds but his scraggly face rarely betrayed emotion. When they drew near enough to be sure it was John who waited for them on the trail, Wally let out a whoop and spurred his horse to a gallop. The others streaked after him and they all raced up to John, bringing with them a cloud of dust as their ponies skidded to a stop all about him.

Rafer McDaniel was the first to speak. "Where yuh been, Stone? Didja get lost? Or maybe you just got skeered and pulled out. I bet that's it! Then you commenced thinking on how you might have to face us again after we come back and got even more scared. So you tried to make up for lost time, from the looks of that mare."

Wally shot McDaniel a disgusted look and returned his gaze to John. "What happened, pard?"

John ignored McDaniel as he briefly told of sighting the Bar BX riders on the trail of the missing cattle and luring them off in the opposite direction. He included more of the details when he told of how he'd escaped the forced march. Some of the men began to snicker, and

McDaniel joined in as if he'd never made his disparaging remark.

"You might say you caught 'em with their britches down," said Speckles with a guffaw, "damn near it, anyhow!" All the rustlers burst out laughing except Beasley, who signified his amusement by widening his eyes and increasing the tempo of his tobacco chewing.

John was caught up in the mirth and camaraderie and found himself laughing with them. It was amazing how a desperate situation could become so hilarious when you looked back on it. "Anyhow, I got so far ahead of them I was able to lead 'em off up a canyon and double back on 'em and came on down here," he concluded when the laughter finally began to settle.

Oates's face turned sober. "How far ahead of them do you reckon you are?"

"A day, prob'ly more," John estimated. "Their ponies was plumb wore out. They'd be obliged to go by the Bar BX for fresh mounts. Unless they could've rode 'em as far as the XT," he added, just then thinking of the possibility.

Wally shook his head. "Ben don't like to be beholdin' to nobody. He'd go for his own hosses."

McDaniel jerked a brand new carbine from his saddle boot. "Well, I hope they come on," he exclaimed. "I'm anxious to try out this here new Winchester." He brought the rifle to his shoulder and loped his horse in a circle while sighting down the barrel at imaginary targets.

Wally shifted his mount to watch Rafer's antics and John's eye was drawn to the new leather underneath his worn stirrup leather and the polished wooden gunstock protruding from the scabbard. "You got one too, huh?" he said when he caught Wally's eye.

"Yeah," Wally enthusiastically affirmed, "a few freighters are still running the Pecos City trail in spite of the railroad. Rafer hailed one of them to see if he had any likker and he got to talking about these new Winchester thirty-thirty caliber carbines. They's not many of them around yet, but he had a few on his wagon. Me and Rafer and Oates talked him into selling us three of them. Scabbards and cartridges, too. Beasley decided to stick with his old Winchester because his pistol takes the same caliber shells. Speckles bought Rafe's old rifle."

McDaniel and Beasley had been the only ones with rifles; now the whole gang was armed with both rifle and pistol except John, who had neither. If they met up with the Bar BX crew on the way back to Abels's canyon there would be quite a battle.

When they got back to the Delaware, John suggested the rest of the gang should ride on to the safety of the canyon, leaving him to rest his mount a day or so before following them. Rafer opined as to how he reckoned all their horses could do with a little rest, not to mention their own bodies, and he figured with all the new artillery they could handle anything the Bar BX could muster.

They'd no sooner settled into their temporary camp when McDaniel became restless and fetched his horse from the graze. He rode out to the prairie looking for something at which to shoot and returned about sundown with a young antelope draped across his saddle bows.

The next day the men lounged about the camp, resting and enjoying the fresh meat. Except McDaniel, who constantly stalked the river bank looking for sunning turtles and surfacing carp to blast to kingdom come with his new thirty-thirty. John sensed that he could hardly wait to try it out on human game. Rafer would welcome an encounter with Ben Bledsoe and his cowboys.

John breathed a sigh of relief when they approached the mouth of the canyon without incident on the following day. He held back to allow the others to pass ahead of him up the canyon and dismounted to cut some brush for dusting out any sign of their hoofprints. He walked to a point on their back-trail where they'd crossed an exceptionally rocky area and carefully worked his way into the canyon before discarding the branches.

As he remounted and reined the bay toward the camp his eye strayed toward the bluff where Emelda's lookout was situated. He wondered if she was up there now, watching him. It wasn't likely, for Abels only sent her up there when he didn't want to take a chance on unexpected visitors discovering something or someone in camp that might incriminate him in some way.

They'd do well to keep a constant vigil for the next several days, at least. You couldn't expect the leaders, Wally and Rafer, to share sentinel duty. Nor Abels either. The sullen Beasley might make a good sentry if you could get him to do it, which was doubtful. John couldn't visualize the young Speckles or the pudgy Grassbelly doing anything but sleeping if either of them were sent to the lookout. He decided the watchdog duties were best left to himself and Emelda to share.

Chapter Sixteen

John slumped in the saddle, content to allow the dun to follow the roan as Wally led the way down the Lonesome Ridge trail. He felt the horse stop and looked up to see that Wally had reined in. The trail was leading them along the rim of the deep canyon on the south side of the ridge.

Wally stood up in the stirrups and peered into the depths of the canyon, as if he might conjure up a scene from the distant past. "Along here is where it happened, ain't it?"

"It was right along here, yeah." John looked about the rocky rabble of the ridge. "That little pile of gravestones I built has long since disappeared, but it was right along here somewhere."

Wally heaved a sigh and nudged the roan into motion. The dun followed without any encouragement from John. John reaffirmed his grip on the saddle horn and gazed across the canyon to the rocky palisade of White Mule Ridge and the outline of the ridge beyond. Memories of the explosive events that took place between those ridges in the main gorge of the canyon surged through his mind. He tried to focus on the area of the far ridge where he'd kept sentry over seventy years past.

The darting maneuvers of the swallows flashing hither and thither about the limestone cliffs contrasted the lazy circlings of a vulture riding the air currents beyond the canyon's rim. "My job would be a lot easier if I could float around up yonder like that ol' turkey buzzard," John commented to himself as he stood up to massage his numb backsides. He'd try to remember to bring a blanket with him to the lookout tomorrow. Maybe he could make his rocky post a little more comfortable. He raised the glass to resume his reconnaissance of the rugged terrain down the canyon.

Abels' hideout was remote and difficult to approach. He said he'd seen no one since he moved here save those currently in camp. But John knew Ben Bledsoe wouldn't give up. As careful as they'd been to leave no tracks leading to the canyon, he might discover some sign, or decide to scout the canyon "jest on case," as he would say.

Already the rustlers were planning another foray. They wouldn't dare round up another herd so close to the Bar BX. It would be difficult to gather a group of cattle from the outlying areas of the open range that all bore the same brand. There was no possibility that McDaniel and his men would be disposed to take only those which wore the Bledsoe mark. One stolen cow was the same as another as far as they were concerned, and the more the better. John expected Wally to justify his participation by saying there were enough Bar BX animals involved to cover his share of the proceeds.

Well, John wouldn't accept any of the ill-gotten loot. He'd scout for them awhile for Wally's sake, and maybe even pack in supplies for the men and grain for the horses now and then. But as soon as Wally was satisfied he'd collected his due from the Bar BX John wanted to talk him into trying their luck over in the Arizona Territory, or maybe even farther away.

A hollow feeling clutched his vitals each time he thought about being so decidedly separated from Gracie. And yet, he didn't have a chance with her as long as Wally was around and he didn't believe Wally would go unless he went. Well, at least he could do her the favor of getting Wally out of her life.

He might never see her again! Would he ever come back? Even if he did, would Gracie forever pine for Wally? And if she did get over Wally, she might be married to someone else by the time John could return.

Feeling a need to desist his pondering of the dilemma, John sought to concentrate on something else, and turned the spyglass toward the recesses of the canyon. Abels said there were pools of clear, living water up there. The goat camp was about as far as you could penetrate on horseback. From that point the walls of the gorge became increasingly narrow and almost perpendicular and the bottom was strewn with boulders, some of them as big as a two-room cabin standing on end. The whole of the upper end of the canyon was choked with shrubs and trees, including manzanita, maple, ash, various species of pine, fir, small oaks, sumac, hackberry, and other varieties. It would be an interesting place to explore one day when Emelda was on guard duty. John traced the rocky bottom of the canyon's wash, hoping for a glimpse of one of the emerald pools of fresh water that were scattered here and there among the rocks and foliage.

The high-pitched sound of Abels' cackle from the camp below broke the spell and John returned his survey toward the mouth of the canyon. Immediately his eye caught a brief glimmer of reflected sunlight. Reflected from what? Another glass? A gun barrel? There were shiny conchos on Ben Bledsoe's saddle. And Muncie had a shiny new buckle. He kept scanning the area until he spotted a sotol stalk that was waving to and fro as if something had brushed against it. He peered through the long tangle of brush immediately before the sotol and discerned movement on the other side. Presently a hat materialized, followed by a rider and a horse as they gained a position on the slope. Two more riders emerged and crowded their horses against the leader when he pulled up to study the narrowing chasm before them. The second man wore a red shirt. They'd changed horses, but not clothes. Red-shirt hadn't, anyway.

Well, Ben, you was bound to come, wasn't you? If you decide we're up here, you'd best go fetch some more back-up! Three of you ain't gonna be near enough! John backed off and shinnied down the slope to warn the rustlers.

They heard him scrambling across the rocks and gathered around as soon as he'd pushed his way through the thick brush that surrounded the camp. He told them what he'd seen. For a moment they just looked at one another, as if each was waiting for someone else to make a suggestion. Abels chewed his quid like a starving man with a tough piece of meat in his mouth.

"I swanny!" he exclaimed, "I knowed you boys'd draw the law down on me." He emphasized the statement with a disgusted spit.

"Ben ain't the law," Wally reminded him.

"One thing leads to another," Abels insisted. "They'll be afetchin' the law if you waddies leave any of that bunch to ride out of this here canyon!"

"What're you spoutin', you old goat?" demanded John. "You want us to lay up somewhere and gun them down in cold blood? *Durn!* We can't do a thing like that!"

"I can," said McDaniel matter-of-factly. "Me and Beasley. And I seen Choctaw practicing with that Colt's and I'll miss my bet if he's bashful."

John saw a flicker of panic in Wally's eyes just before he ducked his hatbrim to hide his face. He interceded before Wally was forced to respond.

"Now just rein up, *muchachos,*" he said in a placating tone, "and let's think this thing out."

"Better not think too long or we'll see how you think with a chunk of lead in yer brain," quipped Abels.

"Those boys're a long way off yet," John assured them. "And if they was lookin' to fight, they'd of brought more men with 'em. They're just on a scout, and from the way they was hesitating and eyeballing up the canyon, I doubt they'll come this far this time. If they do ride this far up the wash, they still won't be able to spot the camp up here on the bench in the brush. *But,* if they don't get back when they're expected, folks are gonna be trailing 'em to see what happened. A dry-gulching will stir things up a heap more than cattle rustling," he emphasized with a stern tone. "I say we get Abels and Emelda to stay with the horses and the rest of us scatter out and hide along the banks of the arroyo where we can keep an eye on 'em. When they see they can't go any further on horseback they'll turn around. Even if they still think we're up this canyon somewhere they'll go back for a posse. While they're gone, we'll change waterin' holes, *pronto!*"

Wally had kept his head bowed, as if concentrating deeply on what John was saying. He straightened up and tried to look like he'd been talked out of something he was on the verge of doing. "I'm convinced. We don't wanna do nothin' that'll hamstring our b'iness."

The two younger rustlers enthusiastically

voiced agreement with John and Wally. Abels looked disgusted and McDaniel grinned impassively. Beasley maintained his indifferent scowl.

Wally assumed the vocal yeas outweighed the silent nays. "All right then, me and John'll go t'other side of the wash. Rafer, send one of your boys with us, will you?" Rafer nodded to Speckles. They all went to their saddles and secured their carbines. Wally also dug out the old Navy revolver and handed it to John. "I know you ain't gonna shoot at 'em, but you might need a iron sometime or another."

John stared at the old pistol for a moment, shrugged and stuck it in his belt. "Everybody stay hid and don't shoot unless you're shot at," he reminded them as they dispersed to take up their positions. "Don't booger — just be patient and they'll pull out, if they even come this far."

They did. They could be heard before they were seen. The scrape and clink of horseshoes on the rocky rubble in the bottom of the canyon preceded their appearance. The progress of the sound revealed they were moving cautiously, and they no sooner eased into view than they stopped to parley. Muncie looked longingly back the way they'd come. Ben gazed ahead, irresistibly drawn by a mesmeric fascination. He nudged his pony forward and motioned with his Winchester for the others to follow. Muncie held his pony and Red-shirt continued a distance, then pulled up when he realized he was the only one following the leader.

John wiped the sweat from his brow and adjusted his position in the bushes to get a clearer view as the hoofbeats of the one horse drew nearer. *Yep, that's ol' Ben, all right. Stubborn as a ox! But them Bar BX hands ain't drawing fightin' wages.*

Ben reined his horse around and hurled some sharp words at the reluctant cowboys. John couldn't make it out, but it wasn't hard to guess the gist of the reprimand: *Them boys won't be drawing any kind of wages from the Bar BX after today.*

Red-shirt gave an indistinguishable answer along with a nod toward the open end of the canyon. He slowly pulled his horse around and carefully picked his way through the slippery rock toward Muncie, who was already turning his mount. John could see Ben's shoulders slump as he exhaled a disgusted sigh, then the hoofbeats of his horse, too, began to fade.

A shrill whinny emanated from the direction of the goat camp. *Damn you, Abels!* John still held the spyglass and he raised it to see better how the Bar BX riders would react.

Ben yanked his horse around, jacked a shell into the chamber of the Winchester and began seeking a way up the bank of the arroyo. He spurred his horse toward the spot where Oates was concealed and John saw the hapless beast go down before the sound of Grassbelly's thirty-thirty reached his ears. Ben kicked free of the stirrups in time to avoid being pinned by the falling animal but took a hard fall on the rocks and lost his hat. He sprang to his feet with his shirt in bloody tatters and blood streaming down the left side of his skull. *Run, Ben, Run!*

Muncie was by this time nowhere to be seen, but the red-shirted cowboy wheeled his horse and spurred toward his boss, who was frantically clambering across the rocks to meet him. A stone turned under his foot and he went down just in time to avoid stopping a slug from McDaniel's rifle. Through the glass John saw fragments fly from a boulder just behind where Ben had fallen and the wild panic in his eyes as he arose and desperately clawed his way onto the horse with his employee. *Please let 'em make it!* They hunched over the saddle and scrambled out of sight as McDaniel and Beasley burned the air around them with bullets.

John and Wally jumped off the bank and scrambled across the wash in time to arrive at the camp along with McDaniel and Beasley. Abels was there ahead of them, little pig eyes gleaming in expectation of the news of the ambush. "Did you git 'em all?"

He should have known the answer from the disappointment in Rafer's eyes. "Oates made buzzard dinner outa one of the hosses. Me'n Beasley scared hell out of a couple of 'em, but we missed. *Hot dammit!*" he exclaimed with a grimace and an angry shake of his rifle.

It was the first time since Wally had put him

on the saloon floor that John had seen him without his insipid smile. John also noted that Abels' grin of anticipation had reversed its configuration. "Abels, alls you had to do was keep them horses still and nobody would've had to fire a shot!"

" 'Twasn't me! 'Twas the gal! There was too many hosses for two people to keep a clamp on, anyways." He didn't know Emelda had sidled out of the bushes and was standing by just out of range of his peripheral vision. She said not a word, but her eyes burned with hurt as she glared at her unseeing accuser.

Emelda's wounded expression was sufficient testimony for John. "I think it was you, Abels, and I think you did it on purpose when you heard them boys turning back."

Before Abels could form a reply, Oates came reeling into camp, huffing and puffing from the exertion of his walk. He chose a grassy spot and plopped himself down. McDaniel immediately confronted him and Oates pulled the hat from his sweaty head, anticipating a tongue-lashing for shooting the horse instead of the man. But the sight of the pudgy red-faced youth gasping for air as he gazed up at him brought the snake-like smile back to Rafer's lips. "Well I'll swun, Grassbelly, if you got as winded on the way down there as you did a-comin' back, it's a marvel you even hit the hoss!"

"It was the best thing he could of done," interjected John. "One of them hands'd already lit a shuck, so there was no way you could get them all, anyhow."

"You boys're gonna have to find yerselves another hole now, that's for shore," proclaimed Abels.

"Well, you're a purty good hand at scoutin' out places to hide," Wally responded.

"You'll have to find yer own hideout this time, Choctaw. I'm staying right here where I'm at."

"But they'll be back with more men," John reminded him.

"Prob'ly not up the canyon, if y'all would do me a favor. Now, I've done treated you boys white, ain't I?" John just stared at him, waiting for him to get to the point. The others nodded or murmured their agreement. "Now, they know we know they's coming back and they know we ain't stupid enough to set around and wait for 'em to show up. Well, all's I'm asking is for you fellers, when y'all ride out of heah, to leave plenty of sign at the mouth of the canyon that you've done hauled yer freight. Thataway, that posse ain't likely to waste no time a-comin' up heah."

"What if they decide to check it out anyways?" Speckles wanted to know.

"Melda'll see 'em way before they get heah. By the time they do, they won't find nothin' but a abandoned goat camp."

"Sure, Abels, we'll leave some tracks so they'll know we've pulled out," Wally assured him.

Abels nodded agreeably at Wally and shot a nervous glance at McDaniel's noncommital smile. "Thisaway, I can keep an eyeball on any goin's on in these parts and you boys can sneak into camp from time to time to find out if I've seed or heard anything."

Rafer McDaniel knew his silence was making the old man nervous and anxious to do anything he could to assure his good favor. "You got any suggestions where we can go when we leave here?"

"I'll do anything I can to help you, Rafe, you know that. Some of the best hideouts in the country is right here in the Guadalupes. If I's you boys I'd go deeper in the mountains and scout me a good place."

Wally looked at John. "We could go up that canyon where we rimmed out last fall when we found them mavericks."

McDaniel gave a negative wag of his head. "I think I know about where you boys come from that day. I sure wisht we could find a way onto the mountain further away from the outfits."

Abels saw another opportunity to ingratiate himself with the smirking gunman. "I know another way up the mountain," he volunteered. "It's steep. They's a lot of switchbacks and slickrock. You might have to git down and lead the hosses every now and agin." He cut a doubtful eye at Grassbelly. "But it's right close by and y'all will be hard to foller. Soon's y'all get clear of the mouth of the canyon, make a welty to the north an look real careful and you'll come across a old Injun trail to the top."

Chapter Seventeen

Winston stood on the cab of the abandoned pickup truck and searched the country westward toward Big Canyon through the field glasses. He reconnoitered to the south across the state line toward McKittrick Canyon and the point of the mountain; then to the north as far as Gunsight Canyon.

"Any sign of 'em?" O.C. was perched on the side boards, gazing across the distances with the naked eye. Winston brought him along because he was the only one who'd gotten a good look at the truck. They'd found it with a flat tire, plunged into a patch of creosote bush alongside a remote and scarcely maintained BLM road. "They's a good spare," O.C. commented when Winston didn't answer right away. "Seems like they'd of unloaded the hosses and put it on and jumped 'em back aboard and kept on goin'."

Winston lowered the binoculars, but continued to survey the countryside. "They must've been close enough to where they wanted to be," he surmised.

"Far as them city fellers knows, one place is as good as another to go lookin' for mule deer," O.C. scoffed.

"I doubt they're what you'd call tenderfeet, O.C. If you'll look closely at the paint you'll see this truck's been pushed through a lot of mesquite and catclaw and such."

O.C. jumped down and scrutinized a door panel after wiping some of the dust away. "You ain't wrong! This here old pickup's been a-ridin' the range, all right. Now, why in the Sam Hill would them hands steal a couple of hosses in town, haul 'em out here, ditch the truck, and go a-gallivantin' off in the toolies?"

"We don't know for a fact that thy're the same horses that were stolen, O.C."

"Then why'd they try to hide the truck?"

"Maybe the blowout forced them into the brush."

"Now do you really think it all could be just a coincidence, Win?"

"No, O.C., I don't. I always try not to jump to conclusions, but to tell you the truth, I've got a funny feeling about this situation."

O.C. would not be satisfied with anything less than a direct admission that Winston concurred with his own conclusion about the horses. "So you think these hands're riding Miz Stonecipher's hosses, eh?"

"This rocky terrain won't show enough in the way of hoofprints to make an adequate comparison with those I saw at her place, but . . . yes, I've got a hunch the dun and the blue roan you saw are sporting the Circle S brand. By the way, O.C., knock the dirt off of the license plate and take down the number. I'll phone it in and get them to run a make on it soon as I get back to the house. I'm going back for some horses. You stay here and watch the truck in case they come back while I'm gone."

While O.C. looked for a stick with which to clean his plate, Winston again peered through the glasses at the rugged Chihuahuan desert environment sloping up to the base of the Guadalupe escarpment. The riders could be anywhere among the myriad washes, knolls, *rincóns,* and patches of tangled brush within the range of his binoculars and never be seen. He and O.C. had no choice but to trail them on horseback if they were to discover what the mysterious horse thieves were up to. For once he would be glad to have the garrulous O.C. at his side.

O.C.'s grunt of surprise brought Winston's attention back to the immediate surroundings. "Well, I'll be switched," O.C. exclaimed, "this here's a Arizony tag!"

"Maybe they're on a trail ride back to Arizona," said Winston sarcastically as he climbed down from the brush-scarred Dodge.

O.C. took a moment to ponder the western horizon, as if taking seriously Winston's facetious comment. "Shoot, they could've taken the old Indian trail to Lonesome Ridge and be plumb on top of the mountain by now."

John lay on his back on a ledge that jutted

from the bluff above the new hideout, peering through the spyglass into the azure heights beyond the rim. He hadn't offered to return the glass when they parted company with Abels. It was tucked under John's belt when they were about to ride out and Abels saw it and started to say something, but Rafer's amused smile and challenging eye made him think better of it.

John focused on a red-tailed hawk buoying on the standing waves of high-country winds thrown up by the canyons and peaks surrounding the new hideout. The hawk was just one of many John had studied through the glass in the several days since they came up the Indian trail and found the sheltered cove with the wide shallow cave. He'd also seen eagles and another hawk-like bird Silverthorne called a falcon. There was an abundance of smaller varieties of bird life, too, including mourning doves. Silverthorne said you could watch the flight of the doves at nightfall to locate water because, unlike the birds that prey on moisture-containing insects, the seed-eating doves roost only where they can obtain drink for the morning and again in the evening.

Silverthorne had come with the cave. He was there when they came, and surprised them by walking out to greet them when they rode up. John noticed that his eye came to rest upon the pearl-handled Peacemaker and silver studded gunbelt at Wally's waist and for an instant he looked as if someone had slapped him. Silverthorne recognized them, for sure! John surmised he was one of the refugees from the cattle wars who'd holed up in the Guadalupes. No doubt he'd seen a number of desperados come and go in the dozen or so years he'd lived in the mountains.

John soon understood why Silverthorne had chosen to stay in the mountain. He was satisfied he'd be contented to spend the rest of his own days among the rugged limestone cliffs and peaks and grassy slopes studded with pine, pinyon, alligator juniper, and small oaks and maples. Silverthorne said there were thick forests of fir, ponderosa, and limber pine higher up and further south toward the point of the mountain. And a man wouldn't have to worry about going hungry. There was an abundance of mule deer and the usual assortment of smaller game, including turkeys. John had seen no elk, but despite the wholesale slaughter by army hunting expeditions sent out from El Paso's Fort Bliss in the 1880's, a few black bears remained, and bighorn sheep in the remotest crags.

According to Silverthorne, a lot of the vegetation could be eaten, such as acorns, juniper and manzanita berries and prickly pear tunas, even the oily nuts of the pinyon pine cone. Although nutritious, the nuts were bitter and hard to chew. That's why the first part of an Apache to wear out was his molars, according to Silverthorne. He'd learned much of what he knew from living among the remnant of Mescaleros who eschewed the reservation for the freedom of the Guadalupes.

Except for his startling blue eyes and frizzy white beard, Silverthorne, with his sun-blackened skin and makeshift attire, looked very much like an old Apache himself. He even had the loose-kneed, catlike moves of an Indian. John didn't think he was really as old as his wind-dried face and snowy hair indicated. He obviously recognized the outlaws for what they were. Yet, betraying not a sign of fear, he welcomed them to share his hideaway. Of course he knew if he didn't they would most likely blast him out of the cave with no more compunction than they'd have for a porcupine or a badger that happened to stand in the way. John had a hunch experience had taught him they would only present a temporary inconvenience. Sooner or later circumstances would take them elsewhere, possibly to their graves, and he would again be left to the peace of his solitary existence. Perhaps he even enjoyed the company for awhile. At least he seemed pleased to share his knowledge of the mountains with John, whose fascination for the high-country environment was obvious from the day they arrived.

A mingling sound of voices attracted John's attention. The gang was assembled before the cave and appeared to be having a serious discussion. "Noisy as a hen house at daybreak," John muttered to himself, and proceeded to climb down from the ledge, careful of the crevices he used for handholds. Silverthorne had warned him of the little "green rattlers" that frequented such fissures.

"Why don't you let me go for supplies?" John heard Oates volunteer as he walked up to join the group.

Rafer's all-knowing smirk widened a little. "Grass, you just been studying on the climb up the mountain on the way back. That's the onliest reason you'd rather go for supplies," he said.

"Wouldn't mind recapturing to mind what a town looks like, neither," admitted Oates.

"That reason too," agreed McDaniel. "We all could do with a little sashay into town," he added, looking at Wally. "I think we'll mosey on down to Pecos City or Toyah after we deliver the herd."

"Suit yerself," Wally responded with a shrug. "John, we're going down to round up another herd and we'll need beans, salt pork, flour, and coffee and such by the time we get back — grain for the hosses, too. I was just telling the rest of 'em we might get you to ride to town for us while we're gone."

"Sure, but who'll scout for you?"

"We'll either take turns or we'll just take our chances. Silverthorne says it's about three days from here to Eddy if you take the trail across the ridges and down Dark Canyon, so you'll be back before us. *Way* before us, if these hands is set on spendin' some time in one of them towns."

"I believe it'd pleasure me to take some time in

town myself, Wallace. I missed my spring visit to town, you know."

"You could stay several days and still get back before we do."

McDaniel's mischievous eyes darted from Wally to John. "Which town you talking about, Stone? Eddy or Phenix?"

"Yeah," joined Oates. "He's liable to lose all our *dinero* at the faro table before he gets around to stocking up."

"Aw, Oates," Speckles objected, "John ain't gonna do nothing of the kind. You just bellerin' 'cause you don't wanna ride off the rimrock with us. I seen how scared you was a-scramblin' up them switchbacks."

"Godamighty, fellers," Oates admitted, "a ol' pony could flat turn over on that old trail. Ain't they a better way?"

McDaniel's eyes steadied on Oates. "*Easier*, maybe, but not near as fast." No one said anything as Rafer's cool scrutiny caused Oates' face to redden and shiny droplets to surface among the downy fuzz of his upper lip. Beasley turned his head to spit a stream of tobacco juice and continued his impassive chewing as he waited to see Oates grovel.

Speckles regretted he'd brought Grassbelly's phobia to light. "Aw, you'll be all right, Oates," he interceded, "just foller me and keep a light stirrup on the downhill side so's you can swing off on the upgrade if yer pony slips. I'll help you through it."

Oates responded with a hangdog nodding of his head and John decided it was a good time to bring the discussion back on course. "I'll need a pack animal or two if y'all want me to bring back much of a grub box."

"Better get two," Wally decided, "we need enough supplies to last us awhile. Silverthorne said the Shattucks'll have some broncs we can use. Their place is on the way."

The sun, rising out of sight beyond the ridges, spread its roseate radiance into the sky above the camp as the rustlers saddled up for their second raid on the Bar BX herd. Silverthorne observed them quietly from a shadowy position against the checkered bark of an alligator juniper. John speculated that he too, was wondering if all or any of them would make it back. He strengthened his resolve to press Wally about drifting on west, although he dreaded the day he must leave these mountains forever. Silverthorne said you could follow the Indian trail down the western scarp and ride the big canyon between the Guadalupes and the Brokeoffs out to the flats. He must talk Wally into leaving before it was too late. His uneasy feeling was aggravated by the gusty wind that had risen with the dawning to whistle across the bluff and angrily toss the heavy boughs of the juniper and pinyon.

Oates hastily tied off his latigo and turned away from his skittish bronc with a resounding sneeze. "Damn windy weather," he complained.

Silverthorne raised his voice to be heard above the sough of the wind in the evergreens. "It's just one of Ma Nature's ways of disseminating pollen in order to propagate various species of plant life," he said matter-of-factly.

"Do *what?*" Speckles blurted.

"She's spreadin' pollen, dummy," said Oates with a snivel. "Like plant semen, you know?" He wiped his runny nose on his sleeve. "I shore do wish she'd just leave it to the bees and butterflies."

"It's a big country. She needs all the help she can get," explained Silverthorne.

Wally pulled his stirrup over and yanked on the saddlehorn as if to make sure he had his hull screwed down good and tight. "Well, I sure don't need none of her help. I can do my own pollynatin', pers'nal-like."

Everyone laughed but Beasley, and McDaniel was reminded of the prospects that awaited after the herd was delivered to his friends in Texas. "I just hope they's enough purty li'l *flowers* to go around when we get to town," he said. Beasley raised his eyebrows and began to chew his plug faster.

Speckles mounted his red roan, looking expectant and eager to be off. "Yeah, the way ol' Wally's a-talkin', he's liable to need a *couple* of 'em hisself," he joked.

Wally tugged his hat tighter against his ears to forestall the gusty wind, stepped to the stirrup, and swung astraddle. "Naw, I'll leave them saloon gals to you waddies. I ain't in the habit of payin' for it and I don't aim to take on new habits this late in life."

There was more laughter and a sardonic comment from McDaniel: "So what're you fixing to do, *ladino?* Make a little *paseo* up the canyon to the goat camp on the way back, or what?"

Wally gave him a cagey look and began turning his horse to follow Speckles' roan. "I might even have a better idea than that."

John felt like his heart skipped several beats. *He* knew what Wally was thinking about. *Gracie!* He was thinking about trying to see Gracie!

John wondered if Wally detected the stunned expression on his face when he looked back to gesture an *adiós.* He composed himself just in time to signal a response before Wally turned away and rode out of sight beyond the trees that encircled the hideaway. John stood and stared after them, his mind trying to cope with the thought of Wally and Gracie together again as he'd seen them the night of the Christmas party. Maybe Wally would decide it was too risky to try to see Gracie, and settle for Emelda. After all, Ben might have guessed that Wally would try to contact Grace and attempt to waylay him. Wally's wisecrack about being "late in life" could prove to be more prophetic than witty.

"Shattucks'll all be abed by the time you get there if you don't snap out of your trance." Silverthorne's voice jolted John back to the present. He'd walked right up behind John without making a sound. He placed a hand on John's shoulder. "He'll be all right, son," he said with empathy.

"I wish I could be sure of it," responded John with a sigh and a wag of his head. "He'll be taking a awful chance if he's determined to see his gal. But you're right, I've got to be getting on with what he gave me to do." He cut a sagacious eye at Silverthorne. "And I expect you're anxious to enjoy your privacy again for awhile."

"I don't mind *your* company, son."

John strode to the cave, picked up his bridle and blanket and heaved the saddle upon his shoulder. The hobbled bay mare lifted her head from the lush grama grass and whickered a greeting as he approached.

"You ain't nothing but a ol' broomtail pet," he said as he deposited his outfit on the grass beside her. He encircled the muscular neck with his arms and pressed his jaw to her cheek, a gesture he'd never risk while the gang was in camp. He wasn't worried about Silverthorne. He'd understand and even approve.

Chapter Eighteen

"Let's don't get in too big a hurry," cautioned John when they'd worked their way into the beeline. "I'd just as soon nobody sees us and you can't tell when you might run into somebody up here nowadays. It ain't likely except in huntin' season, but we'd best be careful."

Wally reined the roan down a trifle and ducked his head for a better view up the winding trail through the foliage. "Was a time you could wander about up here for weeks, even months, and never see another human. There wasn't hardly anybody running cows in the mount'ins in them days, neither." Wally gestured with his chin at a dried-out cow patty alongside the path.

"Nope," John agreed, "just Cap Shattuck and Elias Queen, as far as I know. Captain Shattuck was the first, I think."

Captain John S. Shattuck, formerly of the army of the Confederacy, moved his family from Texas to New Mexico in 1885, settling on a spring in Dark Canyon in the Guadalupe Mountains. He was elected the first superintendent of schools of the newly formed Eddy County in 1890 and subsequently remained active in the affairs of the burgeoning Pecos Valley. Therefore he and Mrs. Shattuck were away on a trip to Seven Rivers the afternoon young John Stone- cipher stopped by looking to buy a couple of pack horses.

The ping of a hammer on metal led John to the corral where Captain Shattuck's two youngest sons were shoeing an uncooperative brown gelding. John knew them, having seen them at Eddy from time to time when the area ranchers threw their herds together for the drive to Amarillo. Dolph held the young horse's head while his older brother struggled with a hind foot.

Edwin, or Ned as he was called, was about John's age, an energetic and enterprising young man. He would be the first in Eddy County to bring in the heavier-fleshed Hereford bulls to crossbreed with the lanky Longhorn cattle, and the first to build a barbed wire fence in the Guadalupes. The cries of protest he would face over the latter project were more than a decade in the future and unforeseen on this late spring evening in 1894. His struggle with the muscular haunch of horse flesh was the one that was on his mind at the moment. He gave John an acknowledging glance as he walked into the corral and returned his attention to the task of clamping the gelding's pastern between his knees. When Ned finally got the hoof immobilized and began driving the nails, the brown reversed his tactics by gradually easing his hindquarter against Ned's back, eliciting some spit-riddled denunciations from around the horseshoe nails in his mouth.

Dolph grinned sheepishly and tried to maneuver the horse's head enough to get him to ease his weight from Ned's back without retracting the captured leg. In a flurry of activity Ned drove the remaining nails home and released the hoof. He'd take a breather before clinching the nails, so he turned to see what had brought John Stonecipher of the upper Black River into the mountains.

When John revealed he was looking to buy a couple of pack animals, Ned sorrowfully wagged his head and explained that they were a tad shy on horseflesh at the moment and he doubted his father would be willing to part with any even if he was at home to make the decision.

Dolph inquired about John's friend, Wally. John guessed it was because they'd heard about the shooting and were curious for more news. John merely told them Wally was laying low since Charlie had died, waiting to see what action would be taken. They hadn't heard about Charlie's demise. It wasn't hard to put two and two together and surmise from John's presence that Wally was hiding in the mountains and John had been sent for supplies and information, so they didn't pry any further. They invited John to stay the night with them and he accepted.

Riding northwest from Shattuck's the walls of Dark Canyon became less abrupt and the bottom of the valley gradually widened so that by the time John approached Eddy on the third day since leaving the hideout the canyon was just a deep arroyo cutting through the flats southwest of town. It served the purpose of conveying to the Pecos an occasional flash flood from the run-off of mountain thunderstorms.

The first thing on the agenda was the purchase of pack horses. They'd cost more in town, but that couldn't be helped now.

Of the two horses John settled upon at the wagonyard, the gray and white appaloosa was much superior. The tough little sorrel was definitely more what you'd normally have in mind for a utilitarian pack animal, and John felt guilty for having spent the extra money from the gang's reserve for the appaloosa. But he was fond of the color and it was unusual enough that you didn't get an opportunity to buy one very often. He was actually seizing the horse for himself and planned to reimburse the rustlers as soon as he was able. Shoot, they owed him *something* for all the peon work he was doing for them, anyway.

As John turned his horses out of the wagon yard he noticed the livery's fancy rental buggy pulled by a high-stepping gray approaching from the west on Mermod Street. Noting the fancy-dressed man and the blond-haired woman perched on the plush leather seat, he surmised some dandy had been sparking his girl with a ride to the Ocotillo Hills. There you could pull up to the summit and pause to observe the greening young town spreading along the meandering blue ribbon of the Pecos and feel good about its prospects and those of yourself and your companion.

John was about to step into his stirrup when he looked across his saddle at the passing buggy and right into the eyes of the man driving. "Mr. Shavalda!" he shouted, recognizing the gambler who'd intervened in the fight between Wally and Rafer in Phenix the previous fall. "Wait up!" He moved around the bay and extended his hand as the man pulled the gray to a standstill.

The gambler deigned a noncommittal return of John's handshake. "John Stone, I believe?" he questioned, releasing his grip.

"Ah . . . yeah. Say. I just wanted to thank you proper for what you did for us that night over in Phenix." He glanced nervously at the young woman. Surely she knew what Shavalda did for a living and where he headquartered. He decided he'd better not say any more, just in case Eli was keeping things from her.

"That's all right John," replied the gambler, his tone a bit friendlier. "But I hear that Choctaw kid has gone a bit farther than barroom brawling by now. You're not still running with him, are you?" When John hesitated to reply he continued. "John, you better be careful of whose company you keep. Many an innocent man has ended up with a bullet in his heart or a rope round his neck just because he was caught with bad company at the wrong time. Word's been passed about in the saloons that Ben Bledsoe's offering a thousand dollars for the Choctaw boy's scalp. He'll be mighty dangerous company from now on." With that he shook up the gray and pulled away, leaving John standing in the middle of the street with his mouth open.

If John thought that was to be his only surprise of the day he was mistaken. Some time later, while he was loading the last of the supplies on the pack horses beside the general store on the corner of Mermod and Canal, he heard a familiar voice in the drug store next door explaining how her youngest son had fallen so ill they'd been compelled to bring him to town to the doctor. About the time his heart jumped smack-dab on top of his Adam's apple with the thought that Miz Porter might be accompanied by her eldest daughter, Gracie spotted him from inside the drug store, hailed him, and sauntered out for a parley. John choked back the lump in his throat in time to articulate an adequate greeting as she approached.

Grace cast a calculating eye upon the loaded pack of horses. "I guess you'll be seeing Wally real soon," she stated.

"Not as soon as you will." John couldn't keep a tinge of bitterness from his voice. He hoped her surprise kept her from noticing.

"He's coming to the Lazy P?" she responded anxiously.

"Should be there in a few days," John affirmed. "Will y'all be home by then?"

"We're leaving town tomorrow, *but you've got to stop him, John!* It's too dangerous!"

John now realized that what he'd taken for excitement over Wally's impending visit was actually fear. "I'd of tried to talk him out of it before now," he admitted, "but I haven't had a chance at him since I found out what he's up to. After what I heard awhile ago . . ."

"You don't have to spare me the news about the bounty," said Grace at John's interruption of himself. "I already know. My father heard about it from a hangover cowboy on his way back to Texas from Phenix."

Mrs. Porter emerged from the drug store, greeted John with a reserved smile and told Grace they needed to get back to the hotel to get Will started on his medicine. John assumed one of the other children was sitting with the sick boy at the Hagerman.

Grace moved as if to follow her mother across Canal Street, then hesitated long enough for a passing freight wagon to come between them. "John," she said anxiously, "one of the hands saw a couple of men hiding out in the brush near our place. They were armed to the teeth and riding big fine horses. You know what that means! You've *got* to get to Wally before he does something foolish!" She glanced nervously in her mother's direction. "How's he doing, anyway?"

"Oh, Wally was pert, last time I saw him," John assured her.

"John, keep 'im that way for me . . . *please*." The expression on her face matched the pleading tone in her voice.

John touched his fingers to his hatbrim as she turned to scurry after her mother. A deep sigh did nothing to relieve the heavy feeling in his breast. He made a final check on the packs, mounted, and turned the mare to lead the other horses toward the road to Dark Canyon. He'd forego even one night in town on this trip.

Chapter Nineteen

"This ol' sorrel's kinda snaky to be a-riding up that old switchback trail, ain't he?" suggested O.C., gaping at the towering ridge that separated Big Canyon and Franks Canyon. By the time Winston had returned with the horses and they'd trailed the suspects to the base of the escarpment, the sun was about to disappear behind the peaks.

"Why O.C.! Just a week or two ago I heard you telling somebody you can still ride most anything that snorts or whinnies if you've a mind to," Winston bantered.

"Not off of no dang cliff!"

Winston chuckled as he returned the binoculars to the saddlebag. "Well, if the Bar BX has a bronc that's not too salty for you, rope him out in the morning. It's too late to follow them up yonder today. I never really thought they'd take off up the Staircase, but they rode straight to the trail and right on up, apparently. They know where they're going and they must've been there before. It's got to be someone from around here, maybe even somebody we know."

O.C. squinted at the heights, as if to conjure up an answer from the rocky palisade. "Don't believe I know anybody with a Arizony pickup and a hankerin' to go sightseeing in the Guadalupes on stolt hosses."

Winston wagged his head in dismay and turned his mount away from the escarpment. "Damndest thing I ever tried to figure out."

"Well, we'll just have to bring fresh horses in the morning and see what we can find when we climb that mountain."

John fairly towed the newly acquired pack horses back to the mountain hideaway, making the trip in two days instead of the customary three. After one day's rest and plenty of corn for Chris he took the trail to the rimrock and impatiently threaded his way down the switchbacks to the lower elevations. He was determined to head Wally off before he tried to sneak into the Lazy P headquarters to see Grace. He reined the bay mare to halt near the base of the escarpment and let her blow while he contemplated the broken land that spilled out before him until it was lost in the slanting rays of the midmorning glare.

Presently the mare blew a deep breath out of her nose and tossed her head as if to signify she was ready to travel. John held her for a few more moments while he finished speculating on the best route to intersect Wally's approach from Texas, then put her into the choppy, ground-eating trot she'd inherited from her Spanish forebears. He only checked the spine-jarring gait when it was necessary to negotiate one of the winding arroyos that cut through the terrain or to ease through a patch of stubby lechuguilla spears.

A long ridge of rising ground near the Texas line south of the Lazy P headquarters finally hove into view. It would provide a good vantage point from which to watch for Wally. John slowed the mare to a careful walk and scouted the knoll through the spyglass as he approached. He didn't expect any of the others who were looking for Wally would be in this area, but it was best to be sure.

There was no sign of anyone on the ridge. John spent the remainder of the afternoon peering through the telescope across the southeastern approaches. Wally's route from the Delaware to the Lazy P should bring him within the scope of John's observation. If Wally had accompanied Rafer and his men to one of the Texas towns, John might have to wait several days. If not, Wally could have already passed. He might already be captured or killed.

When the sun touched the western peaks John took the mare to water at a spring just inside the territorial boundary. The evening shadow cast an eerie pall on the land by the time he brought her back and staked her out in a grassy draw below his observation point. The fear that he'd missed Wally continued to gnaw at his insides, compelling him to make one last survey in the failing light before settling down for the night.

If anyone was out there, he couldn't see them. He made his way back to the draw, built a small campfire that could not be seen outside the hollow and sat down to munch on some of his provisions while he stared into the flames and contemplated how long he could stand to wait and watch and wonder. The flames had turned to ashes before he finally spread his blankets. Still his mind would not rest, and several hours passed before he drifted off to fitful slumber.

He awoke for the umpteenth time, this time in a cold sweat. When he kicked free of the tangled blanket the cold air on his sweat-moistened skin helped to clear his head and told him daybreak was near. No matter how warm it got during day, the nighttime air could turn downright chilly just before dawn. After a brief interlude of yawning and stretching he fumbled through the darkness to the fire pit and got a blaze started. He felt worse than when he'd gone to bed. Maybe a little coffee and a bite to eat would help.

By the time the sun cleared the eastern hills John was at his post, perusing the receding shadows of the landscape for the emergence of a familiar black horse. Occasionally he would turn the glass to stare in the direction of the Lazy P, as if to conjure up an answer to the questions that plagued his throbbing head and fueled the uneasy feeling in his gut.

Was he too late after all? Had Wally already passed by? Was he wasting time here while Wally needed him elsewhere?

After several hours John lowered the telescope, heaved a disgusted sigh and headed for his horse. He would feel a lot better mounted and doing something than he did just waiting and watching. If Wally had already passed through the area, perhaps John could cut his trail by angling back and forth across the terrain. He didn't consider himself much of a tracker, but he could look. If he was able to find the black gelding's hoofprints he'd recognize them. He could check for hoofprints and still reconnoiter the countryside from time to time whenever he happened upon a good vantage point.

John rode first to the spring to water the bay and fill his canteen. He'd found no shod hoofprints around the spring the previous evening, but he double-checked. It wasn't absolutely necessary for Wally to come by the way of the spring. He could make it from the Delaware to the Black River in a day's ride. But if he came alone he would use the most direct route and he would surely cross the broad hollow that ran along the Texas line just south of the Yeso Hills. The softer ground of the hollow would yield some good tracks.

The hollow led John into Texas and veered to the east. He rode slowly back and forth across the bottom looking for a sign, continuing the search until the draw began to angle back into New Mexico. Tracks of cattle and deer and smaller game were abundant, and even some older horse tracks, but no indication of a recent rider. It appeared that Wally had not come back yet.

The tight fist in John's stomach began to relax its grip. But he still had to intercept Wally and warn him of the trap that awaited him at the Lazy P. He raised his eyes to the Yeso Hills. Those high bluffs would give a man a good view of the surrounding landscape. He took the spyglass and began to scrutinize the approaches to the higher ground, ascertaining how best to make his way to the top.

A shrill whistle suddenly pierced the air and John almost dropped the telescope. Although he was familiar with the sound, it always unnerved him when he wasn't expecting it. He reined his horse around to face a grinning Wallace Bledsoe who hailed him from atop the southern rim of the draw. Wally eased the black down the slope and kicked him into a brisk trot that quickly closed the distance between them. "You lost agin?" he chided as he rode up to John.

John chuckled and stuffed the glass into a saddlebag. "I know where I'm at. I figgered you'd be comin' through here sooner or later."

Wally's expression turned serious. He knew John wouldn't cut short his visit to Eddy in order to intercept him without good reason. "What's wrong, John?"

John hesitated for a long moment, merely returning Wally's questioning stare. He'd been about to bust a gut to find Wally and tell him and now he didn't know how to begin. Finally he just blurted it out: "Ben's gone and put a price on your head."

Wally considered for a moment before he responded. "How did you find out about it?"

"Eli Shavalda told me. You know, the gambler that helped us out that night at Barfield and Rhodes' Saloon."

"So you did go to Phenix?"

"Naw, Wally. I saw him in Eddy when I was buying the pack horses. You see, Captain Shattuck wasn't to home and Edwin and Dolph didn't know which horses their paw wanted to sell, if any. So I went into town and bought a couple from Jake Owens at the wagonyard. That's where I saw Shavalda. He said the word is out on the sly that Ben's put a thousand dollars on your scalp."

"A thousand dollars? That's a considerable sum." Wally said it in a way that was almost prideful.

After thinking it over for a moment an amused smile crossed Wally's face and he shook his head in disbelief. "That tightwad? Naw, 'tain't so."

"Gracie said her paw heard about it, too," said John defensively.

"*Gracie?* When did you see her?"

"In Eddy, after I saw Shavalda. Her and Miz Porter was in the drug store next to the general store I was at."

"What was they doing in town?"

"One of the boys — the least one, Will, she said it was — was ailin' and they brought him in to see a doctor."

"Do you think they're still in Eddy?"

"No, they was fixin' to leave for the Lazy P the next morning."

"Good. She'll be to home by now, then."

"Wally, you can't go over there!"

"How come? I been over there lots o' times and nobody ever knowed about it but me and her. I just sneak in at night and tap on her window and she comes out to our secret meetin' place."

"Yeah, but nobody was watching for you then."

"What do you mean, *watching* for me? She didn't tell off on us, did she?"

"No, course not! But she told me one of their hands saw some strangers out in the brush near their place. They had pistols and Winchesters and high-blood horses. Seemed like they was watching the house, he said. They're bounty hunters, Wallace! They're *expecting* you to try to see Gracie."

"Why? How would *they* know about me and Gracie?"

"Everybody who went to that Christmas dance at Rattlesnake Springs knows about you and Gracie. If he don't, he's blind in one eye and can't see outa the other. Folks don't have a lot to talk about in these parts and they carry on about such as that. Too, you gotta remember that shootin' a feller is one of the best ways to get yourself talked about. 'Specially if the man you shot happens to be your own brother. Folks're gonna tell everything they know about you.

Shoot, they're even talking about that fancy shootin' iron. It sure did capture Charlie's attention and he spread the word before he died. Those men waiting in the brush are *professionals,* Wally. It's their *business* to know all there is to know about the man they're hunting, and they're *expecting* you!"

"To hell with *them!*" Wally put his hand to the butt of his now-famous six-shooter. His face was a determined scowl and he looked off in the direction of the Lazy P.

"Wally, don't try it! Grace don't even want you to. I told her you was planning on it and she said tell you not to try it as long as them hardcases are hanging around."

"I reckon I can sneak by 'em. My Injun blood's bound to be good for *something.*"

John sighed and wagged his head in dismay. "Gracie said you wasn't one to go out of your way to stay out of trouble."

"See there? She knows them bounty hunters can't stop me. She'll be disappointed if I don't show up."

"No, that ain't it. She didn't even know about the bounty hunters when she said that."

"What do you mean? When *did* she say it?"

John could have bitten his tongue off. His face turned red and he averted his eyes. He wished he'd told Wally about the chance encounter before. Now it would appear as if he'd been hiding something. "It was the day I followed Charlie. I surprised her at the tank south of the Lazy P."

"At the *tank?* What were you doing way over there?"

"Just killin' time. I had no way of knowing she'd be there," said John defensively.

"What was *she* doing over there?"

"Swimming."

"*Swimming?* You mean skinny dippin'? And you *seen* her?" Wally's tone was incriminating. "John, just because I was willing to share Emelda don't mean I aim to be Father Christmas!"

John felt like he'd been slapped in the face. "Aw Wally, nothing happened!"

"I reckon I'll just ask *her* what happened." Wally nudged the black into motion. "You sure are anxious to keep me away from the Lazy P!"

"Grace don't have anything to do with that!" proclaimed John. Then he remembered how he'd felt when he first realized Wally intended to visit Grace, before he even knew about the danger, and he silently acknowledged that the statement wasn't entirely truthful.

He reined the bay to follow the black. Whatever awaited at the Lazy P awaited them both. There was no stopping Wally now.

Chapter Twenty

"Shore looks different," was Wally's dry comment when they broke through the pinyon and juniper screening the grassy cove beneath the bluff. He knew as well as John how the look of an area can change over a period of time and yet he seemed mildly surprised.

John wasn't. But then, he'd had occasion to ride by the old hideout a number of times over the years, and found it a little different each time. "A place changes a lot in seventy years, Wallace, especially compared to the way a feller has it built up in his mem'ry," he reminded.

They pulled their horses up and paused to gaze about. The grama was still good, though not as lush as in former times. A tangle of brush obscured the shallow cave which had shielded them from the elements so many years ago. "Still looks good to me," said John, and raised his eyes to the ledge from which he'd exchanged inspection with the red-tailed hawk.

A shadow flashed across the rocks. His old heart leapt and he cast an expectant eye to the sky. "Buzzard!" he said disgustedly. "Well, ol' son, just let me get back up yonder on my perch one more time and you're welcome to this here old carcass. Tough and stringy as 'tis, I doubt you'll do me the honor of saving my flesh from the usual dissolution."

Wally's eyes followed the direction of John's gaze and he joined in watching the lazy circlings of the vulture for a few moments. "So the ledge is what you've got in mind, eh? Kinda like the old Plains Indian way." The satisfaction in his voice bespoke his approval.

"Yep! I may be the only one ever to put to rest in such a fashion in these hills, seein's how the Apaches buried their dead."

"The last time I was up here a few Injuns was still living in these mount'ins," said Wally with a dismayed expression.

"The gov'ment cleared the last few families of Mescaleros out of the Guadalupes in 1912. I remember the year 'cause it was the same year New Mexico became a state. Reckon they didn't think it was fittin' to be a part of U.S. of A. without having all the 'savages' on the reservation. Shoot, them poor folks wasn't bothering anybody. I felt plumb sorry for them."

"You always was one to trouble yourself over other folk's problems," recalled Wally. "And feelin's," he added. "Which reminds me of something that's been chewing on my thinker."

John cocked a surprised eyebrow at him. "Spit it out, then."

"It's Grace. Now, I know I got no right to say nothing at all where she's concerned, but I can't help thinking about her down there in Carlsbad frettin' and a-wondering whatall's become of you." John just kept staring at him for a few moments. Wally ducked his head. "I know, t'ain't none of my concern, but . . ."

"No, it's okay Wallace," John quietly interrupted. "I'm *proud* to see you taking on other folks' concerns. And I 'preciate what you're doing for me."

"Well, I *have* growed up a little bit in the last seventy years," said Wally with a relieved chuckle. "But what about her, John?"

"I expect Grace has figgered out what I'm up to by now," John assured him. "I'll have to admit she's prob'ly fit to be tied trying to figger out *how* I done it!" John had to laugh at the thought.

His laughter was cut short by the pain and stiffness in his back and legs when he moved to dismount. Wally stepped off the roan and came to his assistance. John eased to the ground and steadied himself with a hand to the saddle for a few moments until his legs quit trembling. He nodded to Wally that it was all right to let go.

"I reckon our luck's holding, from the look of that greener patch of grass down there," said Wally with a thrust of his chin.

"Far as I know, that little spring's never failed."

"From here it looks like it ain't much more than a wet spot in the soil."

"I expect it'll need some cleaning out," agreed John. "Them forest service boys wouldn't like us messin' with the nature like that, but these ponies are thirsty!"

"We should take these ponies to water, Wallace. It's too early to try sneaking up to the Lazy P. anyhow." It was the first time either had spoken since leaving the hollow at the Texas line.

"I s'pose," mumbled Wally, and turned the black toward the river.

After they'd watered the horses they staked them on the grassy riverbank and reclined themselves on the grass to while away the remaining time until dark.

Finally John's weariness overcame his distraught state of mind and he drifted off to slumber. He awoke to find Wally pacing the riverbank. When Wally saw him raise up on an elbow he stopped and squinted at the sinking sun.

"Let's go!" He hitched his gunbelt and started for his horse.

John got up and fetched the mare. "There's a awful lot of light left," he commented matter-of-factly as he swung astride.

"I aim to have a look-see at the layout before it gets too dark."

That comment made John feel a little bit better. At least Wally was taking the warning seriously, whatever he thought about the motive behind it.

John let Chris have another long drink before leaving the river. Wally had disappeared from the river bottom by the time she was satisfied. John touched up the mare to a fast trot in order to catch up. Once they'd caught up John was content to let the mare follow along in the black's wake as Wally carefully made his way toward the shallow hollow where the Porter's ranch house, outbuildings, corrals, and hayfields were situated.

As soon as the Lazy P headquarters became visible Wally reined in and motioned for John to come abreast. "Borry me that spyglass, will you?" he said, holding his hand out while he gazed ahead with the naked eye. John extracted the glass from his saddlebag and placed it in Wally's palm.

Wally would never admit it, but John could tell the report about the bounty hunters had him worried. He carefully picked his way from one place of concealment to another around the perimeter of the hollow, pausing at each one to visually probe from all angles the lengthening shadows of the brush and manmade structures surrounding his destination. Finally the circuit was completed.

"I've not seen any strangers about the place," said Wally in a dubious tone as he handed the spyglass back to John.

"Well, they're not gonna be settin' out in the open like ducks on a pond, you know."

"I looked real careful, John. They ain't nobody about but them what's supposed to be there."

"Well, I just told you what Gracie told me," replied John defensively.

"I'm going in."

"You're not even gonna wait for it to get dark?" asked John anxiously.

"I'm gonna work in closer first. Then I'll set tight and study the layout awhile longer. If you've a mind to wait on me, stay right here and I'll pick you up on my way out. About midnight, I reckon." He said it as if he really didn't give a tinker's damn whether John waited or not, and worried the black on through the brush toward the Lazy P without so much as a backward glance.

John stared after Wally until he disappeared over the brow of the brushy slope which descended to the terraces of the Lazy P hayfields. He heaved a sigh and dismounted. It was a long time until midnight. It would be a good while before it even got dark. If there was anything he hated worse than "settin' and waitin' " he couldn't think what it might be. Even the day Ben Bledsoe was loose-herding him cross-country, the waiting for something to happen was worse than the run-for-your-life part of it.

He would think differently about this day. For one thing, he didn't have long to wait. Only a few minutes. And the pursuers were not mounted on weary cow ponies this time.

They were close behind Wally when he came boiling back up the slope from the hayfield, laying the bushes down, scattering stones, and kicking up dust as he leaned over the black's neck and raked his spurs. John had been forewarned by the sound of a smattering of shots and was already mounted and poised to fall in beside him for their mad dash to escape.

Wally jerked his Peacemaker out and twisted in the saddle to send five random shots in the direction of the two long-legged horses that crowded their dust. One or two rounds must have come close, for the big horses were reined down for just a moment, enabling the bay and the black to gain a slight increase to their lead. Wally jabbed the pistol back and the fugitives concentrated on maintaining the pace and gaining more distance, if possible.

No more shots sounded from behind them. The manhunters were confident their blooded horses could run down a pair of ordinary cow ponies in short order, so why waste ammunition?

That was their first bad judgment. The next was when the fugitives swung wide around a rocky slope, knowing it was crusted with a dense patch of lechuguilla spears, and the professionals sought to drive straight across on their strong-legged animals. They pulled up short of crippling their mounts, but by the time they resumed the chase in earnest their prey was out of ordinary rifle range.

The black gelding led the way. John could hear the creak of the bay's water-logged belly amidst the hard gusts of her breath and the drumming of her hooves. He knew she was giving him all she could under the circumstances. He regretted having tarried at the river. The mare fell further off the pace, then suddenly she was crowding the black and John realized Wally was looking back over his shoulder and reining in. John hauled Chris to a halt beside Wally's horse and turned to see what had caught his attention.

Wally let go an elated yell and pulled his hat off and waved it in the air. "Ain't nothing in the country gonna ketch these two hosses," he laughed. "They done give up!"

"They've pulled up all right," agreed John, peering through the gathering twilight at the distant riders, "but one of 'em's dismounted and commenced messin' with something on the ground." He pulled the spyglass from the saddlebags and put it to his eye. *"Durn!"*

"What is it?" Wally's tone quickly changed from elation to alarm. He jammed his hat back on his head.

"We better git," said John, nervously stuffing the glass back into the pocket. "He's settin' up a tripod. They must have one of them high-powered buffalo guns or something. Something with a scope!"

"Hi-yi!" Wally clamped the spurs to his mount and John streaked after him. Again the mare lagged behind, struggling, but giving it all she could muster. He felt her break stride, stumble, then catch herself. She gallantly surged forward, suddenly gaining on the black. John just had time to wonder what had given her the extra impetus when she crashed to her knees upon the rocky ground. He managed to kick out of the stirrups and push himself clear an instant before she spilled onto her side. He came to a bone-jarring, rump-first landing beside her and one look at her belly answered his question. She lay there trembling, ribs heaving in rhythm with her hard breath as blood and entrails welled from a gash that a fifty caliber slug had ripped in her abdomen. She made a pitiful attempt to rise, then sank back to the turf.

Wally sensed that John had faltered from the pace and ventured a glance over his shoulder. He hauled the black to a skidding stop, spun him around and galloped back to John and the fallen mare. John had loosened the saddlebags and was tugging them free. "Leave it!" yelled Wally, and offered him a hand and a stirrup.

With a final yank, John dislodged the saddlebags. He looked dumbly at Wally, as if he didn't comprehend. When he finally spoke his voice was choked with emotion. "I can't leave her suffer. I just can't." He fumbled at the flap on the pocket where he'd stowed Wally's old Patterson.

"Godamighty, John!" exclaimed Wally with a nervous glance at their back trail. "Them fellers is comin' on agin!" He jerked the Winchester from his saddle boot, levered a shell, put it to his shoulder and shot the bay between the eyes before John could unbuckle the flap. "Now let's *go!*" He jammed the thirty-thirty back in place and reached out his hand again.

A bullet whined overhead. John slung the saddlebags across his shoulder, gave the dead mare a tearful goodbye look and swung up behind Wally, barely getting a grip around his waist before the black lurched into a flat-out dead run.

"We can't outrun 'em riding double," he shouted in Wally's ear. "We're gonna have to make a stand."

"Where?"

John was silent for a awhile, looking over the bleak terrain as the black streaked onward. There appeared to be no outstanding feature that would offer substantial cover. Then he spied a familiar-looking slope.

"Wally! On the side of that little ridge, yonder! There's a old mescal pit, remember?"

With a curt nod of his hatbrim Wally reined the black toward the slope. They rushed the grade and plunged into a shallow depression created when the ancient Indians cooked the heart of the mescal agave plant in stone fireplaces, periodically replacing the firecracked stones and casting the used ones aside to gradually form a circular wall a couple of feet high and about twenty feet in diameter.

John slid off the gelding's rump before Wally got him stopped. Wally pulled the carbine out, bailed off and flung himself against the mound of rocks and commenced firing at the oncoming riders. They spread out, dismounted and took cover in the brush to return the fire.

John squatted in the middle of the crater, wincing at the "spat" and "zing" of flying lead while clinging to the reins to prevent their frightened mount from abandoning them.

The hunters were in the disadvantaged position of having to shoot uphill, but all the same a bullet careened off the cantle of Wally's saddle, taking a chunk of leather with it. The nervous horse tossed his head and danced about at the end of the rein, a rolling sound of protest vibrating in his nostrils. John rose to a hunched position and carefully extended a hand to remove the lariat from the saddle. He shook out a loop and eased it over the black's head. "Easy, boy, easy now," he repeated as he passed the reins through and slid the loop down to settle it around the base of the horse's neck.

Wally rolled around with his back to the barricade. "Pitch me a box of cartridges, will you? What th' hell you doin', John?"

John eased along the animal's flank and dug a box of thirty-thirty shells out of Wally's saddlebags. "Gonna throw a scotch hobble on 'im and lay 'im down," he answered, pitching the box to Wally's outstretched hand.

Wally set the box between his knees and commenced reloading the rifle. "You're liable to peel him up a-droppin' 'im on them rocks."

"Better peeled than shot," said John, picking up a hind foot and easing the rope around the fetlock. He looped the end of the rope through the noose he'd draped around the neck. Being careful not to burn the fetlock, he slowly drew the hind foot up against the black's belly and tied off the rope.

"You just give me a dandy idea!" exclaimed Wally. "Should've thought about it sooner!" John's breath caught in his throat as Wally raised up and exposed himself above the mound of rocks. Amid a hail of rifle fire he took deliberate aim, squeezed off a careful shot and dropped back to safety facing John. A satisfied grin spread his dark moustaches and the terrified scream of a mortally wounded horse replaced the sound of the barking guns and whizzing bullets. "There's one for Chris," he said dryly.

"Wish you'd got the buzzard that shot her instead of a horse," replied John vehemently. "Just so they don't one-up the score . . ." He pulled the black's head to the opposite side from the tied-up leg, forcing the excited animal to the ground and out of harm's way.

Wally peeked over the barricade, thinking he might get a shot at the other horse. A fusillade of shots from the brush bespoke the anger his marksmanship had already evoked. He pulled his head in like a startled terrapin. "Them boys musta been right proud o' that pony!"

John crouched over the black's neck to keep him from rising and Wally crawled from place to place along their rocky defense, popping up here and there to squeeze off a quick shot at the brush where the gunmen were hiding.

"Light's failing fast now," said John with an eye to the west. "I s'pect they plan to sneak up on us when it gets too dark to see 'em."

"They can't see no better'n we can."

"Yeah, but they know where we're holed up and we don't know from whichaway they'll be coming."

Wally sat with his back to the rocks and the Winchester across his lap and studied the ground between his knees. "Well, I can't abide just settin' and waitin' on 'em," he said after a while. "They's gotta be something better'n that."

John stroked the black's neck as he thought. "Wally, I get the notion them boys're strangers to these parts; they don't know this country none too good."

"So?"

"Well, if we ride outa here after nightfall we'll know where we're going and they'll be guessing. They won't be able to see us and they won't be able to read our sign 'til morning. We know the lay of the land good enough to get from here to yonder in the dark, but I'll bet them hands'll get bumfoozled again just like they did in the lechugui awhile ago."

Wally turned and raised up on his knees to throw a few shots in the direction of their adversaries. There was no response. "*They* ain't fool enough to waste bullets in this light," he said cynically.

"Keep on shootin'! Let 'em know we're still

here so they won't worry about it. If they think we're stupid enough to waste ammunition and too scared to stop shooting maybe they won't be so careful."

Wally raised his eyebrows and nodded an affirmation. He kept up a sporadic rifle fire until it was pitch dark.

John released the black gelding to its feet and took the rope off. Wally felt his way to the saddle horn and mounted while John coiled the lariat. He passed the rope to Wally, then his own saddlebags, which Wally draped across the pommel of the saddle. Wally could make out that John was bent over groping for something on the ground. "Wha'd you drop?" he whispered. "We'd best git outa here!"

John came up with a fist-sized stone and held it up for Wally to see. Then he hurled it down the slope in the direction they'd last seen the manhunters. "When they hear that, maybe they'll think we're trying to turn the tables and sneak in amongst *them*. It might freeze 'em for a short spell anyways."

He fumbled in the darkness for the stirrup and eased on behind Wally. Wally slowly prodded the horse out of the mescal pit and toward the black bulk of the mountain, barely visible against the western sky. The clink of horseshoes on rock as they moved away elicited a stream of vehement oaths and a spatter of inaccurate shots. Later they heard the sound of distant hoofbeats along with more cursing. Finally they were all alone in the inky blackness of early night.

"Shore hope we get some starshine 'fore long," ventured John. "I'm gettin' spooky as ol' Grassbelly about that mount'in trail now that it comes to climbing it in the nighttime."

"You can quit studyin' on it, John; ol' Ebony's been too far too fast with too big a load today. He'd never make it."

"What you got in mind, then?"

"We'll go up the trail far enough to leave 'em think we went up the mount'in. But we'll pull off and cross over to Abels' canyon. We'll hole up with him and Melda for a spell."

Chapter Twenty-One

"You really think Grace has figgered out what-all you're up to?" asked Wally as he finished cleaning out the spring.

John released his grip on the bridles and allowed the horses to lower their heads to the water. "I'm pos'tive it's come to her by now, Wallace. Many's the time I told her I'd sooner been shot down or bucked off on my gourd than to've ended up the way it was."

"Do you think she knows where you're at?"

"She knows I'd head for the mountains if there's any way I could pull it off. She'd guess it would either be here or down in the canyon where Abels had his camp."

When Augustus Alonzo Abels was awakened in the wee hours by a "halloo the camp" he knew it must be someone who'd been there before. It wasn't likely a stranger would happen upon his covert in the daytime, much less at night. And when John and Wally struggled into sight riding double on the drawn and stumbling black horse, he could guess they'd been shot at and pursued. He didn't much cotton to the idea of men on the run laying a trail to his wickiup, a sentiment he was wont to reiterate as he shared breakfast with the fugitives in the morning. Wally explained how they'd laid a false trail up the mountain a way and cut across a saddle in the lower ridge to descend into the canyon, but Abels had no confidence in their ability to obscure their tracks in the dark. He sent Emelda to the lookout as soon as she'd finished eating.

Abels was so anxious to be rid of his uninvited guests that he agreed to let John borrow his old mule to ride back to the mountain hideout. He even agreed to let John use the saddle he'd scavenged from the horse Oates had shot out from under Ben Bledsoe. John promised to return the mule as soon as possible and the saddle too, if and when he could retrieve his own from his dead mare. In the event that the bounty hunters or someone else had confiscated his saddle, he'd return the borrowed saddle just as soon as he could get another. He certainly didn't want to take a chance on anyone recognizing Ben Bledsoe's saddle on a horse he was riding.

John and Wally promised to leave the next day. They lounged about the camp, eating and sleeping and recuperating. About midafternoon Wally slinked away on the path Emelda had taken to the lookout. John wondered how they'd manage on the narrow ledge. He envisioned them bouncing around up there until they fell off the mountain and he laughed out loud.

He didn't laugh when he saw the look on Wally's face as he came charging back into camp about an hour later. "They found our tracks," John guessed.

"New, 'taint them. It's Gracie!" exclaimed Wally. "How in tarnation did she know we was up here?"

"Ah . . . I told her where you was that day I seen her at the stock tank," admitted John, "and I didn't get a chance to tell her about us moving our nest to the top of the mount'in when I saw her in Eddy."

"Thanks a *lot,* pardner. Just what I need, both women in the same camp! What's she *doing* up here, anyway!"

"I expect she heard them shots yesterday evening. She knowed them boys wasn't trying to help her paw control the coyote population, so she came up here to see if you's still kickin'. I'd be proud if she come looking for *me.*"

"I just bet you *would,*" Wally retorted. "We gotta get her away from here!"

"Well, why don't you run off out there and chunk rocks at her," John sarcastically rejoined. "Maybe she'll just rein that little palomino around and hightail it back to where she came from."

"Too late for anything like that," said Wally as if he'd actually considered some way of heading her off. "Melda's done gone to fetch her in." He strode to the fire and poured himself a cup of coffee, then seated himself on the ground across from John and assumed a nonchalant attitude. "I gotta look surprised to see her; I don't want her knowing I was up there with Melda."

You better be glad Melda don't hardly ever say anything to anybody, thought John. *You just might pull it off if Grace don't stay very long.*

But it didn't take Gracie long to announce that she had more than a brief visit in mind.

John and Wally arose to greet her as Emelda led her into camp and she hugged them both simultaneously, although Wally's lips were the only ones she sought. A puzzled frown creased her brow when he avoided her kiss, but he made it appear as if he didn't realize her intention, so she shrugged it off and proceeded to express her relief at finding them unharmed and fit. Then she made it plain that she'd come to stand by her man through thick and thin, and had no intentions of returning to the Lazy P. Ever.

Wally was pleased at the idea of having her with him at the mountain hideaway and at the same time anxious to get her away from the goat camp before anything should arouse her suspicion about his relationship with Emelda. He even suggested they leave immediately. They could make the ridge by nightfall, sleep under the stars, and go on to the cave come daylight. John reminded him that Ebony needed a little more rest before attempting the climb and Gracie expressed her reluctance for any more riding on this day. Besides, her mount also would be in better shape for such a climb after a night's rest.

When the time came to spread their bedrolls

Wally managed to get John to himself long enough to suggest that they station themselves on either side of her for the night. Gracie accepted the arrangement as an expression of their mutual concern for her protection from the creatures of the night. To Emelda the seemingly three-way platonic relationship was an enigma, and as they all sat around the fire eating their breakfast in the morning her puzzled eye constantly drifted from one to another of the three young Anglos.

About the same time Grace was feeling real sorry for the pretty little Mexican girl who was obviously dreading the departure of those of her own generation and her subsequent abandonment to the company of that horrid old man, Emelda uttered the inevitable question. She asked it of John, who was the closest to her and who understood her native tongue, *"Es tuya la mujer rubia, verdad, Juanito?"*

Wally choked on his salt pork, for he understood what she'd asked. He signaled to John with a quick bobbing of his head, but John refused to admit that the blond woman belonged to him. He just said, *"Es una amiga de nosotros."* He could tell his answer was not satisfactory to Emelda and also noted that Grace had taken in the whole exchange, including Wally's reaction. The perplexed frown once again wrinkled her forehead.

"She's just curious about you," Wally hastened to explain. "She don't never get to see girls her own age. Or any women a-tall, far as that goes. And she's taken with your yellow hair, too."

Gracie nodded that she understood and smiled at Emelda, but afterwards her face betrayed a lingering suspicion.

Wally cut short his breakfast and hastily made ready to leave the camp. They were quickly on their way, with Wally in the lead on the black horse, Gracie in the middle on the palomino mare, and John bringing up the rear on Abels' mule. *Just like old times,* thought John. Then he suddenly realized he didn't feel any less of a man because of the caliber of the animal between his knees. He sat straight in the saddle and tapped the mule on the haunch with his stick. "Hi-yi, Hezekiah you on'ry critter, you keep up with 'em now."

The procession passed out of the canyon and wended its way up the lower reaches of the trail to the ridge. They paused to let the animals blow before embarking the final ascent. Wally dismounted, lifted his canteen from the saddle and turned away from his companions to scrutinize the steep tangle of rocks and scrubby brush that obscured the dim switchback trail to the rim as he slaked his thirst.

John stepped off the mule and hurried to assist Grace from the palomino. "We're gonna have to get you a straddle saddle, Gracie. A side saddle is tricky for your balance on these mount'in trails, I'd suspect."

"You'd suspect right," she said, pulling her bandana loose to wipe the sweat from her neck and face as she stared wide-eyed into the chasm below.

John held to her elbow and steadied her to a smooth boulder. When she was comfortably seated he returned to the mule for his canteen. "Pour a little water on that kerchief after you've had a drink; it'll help cool you off," he suggested as he handed her the canteen.

"Thanks, Johnny. I'm afraid I drained my canteen on the way to the canyon yesterday and we left in such a hurry this morning I forgot to go to the spring to refill it."

"I could tell it was empty by the way it was bouncing around when you'd strike a trot. I should've remembered to fill it for you this morning."

"Well, *somebody* should've," she said, cutting her eyes in Wally's direction. "But somebody was in such an all-fired hurry to leave it's a wonder he even remembered to take me with him!"

Wally finally turned toward them, but if he understood what Gracie had said he didn't let on. "The last couple of hunnert yards is always the worst," he commented.

"From here it looks like it's straight up," responded Gracie with a nervous tremor. "And straight down," she added with another wide-eyed glance at the chasm. She handed the canteen to John.

"It's steep, all right," he agreed. "Lotsa

slickrock, too." He took a deep pull on the canteen. *Closest my lips'll ever come to touchin' hers,* was the sad thought that flashed through his mind as he swallowed the precious liquid. "Wally, my paw always said a mule's a lot more surefooted on the rocks than a horse. Maybe we should switch Grace over to Hezekiah 'til we rim out."

"I swear, John, you'd do anything to get out of riding a mule," said Wally with a derisive laugh. "Mount up and let's get on with it!"

"Maybe we should just lead 'em the rest of the way."

"*Walk?* Are you crazy, John? You're getting as shy o' grit as ol' Grassbelly. Now come on, will you?"

John saw the worried look in Grace's eyes when he helped her to mount and he regretted having said anything to upset her. He climbed aboard the mule and followed her up the trail.

The mule proved so adept at picking a surefooted path along the winding switchback trail that John had to hold him back from crowding the palomino too much. The mare had never been ridden in the rocks before and John could hear Gracie catch her breath every time her mount slipped a horseshoe on the slick surface of the steep mountainside. "If you feel her falling, Gracie, just jump off on the uphill side and start grabbing for a handholt," he cautioned. Wally and the black were getting farther and farther ahead of them.

Gracie bit her lower lip and nodded to indicate she understood John's advice. A few seconds later she had to react to it, for both of the mare's hind feet shot out from under her at the same time. John jerked the mule to a halt just in time to avoid being knocked off the mountain by the falling beast. Gracie was close behind, screaming at the top of her lungs and grasping at anything she could in a futile effort to break her sliding descent. John flung himself off the mule and landed nearly of top of her back, grabbing a fistful of blouse in one hand while digging with his toes and grasping at passing rocks and brush with the other hand. They finally skidded to a halt just short of where the steep slope suddenly became a perpendicular plunge for several hundred feet.

John eased his weight off her back, but maintained his grasp on her blouse, and they just lay there clinging to the mountainside for several minutes, ribs heaving from exertion. "Come on," he said when their breathing had returned to normal, "let's ease our way back up yonder. One step at a time, now. Easy does it."

Wally had ridden back down the stretch of trail nearest them. He dismounted to heave his lariat rope as soon as they climbed far enough to be able to reach it. John followed Grace up the rope and braced her as she reached a hand to Wally for the final step to the trail. As soon as she was clear he grasped Wally's outstretched hand and gained his footing on the trail between them. He followed Gracie's open-mouthed stare to the miniature form of the yellow pony limply impaled upon a jagged crag far below.

"Clumsy as a sorry ol' town hoss," said Wally with a wag of his head.

He never knew how close he came to having his head explosively wagged in one direction only, for at the very moment John sucked in his breath to start his swing Gracie burst out in tears and he turned to her instead. She fell into his embrace and clutched her arms about his neck as deep sobs shook her body and tears flooded the cuts and bruises on her face. He would have expected her to step past him into Wally's arms. She probably would have if he hadn't made that callous remark, John figured. Well, she should know John could sympathize with her; she'd been told about the loss of his bay mare.

John didn't know what to say; he just held her and gently extracted the leaves and twigs from her golden hair. Out of the tail of his eye he could see Wally standing behind him with hands on hips, the muscle clenching in his jaw and the fire dancing in his black eyes.

Presently Grace willed herself to composure and relaxed her grip from John's shoulders. "I'm sorry," she whispered as he released her to stand on her own. "It's all right, I understand," he murmured.

Wally stepped forth and took her by the hand. "Come on, sweetheart," he said with a smouldering glance at John, "you can ride ol' Ebony outa here." She gave him a steely look but allowed him to lead her to the black and assist her to mount astride, with her skirts tucked beneath her legs.

Wally wasn't so foolhardy as to expect the horse to carry a double load up to the precipitous trail, so he submitted to making the climb on foot. There was really no need for John to walk. He rode the surefooted mule and followed along while Wally led the black up the switchback trail to the rim.

Gracie ventured a woeful glance at the dizzying depths as they scrambled over the rim to gain a secure footing on top of the ridge. They stopped to let the animals blow. No one dared to test the atmosphere with conversation. The only sounds were those of the animals' breath and the gusty wind whispering in a lonesome juniper tree. Then the creak of saddle leather when Wally swung up behind Grace to press on to the hideaway.

Chapter Twenty-Two

For the second time in as many days the Bar BX pickup roared down the El Paso highway in the early morning darkness toward Carlsbad. The late model Chevy towed the homemade stock trailer loaded with two fresh horses in the opposite direction from that which had been anticipated the previous evening. This time it was O. C. Kirkes who shared the cab with Winston and O.C. had no difficulty finding his favorite kind of music on the radio.

Well the race is on and here comes pride up
the backstretch,
heartache's movin' to the inside,
my tears are holdin' back, tryin' not to fall . . .

Winston reached over and turned the volume down a tad. "Well, I guess you're somewhat relieved, O.C."

"Hey, George Jones is my favor-rite singer!" The light from the dashboard cast an eerie reflection upon O.C.'s frown. "What you mean? Relieved about what?"

"About not having to make that ride up the Staircase."

O.C. snorted and looked out the side window.

No sooner had Winston and O.C. rolled up to the corrals the previous evening when Barb had come out from the house to tell Winston that Sheriff Hawkins had called and requested he get in touch as soon as possible. Winston left O.C. to unload and see to the horses and walked back to the house with Barb to return the sheriff's call.

The conversation was brief and to the point. There was no information as yet on the Arizona license plate, but Mrs. Stonecipher had called and insisted she didn't want the case of the missing horses pursued. She would file no charges in the affair and wanted the search called off immediately. When she wouldn't be pinned down as to exactly why she'd made such a demand and hung up on him, Hawkins had sent a deputy out to talk to her and make sure she was all right. Everything seemed normal, including her taciturnity.

The sheriff wanted Winston to talk to Mrs. Stonecipher again and, unless some satisfying explanation of the affair was forthcoming, to continue the search for the alleged horse thieves.

Winston expected that further pursuit of the phantasmal riders would be in order and since he would already be in Carlsbad the practical thing to do would be to trailer the horses to the top of the escarpment by way of the Rocky Arroyo road north of town. There was only one trail on the narrow backbone of Lonesome

Ridge and it would be much easier and quicker to approach it from the top of the mountain and look for a sign of the riders' passing.

O.C. turned his gaze from the window and refocused on Winston. "That Staircase trail don't bother me none. I just didn't see no percentage in trying it on a bronc that's liable to take a notion to chin the moon if'n he gits boogered."

"Haven't I heard you say there's not a horse on the Bar BX that can put you outa shape?"

"Don't do you no good to stay in the saddle when a bronc goes cliff jumpin'."

"I reckon you've got a point there," conceded Winston with a chuckle. "Well, that bay horse you're riding today is mountain-bred, so you've nothing to worry about."

With another snort O.C. reached to turn the volume back up.

"And the winner loses a-all."

"I can't win for losing," John mumbled to himself.

Once again he found himself whiling away the time perched upon the ledge in the bluff overlooking the camp. But this time the spyglass was set aside and his gaze was fixed, not upon the soaring raptors in the cobalt expanse overhead but upon the wickiup Silverthorne had helped Wally erect so that he and Grace could enjoy their privacy. For a moment John willed his vision to penetrate the hides Silverthorne had provided for covering the framework of limbs, then he decided it was best that he couldn't see as he'd seen on the night of the Christmas party. For an instant he was sure he heard angry words emanate from behind the covering of animal skins. He consoled himself with the thought that perhaps their relationship was not as blissful or passionate as his imagination would lead him to believe. But even that consolation could do little to ease the tortured heaviness in his breast, nor could it forestall the sickening tug at the pit of his stomach when he saw Grace emerge from the shelter.

He couldn't be sure from his point of observation but he thought the look on her face would support his suspicion that they'd been arguing. The contrasting flash of her smile was unmistakable when she looked up and waved at him. *Durn!* Most people were so concerned with what was right in front of them that they rarely ever looked up. What would she think, catching him sitting up there staring a hole in their tent? He was glad she was too far away to see his face turn red. He returned her gesture and picked up the glass to pretend to study something among the talus rubble along the base of the bluff. Ignoring the vision presented through the telescope, he watched her with his other eye until she picked up a bucket and turned away toward the spring further on down the slope. Breathing a sigh, he again put the scope aside, eased his back against the ledge and stared at the drifting clouds while he contemplated his predicament.

Perhaps it would be best if he just left, quit torturing himself and went on back to the Circle S where he couldn't see her with Wally. He could accomplish nothing by hanging around. On the afternoon they went to the river after school, his presence had served as a restraint to their intimacies, but it would make no difference this time. Nevertheless he felt the same reluctance to turn his back on the situation that he'd felt before. Well, he'd have to leave for a little while anyway. He must return the mule to Abels and retrieve his saddle, if it was still there, before it was excessively tainted with the rotting flesh of the dead mare. Also, Gracie had had some personal things packed on her saddle and he might be able to salvage some of them for her. Those dead horses weren't going to stink any less for his dalliance so he might as well get to it. It was early yet. He could check both carcasses and still make Abels' camp by nightfall. He stuck the glass in his waistband and climbed down from the ledge.

With the mule in tow the appaloosa carried John away from the camp and down the length of Lonesome Ridge to the rimrock. He dismounted and took some time to scan the countryside. When he was sure there were no riders in the vicinity he descended the narrow trail to the bottom of the escarpment and worked his way back up the northern rift to a point below the crag that had smashed the life from Gracie's palomino. He dismounted and climbed the jagged rocks, pulling his bandana over his nose to stifle the odor and slapping his Stetson against his thigh to scatter the buzzards as he approached the bloating carcass.

Gracie's packs had burst upon impact and the wind had scattered items of clothing among the rocks and impaled many of her garments upon the thorny brush. John loosened her blanket roll from the saddle, spread it out on top of the flattest boulder he could find and selected another rock that he could keep on top of the material as he collected it and piled it upon the blankets.

He'd almost finished with his gathering when he noticed a sparkle in a crevice nearby the fallen mount. A few moments on hands and knees groping in the fissure produced a shattered mirror. He'd already found some combs and a hairbrush fashioned from some sort of bone. Ivory, he guessed it was. The mirror was obviously part of the set. The handle was broken off and must have slipped out of sight and out of reach into the narrow recesses of the split in the rock. One piece of glass remained that was large enough to reflect a general idea of her appearance. It would be better than looking at herself in the spring. He arose and placed it in the bundle with the rest of her personal effects.

When everything was piled on the blankets he discarded the rock and began pressing the clothing into as tight a pack as he could. When his fingers touched some of her most intimate apparel he paused for a moment and let his imagination wander.

This is as close as you'll ever get to touching anything more than her hand! With that thought he slapped himself back to reality, pulled the corners of the blanket together and secured the bundle with a latigo string he'd pulled from Gracie's saddle. John left the saddle itself to rot with the mare for the sidesaddle tree was not bound in rawhide like a roping tree and had not withstood the fall. When he got back to the roan he fashioned a loop in the string, hung the bundle from the horn of Ben Bledsoe's saddle, and mounted to lead the mule to the other equine corpse, keeping an eagle eye all the way to make sure he wasn't seen.

The vultures ascended in a pandemonium of flopping wings at the approach of the horse and rider. John marveled at their clumsiness on the ground compared to their lazy agility when riding the currents of the high thermals. He tried to keep his mind on the buzzards and other things and his eye averted from the empty eyesocket and exposed teeth while he hastily extracted his saddle and bridle from the ravaged carcass. He stumbled to the horse and mule and led them out of sight and smell of the disintegrating mound of horseflesh before he stopped to put the saddle on the mule.

Old Hezekiah didn't much like the idea, but John grabbed one of his long ears and twisted it until the fidgety beast lowered his head and stood steady. John swung the saddle into position with his other arm and quickly grabbed the girth when it swung under the mule's belly. He managed to pull the latigo through the ring with the one hand and jerked it tight before letting go the ear. He tied if off as Hezekiah brayed a hee-hawing protest to the way he was being mistreated. Well, you couldn't blame him. That rigging would require some airing out before the stench of decay left it. That's why John didn't transfer Ben's outfit to the mule and ride his own. He'd have to fork the smelly hull soon enough, for he doubted very much of the odor would dissipate during the ride to the goat camp.

John stole a final glance at the remains of the mare, then lifted his eyes to the sky as he pulled away. The sun was well past the midway point of its daily journey.

The shadows of evening were claiming the canyon by the time he dismounted before Abels' lean-to. The old man seemed real pleased to see him. John figured it was because he was glad for the return of the mule and the saddle. When you loan something to a couple of owlhoots you can't help but worry that you might never see it again.

"I'll say one thing for you, Stone — you got good timing, boy! Always draggin' up about suppertime," Abels laughed. "Lemme help you shuck them riggin's." He started for the mule, then wrinkled his veiny nose and turned toward the appaloosa. "Believe I'll swap chores with yuh, boy. The smell o' that rig recollects me too much of my buffler huntin' days. Pew!"

"Yep, I pert near waited too long to go fetch it," admitted John, relinquishing his position beside the appaloosa.

"Wal, you won't be in the market for this'n," said Abels regretfully as he threw the stirrup over. "Reckon I best lift this here pack off fust of all." He moved around the horse to remove the blanket-wrapped bundle. "One thing for shore, you ain't packin' gold," he commented, hefting the pack with one hand to emphasize the lightness of it.

John obliged the old man's curiousity. "It's clothes, mostly. That gal of Wally's lost her mare off the Staircase and I went by to fetch what I could of her things for her." All of a sudden he remembered that Emelda was standing in the shadows and she understood enough English to know what he'd said. *Well, the cat's out of the bag now! Wally won't like that!* Then he realized he didn't give a damn whether Wally liked it or not. In fact, he was glad he'd let it slip. The truth would be painful for Emelda, but she suspected it anyway and he believed it was better to know for certain than to wonder.

"You need a good rock hoss in them mountains," Abels opined. "Y'all should of put the gal on the mule. She all right?"

"Black and blue and all scratched up, but she didn't break anything."

John used his pigging string to suspend his

saddle from the limb of an oak tree so it could benefit from the evening breeze. Abels deposited the other one on the ground until he could stow it in the lean-to and they led the animals to a grassy clearing and staked them out.

"So you've done fetched that blond-headed gal's stuff and you've done fetched your saddle, besides bringing my stuff back. You've covered some ground today," quipped Abels. "You best keep a owl neck when you go sashayin' around the countryside like that, because, like it or not, you sure are *implicated* as part of that wild bunch by now!"

"*I* haven't stolt any cows!"

"Maybe you ain't done nothing direct-like," allowed Abels, "but most folks goes by that 'birds of a feather' saying. Folks know you run with the Choctaw Kid."

John started to protest, then thought better of it. The old goatherd's conjecture was even more accurate than he realized. Ben Bledsoe believed John was still keeping company with Wally. The Shattuck boys had surely known why he wanted those pack horses. By now a lot of folks were probably convinced that the best way to get at the Choctaw Kid would be to catch John Stonecipher and make him talk.

Abels persisted with his harangue. "You'd best heel yourself, Stone. Especially if you're gonna keep on riding around the countryside scoutin' and fetchin' for that wild bunch. I'm telling you, you'd better get yourself a sidearm!"

John thought about Wally's old Patterson, stowed away in his saddlebags with cap, powder and ball in all but one of the chambers. It wasn't worth mentioning, considering the low esteem Abels had for the old pistol. "I reckon I'll get along all right by just being extra careful," was John's reply.

With a doubtful wag of his head Abels led the way to the cook fire.

Mealtime was one thing to which John looked forward whenever he was obliged to pass some time in the goat camp. Abels had a knack for preparing even the most ordinary campfire fare in a way that was exceptionally tasty. He was partial to his own cooking and he seemed to enjoy preparing it almost as much as he enjoyed eating it. Emelda assisted him, but he preferred to do most of the cooking himself.

When the three of them were seated about the fire John noticed that Emelda helped herself to very little food and wasn't doing much with what she had. Discreet appraisals of her supple body, scarcely concealed by the flimsy cotton shift, was the other decided pleasure of his visits to the goat camp.

Occasionally Emelda's teary eyes lingered upon John for a few moments. He had an idea that if he should hang around for a day or so until she began to get over her disappointment in Wally, she would take consolation with him in a very pleasureful way. At the same time he knew Emelda could never soothe his own churning emptiness which even now made him impatient to be on his way back up the mountain. Although it would do nothing to alleviate his disconsolate feeling, he felt compelled to stay as close to Grace as he could. He would leave at first light.

Chapter Twenty-Three

"Wal, wha'd she say?" O.C. straightened up in the seat and turned the radio down when Winston opened the truck door upon his return from the Stonecipher house.

Winston slid under the wheel, slammed the door, and turned the ignition. "I sure wish Barb could've come with us. Getting information out of that old dame is like trying to punch a gopher out of the ground with a piece of baling wire."

"Didn't find out nothin', didja?"

"All I know is there's something she's not telling us." Winston put the truck in gear and eased it out onto the road, the stock trailer clanging a protest as it swayed across the uneven shoulder.

"Reckon she'd tell Barb?"

Winston mulled over O.C.'s question for a while as he pointed the truck toward the Artesia highway. "Maybe she *already* told her! Maybe she told her before she even figured it out for herself."

"Now you're talkin' in riddles, boy." O.C. reached for the volume knob.

"No, just listen for a minute, O.C. When Barb talked to Miz Stonecipher yesterday she mentioned as how John had been protesting the fact of spending his final days cooped up in a nursing home."

"Yep, I bet ol' John would sooner go down in a cloud of gunsmoke and a blaze of glory, like in the good old two-gun times!"

"That's just what he'd told Miz Stonecipher, according to what she told Barb. When Barb told me about it I commented as to how it would be less likely that anyone would see John if he'd left on purpose and didn't want to be seen. And yet, I wondered how a weak, sick old man could get very far. Now two of his horses have disappeared — stolen, we thought — and hauled away in a truck."

O.C.'s pale blue eyes widened. "That old buzzard's gone and got hisself somebody to help him, ain't he?"

Winston slowed the pickup for the turn onto the Artesia highway, then accelerated, heading for the Rocky Arroyo turnoff and the road to the Guadalupes.

"But how? And who in the world could it be?"

"Somebody from Arizony."

"I shouldn've asked Miz Stonecipher if she knows anybody in Arizona."

"Looks like she's trying to help him too, now that it's dawned on her what he's up to. She prob'ly wouldn't tell you nothing anyhow."

"I guess not. Well, Carl said to keep on hunting those horses, so we'll go up yonder and see if we can figure out where they went."

O.C. reached for his makings. A grin creased

his freckled cheeks as he sprinkled the tobacco on the paper. "They're prob'ly headed fer some place they knowed in the good ole two-gun times, one of them owl-hoot hideouts!"

The first thing John noticed when he arrived back at the mountain hideout was that Rafer McDaniel and his boys hadn't come back yet. Then he saw Wally and Gracie lounging upon a rough-hewn bench in front of their wickiup and reined the appaloosa toward them.

Wally put a hand to his nose as John drew rein. "You a mite whiffy on the downwind, hombre!"

"Well, this old riggin' was purty ripe by the time I got back to where my mare was shot," John admitted. "But it'll air out sooner or later, I reckon. I expect Silverthorne'll know of some sort of concoction that'll help."

Gracie's eyes softened with empathy at the mention of John's dead pony, then brightened with recognition when he lifted her bundled-up blanket across his pommel and leaned over to deposit it on the grass in front of her. She went to her knees before the pack and hastily untied the latigo string. "Oh Johnny! Thank you!" she said with a broad smile. "How'd you ever get down there to get this stuff?"

Her exuberance was contrasted by the sour expression on Wally's face. "Hell, he's half monkey. Can't you tell by lookin'?"

John ignored the comment. "I captured everything I could get aholt of. It was bad scattered, so I reckon you'll be missing some stuff. Your saddle was busted, so I just left it."

"So what do you expect her to ride if we ever have to drag outa here?" queried Wally sarcastically.

"Well, she shouldn't be riding a sidesaddle in these mount'ins anyhow," John parried. "I saw a old M'Clellan stashed in the cave and I reckon Silverthorne would let us use it if we ever need to."

Wally started to frame a rejoinder but was interrupted by Gracie's gasp. She set the broken mirror tenderly upon her lap and her eyes welled with tears as she bit her lip and fingered the jagged edge where the ivory handle had broken off.

"That's how I found it," said John in a subdued tone. "I didn't break it."

"Oh I know you didn't," she hastily reassured him with a sad smile. "Why, I didn't even expect to ever see any of this again," she added, gesturing to the pile of linen and resting a hand on the brush and combs she'd discovered. "It's just that these were my mother's, and her mother's before her. I'm just being sentimental, Johnny. I'm sorry."

Wally looked bored and gazed off toward the bluff.

"Oh there's no need for apology," John assured Grace. "And someday you'll have another mirror just like that one."

"Thank you for the thought, Johnny, but I'm afraid it isn't possible. You see, it's sorta like a family heirloom. I doubt I could find another just like it in a million years."

"I'm gettin' sick," interrupted Wally, turning his sullen black eyes on John. "I'm expecting to see some big fat maggots come a-rolling outa that hull of your'n any secont."

"Oh Wally," said Grace disgustedly, "it doesn't smell *that* bad!"

John felt his cheeks redden. What kind of an imbecile was he, sitting there subjecting her to the odor of the tainted saddle? He guessed he was getting used to it, but it must smell terrible to Grace. He tugged his hatbrim at her and nudged the appaloosa on to the pasture ground.

After he removed the saddle and bridle John allowed the horse to roll a few times to ease his sweat-soaked back before looping his stake rope around the animal's neck to lead him to water at the spring. "You'll do, spotted pony; I'm claiming you for mine. This outfit owes me that much, at least," affirmed John, patting the appaloosa on the shoulder.

After he hobbled the animal he hung his saddle from a juniper limb and went to the cave for some of the shell corn he'd packed in from Eddy. He was about to head back to the pasture when he heard Rafer and his boys trailing into camp, so he scooped enough corn into the bucket for their mounts also.

By the time John walked back to the pasture ground they were unsaddling, all the while stealing curious glances at the wickiup and the fair-haired girl sitting out front with Wally.

"I'll swun, Choctaw wasn't lying when he said he had a better idea than going sally-hootin' with us, was he?" commented Rafer to the group.

Speckles nodded agreement. "She's some better lookin' than any we seen in Pecos City, too."

"She's *nothing* like what you boys saw in those Pecos City sally joints," John protested. "*She's* a lady."

Beasley nearly swallowed his cud. He hadn't noticed John when he walked up, so intent was his scrutiny of the girl.

Oates shoved his hat back and squinted hard. "I reckon she's a lady, for sure. It appears Chocktaw had to give 'er a frailin' to make her come with him."

John didn't like the way they were staring at Gracie, yet he had to chuckle at Oates' comment. "Naw, she came of her own accord. But she took a hard spill on the Staircase. That's how she got bruised up. Y'all prob'ly seen her pony on the way up the mount'in."

Some of the color drained from Oates's face, as if the paleness of his forehead was diluting the sunburn on his cheeks. "Yeah, we seen it," he recalled. "Rafer thought maybe Choctaw'd dropped somebody who was chasing him for that reward."

John's mouth fell open. "Y'all already heard about the bounty?"

"Word had already reached Pecos City," affirmed Speckles, "with some *borracho* cowboy who dragged in from Phenix."

"Durn." John wondered if it could be the same inebriated informant who'd told Mr. Porter.

Rafer removed his bridle and slapped his hobbled mount on the rump. "Don't that beat all," he said with an envious tone and a wag of his head, "the Choctaw Kid and his fancy six-gun have gone and got plumb famous. All for killing one man, and him sorta indirectly, seein's how *la gripa* is what really finished him." Once again he cast his eyes toward the wickiup.

John could contain his irritation no longer. "What's the matter with you waddies? Y'all eyeballin' that gal like you would a coiled-up rattler on the foot of yer bedroll. Don't you know it's not mannerly?"

"Well what do you expect?" countered Oates. "We didn't figure to see no woman in camp when we come draggin' in."

"Yeah," responded Rafer, "it ain't like she's somethin' special, just unexpected."

Speckles had released his horse and picked up his saddle. "I reckon her being a surprise ain't no excuse fer us actin' unneighborly," he admitted, replacing his rigging on the turf.

Rafer realized what the red-haired youth had in mind and seized the initiative. "You-all can stand around here chinnin' about her if you've a mind to. I'm fixin' to go make the acquaintance of this here 'lady'." He strode toward the wickiup with the other members of his gang at his bootheels.

John dumped the corn into a makeshift trough and turned toward the cave with the empty bucket. "She *is* somethin' special alright," he proclaimed with a glare at the backs of the departing men. "Too special to be nesting with a man on the dodge in a camp of durn owl-hoots," he mumbled to himself.

"Sounds like the presence of that girl has compounded your worries, John," said a voice from the shadow of a nearby pinyon.

John almost dropped the bucket. "Silverthorne! *Durn!* I thought you was off huntin'."

"I came back. How about helping me skin a buck, John? Bring the bucket; we'll use it for the edible viscera."

"For the *what?*" asked John, following him toward a large grey oak from which he'd suspended the carcass by its hind feet.

"The liver, heart, and kidneys. My favorite parts."

"Well, you'll most likely have 'em purty much to yerself, Silverthorne. My paw raised me to make use of most every part of a animal except the beller, but I expect the other boys'll tell you they don't eat guts."

"Good! We'll have the best for ourselves. Did you ever notice how a wild predator will usually eat the viscera of a fresh kill first? They know what's good for them."

Most of the deer's entrails had been dumped before Silverthorne carried it into camp. He deftly separated the liver, heart, and kidneys from the hanging carcass and severed the head; also the front legs at the knee. Then he proceeded to cut the hide away from the hindquarters. John grasped the loose skin of one quarter and Silverthorne the other. Together they pulled downward on the hide, with Silverthorne assisting the separation of skin from flesh wherever necessary with deft slashes of his razor-sharp knife.

"Did you ever skin a buffalo, Silverthorne?" asked John. "You're purty handy with that Green River knife."

"A few. I hunted them briefly. But it made me sick to my stomach the way they were being slaughtered. The Western Plains were made for the buffalo, and the buffalo for the Plains. Nothing the white man can do with the prairie will ever top that arrangement."

"That old goatherd Abels we nested with down in the canyon told me he was a buffalo hunter the day I took back his mule."

"He was. Among other things."

John's surprise and expectant look failed to prompt further comment. "You know ol' Triple-A?" he carefully ventured.

Silverthorne nodded a slight affirmative, keeping his eyes on his skinning. "Did you or Wally happen to mention my name when you were down there?"

John took a few moments to mull over the two nights and a day he and Wally had spent in the goat camp and the few hours he'd been there last night. "I reckon not . . . I'm pos'tive we didn't. I take it he don't suspect you're in the same neck of the woods, then," pried John.

"Not unless he believes in ghosts."

John waited for more but Silverthorne offered no explanation. John was trying to think of some comment or question by which he could judiciously probe a little deeper when Silverthorne abruptly changed the subject.

"So what are you going to do about her?"

"Huh? Who?"

"You know who I'm talking about, John — the Porter girl, of course. You admit she shouldn't be here in the middle of this nest of thieves."

John squatted on his spurs in order to maintain his pull on the deerskin as it peeled away from the back and ribs. "She's Wally's woman, she's no concern of mine," he replied, for in truth he had no idea of anything he could do about the situation.

"But you *are* concerned, nonetheless. That's plain to see."

John heaved a deep sigh. "Silverthorne, I got no strings to the rest of this bunch, but Wallace Bledsoe and Grace Porter's both good friends of mine. It's not easy seeing him going to the dogs, but it's pure hell to see him dragging her down with him."

Silverthorne kneeled down to get at the remainder of the skinning job. He paused and fixed his piercing blue eyes upon John. "So why watch?"

John glanced away for a moment. "I just can't turn my back on them, Silverthorne. I was gonna see if I could get Wally to move on before his luck runs out and they catch up to him. But now she's here, and . . ." John didn't know how to say it.

"And he suspects how you feel about her and that complicates things," summarized Silverthorne.

John released the hide and let his hands dangle between his knees. "You're a reg'lar eagle-eye, ain'tcha?" His chin slumped to his chest. "All I can do now is stand by in case Gracie needs me. . . . Maybe I can figger some way of getting her outa here. If she'll go."

Silverthorne resumed his dexterous knife work. "She might be willing to leave someday. By then it may be too late. In any case you'd have to defy Wally to take her away. Maybe the whole crew."

John shoved his hat back on his head with a forearm and slowly nodded his agreement. "And me the one who don't wear a gun." He considered a moment, then cocked an eyebrow at Silverthorne. "I've never seen you with a side arm neither, come to think of it."

"Once upon a time I had a very fine pistol," Silverthorne stated factually, "but I lost it. I came to these mountains soon thereafter and I've had no need of a firearm since. The primitive but silent bow and arrow serve me just fine."

"So that's how you killed this buck. You must

be as good with your bow and arrow as you are with the knife."

"I was taught by experts."

"Onliest thing I'm real handy with is *la reata,*" remarked John with a note of irony. "And I can't rope and tie everybody who stands in my way."

"Well, if push comes to shove, don't look for me because you won't see me," said Silverthorne, adroitly making his final slashes with the Green River knife. "Of course, that doesn't necessarily mean I won't be there," he added as the hide fell free of the carcass.

Chapter Twenty-Four

At the same time Winston Brittain made the turn onto the Rocky Arroyo road the aged John Stonecipher awoke from the soundest night's sleep he'd had in many a moon. He seemed less sore than on the previous morning and wondered how that could be. But he knew that the high mountain atmosphere had always been a tonic to his soul, and that when the inner man is serene it goes a long way to the healing of the body. John Stonecipher felt serene. Tranquil in mind and heart.

John didn't understand very much about all the conflicting things he'd heard about the hereafter. He wasn't even sure if there really was a hereafter. Maybe the loss of all knowledge and awareness was the worst thing that could befall a human. He didn't know. But he was ready to face whatever lay before him. And the first thing, if not the only, was the simple act of dying. He was ready now. Lying on those wearisome sheets in the depressing confines of that sick room was no way to go and he'd dreaded it then. Now he was ready.

Well, might as well have a cup of coffee first. John chuckled and threw the flap of the sleeping bag aside so he could rise and go to the campfire where Wally had left a pot warming. Where was that old Choctaw anyway? John had just finished pouring himself a cup when he saw him coming up from the direction of the spring. When he got closer John saw he was turning something in his hands.

"Whacha got there, Wallace?"

"Aw, just a old rusty horseshoe I found down there where we used to pasture the horses."

"Better hang on to it! Might be a antique. Could be one of them old shoes I took off the ol' ewe-necked sorrel Grace rode on that last roundup we made."

"You stand still now or I'll dump you on the ground and hogtie you," John threatened the little ewe-necked sorrel. "Durn, your feet's in sorry shape. I can see why nobody'd want to mess with 'em too much, snaky as you are about it."

The fidgety little mustang swung his head around and rolled an eye at John, who was hunched over a rear hoof administering the final touches with his rasp. John released the leg and put a hand to the small of his back as he stood erect and flexed out the kinks. For a moment he stared at the group of men confabulating in front of the cave. It had been less than two weeks since the last rustling foray and they were already planning another. His attention was attracted to the wickiup when Grace stepped out. A scowl of concern crossed his face as she walked toward him.

"You getting him all fixed up for me?" she asked as she walked up.

"Yeah, doing what I can. His ol' feet's awful brittle. That offside front hoof's in purty bad shape. I won't have much to nail to in one spot there."

"What if he throws a shoe, John? We can't be riding double on this journey."

"Oh I'll put my tools and some extra shoes and nails in a saddle pocket just in case," he assured her. "But I sure do wish you wouldn't go on this gather, Gracie. It could be dangerous you know."

"I know. That's exactly why I'm compelled to go. I just can't stay up here waiting and worrying and wondering. I'd rather be there."

John grimaced and ducked his head. "*Durn* that Wally! I can't *believe* he'd take you with us!"

"*He* understands how I feel, John. I just wish you'd try to be as understanding as he is." With that she turned on her heel and marched back to the tepee.

She might as well have slapped his face. He stood slack-jawed and watched her back until she sat down on the bench to wait for Wally. *How can you say that? Don't you see by now that I'm the one who really understands?* I'm *the one who really cares what happens to you!* But the words were confined to his mind. What would she do if he spoke them aloud? Maybe she'd give him more than a verbal slapping. He could even provoke a situation whereby he'd be denied any access to her whatsoever. John picked up the nippers and headed for the problematic front hoof.

The seven riders came off the mountain by the light of a full moon and began chasing cattle out of the brushy draws and off the grassy flats in the first grey reflections of an illumining eastern sky. John rode along with the rest of them, not actually prodding any specific head of cattle, but a part of the moving force just the same. When the first fiery sliver of morning sun peeked over the eastern horizon he took the spyglass in hand and reined the appaloosa toward the nearest ridge. Grace turned the sorrel and followed him to the crest. She sat her horse in silence and waited until he'd completed his initial survey before she spoke.

"Johnny, I'm sorry I was so abrupt with you yesterday," she began with a conciliatory tone. "I know you're only concerned about my safety, but I just had to come. I'm not one to wait around to see what happens. I like to know what's going on; to be able to do something about it if need be."

There's some things you just can't do much about, thought John. *But if anyone can understand wanting to be on hand just in case, I reckon I should.* "All right," he said with a slight smile, "but you stay right close to me and do what I tell you if there's trouble."

"I expect Wally will look after me," she said, searching for him among the working cowboys. "Why, you don't even wear a gun, Johnny."

"Well, I'll be there anyways, just in case Wally ain't handy . . . again."

If she noticed the implication of his last comment she showed no sign. She continued to gaze at the activity below them for a moment. "Johnny, how can they be sure all those cattle they gathered before sunup are Bar BX?"

John had lifted the glass to his eye for another look-see. He lowered it and when she looked to him for the answer, she saw it in the disbelieving expression on his face.

"But Wally said . . ." She looked again at the growing herd, as if to find something that would disprove what John said with his eyes.

"Wally told you he's just collectin' his fair share of the Bar BX stock, didn't he? But do you really think those are *all* Bar BX cows? And do you see the hands throwing any of 'em back? The next thing Wally'll tell you is there's enough head of Bar BX to make up his part of the take."

"Why, of course there is. That's what he meant," said Grace in a disconcerted voice. She jerked the sorrel's head around and kicked her pony down the hill.

Grace tried to stay near Wally for a while, then contented herself to following along on the least dusty side of the main body of the herd. John moved along from vantage point to vantage point, keeping a wary eye on their back trail. The drovers drifted the gather eastward and a little bit south, loose-herding and adding stock as they went. They'd planned a more direct route for this foray in order to get the stolen herd out of New Mexico and delivered to McDaniel's friends as quickly as possible.

By the time they crossed into Texas, John estimated they'd accumulated over two hundred head. They bunched the cattle and held them in a grassy hollow south of the Yeso Hills, where they would pause for a quick midafternoon meal before pushing on to the Delaware.

John rode down from his lookout and reined in next to Grace to watch as the drovers settled the herd in the hollow. He gazed at the milling cattle for a few moments. "There!" he said gesturing toward the herd. "Does the brand on that brindle cow with the knocked-down horn look familiar?"

Gracie sucked in her breath and stared dumbly at the Lazy P emblazoned on the animal's side.

"And that's not the only one of your paw's cows in this herd. Not by a long shot. Not to mention the stock that belongs to your neighbors. Shoot, there's prob'ly even one or two Circle S cows in the bunch. Gracie, what I'm trying to say is this has gone too far. You gotta help me talk some sense into Wally. I know he's got his ways of telling hisself that he's not doing anything wrong and I know he thinks he's so cagey that nobody'll ever catch him; but somehow we're gonna have to convince him it's time to move on. Y'all could get a fresh start somewhere else. Arizona Territory, maybe. I'd go too, if you'd want me to; at least long enough to see you settled."

Gracie hadn't varied her dumbfounded gaze. When she realized John had finished his little speech she gathered her reins. "Help me get a fire started, will you please, Johnny? The boys'll want coffee." John gave a disgusted huff at her refusal to respond to his appeal, shrugged his shoulders, and turned to help her make ready for the hungry crew.

The cattle quickly settled down to graze on the lush grass of the hollow and the men rode to the campfire. They gulped the hot coffee, hastily consumed the cold provisions, and were quickly back in the saddle, pushing the cattle hard and fast across the rough, brushy terrain toward the river. With the faster pace the dust boiled up even thicker than before. Grace found herself edging closer and closer to the point of the herd and farther off to the side. With the herd mostly behind her, she felt harried, as if she were being pressured to stay ahead of the dust cloud and yet obliged to hold back so as not to actually get out in front of the bawling cattle. She felt isolated and lonesome. She saw John pull up atop a rise just ahead and off to the north. He'd stay there on lookout until the herd passed, then he'd ride on, skirting the dusty procession to take up a similar position farther along. His job was the least monotonous of all, it seemed to her, certainly less tedious than her own course. When she came abreast of his position she pulled out and nudged her pony up the slope.

John lowered the spyglass and turned a surprised eye when she rode up. "Gettin' a little dusty down there, ain't it?"

"I could use a breather," she agreed, "excuse me." She pulled a handkerchief from the pocket of her long skirt and blew her nose.

"You need to get you a pair of trousers," John commented matter-of-factly, "since you've give up riding sidesaddle."

"Well, maybe a divided riding skirt at least," she allowed. "But there's no telling when I'll ever see a dry goods store again."

John raised the scope to his eye. Maybe the realities of life with the back-trail bunch were finally sinking into that pretty head of hers, he thought. "Well, when we get shut of this herd, I was thinking of going by a town I heard about. It's up there on the railroad near where the Black River runs to the Pecos. I need to get some oil for that sorrel's feet. If you'll tell me what size, maybe I can get you some riding togs that'll be more comf'table for straddling that old army saddle. That is, if you'd want me to."

"I'd appreciate it if you would, John."

Grace turned her attention to the passing herd, deciding it best not to distract him with further conversation as he surveyed the countryside through the telescope. Finally he again lowered the glass. "Johnny," she exclaimed in a concerned tone, "look out yonder behind the herd! The drag rider's lettin' some of the calves get by him."

He just gave her a blank look, not unlike the one he'd shown when she questioned if the rustlers were taking only Bar BX cattle.

"You don't mean . . . ! He's leaving them behind on purpose, isn't he?" she asked incredulously. "Why, most of them will die of thirst or starve!"

John nodded gravely. "At the least they'll go dogied and be stunted. But like you said, most of 'em'll die."

"But why does he let them straggle?"

"Stolt cows got to be moved so fast the younger calves can't keep up. The small stuff won't bring much money anyway, so them boys can't afford to fool with 'em."

Gracie looked stunned.

"Welcome to the cow-thievin' profession," said John dryly, and turned his horse to move ahead to another vantage point.

Grace followed him off the slope and trotted the sorrel to regain her previous position alongside the moving cattle. The break in the monotony by the diversion to the hillside had been calculated to revivify her enthusiasm for the trip, but the picture of exhausted calves littering the dusty wake of the rushing herd despoiled the effect. Although an increasing breeze arose to cool her grimy face and drift the dust away behind her, her mood continued to darken along with a lowering sky. Her thoughts about the wasted calves opened the doors of her mind to other dark considerations; some she'd been studiously avoiding. She paid little attention to the gathering cumulus.

The buildup of thunderheads had certainly not gone unnoticed by the rest of the party however, and when Wally yelled at her to get out of the way she looked to see where John had stationed himself and loped her mount to his side. "I didn't realize it was getting so dark," she exclaimed. "Are they gonna bed the cattle already?"

"I reckon," affirmed John. "At least get 'em settled in case we get a storm. We can't make the Delaware today anyhow."

Gracie flinched when a glimmer of lightning pulsated within a black cloud. "I don't even have a slicker, John."

John loosened his own raingear from back of his cantle and laid it across her pommel. The sorrel rolled an eye and sidestepped several paces. "Your ponie's kinda spooky about that thing, ain't he? You'd best dismount and tie 'im up when you go to put it on."

"I can't take your slicker, John!" Gracie protested.

"That's right! You can't. You already got it. And you'd best put it where it'll do some good," he concluded as a few large drops began to spatter on the dusty ground. "I'm gonna go help them boys hold that herd. You stay up here, 'cause there's no telling what them cows'll do if we get some of that skyfire."

The thirsty cattle lowed plaintively as they milled about, their restlessness aggravated by the spattering drops of cold rain, the rumble of thunder, and shimmer of lightning. The normal light of day quickly turned to an eerie yellow twilight although the unseen sun had yet to fall below the horizon. The atmosphere felt charged with anticipation. John shivered, sat ramrod straight in his saddle and breathed deeply of the rarefied air. Why was it a man felt most alive in the very face of the impending wrath of nature?

As if on cue the sprinkle became a torrent with a dazzling shaft of lightning and an explosive clap of thunder. The nervous cattle responded as one and there was no holding them back. The men raced their horses headlong with the seething horde of fear-crazed bovines, hoping to keep them from scattering and somehow to turn the leaders and bring the runaways into a rotating mass that could be slowed and finally settled.

John touched up the appaloosa and raced through the driving rain toward the front of the plunging herd. At a full gallop there was no way he could extract the pistol from his saddlebag, but he might be able to turn a few head by slapping them with his rope. He pulled his horn string and freed the coil. Through the sheet of pouring rain he discerned the silhouette of a horse among the charging longhorns just ahead.

A horse, *but no rider!* He wondered which hand might be lying in the trampled mud behind, pulverized into a mass of bleeding meat and splintered bones by hundreds of pounding hooves. *It looked like a black horse!* He crowded the roan in closer. No, not black, he realized, and his racing heart seemed to settle back in his rib box where it belonged. The horse had just looked black in the scant light because the hide was so soaking wet. It was a brown or a red horse. *It could be a sorrel!* His palpitating heart leaped back into his throat. *I told her to stay on that hill!* He had to be sure. He risked casting a loop into the melee of charging animals, saw it settle around the long neck with the flying mane and raced ahead, gradually leading the plunging horse out from among the stampeding cattle.

The horse came clear of the surging herd just as another deafening crack of thunder exploded directly overhead. In a blinding flash of lightning John glimpsed the terrified animal lunging past him just in time to set the appaloosa against the end of the rope. The slack whipped tight and spun the hapless beast to a standstill facing the appaloosa.

"*Calmase, calmase,* you just calm down now," said John consolingly as he rode toward the captured cayuse. "You're gonna get yerself all choked down if you don't quit fightin' this lasso." He flicked the rope to loosen the noose a bit. The nervous animal trembled and backed away to the end of the rope. But John had seen the burlap tow sacks tied on behind the saddle and he knew he had Gracie's sorrel. Most of the provisions for the drive had been entrusted to Gracie's mount since she was not expected to take an active part in the work and would be the least encumbered by the extra baggage. He'd also observed the tied-up reins dangling halfway to the ground from the bit with a short piece of brush still hanging in the knot, so it wasn't difficult to guess what had happened. *I sure hope she stayed on that high ground!* It would be impossible for him to go on without knowing for sure that Gracie was safe. He reined the ap around and clucked him into a trot, obliging the balky sorrel to stumble along behind.

The storm blew over even more quickly than it had developed. The nippy wind pushed the clouds on to the north and slowly began to dry John's clothing. By the time he topped the hill where he'd left Gracie the vertical rays of the setting sun cast an orange hue upon the back of his yellow slicker where she sat in the churned up mud below. *My God! What's she doing down there?*

Grace turned a tear-streaked face when she heard his hoofbeats descending the grade. She dabbed a finger at an eye and left a smear of blood on her cheek. Only then did John's vision register the crumpled form half buried in the mud in front of her. He dismounted and dropped the reins. When he gently grasped her shoulders and tried to persuade her to relinquish her support of the bloody blond head upon her lap she stiffened with resistance. John relaxed his grip and lightly rubbed her shoulders for a moment before going to a knee beside her. He removed his hat and bowed his head.

"How'd it happen?" he quietly asked after a few minutes had passed.

"Don't know," she said with a sob. "I didn't even see him till after the clouds lifted."

John raised his head and looked all about. "Well, if his pony went down it managed to get up and get away before it got tromped. He might've just lost his seat; he wasn't the best rider I ever saw."

Grace shot him an accusing look.

"I didn't aim to speak disrespectful of the dead," he apologized. He didn't say any more for a few moments, thinking how best to frame his next words. "Gracie, it's coming on dark, you know," he began with a gently persuasive tone. "If I don't get him covered the varmits'll be at him tonight."

She nodded her understanding and eased Grassbelly Oates' swollen and discolored head to the turf. John replaced his hat and helped her to stand. He kept an arm about her waist and walked with her to a drier position on the rocky hillside before beginning his gruesome task.

John didn't have anything with which to dig a proper grave, so he rolled the corpse onto its side to make use of the depression already created by the pounding of the body into the ground. He scooped out as much soil as he could with his hands. When he rolled Oates back over he noticed his pistol was gone, lost in the mud somewhere no doubt. When John went to the hillside for the first of the rocks, Grace returned to the grave with him, bowed her head and began to recite the twenty-third Psalm. John whipped his hat off his head and stood alongside until she was finished. He returned with her to the hillside and objected when she insisted on helping with the rock-hauling chore.

By the time the mound of rocks was sufficient to deter any marauding scavengers of the night the afterglow of the departed sun had almost completely dissipated and John was glad Gracie had pitched in. "I saw some good grass we can stake these ponies on just over the hill," he told her, "and we'll be more comfortable over there, too."

"Oh, he doesn't bother me," said Grace with a glance toward the rock pile.

"He don't bother me, neither, but I'm a mite dampish you know, and the wind's downright chilly after that storm and the other side of the hill's the leeside so I'd lots rather spend the night over there."

Grace chuckled upon realizing she'd misinterpreted his former statement. He was glad to know her sense of humor was intact. She'd be all right now.

Chapter Twenty-Five

"Well, what do we do now, pard?" Wally kneeled to punch up the fire under the coffee pot.

"I'm ready, pardner. All I need to do is get up yonder on that ledge."

Wally slowly wagged his head as he added some sticks to the fire. "I don't think I'll *ever* be ready."

"I'd feel the same way normally. Especially if I was as well preserved as you are. But there comes a time when you just get tired of fighting it."

John took a deep breath and held it a second before he expelled it. "I'm just plumb wore out, Wallace. Onliest way I've helt out to now is knowing in my heart that you'd come so's I could do it my way. I'm beholden to you, pard." John laid a hand on Wally's shoulder as he said it.

Wally fed the last stick into the fire and looked at John, but when he tried to speak his voice caught in his throat. He turned his face to cough. "The least I could do," he finally managed in a husky voice, staring at the flames.

John gave him a gentle pat before removing his hand from his shoulder. He looked up at the ledge and wondered if he had enough strength left to get up there. His gaze traveled on up the monolith. The bright rays of the sun rising above the crest brought tears to his eyes.

The yellow light of early morning seeped in between John's slightly parted eyelids. What was that smell? His eyes opened wide. Hair! No wonder the light seemed so yellow. He had his nose stuck into a big gob of yellow hair! Then he remembered. Neither of their bedrolls included a waterproof ground sheet so they'd been obliged to sleep next to each other on top of his spread-out slicker.

They'd slept fully clothed, of course. How they'd managed to end up together beneath both blankets with his body curved against her back and his hand on her breast he did not know. *Hand on her breast!* Instinctively he jerked it away, awakening her with the action. Too late he realized she'd had a hand upon his own hand. Had she put his hand there? Well, maybe. But only in her sleep. What would she think of him? He rolled away from her and sat up, throwing the blankets aside and staring at the offending member.

Grace sat up and gave him a quizzical look. Then she remembered how a quick movement had interrupted her slumber and where she'd felt it. Her pealing laughter shattered the early morning silence. "What's the matter, John, burn your hand?"

A foolish grin spread across his face. If he'd known she would take it so lightly he would've stayed put awhile and savored the situation. After all, it was as close as he would ever come to the fulfillment of a certain cherished dream.

They didn't take time to boil coffee or cook anything to eat. A quick breakfast of cold canned goods sufficed and they were soon mounted and following the direction of the stampede in search of the rest of their party. Presently they encountered a few head of stray cattle. John rounded them up and drove them ahead, adding another one or two here and there as they went along. Obviously the herd was badly scattered. Finally he heard the lowing of a larger group of cattle ahead and off to the east. He turned his small bunch in that direction and it wasn't long before the other cattle were visible on the horizon. John approached cautiously until he could identify some of the drovers, then pushed his band of strays on to the main body of animals. When he'd finished that chore he pulled away to make sure Grace had joined the procession without mishap.

Wally had already found her. "Where th'hell you been, John?" he shouted as soon as John was in earshot. "If we'd just had a little more help we coulda helt that herd last night," he continued as John rode up to them. "Them cows've scattered from here plumb back into New Mexico. We ain't found more'n half of 'em and we can't take a chance on gettin' caught riding around looking for the rest of 'em. Where *was* you, anyhow?"

"I saw Gracie's hoss running riderless in the stampede so I roped him out and went back to see if she was all right."

"Went back to spend the night with her you mean," said Wally accusingly.

"*Wah*-lee!" exclaimed Grace with a look of outrage. "What are you saying?"

"Don't pay him no nevermind, Grace," said John. "He don't mean nothin'. He's just fractious 'cause he's had the silver lining pulled out of his cloud on account of them cows, is all. He knows you good enough to know nothing untoward happened betwixt us last night."

John's comment effectively thwarted Wally's pursuit of that tack, so he returned to his original complaint. "Well, I wasn't surprised to see that Oates had turned yeller and run out on us, but you —"

"Oates is dead," interrupted John.

"I found him trampled to death," confirmed Grace. "Me'n John buried him. It was just horrible!"

Wally took only a moment to absorb the news before continuing his sarcastic commentary. "Well I ain't surprised. If snails was as big as cows he'd got run over when he was a kid picking peas in his daddy's pea patch. It's a wonder he didn't get hisself killed a long time ago!"

A look of outrage flashed upon Gracie's face, but before she could voice a protest to Wally's insensible comment, Rafer McDaniel came loping up on his big sorrel and reined in before the threesome. "Ma'am." He tugged his hatbrim at Grace before shifting his eyes to John. "Seen Oates?"

"He must've come unglued of his saddle in the middle of the stampede. Me'n Grace buried him last night."

"Well, I'll swun," responded McDaniel, "I thought Oates would get his falling off a mountain. See, my old grandpappy had this here saying: 'What you fear the worst will surely come upon you.' "

"I never heard that one before," said John. glancing at Grace and thinking it must be true.

"Yep, that's what he used to say. That's how come I made sure not be scared of nothing at all! But Oates, he was afraid of lots of things."

Gracie's outraged expression turned to one of dismay. "Why, you're all just alike, aren't you?" She pounded her horse with her heels and headed for her usual position alongside the herd.

Rafer raised his eyebrows at her angry departure. "What put the burr under her backsides?"

Wally shrugged. "I ain't got time to worry about it. We gotta get the few cows we got left to water as quick as we can. And we need all the help we can get." He cast a smouldering look in John's direction.

John didn't answer. But he fell in behind them and rode back to the herd. "These boys are dee-termined to make me out a cow thief," he grumbled to himself.

The drovers pushed their decimated herd on to the Delaware, watered them, and pressed on for several miles before bedding them down for the night.

At the cookfire that night John announced his intention to leave the party on the morrow and ride north to the new town on the railroad to purchase a few things he needed. They were well enough on their way and would be trailing the small herd at a more leisurely pace, so they really didn't need him anymore. He'd be glad to obtain any small items the rest of the group might want from town and bring them back to the hideout. Rafer revealed that he and Beasley and Speckles would detour to Pecos City again after the herd was sold, so they could do their own shopping. Grace said there were several things she needed, if purchasing some articles of a feminine nature wouldn't be too embarrassing for John.

Before John could say yea or nay Wally spoke up. "He's done put his grimy hands on your personal things enough, fetchin' that stuff back from where you lost the mare."

"Why Wally —" Grace cut her exclamation short. She didn't want to get involved in an argument in front of everybody.

Rafer's pernicious smile diminished somewhat when he realized she wasn't going to respond in kind to Wally's provocative statement. "Why don't you just let her go on into town with Stone, Choctaw?" he suggested, hoping to keep the pot boiling.

Before Wally could respond with another sarcastic remark, Grace interjected her own suggestion. "Let's both go, Wally. Three hands can handle the herd from here on and Mr. McDaniel can bring the money for your cows."

"Sure," said Speckles, " 'twouldn't be no problem a-tall, no more cows than we got left. And thanks to that storm we don't have to worry about nobody tracking us out of New Mexico."

"*Please,* Wally?" Gracie pleaded.

John risked the chance that his encouragement might make Wally balk at the idea. "It's not likely anybody would recognize you in those parts," he ventured.

"So what if they do?" Wally retorted, putting his palm to the grip of his pistol. "I can take care of myself."

John knew he'd said the right thing. "Then why not go?" he challenged.

"I'll sleep on it."

Chapter Twenty-Six

The sun was almost all the way to its zenith by the time Winston and O.C. rode to the point of Lonesome Ridge. Winston knew they were wasting time, for they'd found signs of the elusive riders' passing a long way back. But O.C. had never been on the ridge before so Winston indulged him the extra time for sightseeing.

O.C. stood up in the stirrups as if to see even farther into the panorama of landscape to the east of the escarpment. "I swear, I believe I can see Malaga over yonder on the horizon."

The Pecos Valley Railway changed the name of the Kirkwell siding near the confluence of the Black River and the Pecos to Malaga in 1891 in honor of a variety of grape which Swiss immigrants to the area were growing in their irrigated vineyards. The village that was founded at the site a year later was little more than two years old on the early summer day the three youths from the upper Black River rode in from the south on the Pecos City wagon road. "All the lungers in the world must be a-flockin' to the Pecos Valley," said Wally as they rode past several tuberculosis tents at the edge of town. He led the way to the mercantile store.

"Ah, Wally," said John cautiously, "like I said the other night, it's not likely anybody over here will know who you are, but that silver-studded gunbelt stands out like the teeth in a catamount's grin."

"There ain't another one like it, that's certain. So what about it?"

"Folks're gonna sit up and take notice of it, that's what. And they'll take remembrance of the hombre who's wearing it. Worst of all, they'll look right careful at the pistol it's packin', and anybody who's heard the gossip Charlie started before he died will likely recognize that fancy Peacemaker."

"Well, I'd be tickled to introduce 'em to it, just like I did Charlie," Wally retorted. "I can —"

"*Wah*-lee!" Grace interrupted, flashing a worried look at him.

"I know, you can take care of yourself," John finished for him, "but Grace would most likely be caught right in the middle of a 'ruption, and you don't want anything like that to happen, do you?"

"I reckon I can take care of Gracie, too," mumbled Wally in a surly voice. "I won't chance being caught unarmed."

"Then carry the old Patterson while we're in town."

"Aw, alright," agreed Wally disgustedly, "if it'll make you feel better."

John wished Wally would relinquish the

gunbelt as well, but the surrender of the Peacemaker was more than he'd expected. He dug the Patterson out of his saddlebag and exchanged with Wally after they reined in at the hitch rail and dismounted.

Inside the store John left Wally and Grace to tend to her shopping while he approached the proprietor to ask him if he had any neat's-foot oil. He had some in his stores, he said, and shuffled off to the storeroom. John browsed aimlessly among the varied trade goods while he waited. He came across a ladies' mirror similar in size and shape to the one Gracie had cherished so highly. The handle and frame were not of ivory, but rather the glass set in handcarved mahogany which had been oiled and rubbed to a beautiful luster. It wouldn't much match her brush and combs, but it would certainly fill her need. It was the only mirror in the store.

In fact, a lot of the shelves in the store were very sparsely stocked. John made mention of the fact to the storekeeper when he returned with the can of neat's-foot oil.

The old fellow wrinkled a hoary eyebrow and explained that Malaga had seen the arrival of an unusual number of consumptives during the last few weeks and most of them were accompanied by at least one family member. Therefore, the demand upon his trade goods had been greater than anticipated. "Food is the thing folks can't do without," he added, "and I've got a shipment of grocery items arriving today from a wholesaler in Eddy. The train should be rolling in directly."

John started to call Gracie's attention to the mirror, then decided to buy it himself and surprise her with it. Wally wouldn't like him giving her a present, but the satisfaction of pleasing Gracie was more important to him than preserving Wally's good humor. He had the storekeeper wrap the mirror up and paid him before Wally and Grace came to the counter with their purchases.

The whistle of the approaching locomotive was stirring the sleepy little village to action by the time the storekeeper had finished with Gracie's bundle. He followed the threesome out the door and locked it behind them and they in turn followed his quick-shuffle gait down the street and around the corner to the siding to watch the train come in.

Gracie counted the cars as it approached. "One, two, three, four, five, six, seven. Only seven cars and a caboose," she said disappointedly.

"And some of those cars are empty," revealed the old man. "You see, they're what we call 'immigrant cars'."

"Immigrant cars?" exclaimed Wally. "You mean them sodbusters are coming to the Pecos Valley by the carload?"

"Well, not exactly," the merchant continued. "You see, they insist on bringing all their earthly possessions with them, so they hire a railroad car. Most of the time there's not enough being shipped out of the valley to fill all the immigrant cars on the return trip. That's why there are so many empty cars," he concluded, peering through his spectacles at the threesome as if to ascertain the degree of their comprehension.

"Except for last year," John guessed, raising his voice to overcome the chug and rattle of the engine. "I heard there was a lot more leaving than there was coming, after the big rise and the dams busted and all."

"I bet they don't take nothing with 'em when they leave," Wally volunteered, "if they's even got anything left by then."

"That's right," agreed the storekeeper, "the ones that starve out usually hold a big auction sale and sell most everything they own, just trying to get enough money to get back where they came from."

The noisy locomotive finally came to a halt and the cars settled in behind with a staccato of clanks. Wally ducked his head and squinted down the tracks at one of the boxcars. "Somebody must be taking their stock back home with 'em. Looks like hosses in that fourth car yonder." He'd no sooner spoken than a smallish man with a metal star on his vest jumped down from the car.

The storekeeper adjusted his spectacles and peered down the track. "Why it's Marshall Harkey!" he exclaimed.

Wally grabbed Gracie by the arm and disappeared around the corner of the station house.

John started to follow suit but at that very moment Harkey recovered from his dismount and looked up. John knew it would seem awfully suspicious if he suddenly turned away. If he did and Harkey gave chase, he might see Wally. John pulled his hatbrim down low over his face and stood behind the merchant, lounging against the wall of the station house and studying the package in his hands.

"Howdy, Dee," the storekeeper said warmly, extending a hand as Harkey came up to them. "What brings you out here? Got a posse with you, I see," he added with a nod toward the three other men who'd jumped down from the boxcar to stretch their legs.

Harkey hooked his thumbs in his gunbelt and turned to look back at the other men for a moment before he answered. "Well, I reckon so," he replied with dry humor, "if they don't cut and run when the lead starts flyin'."

"Who're you chasing this time?" the merchant persisted.

"Rustlers this time, George."

"Rustlers are no business of the U.S. Marshall's office, Dee."

"That's so, George; but Porter, one of the ranchers over on the upper Black River, sent a rider in to tell me him and Bledsoe thinks that half brother of Bledsoe's has something to do with it."

George wrinkled his eyebrows. "So what difference does that make? It's still rustling."

"The boy's also wanted for murder," explained Harkey.

"Bledsoe . . ." George repeated with a hand to his jaw. "Isn't that the name of the young fellow who shot his brother? The one they call the Choctaw Kid?"

"That's right, George. He's the reason I'm out chasing cow thieves."

"You're not the only one after the Choctaw Kid, Dee. He's bound to get caught before too long anyway."

"Caught or killed. I'd prefer he stands trial. Also, Porter's daughter has run off and he thinks she's with the Bledsoe boy. If so, she could be shot, either by mistake or by carelessness. I'm hoping to capture them before that can happen."

"I see your point, Dee, but you're a long way from the upper Black River," George pointed out.

For a moment Harkey fixed a narrow-eyed look upon John. "I've got a hunch about where they've been going with those cows," he explained to George, "and I plan to get down there by rail soon enough to pick up their trail before they get too far."

A couple of townsmen sauntered by and John turned his back and walked away with them, striking up a conversation so as to appear to the lawman that he knew them and had been waiting for them to come along. He continued walking with them until they were out of sight from the railroad siding, then he made a beeline for the mercantile store and the appaloosa. He discovered that Wally and Gracie had arrived just ahead of him, for they were in the process of mounting up. He ran to the hitch rail and jerked his reins free. "You must have eavesdropped long enough to hear what Harkey's up to," he guessed aloud as he tightened his cinch.

Wally had already traded the Patterson for the Peacemaker. "You better believe it," he affirmed. "And I don't know how we're gonna warn them boys before he sniffs 'em out. We sure can't outrun that durn train."

John stepped to the stirrup and swung astraddle. "Maybe Harkey don't know as much as he thinks he does. We know exactly where they're taking that herd. Maybe we can get to 'em ahead of him." He reined over to Grace and handed her his package. "Put that in one of your packs, will you? Grace, I sure do wish you'd wait for us here."

For once, Wally concurred. Before she could voice a protest to John's suggestion Wally issued a mandate. "You stay at the hotel till we get back. We're gonna be riding hard and fast and you're already sore and stiff from follerin' the herd. You just ain't used to being in the saddle all day long and you'd slow us down too much. Here," he said, producing a roll of bills, "this'll put you up at the hotel for a spell and pay the liv'ry."

John thought she was going to cry. But she

knew what Wally said was true. She bit her lip and accepted the roll from Wally's hand. He just turned away and rode off. John lingered a moment and his eyes met hers with a look of empathy and goodbye. Then he touched the steel to the appaloosa and streaked away after Wally and the black.

They loped the horses until they were out of sight of the town, then settled to an easy trot. They had a long way to go.

"It's a wonder Harkey didn't recognize you, John," Wally marveled. "Course, the onliest time he's ever seen us up close was that day at Abels' old camp. But he sure enough give us the once over that time."

"Well, I stood behind the storekeep and didn't show my face to Harkey. And I ducked out soon as he commenced studying me.

"Wallace, they don't know for certain who's been stealing them cows. But they *will* catch up to you sooner or later if you don't stop." John hesitated, thinking Wally would protest the idea that anyone would be able to catch him. But Wally just rode along in silence with his eyes studiously fixed upon his horse's ears, so John continued.

"Since you've got no intention of trying to clear yourself with the law about the difficulty with Charlie, we'd best fade outa this part of the country while we're still on top of the ground and kicking. We could drift on over Arizona way and have us a look-see."

John couldn't tell if Wally was ignoring him or contemplating what he'd said. "Think about it," urged John, twisting in the saddle to watch the train steaming out from Malaga.

"Harkey's gonna stop that train and jump them hosses out when she gets close to Pope's crossing," guessed Wally. "Unless he thinks we been taking them cows all the way to Emigrant Crossing, or Horsehead."

"Naw, he's thinking Pope's, I'll wager. It's less traveled than the others. Not as spooky for somebody crossing a herd with mixed brands. He's hoping to pick up our trail down there. And unless he has some trouble finding it we're gonna be too late!"

"Yep, he's on his way to Pope's, all right," Wally agreed with a frown. After a moment his face brightened. "But he don't know we been turning them cows over to another outfit. He prob'ly thinks we've been stopping over there on the prairie somewhere to burn the brands and sharpen the ears before we push 'em further east to sell 'em." A broad smile spread across Wally's face. "Now that'll be just dandy, won't it? Even if he does strike the trail of the herd without no problem he'll likely catch the other gang with them stolt cows after our hands have done got the money and lit a shuck."

"Let's just hope our boys deliver them cows and cut 'cross country to Pecos City instead of coming back to the river crossing to take the wagon road, else they're liable to meet up with the posse follerin' their trail."

"So? Harkey don't know the hombres he's tracking. Except me. He'd expect me to be with the bunch he's after. And Rafer's almighty good at stretching the blanket; he'll talk his way around him and send 'em on down the trail to them other hands."

"I expect Harkey's too long-headed for that," John disagreed. "He'll compare their hoofprints with the ones that belong to the horses pushing the herd."

Wally heaved a sigh. He knew John was probably right. "Well, let's just hope Rafe and his boys don't turn back for the wagon road."

They did.

Chapter Twenty-Seven

Winston looked at his watch. Since it was already nearly noon they might as well eat the lunch Barb had sent with them. He dismounted and removed the foodstuffs from his saddlebag. "Climb down, O.C. You can chew and gawk at the same time."

O.C. disengaged his foot from the off stirrup and slowly dragged his leg over, still peering at the distant horizon. "Yep, a feller can see all the way to Malaga from up here."

"If you keep on gaping you'll be tellin' me you can see all the way to the other side of the Pecos!"

John and Wally were east of the Pecos and proceeding with due caution when John sighted the riders coming toward them. He handed the glass to Wally to see if he agreed with his identification.

"Yep, that's Speckles and Beasley, all right," Wally confirmed, "but I don't see hide or hair of McDaniel. It don't look like Beasley's in too good of shape, the way he's riding all hunkered over." He handed the telescope to John. "They must've met up with the posse, sure 'nough."

"We best let 'em get close enough to recognize

us before we show ourselves," John cautioned. "If they've been in a fight they'll be spooky and if we was to booger 'em they'd run."

"They might even start shootin'," Wally concurred.

They reined their horses into a swale and behind a large patch of mesquite. As soon as the approaching riders were close enough to be able to recognize them, John shouted Speckles' name and rode out from behind the bushes. The freckle-faced cowboy yanked his reins with his left hand and clutched at his pistol with his right, but in the same instant he saw it was John. He relaxed and pushed his hat back to wipe the sweat from his forehead as John and Wally rode up.

Beasley's brown gelding had come to a halt behind Speckles' red roan. His chin was slumped on his chest and his right sleeve was soaked in blood from the shoulder to the wrist and strings of red coaglum oozed from his fingers upon his chaps where his hand dangled uselessly against his knee.

Wally reined in with an open-mouthed appraisal of Beasley's arm. "Damn! He got plugged purty bad, didn't he? Where's Rafe? Did they get 'im?"

Speckles pulled his hat down and breathed a sigh of relief. "Y'all scared the pee out of me, riding outa the brush like that! If you hadn't've hollered my name I'da prob'ly shot you before I seen who it was."

"We was afeared you'd run if we showed ourselves too soon," Wally impatiently explained. "Where's Rafe? What happened?"

"I take it you know about the posse," Speckles assumed. "Else you wouldn't've rode back down here."

"Saw 'em in Malaga," affirmed John, "heard what they was up to. We came as quick as we could, but they rode a boxcar to the crossing."

Speckles raised his eyebrows and nodded his understanding. "So that's how come their hosses was so fresh. We was coming back to the crossing when we run into 'em. We'd been follerin' along the bottom of a little coulee for a way and when topped out, why, there they was. Seemed like it surprised them as much as it done us."

"They didn't figger on you leavin' the herd with them other hands and turnin' back," John interjected.

Again Speckles nodded. "Why shore. Anyhow, we just cut and run like a bunch o' jackrabbits and it didn't take them boys long to start making like a bunch o' greyhounds on them fresh horses, and they was shootin' whilst they was chasing. We seen we couldn't outrun 'em, so when we come up on a rocky ridge where we could hide the hosses we hauled in and scattered out amongst the rocks and done some shootin' of our own."

"So what happened to Rafer?" Wally interrupted. "And how'd y'all get away?"

"I'm gettin' to it," said Speckles with a hint of

irritation. He cleared his throat. "The posse took cover in a cutbank ravine down below us and we had 'em in a purty bad jackpot. The gully wasn't deep enough to hide their hosses too good so Rafer started taking aim at 'em with that thirty-thirty. Well, they laid them ponies down lickety-split, whilst one of 'em kept us dusted with rifle fire. But they was really in a pickle, trying to keep them broncs on the ground and throw lead in our direction at the same time. Rafer says he's gonna lead his pony around them, keeping to low ground, and come up on 'em from behind. So me'n Beasley keeps 'em busy 'til our rifle barrels commence to gettin hot, then we commence to wondering what's happened to Rafe. Finally Beasley spies a dust cloud away off yonder on the skyline and it don't take us long to figger out what that means, so we decide to lead our ponies off a ways back of the ridge and fade outa there, *pronto.* Only them boys in the ravine gets suspicious when we quit shooting and I figger they stuck a hat up on the gunbarrel or something and when it didn't draw no fire they come a-gallopin' over the ridge. They plugged Beasley right off and I was saying my prayers when one of 'em hollers and they all yank their broncs around and head off after Rafer. The one who hollered must've looked around for him when he seen there wasn't but two of us behind the ridge."

"Damn! Rafer's got my money," said Wally disgustedly. "Now why would they leave y'all and go after him?"

"I ain't got the slightest notion," admitted Speckles, "but I sure am thankful they did. They'll never catch him, though. He got the jump on 'em and he surely lost 'em once he got into that country west of the Pecos."

John gave Wally a somber glance. "They're not after Rafer," he said matter-of-factly. "They think they're chasin' Wally. Dee Harkey's leading the posse and we heard him say he expected to find Wally when he caught up with y'all. It's what you call a case of mistaken identity."

"Naw, 'tain't so!" objected Wally. "Rafer don't look nothing like me!"

"I've mistook him for you from a distance," John argued, "and you heard Harkey say it was you he was really after."

Wally considered a moment. "I reckon that's the only way it tallies," he admitted. "Well, I hope Rafe makes it back to the hideout with my money!"

A crooked grin spread across Speckles' face and he slowly wagged his head. "If I know McDaniel, he'll not tarry on the mount'in for long, so if you want that money you better catch up to 'im *pronto*. There ain't no doubt he seen the posse's dust on his backtrail. He don't know why they singled him out and I betcha he don't hang around these parts long enough to find out."

"Well, let's quit chinnin' and git on back up there," said Wally. He gave Beasley a doubtful look. "You gonna be able to ride with us, Beasley?"

Beasley's reins were tied together and hanging on his pony's neck. He took a white-knuckled grip with his left hand on his saddle horn and nodded his ashen face. "Go fer it. My ol' pony'll keep up."

"Hold it, Wally!" exclaimed John. "What about Grace?"

"Grace? Oh yeah, Gracie's waiting in Malaga, ain't she? John, you fetch her back to the mountain for me, alright pardner? I gotta get to McDaniel before he jumps the border with my cash!"

John gave him a disapproving look. "Whatever you say, Wallace," he said evenly.

"Hey pardner, we're gonna need that *dinero* when we go to Arizona, you know." Wally touched the steel to the black and led the way west.

They all rode together back across the Pecos and when they arrived at the wagon road John turned the appaloosa to the north. Wally reined alongside him as the others crossed the road. "John," he said with a direct look, "now I'm trusting you to bring Grace back safe and sound, so don't you be gettin' no ideas about her on the way. You know what I mean. Remember, I'm *trusting* you." With that he pulled away to catch up with the others.

"Won't be gettin' no ideas I've not already had," said John under his breath.

Chapter Twenty-Eight

"Here it is!" O.C. reined in where they had first detected some hoofprints in a stretch of softer ground on the rocky trail.

Winston nudged his horse over to O.C.'s. "Yep, that's it! We'll just stay on this trail and watch for any sign that they left it. Whenever another trail intersects with this one we'll have to study both paths until we find an indication as to which way they went."

O.C. lifted his hat and wiped the sweat from his forehead with his forearm. He reset the hat and looked again at the two sets of hoofprints. "I wonder who the Sam Hill ol' John got to bring him up here? Maybe we'd already be a-knowin' if we hadn't made that welty out on the ridge."

"With the head start they've got I doubt we'd have caught up to them by now anyway."

O.C. glanced at the sun. It was well past its highest point. "What do you think our chances are of catching up to 'em before sundown?"

Winston peeked at his watch. "Slim to none."

It didn't take Deputy U.S. Marshall Dee Harkey long to realize that the cow thief on the big sorrel horse had such a head start that the chances of catching up to him in the rugged country west of the Pecos were slim to none. In fact he never even got close enough to see the color of the fugitive's horse. He knew the rider who fit the Choctaw Kid's description was riding the sorrel only because of having seen the rustlers up close when they suddenly rode up out of the coulee.

From what he'd been told about the sign the ranchers had seen when they discovered the cattle had been driven off, there should have been more than three rustlers. And although it was certainly possible for a man to acquire an extra mount, it had also been mentioned that the Bledsoe boy rode a black horse. Well, at least he could assure friend Porter that his daughter was not riding with the gang. Harkey mentioned these things to George the storekeeper after the disappointed posse had ridden back to Malaga empty-handed. George's hoary eyebrows rose above the wire rims of his spectacles as his brain computed the dearth of rustlers, black horse and girl with the young customers he'd served the same day Harkey had passed through on his way south.

The slump of exhaustion faded from the deputy marshal's shoulders and he squared himself upon the wooden bench in front of the general store when George related his sudden suspicions. "You told me you'd heard the story about the Bledsoe shooting, George. Didn't you notice the kid's pistol?"

"Yes, I noticed the pistol, Dee. But not because it was the fancy one they tell about when you hear the fratricide story. I noticed it because it was an old cap-and-ball model and he was carrying it in the fanciest silver-studded black gunbelt I've ever seen. It was incongruous, like putting a silver-mounted parade saddle on a bandy-legged, buck-kneed, broom-tail mustang."

"It was the Choctaw kid, George! I'd bet the farm on it. He's prob'ly heard that his brother described that flashy pistola before he died, and if so the kid's surely precautious enough not to go struttin' around in public with the gun on his hip."

"Yep, it was probably him. He and the girl were standing beside me when you jumped off the train. I guess they lit out when I turned away to greet you."

Harkey slumped against the wall of the store. "So they were right here in town and I went off chasing the wrong man. I could've taken the Porter child back to her mother and father by now!"

"Child?" George flared his pale blue eyes and peered sideways through his lenses at the diminutive lawman. "How long has it been since you've seen the girl, Dee?"

"Not long —"

"Well, you better take a closer look. *She's* still in town."

Harkey came off the bench like he'd been shot from a catapult. "Why didn't you say so?" He hitched his gunbelt on his skinny hips. *"Where?"*

"She took a room over at the hotel."

Harkey took a step, then stopped and put a finger to his temple. "She's waiting on the Kid to come back for her, George."

"If so, all you need to do is to stake her out till he shows up."

John was in no hurry to get back to Malaga. He took two days for the trip, stopping frequently to rest his jaded horse and allow him to graze upon the strengthening grama and tobosa grasses. He intended to treat the appaloosa to a night at the livery with a trough full of grain when he got to Malaga, for it was a long way back to the mountains.

Squares of yellow lamplight identified the hotel restaurant when John rode into the main street of the little town in the gathering dusk. He came abreast of the windows on his way to the livery and leaned over his pommel to peer between the gingham curtains. Sure enough, Grace was seated at one of the tables having her evening meal. He resisted the urge to tie up at the hitchrack and go on in to join her. Better to take care of your mount before seeing to your own needs. He rode on down the street and dismounted before the open doors of the livery barn. A tow-headed youth put aside the harness he was mending and picked up his coal-oil lantern to show him to one of the few remaining empty stalls.

"Must be having a *baile* in town tonight," said John, observing the other horses, one of which was Gracie's sorrel.

"Oh, no sir," replied the youth. "We never have dances on any night but Saturday."

"Lots of horses been put up for a little burg like this, seems to me," John insisted, "unless something special's going on."

"Well, four of 'em belongs to Marshall Harkey and his posse. They've been down in Texas chasing banditos or something, and they're on their way back to Eddy."

Durn! John thought there'd been plenty of time for the posse to have already passed through town by now. That was one reason he'd been in no hurry to get back. He would have to be very careful. He felt sure Harkey was on the verge of recognizing him the time before. He'd recognize John for sure if he saw him again.

As soon as he finished tending to the appaloosa John exited by the rear door of the barn and kept to the shadows as he made his way back to the hotel restaurant. He put his back against the wall and cautiously looked through a crack where the curtain failed to meet the jamb of the window nearest the corner of the room. Grace was still there. But so were a number of other people, including a man who looked a lot like one of the posse members he'd seen dismounting the boxcar a few days ago. The man was seated with his back to a wall, positioned so as to have a clear view of the adjoining hotel lobby, the staircase to the second floor, and the front door.

Gracie finished eating, paid for her meal, and ascended the steps to the upstairs rooms. The man John thought he'd seen with the posse watched her carefully. Well, she would naturally attract a man's attention, but could it be that his interest was more than casual? Did he know who she was? John knew that Harkey knew her. Had Harkey seen her and assigned someone to watch her, thinking that if she was in town Wally would not be far away?

John rushed into the street and looked up at the windows of the hotel rooms. He doubted that Gracie had lit a lamp before going down to supper, therefore she would light one upon returning to her room. Only one room on the front had a lamp already burning. He ran around to the back of the building. Two rooms on the back side showed some light behind their window panes. He watched until he was sure Grace would have had plenty of time to get to her room and went back to recheck the front windows. A yellow glow now filtered through the flimsy curtain of a second window on the front. That must be her room!

John went back for another look at the inside of the restaurant. The man who'd watched Grace ascend the stairs was still there, nursing a cup of coffee and keeping an eye on the staircase. John was convinced he was a spy. He might even have John's description as well as Wally's. It would be best not to take a chance on being recognized or arousing suspicion.

The porch would be John's way to the second floor. He pulled off his boots and set them out of sight in the darkness by the side wall of the hotel. After double-checking to make sure no one was around to see, he shinnied up a post, climbed onto the split-shingle roof of the porch, and carefully made his way on silent sock feet to the window of the room he thought to be Gracie's. The window was slightly opened to allow the cool night air to circulate through loosely woven drapes. He paused to listen and was rewarded by the sound of a familiar voice humming the sad tune of "Little Joe the Wrangler."

The poor girl's still thinking about what happened to Oates, thought John, and lightly tapped on a window pane. The humming stopped abruptly and he tapped again.

"Who is it?" she asked nervously from behind the curtains.

"John," he said just loud enough for her to hear, and made a quick surveillance of the street below to be sure there was no one to see her toss the drapes apart and lift the window.

She stepped back to make way for him to slip inside. As soon as the curtains closed behind him she threw her arms around his neck and hugged him. "Oh, Johnny, I'm so glad to see you! Wally's safe, too, isn't he? Why didn't you just come through the lobby?" She jerked away from him and took a couple of steps back, a look of horror expunging the happy welcome from her face. "What's happened, John? Where's Wally?"

"Calmase," said John with a chuckle, "Wally's all right."

She let go a deep breath and sat down on the bed, a look of relief flooding her features.

"He went back to the hideout to get his money from Rafer," explained John, "and he sent me to bring you back up there. You see, the posse run smack-dab into Rafer and the boys out east of the crossing when they was coming back from turning the herd over to Rafer's friends. Rafe made a run for it and got away, but the posse took out after him, thinking he was Wally. We found the other two and Speckles thinks McDaniel is so boogered he'll pack his war bag and keep on running. Wally's determined to catch up to him and get his money before he leaves the country."

Grace slumped her shoulders. She suddenly looked very tired. "Maybe we *all* should leave," she said with a disconsolate tone, "like you suggested before."

"I made mention of it to Wally after we left you here. I think he's finally coming around to our way of thinking."

Grace blinked her eyes and took a deep breath. "Well, you still haven't told me why you sneaked in my window in your stocking feet," she stated with a little more brightness.

"The posse's in town and I think Harkey

knows you're here," said John matter-of-factly. "I saw one of his men downstairs guarding the staircase. They think you'll lead them to Wally or he'll come for you."

Gracie's eyes widened and she immediately got up and began getting her things together.

"Maybe you should let the marshall take you home," John suggested. "I could come back and get you after me'n Wally are settled in Arizona."

"I can't go home, John," Grace stated flatly as she busily prepared to leave.

"Why not? Your maw and paw would be relieved. They'll forgive you for running off."

"I'll not shame my mother, John."

"Shame her?" Suddenly John thought he knew what she was talking about. "Well, she wouldn't have to know that you and Wally been . . . you know." He didn't know how to say it. He wished he hadn't even brought it up.

"I know, John." Her back was to him and she was bent over the provision packs stuffing her belongings inside. She straightened up, as if composing herself for what she was about to say. Her voice trembled nontheless. "In the first place, if she asked me I couldn't lie to her. And even if she didn't ask, she would know before very long." She bowed her head.

John's mouth fell open and all the blood seemed to rush to his head. He was so dizzy he didn't know if he could walk across the room to her. But he did, and he gently put his arms around her. "I don't know why I'm so surprised," he said to himself as well as to her. "Such things just natcherly happen. Does Wally know?"

"Not yet. I'm not a hundred percent sure myself as yet. John, don't you dare say anything. Let me be the one to tell him. And don't you ever let him know I told you first. I didn't mean to; I don't know what got into me!"

"You just needed to tell somebody and I just happened to be handy, that's all. Now let's see if I'm handy enough to get you out of here." He released her and picked up the packs. They weren't very heavy, as most of the remaining foodstuffs had been taken by Rafer's party when they split up, but the one with their purchases was rather bulky.

After he peeked through the curtains to be sure no one was about, John eased the packs outside onto the roof of the porch. Gracie pulled her boots off and gathered up her skirts and he helped her across the windowsill. "Didn't you get some trousers?" he whispered as she stepped onto the roof.

"I got a riding skirt," she replied when he was outside. "But it's still in the pack."

John slung the packs over his shoulder and took her boots from her hand. He tiptoed to the corner of the building and dropped the boots into the darkness where he'd left his own. Then he took her by the hand and led her to the corner of the roof.

"I'm afraid I'm not much of a climber, John,"

she admitted nervously.

He slipped the packs off his shoulder and onto the roof. "You don't need to be. Just ease over the edge and wrap your legs around the post. I'll get down on my belly and hang on to your hands until you slide down as far as you can. You won't be more'n a couple of feet off the ground when I let go. Go find your boots and put them on soon's you get down."

When he'd help her over the edge and down to the ground he got up and replaced the packs on his shoulder. He was afraid they'd make too much noise if he dropped them from the roof. And it might break Gracie's mirror. He didn't realize how awkward they would be. He'd just lowered himself over the edge and made a tentative grasp of the post with his knees when the bulky pack swung between him and the post, causing him to lose his grip. He tried to grab the post as he fell and only succeeded in spinning his body around so that he crashed noisily onto the railing of the porch, breaking a section of it away from the posts with a resounding crash.

Gracie pulled her last boot on and ran to help him to his feet, but he was already up by the time she got there. He could hear chairs scraping inside the restaurant and boots drumming on the wooden floor. "Run for the stable," he told Grace, and dodged around the corner to pick up his boots before anyone could get outside the door of the hotel. With his boots in one hand and her wrist in the other he scurried to the back of the building so they wouldn't be seen if anyone looked around the corner of the front wall. They ran across a vacant lot and to the other side of the next building. He stopped in the dark shadow of the eaves and sat down to put his boots on. They could hear the voices from the front of the hotel where the group from inside was speculating as to who or what could have broken the railing.

"Go on and tell the stable boy to saddle your horse," he told Grace. "And pay up if you owe him anything. I'll catch up before you get there, most likely."

"But won't the marshall's man be coming after us?" she asked in a frightened voice.

"He'll check your room first. And he'll have to explain to the desk clerk before he can get a key. We got a little time, but not much." By then he already had his boots on, so he jumped up and grabbed her by the hand and they ran down to the stable.

John deposited the packs outside the back door of the livery and they quietly crept into the barn. They could hear the tow-headed youth snoring and saw that he was slumped against the wall near the front door, his mending job on his lap and the lantern by his side on the bench. The lantern provided just enough illumination for them to see their way around the barn. John put a finger to his lips and motioned for her to follow him to the tack room. He got her bridle and handed it to her and whispered that she should fetch the sorrel. The stable hand snored on blissfully as John retrieved the remainder of their tack and carried it to where Grace was leading the sorrel out of a stall. John sat his own gear down and placed the blanket and saddle on Gracie's mount. When Gracie saw that he intended to saddle her horse for her she shook her head vigorously and pointed at the appaloosa. John left her to cinch up the sorrel and went for his own horse.

When he'd finished saddling up he looked at Grace, nodded toward the rear opening of the stable and followed with the appaloosa as she led the sorrel outside. He paused in the doorway and dropped the reins long enough to tie the packs back of her saddle and assist her to mount.

Just as John gathered his reins and stepped to his stirrup several men rushed into the street entrance of the livery.

"There they are," one of them shouted, and squeezed off a shot that zinged past John's ear. The stable boy bolted upright with mouth agape and eyes wide, upsetting the bench and spilling the lantern upon the dry straw that was scattered on the ground.

"Hold your fire," John heard Harkey's voice command. "You might hit the girl! Put out that blaze!" John's toe found the off stirrup and a touch of the spur sent the excited appaloosa streaking into the darkness with the spooky sorrel close behind.

Chapter Twenty-Nine

John propped himself up on an elbow and cocked an eye at the bluff. The sun had long since cleared the summit and was already settling into the tops of the trees on the west side of the clearing. It was too late to do any rock climbing today.

He'd gone back to sleep after breakfast and again after the noon meal. He guessed he needed the rest after the long ride up the mountain. Maybe he'd feel like trying the cliff tomorrow.

Wally was nowhere to be seen. Probably off on another of his sentimental explorations. John was all alone in the clearing. Well, he'd be all alone up there on that ledge. There wasn't room for two people up there, especially if one of them was stretched out. The only advantage of dying in the nursing home or the hospital would be having Grace by his side at the end.

Gracie! She'd probably guessed where he was by now. But she wouldn't tell. He was sure of it. She wouldn't have let him do it if she'd known what he was up to. But now that it was done she wouldn't tell. In a way she would probably like to escape to the mountains with him, but she'd become too practical to actually try it.

John thought back on the time when they did escape together.

"I would've walked right into their trap if the stable hand hadn't said something about those horses belonging to the posse." John fed a few more sticks to the small fire and looked up to make sure the smoke was dissipating unnoticeably in the boughs of the cottonwood trees where they'd stopped beneath a bluff overlooking a bend in the Black River. They'd ridden all night by the light of the moon and stars, generally following the river's meandering course upstream toward the mountain. Only when the dawn revealed there was no one following did they dare stop to rest.

"Mister Harkey's man at the hotel would've stopped us if we'd tried to leave by the staircase," agreed Grace. "But they've got no valid reason to arrest you. They were expecting Wally. Maybe that's why they're not following us. I mean, they saw you at the livery. There's no mistaking you for Wally." She went to the water's edge and dipped a kerchief to wipe her face.

There were yet a few canned goods in the tow sacks on the sorrel's saddle and John went to see what he could find for them to warm over the fire. "I reckon Harkey wants to get you back to your folks just as bad as he wants to capture Wally, and I'm sure he wouldn't mind asking me a few questions. But by the time they got that blaze put out last night we was long gone. He prob'ly decided there was no use trying to catch us in the dark."

"Do you think they can make out our tracks today?" Grace was looking at her distorted reflection in the water trying to put her wind-blown hair back in place.

While rummaging in the pack for the canned goods, John came upon the package which contained the mirror. He tore it open and pulled the mirror out, relieved that it was still in one piece. "Maybe. But tracing out our trail would be mighty slow going." John shined the mirror with his shirt tail as he pondered the situation. "Considering what he's done so far, and if he can pick up our tracks for a little way to see which direction we've took, I'd guess he'll figure we're running back to our old stompin' grounds."

"You mean the upper Black River country?"

"There and beyond." John walked quietly toward Grace. She was squinting at the surface of the pool as she tried to smooth some reluctant wisps of hair into place. "He's smart enough to know we've got a roost in the canyons somewhere, or else higher up," he continued. "He needs to catch up to us quick, before we have time to get to the others. He don't want you getting caught in the middle of a shootout. So I believe they'll fan out and make a fast sweep of the country along the river between Malaga and where he thinks we're going. When their horses get tired he'll use his authority to trade for fresh mounts at the ranches along the way."

"Then he'll catch us."

"Nope. Because we're going back another way." John kneeled down beside her and held the mirror in front of her. "This might work a little better."

"Why, John! For me?"

"I know it's nowhere near as fine as the one that got broke, but at least you can see your pretty face." He gently eased his arm around her waist.

"It's beautiful," she exclaimed, taking the mirror from his hand to run her fingers over the polished mahogany and its intricate carvings. "Johnny, you're so thoughtful. Thank you!" She leaned against him, lightly kissed his cheek and started to pull away.

John's arm tightened and he held her there, his eyes searching her face. "Gracie, Gracie, what have we got you into. Carrying a desperado's child and on the run from the law." He blinked at the moisture in his eyes. "You deserve better. Lots better."

She lifted a hand and tenderly caressed his cheek with her fingertips. "It's not your doin', Johnny. I made my own choices." For a brief moment she gently touched her lips to his.

John's breath caught in his throat and he pulled her against him with both arms. "Grace, I —"

"Dear, sweet John," she interrupted. "Some of my choices were not wise ones, I'm sure. But things are the way they are. It's too late for second guesses."

Reluctantly he released her. "Grace, if you ever —"

She put a finger to his lips. "I know," she whispered. "And it means a lot to me. But right now we need to be thinking about eluding that posse and getting back to the hideout." She stood up and went to put the mirror away and see what he'd found to eat.

"Yeah, and Wally's *trusting* in me," muttered John bitterly. He picked up a small flat stone as he got to his feet and skipped it across the surface of the pool with a jerk of his arm.

The horses needed rest and circumstances had denied John his supper, else they wouldn't have taken time for breakfast. As soon as they finished the meal he kicked dirt on the fire and they mounted and left the river bottom, abruptly abandoning their southwesterly course to forge to the northwest and strike the Dark Canyon trail.

The midafternoon sun beat down mercilessly between the canyon walls by the time John called a halt and dismounted. Grace slid from her saddle with a sigh of relief. When her feet touched the ground her knees buckled, and John reached her just in time to break her fall. He helped her to stand and walk through the rocks and brush to a tiny pool of still water.

"How'd you know about this spring?" she asked as he helped her find a place to kneel down among the rocks.

"The Shattuck boys told me where to look. I passed the night with 'em when I went to Eddy for supplies," he explained, carefully releasing his grasp upon her waist and hand. "You're a little wobbly in the hocks from all the hard riding, I reckon. Just you rest here and I'll get the canteens and something for our bellies. I hope you like beans and tomatoes, cold and with a little taste of tin," said John with a grin.

Gracie's face paled and she looked as if she might lose her breakfast. "Nothing for me, John, thank you."

"You're sick!" exclaimed John, his grin abruptly changing to an expression of alarm. "Why didn't you say something?"

"It's nothing to be concerned about," she replied reassuringly. "Most women get sick in the morning, but for others it happens at different times of the day. It'll pass."

John remembered enough about his mother's last pregnancy to understand what she was talking about. "We don't have to be pushing so hard, I reckon. Even if Harkey was to figure out how we changed direction on him, we've still got a big lead on the posse."

"Don't worry about me, John, I'll be all right. Just get me back to Wally as quick as you can. I've got to convince him to get away from here before he gets caught. I don't want anything to happen to the father of my child!"

Her allusion to Wally's inexorable claim on her provoked a bitter pang in John's chest. He decided he wasn't hungry either. The canteens were quickly fetched and filled, the horses watered, and they were back on the trail.

Gracie's sickness did not pass as she'd predicted. From time to time she had to stop and John held her head and steadied her shoulders as she tried to purge an already empty stomach. Each time she insisted she would be all right, that they must keep pressing on and try to make up for the lost time. John kept a worried eye upon her pallid countenance, his concern growing with each passing mile. He was afraid she might faint and fall out of the saddle and so took to riding alongside her wherever the trail would permit. As they approached another spring the Shattuck boys had told him about she was swaying in the saddle and he decided they would stop for the night, even though there was an hour or so of good light remaining. Grace did not protest.

When John helped her down he realized with a start that in spite of the perspiration on her brow she was trembling all over. "You're having a chill!" he exclaimed with alarm.

Grace nodded gravely and accepted his assistance to sit down with her back against the trunk of a limber pine. "Must be something more than what I thought it was."

John gathered up a bed of pine needles, spread Gracie's blankets upon it and helped her change positions. He fetched his own blankets and covered her to the neck. "Maybe this'll keep you from shivering so bad."

"Thanks Johnny," Grace managed through chattering teeth. "At least the nausea has settled," she added hopefully.

"You feel like eatin' a little something?"

She gave him a you've-got-to-be-kidding look.

By the time John had tended the horses Gracie was asleep. Evidently the chill had passed and her exhaustion had given way to blessed slumber. As soon as he finished a cold supper he built a small campfire so they could see what they were doing in case she had more problems during the night. Then he spread his slicker on the ground next to her and eased his lanky frame upon it, being careful not to wake her.

He fought against going to sleep, afraid to lose touch with the reassuring sound of her breathing. But the long ride and agonizing worry had taken their toll, and the next thing he knew he was waking up to the sound of her body stirring the pine needles with the throes of another chill.

"Gracie, Gracie," he soothed, tugging at the blankets as if he could pull them snugger than they already were.

"It's all right, J-John. I'm j-just so cold!"

John turned away long enough to stoke the embers of the campfire and pile more brush on them. The heat probably wouldn't reach her, but perhaps the sight of the flames would counteract the bleakness of the night and be of some comfort to her spirit.

"Shiverin' and sweatin' all at the same time,"

he muttered as he returned to kneel beside her.

"F-freezing to death."

John slipped under the blankets and snuggled against her, hoping the warmth of his body would help. "You just hang on Grace; the fever's bound to break before too long." Finally the chill subsided and she was once again released to a merciful slumber. And so it went on into the night, with John sleeping when she slept and awakening at the onslaught of each feverish chill to hold her in his warming embrace and reassure her with his consoling words.

When John awoke at break of day he realized it had been some time since the last shivering go-round, and took it as a good sign. His attempt to ease himself away from her side without interrupting her rest was not successful and upon awakening she confirmed that the fever had broken. John fetched her canteen and she found that she was able to keep a little water in her stomach. Encouraged by that success, she insisted she was ready to move on.

Grace staggered several times as she prepared to leave and John had no confidence that she could stay in the saddle for very long. Yet he did not wish to remain where they were. Grace needed to be somewhere she could rest and be fed properly so as to regain her strength. He transferred his baggage to the sorrel and tied a lead rope from the sorrel's neck to the appaloosa's tail. Then he lifted Grace to his saddle and mounted behind her so as to support her swaying torso as they wended their way up the canyon to the log house of the Shattuck family ranch.

It was past noon by the time they rode up to the ranch house. Ned Shattuck was picking his teeth with a dried-out snake fang when he stepped out the door to greet them. "Hush!" he shouted at the pair of black and tan hounds that had announced their arrival. "I thought they'd treed a rattler or something," he said to John.

"Y'all just missed dinner time, but I reckon Aunt Pop can rustle you a little something to line the ol' flue pipe," he added, referring to his mother's old maid sister who lived with them. "Light down, John, Miss Porter. Y'all come on in out of the sun. I'll get Dolph to see to your horses."

There was a quizzical expression upon Ned's face and John knew he was wondering why they were riding double on the one horse and leading the other. More than that, he was wondering what had brought them to his doorstep and where they were going. But Ned wouldn't ask any questions unless John first volunteered an explanation. Shattuck hospitality did not depend on knowing their guest's business.

"Much obliged, Ned." John dismounted and assisted Grace to the ground. "Grace took a fever on the trail. It's done broke, but she's not been able to eat anything and she's awful weak." He continued to support her as she proceeded to the house on unsteady legs.

"Poor child!" said Aunt Pop from the doorway where she'd been watching and listening. "I *thought* she looked almighty peaky." She bustled past Ned and took charge of Grace. "Let's get you in the house and cleaned up and put to bed. Aunt Pop'll boil you up a pot of chicken broth. Best thing there is for dehydration. Randolph, you fetch me a bucket of water as soon as you've seen to the horses," she said to Dolph, who was on his way to take charge of the mounts.

Ned gestured for John to follow the women into the house. "Seein's how Aunt Pop's got a patient you'll have to look to me to rustle you some grub. Hope you don't mind cold biscuits and leftover beef."

"That'll be fine and dandy, Ned. Much obliged. I take it your folks've not made it back from Seven Rivers yet."

Ned followed him inside and gestured for him to take a seat at the table. "Not yet," he affirmed. "They had some business to attend in Eddy, also. Prob'ly decided to do it all in one trip and be done with it."

When John had been served Ned took a chair on the other side of the table, observing him with an expression of mild amusement. "I'd say it's been a spell since your last meal," he commented with a chuckle. "You're packin' it away like a owlhoot on the dodge."

The comment was as close to a direct inquiry as Ned would make.

"We don't aim to cause you any trouble,

Ned," said John around a mouthful of beef and biscuit. He paused to chew and swallow. "There's no wants on me and I don't believe anybody's on our trail." John forked up another mouthful of beef.

Ned studied him for a few moments, then crossed his legs and contemplated the toe of his boot. "I reckon the girl's almighty wanted," he said quietly, "by her folks."

John carefully set his fork down and leaned back in the chair. "Ned, believe you me, I wish to God she was with her folks. I'd take her there myself. But she's got notions of her own, and —"

"And she's gonna have to *change* her notion," interrupted Aunt Pop, coming into the kitchen from the room where she'd put Grace. "She insists she'll be ready to travel once she's had a little nap and something to eat but I told her she needs several days in bed to convalesce and she'd gonna get it if I have to *sit* on her to keep her there!"

"Once Auntie captures a patient she don't like to give 'em up," said Ned with a wry grin.

"She finally agreed to stay put," continued Aunt Pop, "on one condition. John, she wants you to go on to wherever you two were going and fetch that Bledsoe boy back here, *pronto!*"

As soon as John finished eating he reaffirmed his gratitude to the Shattuck household and went to the bedroom for a final parley with Grace before riding on to the hideout to get Wally.

Chapter Thirty

John lounged on his sleeping bag thinking back on the old times. Wally still hadn't returned. John's eyelids began to feel heavy and he started to drift off to slumber again. A sudden thought startled him to wakefulness.

What if he died in his sleep? Maybe he should have tried climbing to the ledge today instead of waiting until tomorrow. Even with all the rest he could tell he was getting weaker and weaker instead of stronger. The ride up the mountain had just about taken all of what little strength he'd had left.

Well, it was too late to do anything today. He'd just have to hope he could make it through the night and manage to get up there tomorrow. Wally had promised to help. "I never took to climbing like you did, but I ain't scared of heights," he'd said. "We've got ropes on the saddles and I'll climb along beside you, or behind you, and do anything I can to get you up there."

"I know you will, Wallace," John had answered. "For all these years, even though you wasn't around, I've always thought of you as my best friend ever. When I sent you that letter I knowed I could depend on you."

Wally had looked away, and when he answered his tone was subdued. "It's the least I could do now, considerin' all the times I *didn't* do what I was asked."

"I *can't* go to Shattuck's right now, John." Wally averted his eyes from John's disbelieving glare. "I've gotta ride down to Abels' camp to meet Rafer and collect my money for them cows. He won't wait around much longer."

Wally and Speckles had arrived at the hideout only a couple of hours ahead of John. Beasley did not make it. The jarring ride had caused his wound to continue to ooze blood and he became too weak to stay in the saddle without assitance. Soon after they'd found a suitable place to hole up he lost consciousness and never regained it.

Beasley died slowly and by the time Wally and Speckles buried him and rode on to camp Rafer McDaniel had already packed his possibles and ridden down to Abels' camp in the canyon. He left word with Silverthorne that he would pass a few days with Abels before jumping the border and Wally could come down and collect his money if he made it back to the hideout.

John wagged his head dismally as Wally explained the situation. " 'Tisn't *that* much money, Wallace. And Gracie's gonna be *some* disappointed if you don't show up tomorrow. Why don't we just pack our stuff on Beasley's pony and go fetch her and cut across through El

Paso Gap and on west to Arizona?"

"Gotta get that *dinero,* John. We're gonna need it. It's bad enough we've got to leave without our cows. I can go see Rafer and be back on the mount'in and over to Shattuck's before Gracie's able to travel, anyhow. Why don't you ride back over there tomorrow and explain it to her for me?"

John considered for a moment. He knew Wally's mind was set. There was no use trying to dissuade him from riding down to the goat camp. And he'd promised Grace if she would stay put until she regained her strength he'd see to it that Wally made it to the Shattuck cabin safe and sound.

"No, I reckon not," John replied. "I know you can take care of yourself, Wallace, but the last thing Gracie asked me was to see that you didn't get into any more trouble, so I'll just tag along with you tomorrow if you don't mind."

"Whatever tickles yer fancy," said Wally indifferently. "Let's go see if Silverthorne's got any venison to go with our *frijoles* this evenin'."

He did, and he shared his cookfire with John and Wally and Speckles. "I suppose you'll be departing for Mr. Abels' camp in the morning," he said to Wally after they'd taken the edge off their respective appetites.

"Yeah," Wally affirmed with a swallow, "John's going down with me to see I don't get tangled up in that li'l *mexicana*'s blanket."

John stopped a forkful of beans en route to his

mouth and gave Wally a surprised look. "I hadn't even thought about that!"

"Well, you said Gracie told you to keep me out of trouble," responded Wally with a humorous wink.

Speckles chuckled and dropped his fork upon his empty plate. "Won't be no trouble if Miss Grace don't find out. You'd best leave ol' John on the mount'in, Choctaw."

Wally and Speckles joined in a laugh, but Silverthorne's face remained serious.

John shot the jovial pair a look of mock incredulity and stuffed the beans into his mouth. Then he noticed Silverthorne's pensive expression. "Whatzamatter, Silverthorne?" he asked as he chewed.

Silverthorne put a hand to his jaw. "Oh, nothing probably. It just seems that McDaniel could've left Wallace's money with me. He knows he could trust me. He knows I have no use for cash."

"Why shore," said Speckles, still grinning. "Rafer understands that. But he's thinking maybe that posse already met up with Choctaw before they run into us. Or they might catch up to him afterwards, before he could get back to the mount'in. He wouldn't want that money to be wasted if it so happened that Choc didn't come back," explained the freckled youth, his grin spreading. "And Rafer's got plenty of use for cash!"

"Perhaps it's as you say," rejoined Silverthorne. "But I've never subscribed to the 'honor among thieves' cliché."

Wally slammed his plate against the ground. "I ain't no thief!" he exclaimed. "I've just been claiming what's rightful mine!" The color rose in his face and he glared at Silverthorne with fiery eyes.

Silverthorne continued to rub his whiskers contemplatively and returned Wally's gaze with his usual phlegmatic expression. He did not rise to the challenge nor did he speak a word to retract or explain.

John moved to break the sudden silence, tossing the dregs from his cup into the flames. "Well, we've got a long way to go tomorrow and we'd best spread the soogans so's we can get a early start."

He commenced scouring his plate with sand and Speckles followed his cue. Wally slowly lowered his sullen black eyes to the cleaning of his own utensils. Not another word was spoken as they deposited their eating tools in the wreckpan and drifted off into the darkness, each one to his bedroll.

John and Wally arose with the first gray light of dawn and made ready to undertake the long ride to the goat camp.

"Silverthorne's already up and gone," observed John as he prepared a greasysack from the previous night's leftovers.

"Maybe I hurt his feelings last night," Wally dryly commented.

"No, I think it was the other way around," quipped John. "I've never seen Silverthorne ruffle his feathers over anything."

"You can't never tell what he's thinking if he don't want you to, just like a damn Injun." Wally inclined his head and spat upon a stone. "I think he lived with them Apaches too long."

"I 'spect living with the Injuns has a lot to do with the way he is," agreed John, "but from the little bit he's told me about hisself I think it also has to do with something that happened to him just before he came to the mount'ins to live."

Wally turned away to mount the black. "Well, you're the onliest one of the bunch he ever had much to say to," he said as he settled in the saddle. "He wasn't worried about me having to go to the goat camp fer the money 'til he found out you was going with me."

John mounted and followed Wally out of camp. "I wonder where he took off to so early."

By the time they rode out of the timber and onto the rocky barrens of Lonesome Ridge the sun was climbing rapidly in the midmorning sky. They stopped to rest the horses and have a few pulls on their canteens, then continued along the ridge, pausing occasionally to peer into the depths wherever the trail skirted the rim of the deep canyon on the south side of the ridge. This was the north fork of the canyon in which Abels and Emelda resided and their camp was on the other side of the ridge that divided the north fork from the middle canyon. It wasn't very far as the crow flies, but the riders were obliged to follow the trail the length of Lonesome Ridge before they could descend to the lower elevations. Then, to reach the goat camp they would make their way up the bottom of the middle canyon in the general direction from which they'd come.

When they came to where the trail dropped abruptly off the rimrock they dismounted to eat and to rest the horses before undertaking the perilous descent. John took out the telescope and studied the rugged terrain that sprawled out from the base of the escarpment into the purple mists of the distant horizon.

"I see something moving off to the east of the XT headquarters," he announced.

Wally bit a mouthful of cold venison off the chunk in his right hand and reached for the scope with his left. He put it to his eye, chewing vigorously as he focused on the area John had indicated. "Yep," he said with a swallow, "I see 'em. Can't tell much about 'em. Ain't likely loose horses would be moving that fast and deliberate in the heat of the day."

"Men a-horseback," concluded John with an affirmative nod. "Betcha it's a posse."

"Tallies," agreed Wally, handing the glass back to John. "If it's Harkey's posse they're prob'ly using the XT for a base of operations. If it's Ben and his bounty hunters, he's just riding by to see if Holderman's seen or heard anything. Either way they'll be scoutin' up these here canyons purty soon. Manana, most likely; no later'n the day after. We best git down yonder and git out, *pronto!*"

"They might head this way soon as they've had their dinner," John gravely commented. He made sure Wally was looking at him before he continued. "Wally, it's not *that* much money. Let's hightail it back up the ridge, fetch Grace, and quit this part of the country before it's too late!"

"Naw," responded Wally with a wag of his head, "they'll wait 'til they can get a early start before they go to searchin' the canyons. We got time." This time Wally made sure John was looking at him. "But I ain't got a noose on you, you know. You can go fetch Grace and wait for me at the hideout, if you've a mind to."

John breathed a sigh and slumped his shoulders. "No, I reckon I'm in for the go-round."

"If you're really worried about that posse showin' up today you should stick that old pistol in your britches when you go to put the glass away."

John followed the suggestion, just to show Wally he was genuinely concerned. He mounted, took a moment to adjust the pistol to as comfortable a position as possible behind the waistband, and reined the appaloosa to follow the black off the rimrock.

Chapter Thirty-One

Wally finally hove into view and walked up to where John was resting. A bemused frown creased his brow. He squatted down next to John. "John, that feller we seen back there working cows, I reckon he owns the Bar BX now?"

John nodded. "Him and his mother."

"I sure hope he didn't take after his grand-paw."

"Him and old Ben didn't even get along very good, from what I hear tell. No, I've had dealings with that boy and he's *bien gente.* Now that Ben's gone I'll have to say the whole family's good, upstanding folks. They even go to church most every Sunday morning, if that means anything."

John sought to break Wally's pensive mood. "Find any more rusty horseshoes, pard?"

Wally chuckled. "Naw I didn't see no more of your leavin's around here nowhere, John."

"Well, I reckon old horseshoes ain't worth much anyhow. Now I did leave something in the brush down yonder in Big Canyon that would be worth something nowadays — a *real* antique."

"You mean that old Patterson cap-and-ball pistol?"

John must have repositioned the old Patterson a hundred times by the time they sighted the rocky spire of the canyon wall that overlooked the goat camp. "I betcha little Melda's up there with a glass on us right now," he said, raising his eyes to the heights.

"Prob'ly already on the way down to tell Abels and McDaniel she's seen us coming," guessed Wally.

"You better hope Rafer hasn't already flew the coop."

"Now that would be *some* disappointin'." Wally nudged the black to a faster pace along the rocky wash of the canyon bottom.

The appaloosa moved to keep up without any encouragement from John and before long they'd climbed to the bench below the spire and breasted through the brush to rein up in the clearing before Abels' lean-to. The tarpaulin sheet which served as a front wall for the lean-to during inclement weather had been lowered. Emelda's dog was bounding about the structure, yelping and trying to find a way inside.

"Seems the onliest one knows we're here is the dog," said Wally, looking all about. His eyes came to rest on McDaniel's big sorrel, tied to a tree at the edge of the clearing. The horse was saddled and Rafer's bedroll was tied on behind the cantle. "Looks like I got here just in the nick of time." He swung down from the saddle. "Where's everybody at? I figgered they'd be waiting out here to howdy us."

The dog stopped barking to concentrate on trying to squeeze under the tarp.

"I think I hear somebody scuffling around inside," said John. He dismounted, dropped the reins and leaned against his mount, facing the lean-to with his arms draped around the seat of his saddle.

Wally palmed his gun and started toward the shelter, but held up when McDaniel pushed back a corner of the canvas and stepped out. A sharp kick in the ribs sent the dog rolling and squealing.

"I'd just about give you up," said Rafer, turning his attention from the dog to Wally with a bright smile. "Stone," he added with a nod in John's direction.

The dog regained its feet and rushed inside the lean-to, almost tripping Abels, who'd appeared at the opening behind Rafer. " 'Light and set, y'all. Glad to see you," Abels greeted them with his yellow-toothed grin.

Wally holstered the Peacemaker, put his hands on his hips and cocked his head as Rafer strode toward him. "What y'all doing in there, taking one of them Navajo sweat baths, or what?"

"Naw," replied Abels, "we got Melda in here. She's done took a chill and we dropped the tarp to keep the air off her." He remained in the makeshift doorway, the right side of his body obscured by the canvas flap.

Emelda's sickness would explain why the

camp was not forewarned of John and Wally's arrival. John wondered if it was the same malady which had afflicted Grace. "Get your dinero and let's get out of here," he muttered to Wally.

Rafer extended his right hand as he approached Wally. "I didn't rightly know if I'd ever lay eyes on you again, Choctaw; I'm glad to see you slipped by that posse. I reckon Silverthorne told you what happened to us after y'all pulled out for Malaga."

Wally ignored Rafer's hand. "Yeah, he told me what you told him. And Speckles told us the rest. Beasley won't never tell nobody nothing again. You shouldn't of run out on 'em, Rafer."

"Hell, Choc, what was I to do? I had them lawmen pinned down for 'em. All they had to do was keep 'em thataway till dark and slip away just like I done. 'Tain't my fault if they got panicky and tried to rabbit." Rafer gestured for Wally to shake his hand. "No hard feelin's?"

Wally kept his hands on his hips. "You knowed they'd rabbit. You shouldn't of run out on 'em," he stubbornly persisted. "Just give me my cut and we can both ride on out of here." He glanced at the saddled sorrel, indicating that he knew Rafer was about to depart with his money.

Rafer raised his right hand, looking at it and wagging his head disappointedly. "I was hoping we could say adios like amigos, Choctaw. But if you're gonna be mule-headed about it, I got your share of the take right here in my shirt pocket." With a flourish he stuck the fingers of his right hand into his shirt pocket and extracted a roll of bills.

John released his grip on the saddle. *If Rafer had given up on Wally and was fixin' to ride out, how come he's got Wally's cut all counted out and separated in his shirt pocket? And he's making a show of that right hand, same as he did with the coffee cup when he challenged Wally at the roundup last year! Rafer's a lefty!*

Wally reached for the roll of bills.

"Watch him Wally!"

The warning was too late. Rafer dropped the money, grasped Wally's gun hand and drew his pistol. Wally tried to wrench away from McDaniel but the gunman's grip held firm and he stepped against Wally and brought his gun up.

John heard Rafer's pistol explode against Wally's body and saw Abels unlimber his carbine from behind the canvas. John's eyes flared wide as the rifle barrel swung to his direction and he suddenly remembered the pistol at his waist. Desperately he clawed the old gun out, grabbed it with both hands and cocked it as the appaloosa shied and bolted away, giving Abels a clear target. John saw the outline of Abels' body beyond the pistol's front sight and pulled the trigger. Abels fired at the the same time, but the plunging horse had made him hesitate and the slug whined past John's left ear. In an instant John saw the shocked expression on Abels' face, saw him sink to his knees and topple over on his face, and swung the sights of the old Patterson to search for another target.

McDaniel was sprinting to his horse. He jerked the reins loose and vaulted into the saddle. John aimed the pistol, but hesitated to pull the trigger and Rafer spurred the sorrel into the brush and out of sight.

"Let him go," said Wally. "I've got the money. Maybe the posse'll get him before he can make it to Texas."

John lowered the pistol. "Wallace! Are you bad shot?"

"Naw, I don't think so. He'd of got me dead center if you hadn't hollered, but I got a hand on his iron about the same time he went to pull the trigger." Wally was clasping his left side with his right hand and holding McDaniel's gun by the barrel with his left.

"You took his gun away from him! No wonder he vamoosed. How'd you do it?"

"Don't rightly know. Must've grabbed it just when he let go the trigger or something. Maybe he was thinking too hard about holding on to my gun hand."

A grunt from Abels attracted John's attention and he went over to the old man, kneeled down, and gently rolled him over on his back. "Thank God you're not dead."

The ball had struck Abels in the right side rib cage, just below the pectoral muscle. His blue eyes gleamed with tears as he steeled himself against the pain and opened his mouth to speak.

" 'Twasn't my idea, I swear it." He raised his eyes to Wally, who'd walked up behind John. "I'm glad he didn't get you, Choctaw."

Wally looked as if he would spit on him. "Th' hell you are."

"I swear, Choc. He'd of killed me if I hadn't gone along with him. He wanted that-there bounty, but he couldn't go collect it hisself."

"How come he couldn't?" John wondered.

"He figgers they's a description out on him for one of the rustlers. He said that-there posse got a good look at him."

Wally nodded his comprehension. "So you was gonna haul the carcass in for collection. How much was *you* gonna get? Fifty percent?"

"Wasn't gonna take nothing, Choc, I swear. I's just trying to save my hide. And Melda's." Abels clenched his teeth and shut his eyes against the pain.

John stood up and stuck the pistol in his pants. "Well, let me see if there's anything around here we can use for doctoring you two. What say, Abels, you got any medical supplies?"

"Nothing much," Abels managed to reply. "Inside. Untie Melda and she'll show you."

"Untie?" John's questioning expression quickly changed to one of realization. "So that's what the dog was so excited about. She ain't sick, she *did* tell y'all we were coming but she caught on to what you was up to and you had to tie her up and gag her to keep her out of it."

Wally nodded at the revelation. "Thanks to

her you wasn't quite ready for us when we rode up."

John picked up Abels' carbine and carried it into the lean-to. He propped it up against a wall and turned to face the growling dog crouching between him and the cot to which Emelda was bound. From the look in her eyes he knew Emelda was pleading with him not to hurt her dog.

"*Now* what am I gonna do?"

"Perhaps I can help," suggested a voice just behind him.

John thought he would jump out of his skin. "Silverthorne! Where'd you come from?"

"Sorry I didn't get here sooner, John. I found my way to the head of the canyon in the dark, but I had to wait for daylight to climb down the cliffs and I just wasn't able to make it this far before the shooting started."

Wally had followed Silverthorne inside. "You clumb down the wall of the canyon?" he asked incredulously.

Silverthorne nodded and turned his attention to the dog. He began to console the animal in a low, reassuring tone and it wasn't long before the dog quieted down and ventured over to lick his extended hand. Silverthorne petted the dog on the head to seal their friendship and was allowed to approach the cot. In a flash he pulled his knife and severed the ropes.

The dog bounded into Emelda's lap as soon as she sat up. She brushed the ropes aside and hugged her pet while Silverthorne removed the gag. Then her eyes sought Wally. *"Ay, Walito! Estas sangrando!"* She released the dog and vacated the cot. "*Acuestate!* You lay down!"

John looked at Wally. "You'd best do like she says. You *are* bleeding purty bad!"

Wally's face turned pale when he lifted his hand and saw the amount of blood that saturated his clothing. He staggered a little as he made for the cot. Emelda helped him to sit down and removed his bloody shirt.

John began rolling the canvas up to allow the air and sunlight to circulate within the lean-to while Emelda showed Silverthorne the scanty supply of emergency medical supplies Abels kept on hand.

"There's not very much here I can use," he said, "except these clean rags. Pull down those cobwebs." He gestured at the ceiling. "They'll help staunch the flow of blood."

"La tela de araña," explained John when he saw that Emelda didn't understand "cobwebs." As soon as he got the tarp tied off he began pulling the cobwebs off the highest part of the ceiling while Emelda concentrated on those within her reach.

They delivered their harvest to Silverthorne. "I don't believe the bullet ruptured an intestine," he commented as he worked. "And it went all the way through. In one respect the bleeding is a good thing, because it has cleansed the wound, which minimizes the chances of infection. On the other hand, we don't want him to lose any more blood."

John and Emelda were listening intently to Silverthorne's evaluation, and so was Wally. "I'm much obliged to you, Silverthorne," he said. "And I'm plumb tickled you're here. But how come you to show up down here, anyways?"

Silverthorne didn't answer right away. He packed the last of the cobwebs into the wound and reached for a jar of ointment he'd selected from Abels' medicine kit. "Well, let's just say I've had some experience with that old goatherd's brand of treachery." He glanced at Abels and a look of contempt briefly flashed across his features.

John followed Silverthorne's glance. Abels was lying on his back outside the lean-to just as he'd left him, his eyes squeezed shut in his pain-distorted face, his chest heaving with the labor of his breathing.

"You *will* try to help him, won't you?" It sounded more like a plea than a question.

Silverthorne gestured for Wally to lift his arms and began to bind his midsection with the rags. "Now *that* would be an antithesis, wouldn't it?" he responded, as if talking to himself. "The exact opposite of the rule of 'eye for eye and tooth for tooth'." He finished tying the bandages and looked at John. "Yes, I'll see what I can do for him."

Wally eased back onto the cot. Emelda brought him Abels' spare shirt and knelt beside him to wipe his brow and console him with soothing words of Spanish. John followed Silverthorne out to see about Abels.

Silverthorne went to his knees, took one look at the bloody hole in Abels' rib box and raised his face to within a few inches of Abels' face. Abels felt Silverthorne's breath upon his cheek and opened his eyes. Just a squint at first, then they flared wide and glistened with fear.

"Didn't expect to see me again, did you, old timer?" An impish smile spread across Silverthorne's face.

"Not this side o' hell," muttered Abels. "Thought I buried you up in the Capitans."

"I guess you did, if you call throwing a little dirt and brush on a body a burying."

Abels looked away from Silverthorne's accusing gaze. " 'Pears to me 'twas good for you that I didn't do too much to save yer carcass from the wolves and the buzzards."

Silverthorne smiled pleasantly and rose to his feet. "Well, I promise to do much better for you. Free of charge. There's nothing on *your* carcass worth taking." He brushed the dust from his trousers and turned away.

John grabbed him by the shirtsleeve. "Ain'tcha gonna help him, Silverthorne? You said you would." He couldn't control the tremor in his voice.

"There's nothing I can do for him, John. You see how black the blood is? He's shot through the liver."

John stared dumbly at the dark stain on Abels' shirtfront.

Silverthorne gently patted John's hand and removed it from his sleeve. "I'm sorry, John, I'm truly sorry. I understand what you're feeling. When you stop reacting that way to the death of a fellow human you're in trouble. This, too, I know from experience." He moved away to catch up the horses.

Abels started an ironic laugh, then choked it off with a cough. "Killed by a kid who don't even tote a gun. Leastwise, I didn't think he did."

John looked at the pistol in his waistband. He jerked it out and held it before him. His hand trembled and his face contorted as if he were holding a handful of stinking feces.

Abels squinted at the pistol. "That old relic? *That's* what you done me in with? Well, I swanny!" Again there was a choking laugh of irony.

John remembered the pealing cackles that had once reverberated within the walls of the canyon, and across the dark waters of the Pecos on the night Abels had first ridiculed the old Patterson.

"Aw, Abels, why did you hafta go and —"

The red-rimmed blue eyes still stared back at him, but they no longer glistened with perception.

John flung the pistol as far away from him as he could possibly throw it.

Chapter Thirty-Two

"We'd best get back to the truck before it gets too dark." Winston reined his horse around. Their camping supplies and the rest of their provisions were in the truck.

O.C. was quick to follow. "Every time I swaller, my stomach says 'thank you'." He kicked the bay into a trot.

Winston's buckskin quickened its pace to stay ahead of the bay, but Winston held him in a moment to be sure he had a fix on their bearings. "We'll come back here and start looking for a sign again tomorrow at daylight."

The light of a new day found John and Wally wending their way out of the canyon, with Emelda following on Abels' mule. Emelda's dog, Chico, brought up the rear.

Silverthorne warned Wally that his wound needed much more than one night's healing before he attempted to ride, but under the circumstances they had no choice. They had to get out of the canyon before the search parties came. Silverthorne chose to leave the canyon in the same way he'd come down, and refused John's offer to ride double back to the hideaway.

The party approached the mouth of the canyon with due caution. John scouted ahead, scanning the horizon with the telescope and motioning the others forward when he saw no movement upon the land. Leaving the canyon, they turned to the north and picked up the ancient trail to the rimrock. They gained the ridge without mishap and dismounted to breathe their mounts and have a go at their canteens.

John took out the spyglass and perused the country below. "I see 'em now," he announced. "Looks like a buncha ants swarmin' out of a stomped-on anthill. I betcha Ben's crew and Harkey's posse have joined up to make a sweep of the countryside. They're definitely headed our way."

"Well, if they catch us that bounty's gonna spread a mite thin, I'd say." Wally eased himself to a seated position upon a rock and Emelda rushed to his side and began tugging the shirttail out of his pants in order to check his wound.

John lowered the glass and returned it to the saddlebag. "Ben's most likely promised every one of 'em something if you're caught," he guessed. "Prob'ly offering a sizeable bonus to the ones that actually nail you."

Emelda uttered a small *"ay"* and John went over to have a look. The brightness of fresh blood showed upon the bandages. "We gotta get you back to the *rincónada,* amigo! Let's mount up."

Wally stood up and stuffed his shirttail back. "It's just oozing a little. I'll make it all right."

"If it don't get any worse," agreed John. He mounted and took another look at the country below, but without the scope he couldn't see the hunters. "*Durn,* they'll be a-climbing up the mountain before you know it," he prophesied.

Chico trotted to the rimrock and let go a few yips as if he understood the situation.

Wally carefully mounted the black, with Emelda standing by until he was in the saddle before she went for the mule. "It'll be a spell before they get around to coming up here," he opined, "but let's get a move on." He rode ahead, taking the lead away from John.

The sun was high and hot by the time Wally called a halt for another water break. Before them the trail dipped into a shallow saddle and looped over to the edge of the sheer cliff of the canyon, then climbed out of the swale and disappeared into a thick stand of young pine trees.

John didn't realize how hungry he was until he'd quenched his thirst. "We could shade up over yonder and open our greasysack," he suggested.

Wally tilted his hatbrim and studied the coppice. "I dunno, them trees is so thick they won't allow much of a breeze. It might be cooler out in the open." He punched the cork back into his canteen with the heel of his hand and nudged his horse forward. "We'll see."

As they rode past the rim of the canyon John gazed down at the thick vegetation that choked the bottom of the gorge. With the telescope emerald pools of spring water could be seen here and there among the trees and brush, but they were not visible to the naked eye. “Better not get too close, Chico,” he said to the dog. “The wind’s liable to suck your fuzzy carcass right off the rimrock and it’s a long, long way to the bottom.”

Chico released a couple of yips into the void and scampered up the trail ahead of the horses.

Wally watched the dog for a distance and turned to John with a grin. “Seems the ol’ dog agrees with you about that there shade. He sure is anxious to git on up yonder.”

John responded with a chuckle and looked ahead for Chico. The dog had disappeared. “I reckon he’s already flopped hisself down under a tree to wait on us.”

Wally lifted his reins. “Hold up a minute.” He stood up in the stirrups, pressing a hand to his wound and cocking an ear to the direction of the trees. “Now what’s he barkin’ at?”

The barking ended with a sharp yelp and Chico burst from the foliage and scurried toward them with his tail between his legs and an anxious look over his shoulder.

“That could spell trouble, Wally,” John warned. “We best turn tail!”

The warning was wasted on Wally for he was already reining the black. John pulled his mount off the narrow trail and let him pass with a “hi-yah!” to spur the animal’s retreat, but Emelda did not react so quickly. Wally reined his plunging horse aside to avoid a collision with the mule and spurred on across the brush and rocks along the edge of the cliff, leaving the trail to John and Emelda. John held the appaloosa behind the mule in order to make sure Emelda escaped with them. He heard the report of a thirty-thirty rifle at the same time he saw the black stumble, but instantly he realized the sound had come too close upon the fall of the horse for the shot to have caused the spill.

Wally was thrown headlong over his horse's neck and barely escaped the crushing force of the black's hurtling body when it crashed to the ground alongside him. Instinctively he scrambled to his feet and twisted away from the panicky beast as it also tried to rise. Somehow the black managed to lift itself from the ground, but when its weight came down upon the broken bone in the shank of its right foreleg it collapsed upon the rocks with a pitiful squall and began kicking and writhing. Wally staggered after his fallen mount as if he was in a stupor.

John pulled the appaloosa to a skidding stop, vaulted from the saddle and hit the ground running. *"No! Hold up, Wally! Stop!"*

Wally grabbed at the black just as the animal's agonizing contortions hurled it over the rim of the canyon.

"Oh, no!"

Chapter Thirty-Three

At the same time Winston Brittain and O. C. Kirkes regained the place where they'd lost the trail the day before, John Stonecipher was making another tardy exit from his sleeping bag a few miles away.

John hadn't slept well. His mind had been too occupied with anticipation for the coming day and too afraid that he might not make it through the night. Exhaustion had finally brought soundness to his sleep just when it was time for country folks to be waking up.

He was thankful for one more day. That's all he needed to do what he'd set out to do.

Wally had stayed by the campfire this morning. "Ready for a cup of coffee, pard?"

"Don't mind if I do," said John, fumbling in his shirt pocket for his eyeglasses. When he got them on he took a deep breath and gazed all about, taking in all the smells and colors of the mountain hideaway.

Wally lifted the fire-blackened coffee pot off the flames, watching John from the corner of his eye. "Hard to leave it all behind, ain't it?"

"At least I got a last look at it, thanks to you." John's gaze came to rest on the ledge. "Now if I can just get up yonder without falling and breaking my neck —"

"I won't let you fall, pard. No more'n you let me fall, seventy some years ago."

John vaulted over the rocks and brush and dashed toward Wally. Too late! The black horse disappeared beyond the brink. Miraculously, Wally missed his grab and maintained his balance. He was standing on the rimrock, his body swaying as he stared into the chasm with a look of stunned disbelief. He flinched when John's hand grabbed his arm, but John anticipated the reaction and pulled him away from the precipice with an iron grip.

Emelda jumped off the mule and ran toward them, the dog at her heels.

"My . . . my horse, John . . . he . . ." stammered Wally.

"I know, Wallace, I know," said John consolingly as he guided Wally toward the appaloosa. "Just be glad you're not down there with him. *Durn!* Your wound's bleeding again. The blood's soaked through your shirt." He could tell that Wally wasn't comprehending. Although he was on his feet, he'd been knocked senseless by the spill. There was a huge welt on his forehead.

Wally's hat was on the ground immediately before them, so John bent over to reach for it with his free hand. That's when he became aware of the hoofbeats. He cocked his head and observed Rafer McDaniel riding up to them on his big sorrel, the thirty-thirty pointed at them across his saddle bow.

"Ah-ah! Hold it right there, Stone!" McDaniel lifted the rifle.

John froze the motion of his hand toward Wally's Peacemaker, then slowly moved it on to his original objective. He straightened up and gently set the hat upon Wally's head.

"You! Melda!" said Rafer with a slight gesture of the rifle barrel. "Git over there with 'em."

When Emelda had taken her place alongside Wally, Rafer dropped the reins, lifted his left leg over the sorrel's neck and slid off the saddle facing the three with his eyes and rifle always on them. "Well, Stone, I'm obliged to you," he said with a taunting smile. "You saved the golden goose for me. 'Twould've been a unpleasant chore if I'd had to go down yonder and scrape his carcass off the bottom of the canyon."

Chico slinked out of the brush and took up a position behind Emelda, teeth bared and a low growl rumbling in his throat.

"Stupid dawg," jeered Rafer. "Damn near boogered up my ambush."

I shoulda got Wally's gun as soon as I got him away from the cliff, thought John, chastising himself. The only thing left for him to do was stall for time and hope for something lucky to happen. "If Wally'd fell, you'd never got 'im, Rafer. There's a posse on the way right now with intentions of searching the canyons."

"If that's so, then I reckon I'm double obliged to you, Stone." Rafer's smile spread even wider. "When they don't find him maybe brother Ben will raise the ante."

"What difference does it make to you?" asked John with a sneer. "Your Judas has played out his hand and run out of chips, in case you was too busy *running* to see what happened to him down yonder when you made your first play. You got no go-between to collect for you."

John's provocation seemed to have no effect on the swarthy gunman. He just kept smiling. "I expect they's others that can be persuaded to do it. Maybe even you, John Stone, if the safety of your green-eyed blond 'lady' was at stake."

John was glad Grace was at the Shattuck's. Or was she? He knew she wouldn't stay put very long. She'd be coming to find out what had happened as soon as she possibly could. "Now you listen here, McDaniel —"

"No, *you* listen, both of you." The smile finally faded from the outlaw's lips and he focused on Wally. "*Choctaw,* what did you do with my six-gun?"

To this point Wally had been oblivious to the conversation, but he seemed to understand that Rafer was now speaking directly to him and fixed a scowling gaze upon his adversary. Still he said nothing.

"I reckon he left it in the lean-to," John volunteered, "like I did with Abels' carbine."

"Seems to me you boys don't look to yer weapons none too good." The taunting smile reclaimed Rafer's lips. "Only one sidearm left between you. I reckon I'd best take charge of that-un before you do something foolish with it, too. Melda, take his gunbelt off him, real careful-like."

"Quítate el cinto con la pistola," John translated to be sure she understood. *"Cuídate!"* He didn't think Wally would stand still for it, but he seemed not to even notice as Emelda removed the gunbelt. He just kept scowling intently at McDaniel as if everything else was beyond his focus now that Rafer had demanded his attention.

The rumble in Chico's throat intensified when Emelda approached McDaniel with the gunbelt.

Rafer balanced the rifle in his left hand and took the shiny Peacemaker from the holster with his right. "Tell her to put the belt on me, Stone."

Emelda moved to place the fancy gunbelt around Rafer's hips without waiting for an interpretation.

"Too bad it's a right-handed rig. But it'll do till I get a chance to put my own belt back on," said Rafer as Emelda fastened the buckle and stepped aside. She flashed a fearful glance at John and Wally, then looked to Rafer to see what he would order her to do next.

John saw the chance for another jibe. "I reckon you shed your own gunbelt 'cause you was afraid somebody'd see you struttin' around with a empty holster and wonder how you lost your iron. You'd be about as comf'table as a duck in a desert, trying to explain how you let a kid take it away from you when you had the drop on 'im."

Rafer's smile diminished, but only slightly. "Choctaw just got lucky, that's all."

"Choctaw?" Wally's chest started heaving, his face turned red and his fiery eyes seemed on the verge of popping out of their sockets.

Rafer took one look at him and shot a nervous glance at John. "You best talk to 'im, Stone, he's done gone plumb loco."

"Cracked his gourd when his horse fell," John explained. "Wallace!" He reaffirmed his grip on Wally's arm. "*Listen* to me, Wallace."

Wally did not vary his outraged stare. He surged forward and John scrambled to get a grip on him with both hands.

Rafer extended the pistol and thumbed back the hammer. Emelda reached to grab his arm but he jammed the rifle barrel into her abdomen with his other hand and knocked her to the ground. Before he could swing the rifle back, thirty pounds of black and white snarling fury shot through the air and attached itself to his forearm. Rafer yelled a curse and dropped the rifle. He tried to sling the dog aside, but Chico held fast his toothy grip.

John saw Rafer turn the pistol toward the dog. He released his grip on Wally and ran with him toward McDaniel. The six-gun roared and Chico fell from Rafer's arm with a horrified squall. Wally slammed into Rafer before he could realign the pistol, knocking him down and falling on top of him. McDaniel's breath exploded from his lungs with a sharp grunt. John pounced on his gunhand, wrenched the Peacemaker from the outlaw's grip and backed away to cover him.

"Let him up, Wally! I got the gun!" John grabbed Wally by the collar with his free hand and dragged him back. Rafer twisted away and tried to scramble out of reach, but Wally jerked free of John's grasp and pounced on the outlaw's back. He grabbed him by the hair and began pounding his face against the rocky turf. *"Choctaw! Choctaw! Choctaw!"* he chanted with each blow.

John set the pistol aside so he could grab Wally in a bearhug and finally tore his hands from Rafer's hair and hauled him away from the prostrated gunman.

"He's beat, Wally. He won't ever call you Choctaw again, I promise. Now settle down!" John felt Wally slowly relax, his terrible, addlebrained fury finally spent.

As soon as John got Wally seated on the ground, he retrieved the pistol and went to Rafer. He kneeled down and laid a finger on his neck. There was no pulse. "My God," said John with a sigh. He stuck the pistol in his belt and sat down on the rocks next to the body and gazed at Wally. "This time you knocked the breath out of 'im for good. *Durn!*" Wally gave John a blank look, then eased his back to the ground and closed his eyes.

John turned his attention to Emelda, who'd recovered sufficiently from the blow to the abdomen to scramble over to where Chico lay. "Melda, you all right? *Estás bien?*" She raised her head and he saw the tears streaming down her cheeks.

" 'Ta muerto el perro?" he guessed.

"Sí," she sniffed and bowed her head and stroked the fur of her faithful companion who'd given his life in her defense.

"Qué lástima," sympathized John with a wag of his head.

"That dog was worth more'n you was," he said to the corpse. "I should leave you to the buzzards." John took a deep breath, let it out in a long sigh, and got to his feet. "I s'pose if I'm gonna throw some rocks on him I'd best quit burnin' daylight." He rolled McDaniel over on his back with the toe of his boot.

"Durn! No wonder you couldn't catch your breath. Wally durn near beat your face off on those rocks!" He straddled the body and bent down to retrieve Wally's gunbelt. "Better get this off you or somebody'll dig you up someday and think you're the Choctaw kid."

The thought froze John's hand as he was about to release the buckle. He contemplated for a moment, then slowly stuffed the billet back through the keeper. He straightened up and looked over at Wally, then back at Rafer. He looked over his shoulder at the rimrock where Wally's black gelding had squirmed over the brink.

John stepped back and grasped Rafer's boots at the ankles and dragged the body to the precipice. A quick search of the pockets revealed nothing that would identify the corpse. John pulled the long-barreled Colt's Peacemaker out of his belt and admired its engraved silver plating and carved mother-of-pearl grips for the last time. Quickly he jammed the fancy pistol into the silver studded holster on Rafer's hips and thumbed the latigo loop over the hammer to secure it. One good push of John's boot was all it took to send the body sailing over the cliff and plummeting down to join the black horse at the bottom of the abyss.

"Y'all show that posse where they're at," said John to the several vultures that soared upon the airy updrafts above the canyon. For a moment he gazed into the distance, as if he could conjure up a vision of the oncoming riders. When he turned away from the rimrock he saw that Emelda had moved to Wally's side and was pulling his shirt up to see how badly he was bleeding.

John piled a mound of stones on Chico's carcass and even fashioned a couple of sticks into a little cross for the grave. It would make Emelda feel better, and after all, it was Chico who'd warned them of the ambush and enabled them to overpower McDaniel. When he walked over to Emelda and Wally she looked at what he'd done and thanked him with an emotional flash of her teary eyes. She helped him get Wally on his feet.

To John's surprise, when they led Wally to Rafer's sorrel he mounted up without any encouragement or assistance. He did not pick up the reins, however, so after retrieving the thirty-thirty and jamming it in the scabbard, John took the reins and mounted the appaloosa. He moved out leading the sorrel. Emelda mounted the mule and followed along.

Wally said not a word all the way back to the hideout. John made him as comfortable as possible in the wickiup, and he and Emelda took turns keeping watch on him all through the night.

Chapter Thirty-Four

John watched Wally pour the cup of coffee for him. It would be his last, one of the many simple pleasures he would never again experience.

Wally passed the steaming cup. "You know, when you mentioned that old Patterson yesterday, it got me thinkin'. Do you reckon they's any chance a-tall my Peacemaker's still down there in the canyon, too?"

John tasted the hot brew before he answered. "Nope. I reckon it's down there at the Bar BX somewhere. The way Harkey told it your brother Ben toted it off along with everything else he could scavenge."

Deputy U.S. Marshall Dee Harkey knew there was no telling what he might be getting into when he decided to commit his posse to Ben Bledsoe's all-out effort to locate the gang of cow thieves that had been plaguing the ranchers of the upper Black River, but he hadn't expected it to include clambering around afoot in the bottom of a canyon. He paused to catch his breath and realized he'd outdistanced the huffing Ben Bledsoe by fifty yards or more. Harkey sat himself upon a boulder and waited for his red-faced companion to catch up. He gazed in awe at the magnificence of the sheer limestone walls that towered above him, and the diversity of trees and bushes that congested the narrow confines along the banks of the canyon's twisting arroyo.

The middle fork of the canyon, which they'd explored the previous day, was much the same. Just beyond the spot where Bledsoe said he and his men had been ambushed several weeks ago, they'd discovered a recently abandoned camp and a fresh grave. There were a few goats in the thickets and upon the slopes about the camp, so Harkey guessed some unfortunate goatherd had been murdered to keep him from describing the rustlers. Could it be the same old goatherd in whose camp he'd found the Choctaw Kid last autumn? If so, he was probably just as guilty as the rustlers themselves.

Harkey cast a disgusted glance at Ben Bledsoe, who stood bent over with his hands on his knees about twenty yards below him on the slope, gasping for breath. Now he knew why the tall, pudgy rancher had wanted to send one of his men up the slope instead of accompanying the marshall himself. But Harkey had insisted that Bledsoe climb with him to inspect the carcass they'd spotted at the base of the cliff where it joined the steep slope. It appeared to be a black horse, and Harkey wanted Bledsoe to be the one to make the identification if it happened to be the one ridden by his half brother.

Bledsoe finally caught his breath and managed

to struggle up to Harkey's position before he had to stop again. He was so bushed that the marshall was afraid he might fall and tumble back down the incline if a stone happened to turn under his boot, so Harkey stayed beside him and set a slower pace for the remainder of the climb to the dead horse.

"Yeah, that's the hoss the half-breed stole from us," Ben blurted between gasps. He was so winded he didn't notice the crumpled human form wedged in a shallow gully not ten yards away, but Harkey did. He climbed over to inspect the body. "Is this your half brother, Bledsoe?"

The rancher's florid face snapped to attention and he scrambled to Harkey's side to gaze at the broken body sprawled grotesquely upon the rocks. "How th' hell should I know? Looks like he lit on his face."

"It appears he bounced off the wall a few times on the way down, all right. Hard to tell what he looked like. The rest of his features match the Kid's description, though." Harkey squatted down and quickly ran his fingers through all the pockets. "All he's got on him is this roll of bills — probably from the sale of some of your cows. But this seems to be the pistol your brother Charlie described." He slipped the thong on the Peacemaker and held it up for Bledsoe's inspection. "And that's definitely the gunbelt George saw the Kid wearing the other day in Malaga."

"I still ain't right sure this here's Wallace.

They's just something about this hombre . . ." he trailed off, unable to explain his doubts.

Harkey's feet were aching in his high-heeled boots and he regretted he'd left his canteen on the saddle. "You know what I think, Bledsoe?" he snapped. "I think you've been hating this boy so long that you just can't bear to let go of it. The evidence is overwhelming, man. They left that camp down yonder in a big hurry, so quick they left a rifle and a pistol in the lean-to. They found out we were coming and they panicked. They fled up the old Indian trail and were riding their horses to the ground along the ridge. You can see that the black horse broke its leg. It went over the rim and this poor misguided young man that lies here dead before us with his face caved in went over the rim with his mount. That's all there is to it and my motivation for being on this chase to begin with has just ended."

"But what about the rest of 'em?"

"Cow thieves aren't my department, Bledsoe. If you want the law to help you run them down, send for your friend Sheriff Kemp. It would be a waste of time, though. I expect what's left of that gang of rustlers is halfway to Mexico by now." Harkey cut his steely eyes at Bledsoe. "You gonna help me cover him up or do you want to carry him home to his mother?"

Ben looked down the slope to where the other possemen waited with the horses. "She maybe could tell for sure if this here's her whelp, but the damn Injun wouldn't say nothing even if she could." He thought about the labor involved in descending the slope with the corpse slung across his shoulders. "Let's plant 'im. But I'm taking that there shiny shootin' iron and the fancy gunbelt, too. And don't let me ferget that carabine on his saddle."

"I reckon they're rightfully yours," said Harkey with a hint of contempt. "He's your brother."

"I still ain't pos'tive about that."

"Well I doubt the Porter girl will stay out here without her beau, so if she comes home now, that should convince you."

On the same morning that Dee Harkey and Ben Bledsoe discovered the battered corpse at the bottom of the north fork of Big Canyon, John Stonecipher prepared himself to break the news about Wallace Bledsoe to Grace Porter. John felt the warmth of the early morning sun on his back as he saddled the appaloosa. It would be well overhead by the time he reached the Shattuck cabin. How was he going to tell Grace what had happened? He'd promised to bring Wally to her safe and sound. He mustn't tell her in front of the others; he'd have to wait until he got her away from Shattuck's. Then he would have to tell her everything.

The appaloosa was feeling good after a bellyful of corn and a night's rest. He tossed his head and swished his tail and shied at shadows on the way out of camp. To make sure John knew how fit he really felt he even crowhopped a few jumps just before they pushed into the fringe of trees that surrounded the mountain hideaway.

By the time they reached the Shattuck's the only tossing and swishing he was doing was at an occasional annoying fly. A short rest accompanied by a loosening of the girth and a drink of cool water was all the respite for the spotted horse, for John only stayed long enough for a noonday meal with the family.

John and Grace expressed their gratitude again upon departing, this time also to Captain and Mrs. Shattuck, who'd finally returned from their business trip to Seven Rivers and Eddy.

As soon as they were on their way Grace turned to John with a furrowed brow. "What in the world were you and Captain Shattuck talking about so seriously when he took you aside just before we left?"

"Aw, nothing much. They just saw my folks in town, is all."

"And?"

John looked away before he answered. "Aw, you know. They want me to come back home before I get too far mixed up in Wally's problems and all. Same old six and seven."

Grace reined the little sorrel to a halt. "I don't believe you're telling me everything."

"What makes you say that?" asked John, lifting his reins.

"I know you pretty good and I think you're hiding something." When she saw that John wasn't going to answer, she continued: "You were hiding something back there at Shattuck's, too! I know you didn't want to say too much in front of them, but you were so vague about where you've been and what you've been doing and why Wally didn't come with you that a body would think something terrible had happened and you didn't want to tell me about it in front of everyone." A glimmer of fear touched her eyes. "Wally's all right, isn't he?"

John's face was somber. "Well, not exactly, no."

Gracie sucked in her breath and the color drained from her face. "What happened, John?"

"Get that old pony moving and I'll tell you all about it on the way back to the *rincónada.*"

John started at the beginning, telling her about Wally's insistence on going to the goat camp for the money McDaniel owed him and the setup they'd walked into when they got there. He didn't waste time on the details of how they'd escaped the trap, and avoided the fact that it was his own shot which had killed Abels. The revulsion he'd felt at having taken the man's life still burned in his gut.

John included all the gory details in his account of what happened on Lonesome Ridge, strongly emphasizing that Wally had been out of his head when he'd done what he did to McDaniel and making it very clear why he disposed of Rafer's remains in the way that he did.

"I left Emelda with Wally this morning, so's I

could come fetch you," said John, concluding his summary of the events of the previous day. "He didn't wake up all night, leastways not enough to where he made any sense. I sure hope he's not perm'nently addled. If anything can be done for him, Silverthorne would know. I was hoping he'd get back before I left, but he must've took a detour to do some hunting or something. Speckles said he'd scout around and see if he could find him, but nobody sees Silverthorne unless he shows hisself on purpose."

To John's surprise, Grace had not interrupted a single time while he told his story. When he finished she continued to ride along in stunned silence.

John bowed his head and rubbed the back of his neck. "I know I let Wally get into a jackpot after I'd promised you —"

"No John," Grace interrupted, "it's not your fault." She bit her lip and blinked at the moisture in her eyes. "Nobody can keep Wally out of trouble, not you, not me, *nobody!*"

John decided to change the tack of the conversation, lest she burst out crying. "Well, now you can understand why I acted like I did back there at Shattuck's. They're gonna hear that Wally's been killed and I want the way I was puttin' on to add up with the news."

Although the ride back to camp must have seemed longer to the tired appaloosa the conversation and the company made the afternoon journey pass much more quickly for John than had the lonely trek of the morning. When they dismounted before the wickiup John took charge of the horses and Gracie hurried inside.

Speckles's red roan was still absent from the horse pasture, but John was relieved to see that Silverthorne had made it back on his own. Speckles would give up his search and return to camp before dark.

Silverthorne approached John with a quizzical look. "What's happened, John? I just got back and I saw that McDaniel's sorrel and the mule were here but not the appaloosa or the black. Before I can investigate you and Miss Porter come riding in. What's Rafer doing here? Where's the black horse?"

"Rafer's dead, Silverthorne; I'll tell you about it later. The black broke a leg and dumped Wally on his gourd and he's been acting crazy ever since, when he's not sleeping. Would you take a look at him?" John left the horses groundhitched and led the way to the wickiup.

When the two men ducked inside, Grace and Emelda moved aside and Silverthorne squatted down to take their place beside Wally. He gingerly examined the huge purple goose egg on his forehead. "From the looks of this contusion and what you said about his conduct after the spill, I expect he's suffered a minor concussion. Has he been sleeping like this most of the day?" Silverthorne looked at Emelda. *"Mucho sueño?"*

"Sí—he sleep—*duerme mucho,"* she replied.

Silverthorne nodded at her affirmation and

shifted his attention to the gunshot wound and began to remove the soiled bandages. He tried to be as gentle as possible, but when the saturated cloth pulled free of the dried blood Wally cried out and his eyes flashed open.

"Where'm I at? What happened?" he asked.

Gracie drew a sharp breath and went to her knees next to Silverthorne. "Oh, Wally, can you hear me?"

Wally turned his head to look at her. "What's goin' on Grace? Why's everybody standing around staring at me?"

Silverthorne smiled and looked up at John. "You'll have to fill him in on most of it. He may remember a thing or two here and there, but not much."

"He's gonna be alright, then?"

"I believe so, if you can keep him quiet for a few days. He needs to remain very still. By no means should he try to ride."

"It don't take a doctor to see that he's in no shape for traveling," John agreed. "I sure hope them bounty chasers took the bait and called off the hunt."

Silverthorne stood up and wadded the soiled bandages. "Bait?" Before John could reply he held up a hand to cut him off. "I've got a feeling this explanation will take awhile and I need to re-dress that gunshot wound as soon as possible, so my curiosity will just have to wait."

"You can tell me, John," said Wally.

Silverthorne promised to return with ointment and fresh bandages and left John to explain to Wally what had happened to him.

Wally absorbed the account with open-eyed amazement, saying very little until John had finished. "Damn! Ol' Ebony's really gone, then." There was a tremor in his voice. "Seems like I woke up knowin' that part of it. I recollect him falling. Not much after that, though. I vaguely recall tussling with Rafe, like it was in a dream. It's hard to believe I killed him."

Grace put a soothing hand on his arm. "You were out of your mind; you didn't know what you were doing."

"Yeah," John agreed, "and besides, if you hadn't started acting crazy we'd most likely never got away from him."

Wally gazed at the roof of the hut. "Do you really think they'll believe I rode Ebony off that cliff? It'll sure enough look like *some*body did. But will they believe it's my carcass in the bottom of that canyon?"

"I don't see how they can tally it any way else," John assured him. "They'll think the head was busted up in the fall. Of course, you can't show your face in these parts ever again, but I reckon you don't have to worry about anybody doggin' your trail after you leave these parts."

"I just wish they was some way I could get my shootin' iron back." Wally continued to stare at the ceiling as he contemplated. "I bet Ben'll fetch it home with him. Unless it come out of the holster and got lost in the canyon. I bet I could find it! If it's not in the canyon I could sneak back to the ranch . . ."

Grace and John exchanged glances. He couldn't tell if it was exasperation or disappointment he detected in her eyes. Both, perhaps.

"Well, I'd best go see to the horses," he said to Wally. "Grace and Melda can keep you company and Silverthorne'll be back in a spell."

Chapter Thirty-Five

About the same time O. C. Kirkes told Winston Brittain he thought he'd caught a faint whiff of woodsmoke on the air, Wallace Bledsoe kicked out the remnants of his campfire and went to get the ropes from the saddles.

John Stonecipher drank the last of his coffee, holding the cup in both hands lest he spill it. From the way he felt, Wally wouldn't have to wait around very long to be sure the mission had reached its ultimate climax. He just hoped he could hold out long enough to get to his chosen resting place. Then he'd be completely satisfied. He'd die happy.

John reached his hand for Wally to help him to his feet. "No sense waitin' any longer. Nothing to it but to do it!"

There wasn't much to do during the days they waited for Wally to recover. John tended to the hooves of the little sorrel and made sure all the animals would be ready to travel. The mule could be used as a pack animal, for the death of Beasley had left them with another mount.

John killed most of one day by riding out upon Lonesome Ridge to assure himself that his ruse had worked. When the spyglass revealed a grave near the dead black horse and no movement upon the lower elevations he returned to camp with an improved sense of security. He rode in to find Grace sitting alone on the bench outside the hut. After seeing to his horse he joined her.

"Well, they buried McDaniel right where he lit. How's Wally doing?"

"He wants to leave in a couple of days." A glimmer of uncertainty seized Gracie's eyes at the thought. "At least you talked him out of going back for the pistol."

"It's a foolish notion, even if he got away with it. If anybody has any doubts about who's buried in that grave, their suspicions would be some agitated when that Peacemaker came up missing. That's the only thing that convinced him not to try for it.

"Well, I reckon I'd best go see what he's got in mind about leaving."

"He's sleeping right now. Emelda's with him."

John raised his brows and cut his eyes at the hut.

A sad smile touched Gracie's lips. "I know what you're thinking. It's plain to see how she feels about him."

"Have you told him about — you know."

"No. No, I haven't. I'll wait till . . . till later."

"When?"

"Oh, I don't know — after we get settled."

"That could be quite a spell, Grace. The baby

might be born before it happens."

Again the look of uncertainty clouded Gracie's features. "Between the two of us we can convince him to settle down to steady work so we can have a home, don't you think so, John?"

When John didn't reply she continued: "Oh, I'll tell him soon, you needn't worry. I know he's gonna have a fit, no matter when I do it, but right now would be the worst time of all. Besides, I'm still not absolutely certain. I'm not used to all the riding and outdoor living and I've lost quite a bit of weight. That sometimes brings about other changes, so I've heard."

At the risk of looking hopeful, John smiled. "I noticed you've been looking a mite lanky."

Gracie chuckled. She always seemed to find humor in the way John expressed himself. "I expect I'll be a mite lankier by the time we get to wherever it is we're going."

Two days later the rising sun promised a torrid day of travel for the three young men and two young women who said their goodbyes and left the mysterious Silverthorne to recapture the serenity of life in his mountain hideaway without the interpose of the problems of others.

When the riders came upon the ancient Indian trail that traversed the backbone of the Guadalupes they eschewed the path to Lonesome Ridge and turned their mounts toward the western rim. Except for John. He reined aside and watched the others pass along.

Grace was the first to realize he was making no move to follow them. She abruptly pulled her horse around. "What's the matter, John, your horse pick up a stone or something?" When John didn't reply she called out to Wally and Speckles: "Something's wrong with John." The three of them spurred their mounts back up the trail, leaving Emelda to look after the pack mule.

"What's the trouble, pardner?" asked Wally when the three reined in before him.

John took a long look down the faint path tracing the way across the rocky terrain toward Lonesome Ridge. "I reckon you could say we've come to a fork in the trail, pardner." He looked at Wally and Grace. "And I'm bound to pull a different rein."

Gracie looked like someone had sneaked up on her and slapped her face when she wasn't expecting it. "You mean you're not going with us, John? *Why?*"

Wally rested his hands on the saddle horn and studied John with an I-might've-known-it expression. "The law's got nothing on him, Grace; why should *he* leave home? He's going back to mammy and pappy."

"Yes, Wallace, I am. But it's not the way you're making it out. It was a hard choice for me and I aimed to make it myself, with nobody giving me advice one way or the other." John's eyes settled on Grace. "That's why I wouldn't tell you all of what Captain Shattuck told me that day I came for you."

"What did he tell you, John?" Gracie's voice was barely audible.

"My paw's in a bad way, Grace. Something to do with his heart. When the Shattucks saw them they was fixin' to go back to the ranch, but the doc's put some tight restrictions on him. I'm obliged to go lend 'em a hand."

"Why certainly, John. We'll just wait for you here in the mountains till you've taken care of things, won't we, Wally?"

Wally gave her a disgusted look. "I ain't hanging around for a sick old man to be wet-nursed back to where he can pull his own freight. John'll just have to try and hunt us up later on."

John slowly wagged his head. "Ma told the Shattucks that Paw won't ever be able to do hard work any more. Somebody's gonna have to run the outfit for him and he can't afford to hire a *mayordomo*. I reckon I'll be at the Circle S from now on."

"So that's it! Got yer own outfit now, so you don't need your friends no more!" Wally spat upon the ground and jerked his mount around. "Let's go to Arizona, Speckles! Come on, Grace!"

The hurt was plain in John's eyes. "That's got nothing to do with it!" He knew there was no use arguing with Wally. He looked at Grace. "*You* don't believe —"

"No, John," she interrupted with a quavering voice, "I know you better than that."

Speckles nudged his pony close enough for a

farewell handshake. "Been good knowin' you, John; *Buena suerte.*" He pulled away to follow Wally.

Grace made no move to leave. She just sat her horse and stared at John. "I'll never see you again, will I?" she sobbed, tears streaming down her cheeks.

John hesitated to answer lest his own voice should break. "I'll never forget you," he managed in a hoarse whisper, fighting back the tears.

Wally pirouetted the big sorrel with a touch of the rein and pulled it to a stop. "You best get on down here if you're going with me, Grace!" he shouted.

Her eyes flickered, then refocused on John. She lifted the reins, but made no move to lay one against her pony's neck.

Suddenly hope welled in John's breast and the sound of his heartbeat thudded in his temples. "There's plenty of room for *both* of us at the Circle S." he heard himself saying, the words sounding as if they were coming from somewhere outside his head.

Gracie closed her eyes and made a quick little negative motion with her head. Her chin slumped to her chest. "Johnny, I couldn't burden you with —"

It was John's turn to interrupt, for he guessed what she was about to say. "Plenty of room for *three* of us, if that be the case."

Wally lifted his hat and reset it with a yank. He was too far away to hear the conversation, but it was obvious that Grace was reluctant to go on without John. Wally regretted he'd sent John to fetch her back to the mountains from Malaga. He suspected something must have happened between them on that trip. "I ain't got all day, Grace," he yelled, "make up yer mind."

Grace lifted her head. Her green eyes glistened with tears, but there was also a glow that hadn't been there before, a shining strength which replaced the uncertainty John had seen in those eyes so often during the past few days. Finally she touched a rein to the horse's neck, but it was after she'd heeled him over to the appaloosa and the motion served to bring her mount around so that the two horses stood side by side facing toward Wally and the others. She raised a hand in farewell and dropped it to her thigh.

"Bitch!" said Wally between his teeth. He snatched the sorrel about and spurred down the trail without a backward glance. Speckles and Emelda had reined up when Wally turned to yell at Grace. Now they hastened after him. Emelda turned in the saddle for a final backward glance. In spite of the distance John could see the flash of her happy smile.

Grace saw it, too. "He'll not want for company," she mumbled.

John could hardly believe she'd chosen to stay with him. He expected that any second she would put the boot heels to her pony's flanks and go galloping after Wally. "I want you to be *sure* about this, Grace. You told me once before that it was too late for second guesses. Well, it *wasn't* too late then. But it's mighty nigh on to it right now."

Grace crowded her pony against the appaloosa and leaned into John's embrace. "There's no guessin' to it, Johnny. Only reality. I love you, John." For the second time her lips touched his, but this time it was more than a fleeting encounter. Much more.

Chapter Thirty-Six

When Winston and O.C. heard the horse whinny it was the only clue they'd had as to the whereabouts of the mysterious riders since O.C.'s whiff of woodsmoke. They'd been searching for hours, but the terrain was too rocky to leave a hoofprint and there were a few cattle in the area, so it was impossible to distinguish whether any disturbance of the ground or the vegetation had been caused by horse or cow. Besides, running a ranch in the modern way provided neither the need nor the opportunity for a man to sharpen his tracking ability.

The dun lifted his head to sound another greeting to the horses he'd heard and smelled a few moments earlier. Now they were in sight at the edge of the clearing.

O.C. followed Winston out of the trees, nudged the bay up beside the buckskin and drew rein. "Dang! I bet we been riding all around this place all day long!"

They sat their horses, taking in the tranquil beauty of the little hideaway.

"One dun horse, no blue roan," Winston quietly commented, breaking the spell.

"Which means one of 'em's done lit a shuck and the other'n's still here. I bet they's a neat little grave around here somewhere."

Winston heaved a sigh. "We'd best check it out. You go around the clearing that way and I'll ride around this direction. Holler if you find anything." He nudged the buckskin into motion.

O.C. held his mount. "Why don't we just let him rest in peace, Win?"

Winston pulled his horse around. "O.C., I can surely understand why old John would want to be laid to rest up here and I wouldn't like it if our investigation should result in the relocation of his body. But I've got my duty to perform."

O.C. continued to hold his mount and scowl at Winston.

"Look, O.C., I don't like it any better than you do." Winston glanced at the sun. "We're gonna run out of daylight if we don't get moving."

"It ain't like you was a *real* lawman, Winston," O.C. persisted.

Winston sighed again, wagged his head and looked hard at O.C. "When I'm on an assignment I have the same authority as a regular deputy sheriff. I'm taking the taxpayer's money and I'll do what I'm getting paid for." He turned the buckskin. "Come on! *I'll* look for the grave and you just follow along and keep an eye peeled in case John's accomplice is still around here."

The possibility suggested by Winston's final comment erased the scowl from O.C.'s face. He kicked the bay to follow, twisting this way and that in the saddle to give a wide-eyed scrutiny to the gathering shadows among the trees surrounding the little clearing. "I wonder who in the Sam Hill come up here with him, anyway? Could be some old owl-hoot from the old days that'd sooner shoot you as to look at you!"

Someone from the old days! Winston pondered O.C.'s speculative comment as he dismounted to check out the brush at the base of the limestone bluff that overshadowed the clearing. There was nothing there, nor in the shallow cave at the bottom of the cliff. Winston emerged from the brush to find O.C. gawking up at the dark shadow of the precipice as he sat the bay and held the reins of the buckskin.

"That old owl-hoot might be up there drawing a bead on you right now, O.C."

"It's gettin' so dark you'd never see 'im if he was." O.C. handed the reins to Winston.

"Yeah, and I don't relish the idea of trying to find our way back to the truck in the dark. We've still got a little grub with us and there's water and good grass for the horses, so we'll just stay here tonight and go home in the morning."

"Thataway we'll get outa going to church *ag'in,* won't we?" O.C. emitted a sly chuckle. "That'll make the womenfolks about as happy as a old settin' hen deprived of her aigs."

Winston swung into the saddle and headed for the place where they'd discovered the remnants of a campfire, and John Stonecipher's saddle hanging from a tree limb.

"That's right, tomorrow is Sunday, isn't it?"

On Sunday morning Winston and O.C. were

about to collect the dun horse and ride out of the clearing when the piercing scream of a red-tailed hawk drew their attention to the bluff.

Winston watched the hawk circle once and drift out of sight beyond the summit. When he refocused his attention on his companion, O.C. was still staring at the bluff.

Winston's eyes followed the direction of O.C.'s gaze. "What are you looking at, O.C.?"

O.C. snapped to attention. "Nothing! Let's get outa here!" He urged the bay into motion.

Winston continued to scrutinize the bluff. "Hold up a minute! There's something up yonder on that ledge, isn't there?"

O.C. drew rein and gave Winston a hard look. "*I* don't see nothing up yonder, Winston."

Winston returned O.C.'s glare for a moment. "Then I don't see anything either, O.C. Dab a rope on Miz Stonecipher's pony and I'll throw that saddle on 'im and we'll be on our way."

O.C. exposed his tobacco-stained teeth and winked a pale blue eye. "Yes *sir!*"

It was well past noon by the time the Bar BX pickup pulled the homemade stock trailer loaded with three horses up to the corrals on the home ranch.

Winston and O.C. unloaded the horses, led them to the tack room and unsaddled them, then took them on to the corral. O.C. held the horses while Winston opened the gate. The Circle S dun nickered a greeting to the other horses in the corral and just as Winston swung the heavy wooden gate wide enough to see them, the blue roan stepped out of the pack with a rolling rejoinder. Winston looked to see if O.C. had noticed.

O.C.'s gape-mouth stare answered the question. "Well I'll be switched. He ain't so much of a owl-hoot after all, is he? Leastways, he ain't no horse thief!"

"If we'd been looking we'd probably found the other saddle amongst our gear in the tack room, too."

"I'll bet that old pickup's halfway back to Arizona by now. He'll probably trust his spare to get him to El Paso before he stops to get the flat tire fixed."

"When he leaves El Paso he'll still have a lot of New Mexico to cross before he gets home. You could put out a A.P.B. on 'im."

"What for? What's he done that's illegal?"

"Nothin', I reckon. I'd just like to know who he is."

"Come on, O.C., let's turn these ponies loose and go see what we can find to eat."

"About five gallons of ice cold Coors would satisfy me."

When they took the bridles to the tack shed they made sure the other Stonecipher saddle was there and continued on to the house. Winston put his hand on the hood of Barb's station wagon as he walked past, ascertaining from the heat that the rest of the family had arrived just ahead of them. They entered the kitchen by way of the back door.

O.C. stopped dead in his tracks and jerked his hat off, peering at the two women sitting at the kitchen table. "I didn't know y'all was taking to church-goin' so serious! Even a couple of sinners deserves a smile."

"Why the long faces," joined Winston. "What's wrong?"

"Someone broke into the house while we were gone," explained Barbara. "The bedrooms are a mess. I guess they found what they were looking for when they got to the storage closet."

"Why do you say that — what's missing?" Winston looked at his mother, for the closet was her domain, the place she kept some things which had belonged to his grandfather and other keepsakes and mementos with which she was reluctant to part.

"They ransacked that box of old relics I was planning to donate to the municipal museum in Carlsbad," she responded.

"They stole some antiques?"

"Just one. That old pistol your grandfather said he found at the bottom of Lonesome Ridge back in 1894."

O.C. looked at Winston, "Wal, it 'pears the owl-hoot's committed a felony! Are you goin' after him now, Win?"

Winston pushed his hat back and a knowing smile relaxed his features.

"Why should I? It's *his* gun!"